PALM SPRINGS

PALM SPRINGS

TOM ARDIES

CUTTING EDGE

ISBN-13: 978-1-954840-19-5

Published by
Cutting Edge Books
PO Box 8212
Calabasas, CA 91372
www.cuttingedgebooks.com

For Bobbe, who always believed, and for
Bogie, who didn't but helped anyway.

"A work of art is never completed. It is abandoned."

—**Valéry**

PART I

CHAPTER ONE

They came over a hill and the billboards started. *Eat at Melvyn's. Drink It Up at Zelda's. Play with Arnie at Ironwood* and *Shop at Wallah Clarke's.*

Waltah? Yes, probably, Sargent decided. Mistakes weren't allowed in paradise.

"What brings you to the desert?" Whadda Hope asked.

"M-m-mental illness," Sargent told her, which was true.

More billboards: *Frank Sinatra—Shhhh! Telephone 327-5489… If You'd Flown, You'd Already Be There… Next Time, Stay at the Riviera…*

"I'm, uh, sorry," Whadda Hope said at last.

"Everybody is," Sargent conceded.

They were in a limousine, the stretched-out kind, five rows of seats, a mixed bag thrown together by the fates, the only common denominator their destination. Fifteen bucks a throw and it is customary to tip the driver.

Sargent knew the driver's name, he had gotten that right, Lewis, but the others were a blur, forgotten as soon as he heard them, given labels instead. The labels were for… What? Surely not amusement? He hadn't had a nice day in six months.

Lewis was alone up front. Sargent had the second row all to himself on account of the note pinned to his shirt. Whadda Hope and the Gingerbread Man were immediately behind him in the third row, the Rabble-Rouser and the Sweet Fuck shared the fourth row, and Mr. Mysterious—hidden for two hours in his Los Angeles *Times*—occupied the jump seat in the rear.

More billboards: *Westward Ho, Sensible Room Rates... ISRAEL, $799...*

Mr. Mysterious had boarded first. He was already barricaded behind his newspaper when Lewis picked up Sargent at Union Station. Sargent caught just a glimpse then, a fleeting image of a dark, craggy, weathered face, shaped by the elements and defeated by something more persistent. He hadn't lowered the paper. He hadn't said hello. He hadn't said anything. A conundrum.

Normally, Sargent would have let it be, too burdened with his own unfathomable past, but that familiar look of defeat, the admission and acceptance of it, had somehow forged a bond. Sargent saw the same look in every mirror, and something else, too. Was it possible that another reluctant traveler shared the same awful secret?

Lewis, busy picking his nose, could never hope to know or understand, and neither could Whadda Hope, none of the others, but Sargent kept wondering about Mr. Mysterious. Did he know?

Not that it mattered (knowing the secret, nothing did), but it was still interesting to speculate. Pssst! Life is a bad joke, piss in a cup ...

"Oh, good," Lewis said, examining a speedometer glued to fifty-five. "Did you see that?"

Sargent caught just a glimpse of a disappearing Rolls Royce, doing eighty, easy. The license place said AVARICE.

"Rock stars," the Sweet Fuck volunteered.

"They live in the Springs?" This from the Rabble-Rouser. Kind of plaintive.

"Only when they're not in Bel-Air or Malibu," the Sweet Fuck assured him.

Sargent wondered how she knew, and why he couldn't remember her name, he'd heard it several times, Jody or Judy Whoever, and he was suddenly reminded of Steve In a Moment thrill having his cock sucked. And Ross. Poor Ross. So poor he had to spell it with one *o*. He was po'r.

"'Frank Sinatra—Shhhh!'" the Sweet Fuck said, changing the subject. "What was that all about?"

"His private jet," Lewis told her. "They claim it's always waking people up in the middle of the night. You know, coming from a party in London."

"If you call the number, who do you get?"

"I dunno."

Frank Sinatra, probably, Sargent thought. That would be justice. Where was he? Oh, yes, the Rabble-Rouser. He fled his wife—an estranged, alcoholic wife—and he also fled other demons. Canada's socialist thrust, and the Quebec separatists who were tearing the country asunder, and runaway inflation and a devalued dollar, and more, much more. The list went on and on. It was endless.

Unlike Mr. Mysterious, the Rabble-Rouser told all—he had to get it off his chest, see?—and he did it quite well, actually. A show. An entertainment.

Initially unattractive, he became ever more pleasing, speaking with graceful hand gestures, the French side of him, his pushed-in face mirroring every emotion. Along the way, he revealed himself as an architect-engineer, a man of solid professional reputation, a long list of design awards, hardly an eccentric, it was just that his personal problems were overwhelming at the moment.

No. Strike that. Not overwhelming. The Rabble-Rouser was perfectly capable of handling his affairs. There was nothing in his dossier that could deny him sanctuary in the only country in the world that hadn't gone commie.

"Did you ever meet Sinatra?" the Sweet Fuck asked.

"Uh, uh," Lewis said. "Just Liberace."

"He took the limo?"

"No. This was in a hardware store."

"He's nice."

Again, Sargent wondered how she knew, and for that matter, who she meant, Sinatra or Liberace, and he also wondered about the Rabble-Rouser. A man like that—educated, gifted, accomplished—he should know better. There was Nicaragua. It hadn't gone commie.

"They used to be a better class," Whadda Hope lamented. and Fred Over the Hill, Hill. Names for you, granted, great names, but *why now?*

"I don't mind blacks, you understand," the Rabble-Rouser said.

"Just niggers, I suppose?" the Sweet Fuck wanted to know.

The Rabble-Rouser was thoughtful. "There is a difference."

"It's nice to see them getting ahead," Whadda Hope said, ever mindful of the other minority present. "I can remember ..." She paused, as if waiting for an argument. "Oh, well. What does it matter?"

The Gingerbread Man, his face a fat brown cookie, raisins for eyes and a frosted icing smile, surreptitiously squeezed her knee.

Exactly, Sargent thought. That was the secret. Or part of it, at least. *Nothing* mattered. They lived in an Oh, wellian world and he could remember when he could remember. Names, addresses, even telephone numbers. The way people looked and the things they said. He ought to get his own personalized license plate, A MESS.

"It doesn't matter," the Rabble-Rouser said firmly, but his retreat was only temporary. When he got his wits about him, he'd be playing the game again, once more into the lists, all together now, follow St. Something.

They'd found him in front of the Beverly Wilshire, his bags on the sidewalk, believe it or not, looking at his watch and as if he hadn't paid his bill. Sargent had immediately pegged him: a hunted man. A sigh of relief when the door clicked shut behind him. And for the first couple of blocks he kept glancing over his shoulder. Running from something. Or somebody.

A woman? Yes, as always, that was part of it, he was to confide as much, he fled his wife, and he also predicted that she would follow, that it was written in the sand, Kismet.

Hold on. Had he actually said that? Sargent paused to sift the rubbish of his tormented mind. Yes, he confirmed, the whole thing was intact, still registering quite clearly: It's written in the sand, Kismet.

Some things you just don't forget.

Sallye, for instance. Remember Sallye? Two days trying to telephone your zip code. And Larkin. So out of it, so far removed. Detached. Harry'd said it all. Larkin got a vicarious "Valentino, Gable. And they kept to themselves. You never knew they were here."

The Gingerbread Man nodded sympathetically, his hand still on her knee, squeezing it.

"I heard Valentino got kicked out," Lewis said, not quite contradicting.

Whadda Hope wasn't concerned. "You always hear stories."

"Yeah, I guess."

"You should have heard what they said about Einstein."

"What?"

"The usual things."

"No kidding."

Sargent refused to watch the stealthy hand at work. Until now, being a victim himself, he'd never been offended by improbable lovers, but this was ridiculous. Did the cad think no one noticed—not even her?

Which was possible.

Whadda Hope, a reference to her chances, was seventy if she was alive. The Gingerbread Man couldn't be much over forty.

They'd boarded next, after the Rabble-Rouser, at Gladstone's 4 Fish in Beverly Hills, and the story had come out with the champagne. Poor tour guide meets wealthy socialite in Mexico City. Whirlwind romance. Marriage that very morning. Now home to bed in fairyland.

Lewis professed to be delighted—he'd said so several times—but Sargent frankly couldn't imagine it. The whole idea was grotesque, obscene, a mockery. A crime against humanity.

For a while, Sargent thought of calling the police, but his own record wouldn't permit that. There was no sense attracting attention. He was here to start over. Afresh. New. Hasty judgments ought to be avoided. The doctor had made mention of that. Had he any real proof that the Gingerbread Man sought to plunder?

Benefit of the doubt. Beauty—you could look it up, Wallace said it?—beauty was altogether in the eye of the beholder. The man might be a history buff. Then he'd want someone who went back, wouldn't he? A repository of ample anecdotes, some of them true. About Valentino and Gable and Einstein and all the rest. And how a camel used to go down to the station to meet the train.

Sargent closed his eyes and pretended to be the Gingerbread Man. He saw a withered throat burdened with the means to finance medical school, and what the liver-spotted hands displayed denied any need to practice. Haw!

"William Holden, that's who I'd like to meet," the Sweet Fuck said. "He's always been my favorite."

"Steve McQueen," Lewis said.

"Ick. He looks like a thug."

"So?"

"You're judged by appearances."

How did she know these things? Sargent demanded, wallowing in his imagery. Whadda Hope limping to bed intent on coupling, the drool staining her nightgown, but worse though, the unthinkable, the Gingerbread Man preparing to oblige, bringing himself to mount her. Aaaargh.

"He's an actor," Lewis complained.

"So is William Holden," the Sweet Fuck said.

Lewis glanced at the rearview mirror. "So is William Holden?"

"Yes."

Sargent shuddered. Dirty pictures, X-rated, hard-core porn, the very pits—nothing had prepared him for such depths. The Gingerbread Man dead aboard Whadda Hope, taken by a stroke, his best performance. Rave reviews in all the trade papers. A posthumous Oscar … hey?

Lewis wouldn't leave it alone. "So is William Holden?"

The Sweet Fuck ignored him, not having to suffer a chauffeur, why should an incredibly beautiful woman, absolutely glorious?

It was true. Sargent still couldn't bear to look at her. Lust was a sin. God was watching. He was married.

The last aboard, they'd fetched her out of the Hollywood Hills, miles up in the high-rent district, almost above the poison gas, and there'd been a terrible scene to go with it. An actor had come running out, pleading with her to stay, begging, threatening.

Well, not exactly threatening, Sargent had to admit. "I won't let you go," that was the strongest thing he said, and there was no real evidence he was an actor. He merely acted like one.

The shouting match had revealed the usual stuff: They'd been living together and he loved her desperately and now she wasn't interested in continuing the relationship any longer./ If she left him she was a bitch dedicated to raising promiscuity to an art form. The idea of a career bored her./ Why the desert of all places? If it was really any of his business, she was just coasting, looking around, which incidentally he already knew, up front./ She didn't know what she wanted. This might be true, but it didn't really matter, when she found it, then she'd know, and the thing he had to understand was, it wasn't him. Any longer./ Did she know what she was? Yes, she did, and he did, too. A sweet fuck.

End of scene. The gentleman had retreated in tears behind a wall of oleanders. The lady, taking due note of the note, chose the Rabble-Rouser, not Sargent, to sit next to. Lewis loaded about half a ton of luggage, remarking that the next time she moved, she might consider hiring a van. And then they wound their way down out of the hills and found the proper freeway and headed for Palm Springs.

The assumptions—all fair enough, Sargent thought—were that the Sweet Fuck had a whole library of how-to-do-it books stashed in her luggage, that she enjoyed, no, relished, experimenting, and that about the only place she drew the line was at making a commitment. And why should she?

After the first rich experience in bed, why should any male, even an actor, think he had some prior call on her services, some reserved place in her heart? The act of love is not love. There is that fine but nevertheless very valid distinction. It should be apparent to anyone. Especially an actor.

Be sensible. It's only a game. She must change partners constantly to learn and progress and excel. Yet this hardly means the lady doesn't discriminate. Ask yourself. Did the Sweet Fuck ever bed a bellboy? Had the world's top tennis pro not been summarily dismissed on account of body odor? Wasn't it foul rumor about that giraffe?

"How about Jerry Ford?" the Rabble-Rouser asked.

Lewis shook his head. "No, like I said, just Liberace."

As always, Sargent couldn't find the courage to look, she was too dazzling, too blindingly radiant, for his weakened condition to risk. A stunning perfection of figure and face. All female and making the most of it. Dressed to the best advantage. Lots of bangles and beads. Intoxicating perfume.

"I guess they keep him pretty well protected," the Rabble-Rouser said.

And she *excelled*, Sargent was certain, physically unable to turn around. She put all of her talents into intercourse and its ample variations. It was what she did best.

"I know Bill," Whadda Hope started to say, but it was too late.

Lewis changed lanes, moving over to the right, leaving the interstate, starting the long looping turn around Windy Point, slicing into the shadow of Mount San Jacinto. There was a hush while his passengers adjusted to the sudden change. It had been day and now it was dusk and in the distance night was already falling, casting across the desert floor, its progress almost discernible.

Sargent watched the first faint lights blink on, imagining that he could feel the day's accumulation of heat, bracing himself for it—and what else?

Touch the silence. You're not alone. Though it hasn't been said directly, other wishes are asked of this fairy-tale place where dreams are supposed to come true, Corporal Sargent. You may seek the ultimate, a whole mind, but Mr. Mysterious asks little less, to be ignored. The Sweet Fuck attempts to end her search, to solve the mystery of what she wants, and to find it, too. The Rabble-Rouser is looking for refuge, a haven, somewhere to hide, a cave where he can lick his wounds and regain his strength. The Gingerbread Man demands wealth and the security it brings. Only Whadda Hope, the old fool, asks the impossible—to keep a man half her age happy.

"You're, uh, going to be met by someone, are you?" Lewis inquired.

Sargent smiled for the first time in how long? "God, I hope so."

The first to come here were the Cahuilla Indians, a large and handsome people, many of the men six feet tall and over, with splendid shaggy heads and faces of much command and dignity. According to the legend, they came from the west, through the narrow San Gorgonio Pass, and then around and down into the valley to the base of Mount San Jacinto, to a spot which is now roughly the center of Palm Springs.

The head man, tired, sick and lame, is said to have taken his staff of power and thrust it into the ground, twisting it around and causing a hot-water spring to burst forth, where he bathed and cured himself and his people also. Then, according to the legend, the people separated and went to different places in the valley, most to Indian Wells, and some to Seven Palms and Palm Canyon, and still others up into the Santa Rosa Mountains. Those who stayed where the head man thrust his staff came to be known as the Agua Caliente, which means hot water in Spanish, and whether or not the legend is true, the hot springs still bubble out of the ground in the Spa Hotel.

The Cahuilla, who had great powers of endurance, an enormous toleration of heat and thirst, had the valley to themselves for untold centuries. The Serrano and the Chemehuevi, the Luiseno and Diegeno, the Kamia and the Yuma, all kept their distance. Even with Father Junipero Serra's entry into Alta California, nothing changed much. Mission padres, the "savers of souls," visited the desert infrequently, and settlers didn't follow the few explorers who had seen the seemingly barren and sterile land.

California had to join the Union, and the War Department to be looking for a route for the Southern Pacific Railway, before anyone bothered to record the existence of the small oasis that was to become Palm Springs, and then it took another decade and "Big Bill" Bradshaw looking for a freight route across the desert from the booming gold-camp country in the New Mexico Territory before it was put to use as a stop and got its first name, Agua Caliente.

Construction of the Southern Pacific finally invited settlement. Two speculators, Byrne and Van Slyke, showed up in 1880, paying $150 to an Indian named Pedro Chino for a small fruit ranch between the oasis and the mountain. "Judge" John Guthrie McCallum, the first actual settler, came four years later, building an adobe home on a half section purchased from the Southern Pacific for $800.

From San Francisco, a prominent attorney, he'd helped frame California's Constitution, gone East to cast California's electoral vote for Abraham Lincoln, McCallum had a purpose. He'd been lured to the desert's dry climate trying to save an ill son. And, once installed, he also had a vision.

He bought an interest in the original townsite from Byrne and Van Slyke and financed construction of a stone-lined irrigation ditch almost twenty miles across the desert from the White Water River. He bought more land from the railway, he set out more orchards, he persuaded an eccentric Scotsman, Welwood Murray, to move down from Banning and build the first Palm Springs Hotel. And he wrote volumes to his friends in San Francisco urging visits to what he called Palm Valley.

Those were boom times in Southern California. "Dr." Murray's small hotel quickly flourished, becoming nationally famous and attracting illustrious guests, among them Charles Fairbanks, later vice-president under Teddy Roosevelt. Promoters came from as far as Boston. New subdivisions and enterprises sprung up everywhere. Lots sold at a public auction for as high as $50. Extensive orchards were planted and the village enjoyed nearly a decade of expansion and prosperity.

Then, in 1894, a terrible ten-year drought struck, reducing the irrigation-ditch water supply to a mere trickle, wiping out orchards and farms alike. The Agua Caliente Indian won a legal fight for exclusive rights to water from the canyon streams, a decision some claim killed McCallum. His Garden of Eden reverted to the desert and most of the early settlers moved away.

Like the Judge, the dream itself might have died, except that a hardy few clung to it, refusing to leave. Though all of the McCallum sons died too, his wife and daughters remained, as did the Murrays, running their little hotel. The village persisted, however precariously, and the winter rains returned after a decade of hardship, and then one day, this was around Christmas, 1908,

Nellie Coffman came in search of the peace and solitude she had
briefly glimpsed from a Southern Pacific coach.

One day, that's all, and Nellie Coffman's heart was pledged
to the desert. While her Santa Monica hotelman father scoffed,
Nellie and her sons, George and Earl, established the Desert Inn
Hotel and Sanatorium, signaling the rebirth of Palm Springs.
The rich and famous came to stay and the town never looked
back.

The McCallums and the Murrays, they were first, after
the War Department's Lieutenant Williamson and Big Bill
Bradshaw, and along with Harvey Wheaton and B. B. Barney
and George Hamblin Fitch, Carl Eytel and J. J. McIntyre, the
Critchlows and the Crockers, some who stayed and some who
didn't, and followed by the Coffmans, signaling the rebirth,
and the White sisters, Florilla, Cornelia and Isabel, carrying
on for the Murrays, and then suddenly too many to keep track,
William Wrigley and Alvah Hicks, Dr. J. J. Kocher and Otto
Adler, D. M. Blanchard and Carl Lykken and Zaddie Bunker
and "Cactus Slim" Moorten, down through the years, the town
growing, a plentiful supply of water found deep underground,
big money coming in, P. T. Stevens building El Mirador,
Hollywood discovering the place, Valentino and all the
rest, Amos and Andy, a city now and sprawling all over, Charlie
Farrell making a success of the Racquet Club, Ruth Hardy with
the marvelous Ingleside, lots and lots of big money now, building big hotels, the Spa and the Canyon and the Riviera, the
rich and famous flocking in, Annenberg and Eisenhower and
Sinatra and Hope, and the nameless poor, too, and all of them
building, castles and shacks, Shangri-la and Mickey Mouse
Town, golf courses everywhere and swimming pools as common as front doors, trailer courts and shanties, a city sprawling and thrusting at the base of towering San Jacinto, changing
with the seasons, a hell and a paradise, crowded and empty,
beautiful and ugly, loved and hated, a city becoming a legend

and starting to believe its own press clippings, an idea more than a place, Palm Springs.

Mallory peered over his newspaper, thinking that the place hadn't changed much, it still was a disappointment. He was never impressed to be suddenly in an oasis, an overabundance of greenery compensating for the harsh blow sand they'd come through. He always expected more—had always believed the legend—but the reality would never co-operate. *Palm Springs,* the sign said, and then the grubby little motels started flashing by, and if it wasn't for the lamppost palm trees he might as well be in Prunedale.

It got better up Palm Canyon Drive, of course. Bullock's Wilshire was there, and Saks Fifth Avenue, and both Magnins. Down selected side streets there were dazzling mansions almost as big as those in Holmby Hills. But here at the gate, where Mallory always wanted to put a rainbow (and maybe a pot of gold, too), he might as well be in Prunedale.

Reflecting on that, Mallory almost wished he was, thinking that this initial disappointment would be just the first of many, that was guaranteed. Next he was going to find that it *had* changed. Which was worse?

One as bad as the other, Mallory decided, not in the mood to search for lesser evils, nor inclined to flee the inevitable. Everything changed sooner or later, himself included. Back in his salad days, tell him he'd be sneaking into town, sitting in the back seat, cowering behind a newspaper, afraid to kiss the bride.

"King" Mallory? Impossible. Absurd. Never. Yet here he was doing it, coming on a dog day, in the dark. Yes, he had changed, all right. One of the mighty who had fallen. He didn't have the stomach anymore.

It didn't show on the outside. To look at him, Mallory was what he was, a big, rangy, brawling kind of man, still young and vital at sixty, still able to take on all comers. Only an expert's eye, that of another victim, might spot the scant tracings left by some distant holocaust, the little telltale signs that all was not well within.

The fact was that it had taken a supreme effort of will to bring Mallory this far. Finally, after four years of self-imposed exile, he had found the strength to come home, but only under the most compelling kind of duress. He needed the money.

And even that wouldn't be compulsion enough if this wasn't the peak of summer when all those who could afford it had fled the scorching heat. Most of his former friends and associates were conveniently out of town. If he avoided them, he wouldn't have to know, not need to be reminded, that the respect and regard weren't there anymore. He wouldn't have to see the disappointment in their eyes, and, what would be the worst part, he wouldn't have to suffer their sympathy.

Once, and not so long ago, either, Mallory had been Palm Springs' leading citizen, movie stars and retired billionaires and former presidents included. He'd grown up with the place, from stable boy to mayor, and if any one man could be said to have "built" this contradictory oasis—the reality and the legend—that man was Mallory. Among the first to realize its potential, he had been and done almost everything: realtor … publicist … land developer … magazine publisher … building contractor … hotel operator … mayor for six years … the district's representative in Congress ….

He'd done it all, it sometimes seemed, and seemingly all at the same time, too. He'd left his imprint everywhere. Most of it was impersonal, concrete monuments, buildings and sidewalks, but there also were reminders of the man himself—even Mallory would have to grant that. He lived on in faded photographs adorning the walls of favorite watering holes and perhaps even in the fond memories of the men who hung them there. Mementos of the good old days. Mallory officiating, dedicating, gracing with his presence. This wasn't to detract from the contribution of other mayors. Charlie Farrell and Frank Bogert and Howard Wiefels, but back in his salad days Mallory was it, Mr. Palm Springs himself.

It was still difficult to comprehend how the end could have come so suddenly, that almost overnight he'd be stripped of his position, influence and prestige. But it had happened just that quickly.

In the bitterly fought campaign for his second term in Congress, he was linked to a sordid Washington sex scandal, reputed to be in the pay of sleazy lobbyists, with doctored tapes and photographs fed to *The National Enquirer*. He was accused of procuring for older lawmakers—supplying high-priced call girls to swing their votes—and it was whispered that his wife, Cissy, always a fragile, ailing woman, was driven to suicide by his conduct.

That it was all bald falsehood made no difference. People believed it, a lot of them—too many, Mallory always thought. Supposed friends and supporters included.

Already pushed to the brink, despondent over Cissy's death, exhausted by the campaign, Mallory took one drink too many and lost all control. He administered a severe beating to the political hatchetman he held responsible, came very close to killing him, and as if that wasn't unbecoming enough for a congressman, he flattened a couple of police officers who tried to intervene. It took six more—and a lot of loose teeth—to put him in jail for the night.

The highly publicized incident, coming in the final days of the campaign, was enough to turn the election, effectively ending Mallory's political career. His opponent's belated apologies and the fact that his name was eventually cleared were no help at all. There was still the assault trial, which dragged on for months before he won a suspended sentence, and it was hell the whole time. The reporters always herding around, the crank telephone calls, the hounding. The rehashed stories and the regurgitated gossip.

The thing became a circus, all the stops pulled out, and while the press had its fun, putting him on the front page day after day, more and more doors started closing to him. It had always been that kind of town. It loved only winners.

Mallory could neither understand nor accept the repudiation after so many years of public service. He'd given his all, the best part of his life, given to the point where he'd neglected his own business affairs, made tremendous personal and financial sacrifices, and suddenly all that was forgotten. They had to have their goddamn circus and make him the clown.

Like a fool—he admitted it now, he should have stayed, weathered the storm—he had said to hell with it and walked away and left a whole lifetime behind. He'd gone to Oregon—Newport, on account of the name, a ridiculous, wispy link—and he had started all over again. The shingle out once more: *Jack "King" Mallory, Realtor, Residential, Commercial & Industrial Sales. Lots of Land in the Land of Lots.*

That hadn't worked. There wasn't the easy money he had been used to in Palm Springs. People didn't drive into Newport with the trunks of their Cadillacs stuffed with thousand-dollar bills. And, after the desert, he hated the rain, of course. If he hung around he could see only a bleak future. Wet and broke.

Moving time again, but he needed a stake, and that's why he was here now, coming to get it like a thief in the night. Unfortunately, it had to be done personally. Spisak, entrusted with the purse, was a careful, prudent man. He wouldn't loosen the strings without an argument.

Also, as Lois had said, if he was really cashing out, once and for all, it was just plain good sense to see to it himself. Why trust letters and telephone calls? This might be his last shot. He needed every blessed dime.

That's what finally convinced him, the need for every blessed dime, that and Lois' repeated assurances that it wasn't going to be the nightmare he imagined, that the town was practically deserted, and that if he actually did bump into a few ghosts from the past, was that going to kill him? Did it mean the end of the world?

Lois Sills had been Cissy's best friend, had stood by her to the very end, and when the rest of Mallory's world collapsed, Lois had stood by him, too. One of the few—and she had hung in ever since.

Mallory could still hear her long-distance badgering: All right, if the papers get onto you, it will be annoying, King. But fatal...? For God's sake, this is still your town, don't you understand that? Nobody can take it away from you. You grew up in its dusty streets and when you became a man you paved them.... Listen, please, I'm sitting out on Rosalie's patio right now, I've got a view of the whole city, and much of what I can see, *you built*. With that kind of legacy—how can you possibly be afraid or ashamed?

How? Easily, Mallory thought. Just as easily as she could ask the question. What she didn't realize, no matter how close to the holocaust, she was still merely a bystander, and like all survivors she could afford to be brave. She hadn't suffered the slashing knives, her guts emptied out in the public square, eaten by the buzzards before she could stuff them back.

No one was more aware than Mallory himself that he had fashioned much of this desert dream world, that what he hadn't built he'd invented. A hundred times he had wanted to thrust the stupid newspaper aside, and if he was recognized, why not? A hundred times—and he didn't have the stomach.

You can't come home again, Mallory mused. Not successfully, anyway. But then he hadn't expected to. The game plan called for a brief visit, in and out, hello, good-bye. He didn't expect to win any battles. He just wanted to lose as few as possible.

Mary Alice whispered in Billy's ear. "Well, what do you think of it?"

They were passing Sambo's. Billy wasn't sure. His main impression, so far, was of an artichoke, the deeper you ventured, the better it got, yet he suspected—as with artichokes—that it would be an acquired taste. And that, the first time, one might eat the thistles by mistake. "It's ... impressive."

"Then you won't mind living here?" she teased.

"If it's with you," Billy said gallantly, aware that others were listening, "forever."

Mary Alice was delighted. He was such a dear, and charming. Her husband, and whatever else he might lack, it wasn't courage.

Everyone should be so lucky, she thought. Filled with generosity, riches to spare, she turned to Jody. "I know Bill Holden. If he's in town, I'll arrange for you to meet him. And if not, someone just as nice."

Jody smiled. "Thank you."

"Where are you staying?"

"The Riviera. For a couple of days, anyway. To see"—again, she smiled—"if you've been telling the truth or not."

"Don't worry, it's everything I said," Mary Alice promised, "and more. I'll call you tomorrow. All right?"

"All right," Jody said, hoping she would, that it wasn't just conversation. Without being obvious, she never was, just the right amount of polite prompting and respectful responses, she had been carefully cultivating Mary Alice, a possible entrée to the Inner Circle.

It wasn't that she had trouble meeting people. The *right kind,* that was the problem. Or sometimes, anyway. And Mary Alice— if she wasn't lying through her false teeth—knew Hal Wallis and Rosalie Hearst and Bob Hope and Darryl Zanuck and Bob Vivian and, well, *everybody.*

"You're sure it's Foothill Crescent?" Lewis asked, driving with one hand, fumbling with his street guide. "There's also a Foothill Circle."

Sargent wasn't certain. Cr. was the only way Em ever wrote it in her letters.

"It makes a difference," Lewis complained. "They're in two different places."

"Crescent," Sargent told him, a guess. It sounded better.

"Then it's in Las Palmas."

"Okay."

"You're first."

"Whatever."

Lewis wondered. Sargent didn't look like he belonged, not with the note and everything, but they weren't paying him to argue. He turned off Palm Canyon, abruptly entering a whole new world, a millionaire's row of walled enclaves, turrets and spires poking into the night, Baghdad American style.

Em was waiting at the door—ladies didn't run to meet the bus—a whole decade gone by without leaving a mark. Weathered well, Sargent decided, wondering how she did it, and then remembering that he'd been told a thousand times. It was attitude. All attitude.

"Jim ...?"

"Yes, it's me, all right," Sargent called. She was in the porch light and he was in the dark on the path, picking his way carefully, the bags too heavy for him. He should have let Lewis—what was the two dollars for?—but he didn't want any witnesses.

"*Jim!*" Em moved onto the porch, taking her apron off, just like in the movies. "Let me see you!"

Sargent struggled manfully, sweating already, thinking yes, before he melted. The heat had been like a furnace when he first emerged from the air-conditioned limousine. What was it? Over a hundred?

"Jim ..." She came down the steps and he just had time to drop the bags before she took him in her arms. "Lord God. How long has it been?"

"A while, huh?" Sargent said. He returned her embrace, collecting all her bones against him, not letting her go. "How the hell are you, anyway?"

"Me? Good. Especially now..." Breathless, she offered her cheek for the ritual kiss, then pushed him back for inspection, anxious to prove the warnings wrong. "And how about my favorite man?"

Fine, he wanted to say, a reflex action from another life, but he only shrugged instead, letting her tell her own lies. He was glad that the yard was dark. If she perceived him gradually it might be less of a shock.

Reluctantly, Sargent presented himself for inspection, a tall, thin man of middle years, bent like the letter S, his nose mashed and his upper lip lifted, scarred by radium to remove a birthmark, giving him the appearance of a battered rabbit. What saved him—or used to—was the intensity he radiated, the joy. His laughter.

"You're ... just the same."

"Am I?"

"Yes."

It had been a trembling, precarious yes, her brave smile already beginning to falter, the distress showing in its place, and a kind of loss, too. One look and she knew, easier in the dark, actually, to see that something had extinguished. He wasn't the same and he never would be, the change was permanent, no one could alter it, not even her.

"Well," she said. "What are we waiting here for? You must be exhausted."

"It's been a long trip," Sargent admitted. He gave her his sling bag and picked up his suitcases, saying the first thing in his head, wishing she would stop staring. "Angie sends her love. And the kids."

"How are they?"

"As always," Sargent said. He hefted the suitcases, anxious to get inside, but she was blocking the way. "Ann's got the tennis bug, and the Squish is into ballet."

"She'll get her fill of that here. Tennis."

"In this heat?"

"It won't last long." Finally, she turned away, starting toward the house. "This is the worst month. August."

Sargent followed. "You're going to love Brodie, all boy."

"Oh?"

"Here's the list for the day—cut off the cat's whiskers and put him in the refrigerator. Started the car and backed it into the street. Drank suntan lotion..."

"God. What is he? Three?"

"At the time. He's four now."

Sargent waited until they got in. "Isn't it nice to be proud of your children?"

Em smiled, blinking back the tears, and Sargent thought, here in the light, maybe she was older, after all. What he wasn't sure of was when it had happened. Over the years? Or coming in from the yard?

"You've got Jack's old room," Em told him, motioning vaguely, going the other way. She stopped just long enough to put down the sling bag. "It's all ready."

"Thanks."

The rest of it came from the kitchen. "You can freshen up while I get dinner. We're having a roast. Okay?"

"Sounds great."

"And you could use a drink, I suppose?"

"Yes."

Sargent waited for her to ask what kind, but there was only a muffled sob, then the clatter of a pot dropping.

"Just a beer will do," Sargent said, making sure he could still speak. He retrieved his sling bag and squeezed down the narrow hall and found what had to be Jack's room. The model airplanes from a forgotten war and the Big Little Books. He got inside, closing the door, leaning against it, and he was all right, handling the whole thing, very calm and cool, rational.

You stupid old cunt, he thought, his own tears starting. You're *supposed* to help.

Jody Walsh sat staring at the black hole that had gobbled Sargent up, thinking that he had disappeared like—well, Alice. For an awful moment, she had almost plunged in after him, calling for him to wait, that she was coming, too.

She still wasn't certain what had stopped her. The fear that he might tell her no? Yes, that was part of it, all right. His very attraction was barrier as much as lure. He might say no. But it was just as disconcerting to think of him saying yes. What if he really was what he pretended? Insanity. That was strange, forbidden ground. Until now, she had never considered—say it—making love to a madman.

There. It was out. The one thing she hadn't done. She had never gone to bed with a crazy.

A strange oversight, Jody thought, smiling faintly. How had she ever managed to overlook that, she being, as Mac claimed, so dedicated to variety? Shouldn't a quick-witted girl hie off to the nearest asylum if she truly quested for the ultimate sexual experience? Wasn't it at least worth a try?

The mocking question brought the kind of answer she might have gotten from Mac. It's a thought, but you should be careful, Empress. They might keep you there.

Dear, poor Mac. Correction: dear, *rich* Mac. Six weeks— a record, wasn't it?—and she just wasn't interested any longer. Actually, be honest, she hadn't been that interested in the beginning, not enough to move in with him, anyway, she had just needed a place to stop and rest for a while. Didn't every traveler?

Yes, and that's enough, no more guilt feelings, it was over and done, and now think about the future. Next stop ... no, not the funny farm, that was too much, but here was her chance to start small, begin with an outpatient.

Jody wondered. What was it that made him so fascinating? He had scared her at first—the note on his shirt—and that haunted, empty look, staring ahead blankly, not seeing anything, not even her.

Oops. It slipped out, didn't it? *Not even her.*

That's what made him different. He hadn't noticed, hadn't paid the slightest bit of attention, and that was ...

Jody felt herself flush. Impossible, the word was there, formed before she could reject it. Unusual, rather. Very unusual. And that was—let's be careful now—fool enough for one day—that was—let's be precise—unfair. It shook a girl's confidence to be ignored. Made her think she might be slipping.

It wasn't easy being a dazzling beauty and he damn well ought to appreciate her. All she asked—all she ever asked—was just a little show of appreciation. Faint, go cross-eyed, fall on the floor. What was so hard about that?

The dumb bugger, Jody thought, the embarrassment past, able to laugh at herself, but the truth kept getting in the way of the joke.

Her beauty had been earned. Certainly it had been nurtured, and what was more important, the difficult part, it had been kept.

From that first discovery in the magic mirror—breathlessly, *Me?*—the treasure had been guarded. Other girls got pimples. Other girls got fat. But the Empress? Never.

When you're perfect, six and perfect, that's easy, but when you're eighteen—"Eighteen and perfect," she would tell the mirror—then you've worked at it. Twenty-five and still flawless? You've toiled.

To stay perfect, you have to pamper, preserve and protect. You have to oil and buff. And comb and manicure. And brush and shine. You have to eat properly, and get enough sleep, and exercise. You have to say no. Two drinks, that's all, and half a dozen cigarettes, the absolute limit, and coffee only in the morning.

There's always temptation. To just lie there, basking. Or to be too busy for yourself. Or to simply run wild. Indulge. But you can't.

A decade can deface and destroy, steal the treasure, waste it. If you'd let yourself go, and so many do, you could have a fat ass, too, Empress. Stretch lines and sagging breasts. Stringy hair and a poor complexion. Flabby underarms. Chapped hands. Pinched toes.

The thing is, it's so fragile. The slightest blemish and it mars. So you have to be very careful, and you have to watch. You have to keep looking in the magic mirror, checking.

The gift is a burden. Carried willingly, of course, and proudly, too, but don't say it's easy. It isn't easy. It's hard. When you're perfect, when you remain so, every day is an achievement.

Did that make her sound ... well, a pain? Because she wasn't. She wasn't haughty or stuck up or anything. She was just happy with herself, pleased, and if it seemed she was shouting, Hey, look at me, huh?, attribute it to the pure joy of being alive and looking so good. That's one thing she always had done. She always had gladly shared. The advice had been her own. It came naturally: If you've got the glory hole, don't sit on it, Empress. Pass it around. Share.

Sargent, he was just a poor dumb bugger, Jody thought, he didn't know what he was missing, but that still didn't make her feel any better. The thing was that it had happened, she'd been ignored, completely and utterly ignored, and she was afraid of the black hole, afraid to find out why.

Lewis got back into the limousine, checking his passenger list, making a mental map. The Riviera, the Mesa, Canyon Country Club, and finally out to Five Lakes in Rancho Mirage.

The girl, Walsh, had to be dropped off next, there was no avoiding it, he couldn't change geography.

Just his luck, Lewis thought. God, what he wouldn't give for a few minutes alone with *that*, pulled over on a dark road. But oh, no—the fates conspired, as usual—it was the fucking frog, St. Pierre, he had to truck all the way to Five Lakes.

"Walsh, you're next," Lewis said, just for the pleasure it gave to speak to her. "Then ..." He consulted his list again. "The Segundos to the Mesa, Brown to Canyon Country—okay?"

For once, a rarity, no one objected. Usually there was a squabble about who went where in what order. Lewis started the engine and backed up slowly, looking in the rearview mirror, but not really watching the road. She had to be the most beautiful woman in the world, he thought. The best he'd ever met, anyway.

Princess Grace, that kind of cool, blonde perfection, but with more going on in the dancing green eyes, a yearning and a deviltry. And the body? Holy Mary, Sweet Mother of Christ. Sophia Loren. In her prime.

Jody hadn't heard him. She kept staring at the black hole as Lewis maneuvered a complicated U-turn against the face of the mountain. The house was the last on the street, or more likely the first, built before the others, its dim outline reminiscent of a Cape Cod cottage, not the Spanish castles they had passed coming up the hill.

St. Pierre asked the question for her. "Is that fellow all right?"

"I guess so," Lewis said.

"There was someone to meet him?"

"Yeah. A lady."

Jody felt oddly relieved and distressed at the same time. What kind of lady? She looked at St. Pierre, waiting for him to ask that, too. It was a natural question. Was she ... nice?

"You're responsible." St. Pierre reminded Lewis. "This is a public conveyance, door-to-door. You don't leave someone standing on the road. Was she competent?"

"Who?"

"You said there was a lady."

"There was."

Jody waited. That wasn't a proper answer. He ought to be made to answer properly.

Mallory wondered why Mary Alice didn't say something. It was Em's house, surely she knew that? Or, instead of cataracts, which would be more seemly at her age, was the old girl blinded by love?

Mary Alice was momentarily at a loss, not wanting to mention names. Em, after all, enjoyed a certain standing, and wouldn't want it bruited about that she was taking in loonies. "Don't worry," she instructed Lewis. "I recognize the place. He's in good hands."

"I've seen that look," St. Pierre said, backing off. "Men returning from the war. Empty shells, nothing inside."

"Well, it can't be that," Lewis said. "There's no war at the moment."

"You're sure of that, are you?" St. Pierre asked. He gestured vaguely, indicating the desert, apparently. "It's a jungle out there."

No one agreed—at best, there was a muffled snicker—and St. Pierre completed his retreat, reminding himself that he was, after all, a foreigner. It wasn't his place to lecture.

"How about you, Walsh?" Lewis said, emboldened. "Will somebody be meeting you?"

There'd be a small flurry at the Riviera, Jody decided, not answering. Someone would think it was a movie star, a natural mistake, all the luggage, and everybody in the lobby would come out, including the night manager. She'd give the bell captain five dollars to take care of her bags and she'd ask the manager if she might check in later because right now what she really needed was a drink.

A man would be at the bar. Serenely, she'd go to him, watching her progress in the mirrored wall, as pleased with herself as the man was, offering her wounds to be healed, kissed and made better. Five minutes, that's all, and then her world would be back to normal again, functioning the way it always did, the way it was supposed to.

"Well, is there?" Lewis persisted.

"Yes," Jody told him, "and he is also competent, thank you."

Jesus, Lewis thought. What had he done wrong? He swung back among the spires and turrets again, retracing his route from Palm Canyon. Ritzville. The old families. Money and class. It must be nice to belong.

As it turned out, he was at the piano, not the bar, and there wasn't any mirrored wall, but it was close enough to make her wonder. Sometimes she believed that there were forces at work and that they could be harnessed. She started breathing again and walked across the lounge.

Watching her come, the man shifted slightly, making room in his private preserve, inviting her to share it, no one was playing—too early for that—and he had it all, amused with himself, waiting.

"Hello," he said, smiling in welcome.

"Hello," Jody said. She took a stool across from him, getting out her cigarettes, looking for matches.

"I'm sure glad you're here," the man told her. He produced a gold-filled Ronson and gave it a shove. "It's been dull, dull, dull. The solar-energy delegates left Saturday, and the air-conditioning convention doesn't start till Tuesday. The Eskimo—an early exhibit—he's been the only distraction."

"Thank you," Jody said. She lit her cigarette and leaned forward to return the lighter.

He made a gesture. "That's okay, keep it."

Jody laughed, taking a better look at him, thinking at least he was original. And fast. The lighter felt very heavy in her hand. A gold bar. "You've more, I suppose?"

He patted a pocket, as if making certain. He nodded. "Yeah."

Sure, Jody thought. On impulse, she kept it, putting it alongside her cigarettes, offering a small casual shrug of thanks. She must remember to be blasé. After all, this was Palm Springs.

"I don't know where the Eskimo went," the man said, looking around. "He was in here awhile ago. Pissed out of his mind, as usual." He finished his drink, an abused margarita, and caught the eye of a waitress. "Louise, do me again, will you?—and you've got another customer."

The waitress had been pretending not to have noticed. She started over.

"Trouble adjusting," the man said, meaning the Eskimo. "Jet lag, and he can't get used to the plastic grass. The way he thinks, if there's plastic grass, there oughta be plastic dog shit." He surrendered his glass and winked at the waitress. "What'll it be?"

Jody thought for a moment. "Have you got any gin?"

"I dunno," the waitress said. "I'll ask." She stood looking at the man, her ass tightening, swaying. "If we have … what do you want in it?"

"Perrier water," Jody said. "And just a touch of lemon. And lots and lots of ice."

"Lots of ice," the waitress said. She gave the man a look and went away.

The man stared after her. "Have you got any gin?" he repeated, laughing softly.

"How do you like me so far?" Jody asked.

"Fine," the man said. "Just fine." He swung back on his stool. "You a working girl?"

Jody shook her head. She ought to be offended, she thought, but she wasn't, quite the opposite. "No. Just another amateur."

"What's your name?"

"Jody."

"Jody," the man said, sounding like Cary Grant. "Jody, Jody, Jody. I can't tell you how long it's been."

"Tell me anyway," Jody said.

"Today," the man said. He was like gold, that kind of tan, his hair the same color, glistening, and he had a good mouth. The mouth was important. "This afternoon. Mere hours ago..." He paused, as if ashamed. "To illustrate. I looked up a mannequin's dress."

Jody laughed. "That long, huh?" She wondered if she should join him now or after the waitress brought their drinks. Fuck the waitress. She'd join him now.

No one said a word—there wasn't a sound—until Lewis, driving too fast, hurtled across Baristo, which drained a wash. The limousine bounced out of the shallow and came down like a rock.

"Hoo, boy," Lewis yelled then, not caring.

Mary Alice smiled, conscious of the reassuring pressure, Billy's hand returning to her knee. "She was a pretty thing, wasn't she?"

Billy nodded, his hand moving higher for an instant, caressing the inner thigh, telling her—what was it?—that gold also glistened?

"Pretty?" Lewis said. "Hey, she was beautiful." He could barely resist pounding his head on the steering wheel. "I mean, you know, I got put down. But something like that... you don't mind."

"Beautiful," Billy agreed.

"That's the trouble with this world," St. Pierre said, always ready with an argument. "True achievement, nobody gives a damn. But a pretty face?"

Lewis was insistent. *"Beautiful."*

"Luck," St. Pierre said. "Chance. Fate. Born that way. It's hardly an accomplishment."

"It's a gift," Billy agreed. He always agreed.

"Given," St. Pierre said. "A present. What did she do to earn it?"

31

"Don't be foolish," Mary Alice told him, becoming angry. "How can you condemn her for the way she looks?"

"I'm not foolish, and I'm not condemning her. The point is, it's meaningless."

Lewis moaned. "Oh, come on."

Only Mallory stayed out of it, watching for new things in the sea of palm trees, thinking that the Riviera had looked pretty spiffy. They'd changed it since he left, remodeled the lobby, put on a whole new front. And weren't those bare-breasted statues in the fountain from the old Chi Chi Club? He wondered how that got past the planning commission.

"You," St. Pierre told Lewis. "You drive this thing. Me? I create." He looked at Billy, another example, and changed his mind. "But a woman like that? You heard what she called herself?"

"Did I ever," Lewis said, leering.

"It's an empty life," St. Pierre mourned.

There it was, Billy thought, the first open slight, unintentional as it might have been. He hadn't qualified for the list of gainfully employed. Yet who was more deserving than a man who married for money?

Briefly, the inner thigh. Hey, put me on your list, you don't think this is work?

He sighed. Not long ago—last week, yesterday?—he would have laughed at his joke, but it had suddenly become a very serious matter. Truly, this was a job, more than that, a business. It provided for him. One should not laugh at that. Nor need he be ashamed if he gave good value.

Love? No, there was none, there couldn't be, but there was affection, regard. Appreciation.

That's why he had agreed.

Mary Alice wanted a companion, a male companion, a younger man, still some fire left, eager to do things, able. An escort and protector. A man.

Why shouldn't an old woman have a man if that's what she wanted? If she had the money and could buy one?

Yes, that was the word she had used, buy, not hire. Billy could remember every word said.

You want to buy a man?

How else do I get one? I'm old, but not blind. There are mirrors.

Well. You can hire a man. That might be better. You hired me, didn't you?

For the day.

Yes, but it's been a week. And it could be longer if you wanted, but I'm afraid there's nothing more to see.

Or do …?

We drink. (Pause) Would you like another?

No. But go ahead. I'll enjoy it too. You become very amusing.

Well. Seeing how you are buying …

(Long silence)

If you were to buy a man, how much would you pay for him, señora?

Mary Alice.

Mary Alice. But it's not the custom.

How much? (Laughter) You're interested, are you?

I have friends in the business. They all dream of this. Rich widows. But it somehow never happens.

Do you?

Dream? Yes. For a long time, that's what kept me alive. Tomorrow, maybe it will be better. It can be very hard here. Perhaps you've noticed. That's why I never had children.

Yes. You told me.

Did I? Pollo! Another drink.

Or married?

It's not necessary. You can buy a man. I can buy a woman.

You just can't keep her?

No. Not one that I would want.

(The drink comes)

You asked how much. Would that be enough?

What do you mean?

To have the woman you want. Eventually.

I don't understand.

Billy. If I have any attraction, it's that I'll die soon.

Are you proposing, señora?

Mary Alice.

Mary Alice. But it's not the custom.

"Well," Lewis decided, "I'll tell you something. If I was a lady, and if I looked like that..."

St. Pierre was ready to pounce.

"Yeah, I'd sell it," Lewis told him. "Why not? It's like you said, we all get paid for services rendered."

"I didn't say that."

"What did you say?"

"I said we *contributed*," St. Pierre said. "I was speaking of talents, skills. Acquired expertise. But a woman like that, she thinks that's all that is necessary, just to be, to exist. She makes no effort to become something more than beautiful. You heard her talk. There's no other dimension."

"Oh, I don't know about that," Lewis protested.

"No, you don't," St. Pierre said. "Take my word for it. I've had some experience. You're fortunate she wasn't interested. All you'd get is what you see—the butterfly."

"Maybe that's enough."

"Is it?"

"Yeah."

"Then I feel sorry for you," St. Pierre said, smiling sadly, as if he was talking to a fool.

Stung, Lewis hesitated. The fucking frog. It was just a conversation, why get personal, start an argument? He put the question as diplomatically as his anger would allow. "If you're supposed to be an architect, how come you can't appreciate beauty?"

"I can if it's functional," St. Pierre answered. "That's my whole point. You may have the world's most beautiful toilet, but if it doesn't work, what good is it?"

"Well, that's a nice comparison."

"Yes, and as I say, your pretty friend back there, I doubt very much if she functions to anyone's benefit but her own. You see the butterfly, and I see the leech."

Lewis gave up. "What are you trying to tell me, that every woman's a toilet?"

"No. Every woman is a mystery, and some are solved easier than others, that's all."

Mary Alice caught herself. She'd been on the verge of flaring again, of telling both they were talking damn nonsense, but the remark struck her as finally demonstrating some small perception. Every woman is a mystery.

Most men—St. Pierre, Lewis, her own Billy—all were open books, their words quick to reveal what their faces didn't show. They'd have had to practice deceit to be other than themselves.

Women, though? Finally, if only by accident, St. Pierre had stumbled upon a bit of truth, and it applied especially to Mary Alice Chambers; or rather, if she ever remembers, to Mary Alice Segundo. Mary Alice Segundo—who is a mystery even unto herself.

In November, she would be seventy years old, and none too spry a seventy, either. A crock, that's what, admit it. Candidate for a rest home. A rouged wrinkled apple for a face, bones brittle, muscles flabby, all rotten inside. The only thing still intact was her mind. So, why had she done it?

A man half her age, a poor cunning innocent, a roly-poly little brown fat man in shiny pants bagged at the knees.

Companionship? God, no, she didn't want for someone around, she saw enough people as it was. Flo underfoot all the time and Graham over at every chance. Meetings, meetings, meetings and, if she wasn't careful, a dinner party every night.

Need of escort? No, Gordon was always available, a loving nephew in the inheritance business, and there were a dozen other men she knew, any one of them happy to lend an arm. She was still somebody and still good fun. If anything there was a lineup.

Nursemaid? Not her, when the time came, she was just going to drop dead, and if the Good Lord didn't co-operate, registered nurses 'round the clock.

Security? Hardly.

Then what?

Mary Alice had asked the question so often, she ought to be bored to death, she thought, but her pulse still quickened at the answer. No, not the answer, but the mystery, rather. Was it just for the sake of a marvelous scandal? Or—God forbid—was she actually in love?

"Hey," Lewis said, laughing. "You know why I threw away my art collection? It wouldn't flush."

St. Pierre shrugged. The young, they knew it all, there was no telling them anything.

Lewis laughed again, turning between the crumbling adobe gateposts that marked the entrance to the Mesa, the small contradictory bastion that was Old Palm Springs. Even in the dark, the scramble of contrasts was apparent, mean shack against elegant mansion, millionaires next door to working stiffs. None of it ever seemed to quite fit properly. An appropriate destination for improbable honeymooners.

Flo was crying. Tears of joy, Lewis thought at first, marriage did that to some people, but she kept blubbering on and on, heartbroken and inconsolable. Lewis couldn't catch all that was wrong, he was too busy unloading, just something about the place not being ready, and it wasn't her, Flo's, fault. Then the three of them disappeared, Mary Alice leading the way, surprisingly sprightly for her age, Flo flying after her, and Billy Segundo following in a kind of trance. It was an awfully big house. Probably bigger than he'd imagined.

Lewis had to make two trips to get the bags inside the door and still none of them had come back. He thought of leaving, he had two more passengers, after all, but he hadn't been tipped. He rang the bell.

No one came.

Jesus, Lewis thought, ringing a second time, wasn't this typical? There was a sign pasted in plain sight on the back of every seat: *It Is Customary to Tip the Driver*. It even said how much, *$1.50*.

"Hey!" Lewis called, becoming angry. He'd let them open their goddamn champagne, and that was a fifty-buck fine, automatic, if he'd been stopped by the CHP. He rang the bell again, longer this time, leaning on it.

Flo finally showed up with her nose in a Kleenex.

"I put the bags in," Lewis told her.

"Oh, God," she said. "Everything's going wrong." She blew her nose, wiping it, sniffing. "You'll just have to put them back."

"What?"

"It's empty!" she wailed, ready to begin anew. "Can't you see? It's *empty!*"

Lewis edged past her. The massive entrance hall did seem overly bare. There was no furniture, nor any plants or pictures, either. Nothing.

Oh, shit, Lewis thought. Had the old girl been robbed? There was a lot of that in the summer. People went away for months, their homes unattended, whole streets deserted en masse, and it was an open invitation to anybody with a truck. He'd considered it himself. One load from the right place and he could retire.

Billy came back, looking a bit uncertain, steel taps clicking on the marble. "It's empty," he confirmed.

"The whole house?"

Billy made a helpless gesture. It was a very large house. He wasn't sure he'd seen it all.

"It's not my fault," Flo said. She blew her nose again.

Lewis went for a quick look at the living room. It was huge, cavernous, empty. Bare wires dangled where fixtures had been removed from the ceilings and walls.

"I wanted it to be so nice," Flo went on. "There was plenty of time. When did you call?"

Billy made another helpless gesture. "Ten?"

"That's when I called," Flo said. "Right after. And they said they would. Even if it meant overtime."

Lewis returned shaking his head. "You called the cops?"

Flo looked at him, sniffing. "What for?"

"Well," Lewis said. He looked at Billy. "Where's, uh …?"

"Mary Alice?"

"The bathroom," Flo sniffed. "She had to go."

"Is she all right?"

"I hope so."

"Well," Lewis said again, thinking this was really none of his business. Whoever had the stuff would be in Chicago by now and the limousine horn was honking (that would be the frog). "Listen. Maybe I shouldn't be getting involved, but if you want my opinion…"

"I called the Ingleside Inn," Flo said, ignoring him. "They're holding a cottage." She crumpled her Kleenex, stuffing it inside a sleeve, wiping her hand on her dress and then offering it to Billy. "Incidentally, I'm Flo. Isn't this an awful way to meet?" She tried to laugh but it was mostly a sniff. "Congratulations."

"I'm Billy," Billy said.

"I know. Anyway, congratulations."

"Thank you."

The limousine horn honked again.

"Listen," Lewis said. "I've got a couple passengers waiting. If you people..." Finally it struck him. "What is this? The furniture's in storage?"

Flo just looked at him. Where was it supposed to be? On the moon?

"Wooo," Lewis said, laughing. "I was going, h-e-y. You know?" He held his head, what an idiot. "I'm.telling you to call the cops? You're saying what for?"

"Tomorrow will be better," Flo assured Billy. The frown was for Lewis. "I'm sure she'd like you to wait."

"How long?"

"Don't worry. It won't be forever."

If she's taking a crap, it could be, Lewis thought. He didn't like the tone now that the crying jag was over. They could afford a cab. They couldn't afford a tip, maybe—but they could afford a cab.

Outside, the horn honked once more, a long, complaining bleat. Flo went to the door. "Hold your horses!" she shouted.

That just started the horn again.

"Bekins," Flo confirmed, failing to see the humor. She turned back to Billy. "When we close the house for the summer, we send them everything."

Billy was still a little confused. "For safekeeping?"

"Listen," Lewis said. "If you don't mind, I'd better get going. You can call a cab when you're ready. Okay?"

"We can take a cab," Billy said at last. He got out a thin, worn wallet. "What is it? A dollar fifty?"

Lewis nodded. Billy gave him two twenty-peso bills.

Lewis stared at them. "Mexican...?"

"I'm sorry. It's all I have."

"Uh, catch me next time," Lewis said, handing the money back. He was sorry now that he had pushed it. The poor little bastard hadn't been given his allowance.

"If you'd wait," Flo said.

Lewis shook his head and left.

Flo followed him out. "Wait. I'll ask the Missus."

Yeah, Lewis thought. Ask her how to stop talking through your nose.

St. Pierre met him at the gate, trying to get it open, his face flushed. "What in the hell is going on?"

"Billy Boy thought he was robbed," Lewis told him, getting into the limousine. "You should see that place. There's not a stick of furniture in it. Nothing."

St. Pierre scrambled in after him. "Robbed...?"

Lewis released the brake, sliding into gear. One thing he had to admit. There was always something. "Naw, the stuffs in storage for the summer, and it's not back yet, that's all, but Billy Boy, he's white, he's dying. He thinks the old lady's been picked clean. They've taken the family fortune, all the money in the mattress, you know? And he's standing there with an empty wallet."

St. Pierre finally got it straightened out. "Oh. He misunderstood?"

"Yeah. You should have seen his face. Everything gone, including the goddamn fixtures. I guess they're made of gold."

Some of them, Mallory thought, amused. He looked back at the house, a huge marble sprawl, worth a million now, probably more? She'd bought it for about a hundred thousand, sure of the future when nobody else was, taking advantage when times were rotten. A wise old bird—yes, she was old even then, wasn't she?—a wise old bird who knew things nobody else knew. But this latest adventure?

Well, if nothing else, it would give the town something to talk about, Mallory decided. It couldn't subsist all winter on just funerals and committals.

Billy wandered through the house in a kind of a daze, room after empty room, seemingly without end. He could barely believe what he saw. Large, yes, Mary Alice had forewarned of that, but this was huge, massive. It wasn't a home. It was a museum. It must be worth ... what?

A lot of money. Billy thought, swallowing. A very large amount of money. What had he done? He started back, suddenly afraid, his steel taps clicking, echoing all around him. This was too much. And when the furniture came?

Billy's mind reeled. For such a house, to fill it up, there would have to be a lot, and it would have to be expensive, too. A museum demanded museum pieces. What had he done?

Mary Alice was on the telephone as he entered the kitchen. She shushed him, pointing to his shoes, indicating that he should take them off.

Billy stopped, frozen to the spot, waiting for her to finish talking.

Mary Alice cupped a hand over the phone's mouthpiece, looking at him despairingly, as if he were a child. The instructions came in a stage whisper. "Just take them off, silly."

Billy hesitated.

"Take them off."

Billy removed his shoes. Both socks had big holes. His toes protruded through.

Mary Alice put down the phone. "Well," she said after a while. "The first thing, we ought to get you some stockings, I guess."

Billy just stood there, asking himself the same question, What had he done?

Mallory put his newspaper away, taking the chance that Lewis, not having recognized him when he boarded, wouldn't do it now in the dark. Lewis would be what?—barely voting age four years ago?—interested in girls, not politics, and that was still the case, apparently.

St. Pierre was lamenting the exchange rate between Canada and the United States, the money he was going to lose when he transferred, the inept policies and practices which had conspired to force his departure, and that of any other rational investor, too.

"You shouldn't think of it as money lost," Mallory said, belatedly joining the conversation. "Think of it as increased purchasing power."

"That's what I keep telling myself," St. Pierre responded, immediately turning to face him, "but it's a sizable sum. Substantial…" He hesitated, wondering why he was discussing his finances with a total stranger, and then deciding that the question was the answer: Because he was a stranger. Who better to know? It was intimates who wronged you. Friends, relatives. Wives.

"You'll be investing?"

"Yes. Real estate."

"Here?"

"Palm Desert."

"The bloom is off there," Lewis advised, sounding like an expert. He was in this job to make contacts. He heard a lot and retained some of it. "Two, three years ago, you could still pick up some bargains. But now?"

"The price doesn't matter, just as long as it keeps going up," St. Pierre assured him. "I have a motto—'You can't lose money making a profit.'" He winked at Mallory. What did this innocent know? "Are you from here?"

"I know the area."

"Business-wise?"

"Yes and no."

"Which means…?"

"I'd hesitate to advise."

Lewis sighed. "If only I had had the money at the time."

The story of my life, Mallory thought. He reached for his suitcase. "Turn here."

"Just visiting?" St. Pierre asked.

"Yes."

Lewis turned, slowing down, waiting for instructions. He didn't have an address other than Canyon Country Club.

As in Las Palmas, it was immediately a different world, the houses very showy, the dominant color white, which made them all look the same. A subdivision for the nouveau riche, and it was easy to imagine that they, like their superficial houses, all looked pretty much the same, too.

"The corner will do," Mallory said. He made sure he had everything. "Well. Good luck?"

St. Pierre smiled. "Thank you."

Lewis looked back at him, thinking that was strange, not to be directed to a specific house.

"The corner," Mallory repeated. He handed two dollars to St. Pierre, indicating that he should pass it along. "You needn't get out. I can manage myself."

Lewis drove to the end of the block and stopped. Mallory made a quick exit.

"Good-bye," he said, the door slamming on the word, and he was gone as suddenly as he had appeared from behind the newspaper.

"Good-bye," Lewis said, still wondering.

St. Pierre handed over the two dollars. "A strange one, eh?"

"Yeah."

They sat watching for a moment. Mallory was walking slowly now, waiting for them to leave, it seemed.

"What's his name?"

"Brown."

"Brown?" St. Pierre repeated, sounding doubtful. "He didn't give you an address?"

"No."

St. Pierre got an uneasy feeling. "What's he hiding?"

"Himself, probably," Lewis said. He waited a moment longer and then pulled away.

❧ ❧ ❧

Lois was sitting on the patio with a bottle of champagne, looking like she might be posing for *Palm Springs Life*, a mature woman of unquestionable substance, beautifully preserved, exquisitely presented.

"Welcome home," she called, smiling.

"For a visit," Mallory reminded her.

Lois was unperturbed. It was all planned. "For a visit. Come here."

Mallory waited to catch his breath, sweating from the long walk, feeling stupid but justified. Sills was a society – and gossip-column name. Let Lewis see it on the mailbox and he might start wondering. Who was the dark stranger visiting the pretty widow? Was this a secret romance after so recent a bereavement?

"You're absolutely paranoid, you know that?" Lois said, coming to get him. "The back door. Honestly..." She laughed, shaking her head, the teasing meant to hide the rush of desire. "And what's worse, I indulge you."

Mallory looked to where she had been sitting, the bucket of iced champagne, the two glasses, and then far back across the golf course, to where he had left the limousine. It wasn't just chance that she was out here? She'd known he would come this way?

Lois ran the last few steps, falling against his chest, hugging him tightly. "God! How are you?"

Mallory bestowed a cautious kiss, thinking that he ought to be careful, a woman who could read minds. "Fine, and you?"

"Good."

They stood looking at each other, searching for the changes, Mallory wondering what was different, and Lois happy that nothing was, that he was still the best damn man.

"Well," Mallory said. "You want me to pop that?"

"Yes," Lois told him. "Yes, yes, yes." She took his arm and led him back up the steps. "We're going to drink and be happy. Here's to us."

Mallory got the feeling that he was being dragged, but that was just his paranoia, wasn't it? He ought to be thankful for this one good woman, solid, dependable. Unlike him, she got what she wanted. She always knew the way.

A friend—and he didn't have that many anymore.

Lewis stopped at the gate to Five Lakes and the guard came out for a closer look.

"St. Pierre," St. Pierre announced. "Staying at the MacPherson condo."

"Oh, yes, you're expected," the guard said. He went back into the gatehouse and returned with a set of keys. He gave them to Lewis, looking in at St. Pierre, bemused. "We usually don't see you snow birds till December."

St. Pierre didn't say anything. He'd already told all, he thought. Everything, the whole trip, all he'd done was talk, blab, blab, blab, and it still disturbed him that he knew nothing about the man who called himself Brown. It somehow wasn't fair.

"How do I get there?" Lewis asked.

"Keep left. Watch the numbers."

The barrier was raised and they drove in, Lewis thinking that it was like a prison. Walls, a gate, a guard. He checked the number and passed the keys to St. Pierre, resisting the urge to make some remark, welcome to the pen, hope you like your cell. St. Pierre wouldn't appreciate the irony, he'd see barbed wire only as protection. After all, it was a jungle out there.

"You renting? Or is this a friend's place?"

"Yes," St. Pierre confirmed, about to say a friend's but he quickly caught himself. There he went again. Telling all.

"I'm sorry. Which ...?"

There was no way out. "Yes, a friend's."

This necessity to purge, why? St. Pierre wondered. Because it was held in for so long? He had exploded—that's why he was here—and then had forgotten to stop the gaping hole. Everything was dribbling out. Names, dates, places. Reasons. Motives.

"I was going to say, I hoped you'd gotten a rate," Lewis said. "This time of year, they can't give 'em away …." He peered into the darkness, trying to find the number. "What's his name again?"

"Who?"

"Your friend."

St. Pierre decided it was time to draw the line. "Why do you want to know?"

"It might be on the mailbox."

"MacPherson," St. Pierre said, feeling like a fool.

They drove on in silence, the place a graveyard, no lights showing. An occasional tarp-covered auto was the only sign that the inhabitants planned to return.

Lewis finally felt obliged to explain. "The season doesn't begin until October."

St. Pierre nodded carefully. In a few more minutes he'd be safe inside. Surely he could stay out of trouble until then?

"Then the migration starts," Lewis said. "They'll come flying in from all over, soon as the first freeze. The summers there, the winters here, back and forth. Rich ducks, they oughta break out in feathers."

Ha, ha, St. Pierre thought. He'd made up his mind. Not another word except good night.

Lewis turned back, checking for numbers again, and finally one was visible, 88. Four more to go. The next cluster. He speeded up. "Here we are."

St. Pierre looked. It was the same as all the others. A low, flat-roofed, concrete-block unit, very spartan in appearance except for the elaborate door. A fortress—and that's what he wanted.

Lewis parked and went around back and got out the bags. St. Pierre led the way and stopped on the steps. The phone was ringing, barely audible over the air conditioner's whirr, but sounding oddly persistent, as if it had been ringing for a long, long time.

Lewis heard it, too. "Maybe it's for you."

No doubt, St. Pierre thought. His impulse was to run, but he didn't have the strength. He unlocked the door and pushed inside, moving like a dead man.

The phone was right there in the hall. He stood with his hand on it for a moment, willing it to stop, but it rang again. And again.

He picked it up. "Hello ...?"

"Elliott?"

Lewis was looking at him.

"My wife," St. Pierre said, telling all.

CHAPTER TWO

Sargent sat in the morning sun, staring ahead blindly, reviewing the past. He lived there most of the time. Reviewing, always reviewing.

Last night: light rap on the door. It's Em, sounding much better. "Ready ...?"

"Yo." Taking a final look at himself, thinking that if he ever made any real money, he'd get the harelip fixed, first thing.

"It's on the table."

"I'm coming."

Dinner in the dining room. Candles and her best silverware, a crocheted tablecloth, music softly in the background.

"You look awful." The first thing, after grace.

"I know."

"We'll start there. Get you looking better. Stick you out in the sun and let you bake."

"Okay."

"And you'll need some new clothes. A good lightweight suit, a seersucker would be nice, and a couple pairs of shorts, some sandals. You've got to dress for the desert."

"Right."

"We can start house-hunting then, get you settled, some roots down, and the next thing will be a job, and ..."

"A job?"

"Yes. A job. And I don't want any stupid talk of suicide."

Hey? Suicidal thoughts, once entertained, mentioned. But there had not been talk of it.

"If you must"—looking him in the eye—"remember you're in Palm Springs. Here..." For a moment, faltering, then quickly: "Here, young man, we put our head in a refrigerator, not an oven."

"Got you."

Em was watching from Jack's window, wondering how he could stay that way for so long, motionless. Sometimes she was afraid he was dead. He wouldn't move.

A small, severe, relentless woman, given to causes, politics and the sun, she had experienced defeat but never accepted it gracefully.

She wanted to scream—Move, damn you, show me you're alive!—but she turned away instead, making the bed, picking up after him. He'd been tidy before, but now he didn't care, another change. Everything had changed. He wasn't the same person.

There was a piece of paper on the floor. She stopped, picking it up, reading the heading as she did so, *The Ten Danger Signals*.

The rest was too small. She got out her glasses and put them on.

It was typed, with handwritten notes in brackets. She began reading.

THE TEN DANGER SIGNALS

—A general and lasting feeling of hopelessness and despair. (Translation: You whine a lot.)

—Inability to concentrate, making reading, writing and conversation difficult. Thinking and activity are slowed because the mind is absorbed by inner anguish. (What was that again?)

—Changes in physical activities like eating, sleeping and sex. Frequent physical complaints with no evidence of physical illness. (Reminder: Tomorrow get cancer checkup.)

—A loss of self-esteem which brings on continual questioning of personal worth. (Will the check bounce?)

—Withdrawal from others, not by choice but from immense fear of rejections. (Farewell, Diana.)

—Threats or attempts to commit suicide, which is seen as a way out of a hostile environment and a belief that life is worthless. (Farewell, cruel world.)

—Hypersensitivity to words and actions of others and general irritability. (The Fuck You Syndrome.)

—Misdirected anger and difficulty in handling most feelings. Self-directed anger because of perceived worthlessness may produce general anger directed at others. (The Fuck You Syndrome, Part II.)

—Feelings of guilt in many situations. A depressed person assumes he is wrong or responsible for the unhappiness of others. (The Fuck Me Syndrome.)

—Extreme dependency on others. Feelings of helplessness and then anger at the helplessness. (The Please Help Me/Fuck Off Syndrome.)

Em finished cleaning up and then went out to the back yard. Sargent was sitting in the same position. He hadn't moved.

"There's a party tonight," she said, fitting into a deck chair beside him. "It's for the Chermaks, some friends of mine, Howard and Ruth, their twenty-fifth wedding anniversary. Would you like to go?"

Sargent shook his head. "No, but you go."

"It could be interesting," Em said. "The host is Stu Bollinger..." She paused, indicating he was someone important, waiting for Sargent's reaction. "That's synonymous with Howard Hughes."

"He's a dead recluse?"

"No. He's a billionaire."

Sargent closed his eyes, thinking that it sounded more interesting his way, and that in any event he didn't want to go.

"I think he is, anyway," Em said. "He keeps competing with Annenberg. If Annenberg gives away thirty million, Stu gives away forty, and when Annenberg built his golf course, Stu had to have one, too."

"His *own* golf course?"

"They say he got mad. Jews weren't allowed, I don't know, somewhere, so he built his own."

"Who's this now?"

"Annenberg."

"Right. He's the Jew. So Bollinger gets mad and builds a bigger golf course?"

"No. I didn't say he got mad. And they're the same size, nine holes."

"So what makes Bollinger's better?"

"Night lights."

Sargent still didn't want to go. He had his most trouble at parties. People invariably asked him what he did, and then he had to lie, make up something. They wouldn't believe him if he told the truth and said he did nothing.

He had cracked up at Christmas and he hadn't turned a stick since, hadn't written a goddamn word. The funniest column in Washington—yes, funnier than Buchwald's—had died aborning. "Play-Doh's Republic," quoted at breakfast, as was Will Rogers. For three lousy months and then something snapped. The barefoot boy from Maine couldn't handle the Big Time.

"I still don't want to go."

"You're sure?"

"Yes."

"All right," Em said, trying something else, "what do you want to do?"

"Get my harelip fixed."

"You haven't got a harelip."

"I have, you're just saying that trying to make me feel better."

Em sighed. "Do you think you ever will?"

"Of course. I'm feeling better already."

"It certainly doesn't show."

"Well, let me assure you, inside, deep inside, I'm very unhappy."

"I see."

Sargent wondered. Did she? It was a difficult notion. In the supreme moment of his life, when he had never been happier, he was a sick man, insane, and now, in the utter depths of despair, he was better, meaning that he wasn't insane anymore. The depression was a mere aftereffect, a proof of the cure, and it would go away. Gradually and eventually it would go away.

Meantime, waiting for the promised miracle, no wonder he wasted so much time in review, remembering what it had been like. A manic high. Towering, gleeful, as if he could accomplish anything (and almost did?).

Well, he had been bright as hell, that's for sure, and very persuasive, he got things done. Not a genius, not brilliant, he didn't have that within him, but operating at his full potential, which as it happened—a surprise—was quite considerable.

It just got out of hand, that's all. There were too many projects. Stealing Hollywood, for example. He should have passed on that. And CONSULT. That was too big. He'd have had to buy IBM, Mother Bell and Ann Landers. How was he supposed to buy Ann Landers?

The historical society. The string of girls. The dog and the teddy bear. That really dubious business arrangement with Klaus Altmann Barbie in Bolivia for the rights to Naked Nazi and Naked Nancy. Well...

But funny? He had 'em rolling in the aisles. I'm peaking, he said, peeking from behind the chair, everybody in the restaurant laughing, and Ross crying real tears, he couldn't stop, and when Diana didn't want him to drive, he got all tangled up in the seat belt, practically hanging himself, asking her, You're sure?, and

Ross, po'r Ross, he couldn't drive either, and by the time the evening was over he'd turned down the best blow job in Baltimore because he was laughing/crying too hard.

Women? At that last party, he was Dr. Henry Sunshine, and they were all watching, couldn't take their eyes off him, and Diana wanted him to leave, she kept calling a taxi, afraid of what was going to happen, and finally Proctor's wife came over—she *had to*—to ask if he was really a doctor, she thought he was a performer, he ought to be, and he asked if she was a cop, and she said sure, she had a gun in her purse, and she was going to take it out, and she was going to pull the trigger, and a little flag was going to pop out, saying BANG, and that's what they were talking about, wasn't it?, and he took her home and fucked her before they got a block away.

Balls? He had balls. Dragging on the floor. You want a diversion, Inspector? Very well. There will be two trucks, one loaded with liquor, the other with live chickens ....

"I found your note," Em said. "It was on the floor."

"You don't have to pick up after me," Sargent told her. He moved imperceptibly, nothing anyone would notice, just enough to dislodge a fly.

Mallory was staring up at Mount San Jacinto, its folds still muted in the morning sun, but looking—as always, he thought—like a slag heap. It was as unreal as the rest of Palm Springs, placed there by man's hand, it seemed, a carelessly painted movie backdrop, rising abruptly to its ten-thousand-foot peak. The joke was that someday somebody would yell, "Strike the set!" and it would disappear.

Not that anyone in his right mind would want that. With San Jacinto gone, Palm Springs the spa would vanish too. The towering mountain was what made the place. It kept out the winter's coastal rains (most of the time, anyway) and deflected the smog (which, when it came, ended up with other undesirables in comfortably distant Indio). Altogether a necessity, and if you looked at it long enough, viewed it in that light, gradually it took on a beauty, even as did the barren desert. Look long enough and you started seeing the goldenbush and the matchweed and the bedstraw and the pennyroyal. Look long enough, the sun on your back and sand in your shoes ... and you'd never leave?

Lois came out with the coffee. In place of last night's gown, she was wearing a simple peasant dress, bright with embroidered flowers. "Now what's wrong?" she asked, laughing.

"Nothing," Mallory said. "I was just wondering ..." He paused to accept the steaming cup. "How could anybody make a mountain ugly?"

Lois laughed again. All she had been doing was laughing. "Anything else?"

"I don't remember it being this hot."

"And ...?"

"That's all."

Lois laughed once more—God, she'd laugh at anything, wouldn't she?—blowing away a stray wisp of platinum hair with unnatural exuberance. She felt good, as good as she looked. Not a beauty, but pretty, a word that had stuck all her life, and which she had hated once and now spent a fortune to hear. A compact, slightly plump, elegantly turned, pretty lady.

Always, even now, blowing the wisp, the perfect Palm Springs lady. When she went out, she carried gloves, and she was always very, very clean. No one would ever imagine Lois Sills with dirty pants.

Their eyes met, for the first time, really. "It's good to have you back."

"If only temporarily."

"Oh, we'll see ..."

Mallory wondered what that meant. There had been two similar hints last night and now she was at it again first thing in the morning. He'd meant to warn her, don't practice your womanly wiles, they simply aren't going to work, but he hadn't wanted to precipitate anything, and besides, Theo, her interminable father, had been there.

Theo was like the mountain. He hadn't changed, either. He'd shown up at the first tinkle of ice and hadn't left until the late show. By then, Mallory was dead, and Lois, too. They'd said good night and staggered off to bed without really having a visit. Theo had done all the talking.

"Well. Now that it's light. You want to show me the rest of the place?"

"Sure."

Laughing, she took his hand, leading him like a child, taking him on a tour. He hadn't seen any of the changes she'd made. They'd all been done after he'd left—and after Jock's death. It was her home now, reflecting her tastes, not his. He'd been a shoe manufacturer, and it showed.

"The gazebo? That's new?"

"Of course. And all that garden. You mean you don't remember?"

"I don't remember the tennis court."

"Paddle board."

Mallory looked closer, sampling his coffee. It was black, something she remembered. "What did you do? Buy Wrigley's lot?"

"Yes."

"That must have cost an arm."

"Mmmmm." She pulled him along, taking him around the pool, pausing briefly before each new addition, letting them speak for themselves.

Yes, and a leg, Mallory thought. Paddle board. He'd never played, and he wondered if Lois did. Jock must have left her a bundle. Theo's wing, it was a whole new house, practically, and the whirlpool, it hadn't been here before, and what was this? A sauna? "Where's the jai alai?"

"It wouldn't fit."

The answer was only half in jest. Space was always a problem in Canyon Country Club. Even with Wrigley's lot, she'd never have a real showplace, forever in the shadow of Joey Hrudka, whose $3 million home was approached via a half-mile-long driveway lined with 500 Italian cypress, whose swimming pool was shaped like a Thunderbird, and whose wife's closet space provided for a thousand dresses and two hundred pairs of shoes.

Mallory grinned. "Well, you've done a good job, anyway. A regular Barbara Marx."

"You heard about that? She did the whole compound over. In *suede*."

"Yes."

"God," Lois said. "What a place..." She looked at him for a long moment. "Did anybody recognize you?"

"In the limo? No. I hid behind the *Times*. The whole way."

That delicious laugh again. He was her secret. "There was someone?"

"Yes. Mary Alice. But she probably wouldn't have noticed. She'd just been married."

"King!"

"I'm serious."

Lois hesitated, captivated by the idea, afraid of being disappointed. "If you're making this up..."

"Honestly. I swear."

"She's seventy."

"Yes, and he's forty."

That was too much. "King! Damn you."

"Fifty, then, but not a day more, and wait till you hear the rest," Mallory said, finally remembering the importance of gossip. It ranked only after money. "He's Mexican, a tourist guide."

"You're serious? Some fat little fortune hunter from the Zona Rosa?"

Mallory laughed, enjoying himself, hardly believing her expression. "Relax, she's got lots, and besides, he's perfectly charming."

"You *are* serious?"

"Yes."

"That silly goose," Lois complained. "Doesn't she realize? I mean, Lord Almighty, she's not just some old lady, she's …"

"Important?" Mallory offered.

Lois nodded. That was the word. "Yes."

Until now, Mallory hadn't considered this aspect, the reverse psychology of not being important himself, or at least not any longer. "And it won't look good?"

"Being followed around by a gardener half her age? No."

"Tourist guide," Mallory corrected gently. He was sorry now that he had said anything.

"What worries me…" Lois paused, as if trying to think of what did. "She's still active. On the hospital board, the Desert Circus, everything. He could manipulate her."

"Her vote?"

"He conned her into marrying him, didn't he?"

"Says who?"

"Well…"

"Don't bet," Mallory said. "Maybe she conned him. As I recall, she always knew what she wanted, and how to get it, too. Why not wait till you meet him before jumping to conclusions? He struck me as a nice young man."

Lois made a face. "Eck."

"It's going to be that way?"

"You're darn right. I've certainly no desire to…" Lois stopped, suddenly aware of Mallory's expression. "I guess that's not very kind, is it?"

No, Mallory thought, not answering. He'd been gone so long he'd forgotten the rules. Nobody cared whether you were nice or not. What mattered was being important. And rich. If you weren't wearing a thousand-dollar watch they thought you didn't know what time it was.

"King. Let's not spoil it."

"It's not spoiled," Mallory assured her, returning the tentative smile. He looked at his own poor timepiece. "How does a man get some breakfast around here?"

"Buy it," Lois told him, laughing again. She twirled about, her dress lifting, showing her legs. "All this—and you think I can cook, too?"

Billy helped Mary Alice from the cab and stood watching while she paid the fare. He still had no money of his own, just the forty pesos, and he owed that to her, having lost at cards.

"Now," Mary Alice said, the cab sent off. "You stay out of the way."

With that, she left him, hurrying over to the Bekins van, her stick held high. She really didn't need it for walking. It was a weapon, not a cane.

"They're here," Flo said needlessly.

"Why didn't you call?" Mary Alice demanded. "The piano, is it off yet? I want it to stay."

"They just came," Flo complained. Her uniform had been thrown on, it was all twisted, and her eyes were still puffy, sleep bugs in the corners. "How did you get up so early? *Careful!*"

The bigger of the two men put his end of a crate down. A patch sewn on his shirt identified him as Al. "The piano stays?"

"Yes, I want it to go somewhere else," Mary Alice told him. She turned back to Flo. "I'm giving it to Graham, he's always wanted it, and after what's happened ..." There was a quick glance at Billy. "I want those two to get along."

Flo looked over to him, taking the time to wave. "Hi!"

"The piano stays," Al said. He picked up his end of the crate. "Okay, let's try it again."

"Whenever you're ready," his partner muttered; a name tag identified him as Tony. He was already sweating, his shirt sticking to his back, circles under his arms. "What's in this sonofabitch anyway?"

Flo checked the crate. There were stickers, *Fragile, This Side UP, Don't Use Hand Car,* and also a number, 36. "Bricks."

"It sure feels like it," Tony said. He took a first tentative step backward, thinking that next time he got to go forward, and also that it was going to be a long day.

Flo went on ahead, to clear a path, apparently. Mary Alice followed.

"I want to hear everything," Flo said.

Mary Alice stuck out her tongue.

Everything...? Billy got the bags, there were just the two of them, Mary Alice's night case, his own battered valise, and waited until they had disappeared inside. Well, she would have to admit something at least, he thought. Nothing would be difficult for someone so garrulous.

Instead of going in the house, he went through the breezeway, depositing his burden on the patio, then continuing into the garden. He was familiar with the layout—he'd had the tour the night before—and already had found his hiding place.

The garden was flush against the mountain, its focal point a cluster of huge boulders, too large to move or disguise, so the only solution was to *want* them there. Lights had been placed under them, the same way the palm trees were lit, and Billy's most vivid recollection, what had impressed him the most, was the long, comforting shadows. The rest of the place was alien. Here he could be at home.

Voices drifted out to him. Flo had opened the whole place up. It was impossible to air-condition with the movers going in and out.

"No. We get it all inside, *then* start opening."

"We didn't do that last year."

"This isn't last year. And everything stays in the entrance hall. I don't want excelsior all over the place."

Billy sat down against the rock he'd picked, the temperature changing immediately, almost cool in the shadows. He hoped they wouldn't start talking about … everything. He didn't want to hear.

More voices.

"Can we change things around? The chow table never belonged in the den."

"Oh, God, I don't want to go through that. Does the den care?"

"Hey, lady. Tell me the truth. Are these really bricks?"

Billy wondered where else he could go. The house empty, a drum, the voices were very loud, nothing to muffle them.

"How about the plants? Did you phone Neel's?"

"Yes. This afternoon, between two and four."

"And the fish?"

"Uh, huh. But I've got bad news, Roger is dead. What do you think of the job on the rug?"

"Super."

No, he had to move, Billy decided. If he stayed, it was just a matter of time, and he didn't want to hear. He pushed himself up and headed back toward the house. He'd offer to help, and if she still felt him in the way, then he would go for a walk, find some other place to spend the morning. There probably was a park.

When he reached the patio, a telephone rang, making him jump. It was right beside him, a few feet from the pool, a long cord trailing back into the house, and he never stopped to think that it might be an extension. He picked it up on the second ring, pausing for just a moment, wanting to do this correctly, and then it was answered in the house.

"Hello?" Flo said, beating him by an instant.

"Flo?" a woman said, laughter in her voice. "I don't care what she's doing. Put her on the line."

"Oh, hi," Flo said. "You heard already, huh?" She also laughed. "Just a minute…"

Billy was going to hang up, Flo's clatter to cover, but the woman spoke, this time to someone with her, harshly. "The silly bitch."

The abrupt change was startling. The laughter had sounded so genuine, but the contempt was real, too. Instinctively, Billy knew it was directed at him, and he couldn't hang up now, that would be cowardice, not good manners. This was something he ought to hear. He covered the mouthpiece, listening to the enemy breathe.

Mary Alice came on. "Mavis?"

"You old fart," Mavis said, the laughter back. "You mean it's not true? You didn't die of a heart attack?"

Mary Alice snorted. "That's the rumor, is it?"

"The story. Three inhalator calls, at ten, twelve and two. And the last time you were dead."

"But with a smile on my face?"

"Yes!"

"God." There was a pause. "Now, do you want to hear the truth?"

"I'm coming right over."

"No, you're not. The place is a mess."

"I'll help."

"You won't."

"Mary Alice," Mavis said, pleading now. "*I'm* the one who's dying. What does he look like?"

"He's handsome. Short, dark and handsome."

"You can't have everything. How old?"

"You mean you don't know?"

"I mean I don't believe it."

"Fifty-two. But he looks younger."

"The night clerk said he was twelve."

Mary Alice laughed, delighted.

"Listen," Mavis said. "I've got to see him. Lunch? Can we have lunch?"

"No."

"Dinner."

"*No*. And what are you doing in town, anyway? You're supposed to be ... where? Madrid?"

"Rome, but it's just as hot, and we can't have dinner, I just remembered, that's why I'm here. The party."

"What party?"

"Stu Bollinger's."

"Oh, great," Mary Alice said. "Is that tonight?"

"Of course. Isn't that why you came back?"

"No, it isn't." There was a pause. "Do you think the Chermaks know?"

"That you're here? Darling, *everybody* knows."

"Then I'll have to go, won't I?"

"Of course. You're bringing him?"

"Don't worry."

"You promise?"

"He's my husband, isn't he?" Mary Alice said, hanging up.

Billy waited.

"You're going to vomit," Mavis told the person with her, and she hung up, too.

Billy put the phone down, feeling guilty already, and angry and confused, and afraid to go into the house. Mary Alice would see it in his face, he thought. She'd know.

The phone rang again.

He backed off, retreating to the garden, taking refuge in the shadow of the rock, thinking that the woman had made him sound like a freak.

You're bringing him?, and he could imagine her grinning, poking a stick through the bars. *You promise?*

The phone kept ringing. Voices came from the house.

"Flo! Will you get that?"

"In a minute!"

Two more rings. Then silence for a long moment.

"It's for you!"

"Who is it?"

"The Desert Sun."

"Well, tell them to start again."

"No, it's not that. They want to know."

"Know what?"

"If it's true."

Billy felt himself shudder. What was the truth?

Lois drove, headed downtown, supposedly for Louise's Pantry, but they really weren't going there, or at least not yet. First, the surprise.

"Oh, and Saks," Lois said, pointing out another change. "The last holdout. They stay open in the summer now."

Mallory grunted. "That makes it official?"

"Yes. We're a year-round town."

Great, Mallory thought. That improved his chances of bumping into someone he knew. What kind of woman wouldn't cook breakfast because she didn't want to get her gloves dirty?

Lois smiled—she could guess what he was thinking—and checked her appearance in the rearview mirror. You'll do, she told herself. Don't worry. You'll do.

"What's that awful thing?"

"Sunshine Fish, Meat and Liquor."

"It looks like a warehouse."

"I know," Lois said, serene. She was an attractive, vivacious woman. Intelligent, personable. Full of life and eager to live it to the fullest. Who would guess she was fifty-six?

"Who'd let them do that?"

"Now, that I don't know."

"God."

"Exactly," Lois said. She was quite a catch, really. Though Jock may have failed her in other ways, he had at least left her well situated, both socially and financially. Top-layer upper crust, her home truly her castle, and the Rolls dependable transportation, not an indulgence.

Mallory cringed at the sight of yet another architectural indignity, remembering his role, twenty years before, in cleaning out the slums on Section 14, Indian-owned land here in the heart of downtown. Anxious to be rid of the eyesore, the city had employed a variety of laws and ordinances to evict several thousand blacks, Chicanos and poor whites living in shacks and hovels. But this wasn't what he'd had in mind as a replacement.

"Thrifty Drugs. Burger King. The place is going to hell. You'll have a McDonald's next."

"Your fault."

"Mine?"

"Yes, you should never have left."

Mallory didn't argue, his displeasure increasing, thinking that no matter how you dressed it up, a hamburger stand was a hamburger stand. Why couldn't they keep just one small part sacred? His mind went back to the evictions and the bitterness they caused. Though not racially motivated, it did effectively accomplish a kind of segregation, some of the blacks moving to Desert Highlands, at the north end of town, but most having to go twenty to thirty miles away, to Banning or Beaumont or Indio.

And that suited the Christian power structure just fine, only then managing to accept the Jews, he remembered. After all, Palm Springs was specifically established for the rich, and if blacks and Chicanos had to live here, the preference was that they do it in the servants' quarters. After the clean-up, economics conspired to keep the largely non-union town about as "white" as it could reasonably hope for, a fifteen per cent minority population, only a third of that black. There wasn't much housing available for

someone making the minimum wage. You could work here. Lots
and lots of menial jobs. But you lived elsewhere.

"Admit it, you should never have left," Lois said. She was
tired of being a widow, Theo her only company, and, one way
or the other, she was going to get herself another man. The right
man this time. The one she wanted in the first place. Mallory.

"Haw."

"Haw, yourself."

Mallory was suddenly alert. "Hey! Do you know where you're
going?"

"Quiet," Lois told him. The thought made her wet inside.
With Mallory in tow, that would be it, Valhalla.

"You missed the turn."

"Did I?"

"Yes. It's back there."

"You're sure?"

Oh, Mallory thought, wanting to be angry, but feeling apprehensive instead. What was she up to?

She kept looking straight ahead. "Don't worry. I just want to
show you something."

"Such as …?"

"You'll see."

She continued for several blocks, finally leaving Indian
Avenue at the turn-around, heading back with the one-way traffic on Palm Canyon.

Mallory sat silent, thinking he should have known. He had
offered to stay put, a stale bun would be fine, then sneak off to see
Spisak on his own, but that wouldn't do. She had insisted on this
sortie, telling him not to be a sissy, it was one-way glass.

"Don't you like surprises?" she teased.

"No."

Suddenly, she veered right, making an abrupt lane change,
swinging into a driveway and braking sharply. "Well, here it is
anyway."

Mallory stared. It looked like a house, *was* a house, but it couldn't be, of course, not in the middle of the commercial district.

"Like it?"

"What is it?" He remembered it as an office of some sort. An insurance agency?

Lois was already out of the Rolls. "Come on."

He emerged slowly—what had she done?—and stood watching as she unlocked the door and pushed it open with a flourish.

Her face was shimmering. "Come on," she repeated.

With an effort, he went inside, easing past her, aware of her anticipation, a kind of trembling excitement.

"Well...?"

It was a real estate office, fully furnished, ready to go. All it needed was a sign across the front window. Mallory moved through it, touching a desk, feeling a chair, examining a picture—all the things he was supposed to do.

"You do like it?"

"Of course," he said, not looking at her. "It's lovely." He opened a door, revealing a smaller private office, half of it taken up by a huge oak desk, an antique showpiece.

"The boss's," Lois said behind him.

"Right." He tried another door, this time finding a small board room, the paneled walls matching the oval table, the high-back chairs.

"For staff meetings."

"Yes."

Finally, he turned around, still not looking at her, or at least not seeing her. What registered was invisible. The sign on the window, the letters reversed (how else to read it from the street?):

 YNAPMOC YROLLAM GNIK EHT

Please, God, Lois whispered, make it work, and she told herself that it *had to*. There was a carefully reasoned argument that she had rehearsed forever. His political campaign blowup had been forgiven if not forgotten, and in any event he was remembered for his larger contribution, his long years of dedicated service, the growth and development he had spurred and guided. The name alone, King Mallory, remained a powerful draw, and she wasn't worried about the social niceties, either. Her friends accepted him back or they weren't her friends. The hell with them, but it wouldn't come to that, it couldn't, wouldn't. Before the fall, Mallory and Cissy ran with the elite, and it was Mallory—raconteur, character, charmer—Mallory who kept the invitations coming. "Say something."

Mallory was appalled. The last thing he wanted was to return permanently. Surely she realized that, accepted it? True, he knew she might try to change his mind. He frankly had expected her to go through the motions. But this kind of pressure?

"Anything," Lois said, waiting.

Mallory couldn't find the words. She obviously had spent a small fortune establishing this business opportunity for him. To dismiss it out of hand was unthinkable. Yet he wasn't going to let himself be railroaded. It was his life, what was left—and he'd live it the way he pleased.

She was still waiting.

"You hungry?" he asked at last.

She nodded.

"Then let's eat."

Quickly, rougher than he meant, he turned her around, not wanting to see her face.

St. Pierre's morning walk—he always took one, it was a creative experience, a preparation for the day—consisted of the long trek down to the gatehouse at Five Lakes. He could have phoned, but a personal confrontation would lend more importance to his instructions, and in case of any slip-ups he wanted to be able to identify the man.

As he cut across the vacant golf course and its empty puddle lakes, past the shuttered fortress condos, blackout blinds drawn till "the season," he wondered how Cleo knew he'd be here. MacPherson, friend and partner, he'd never tell, and so Cleo had to somehow instinctively know that out of a whole world of beckoning places, he'd be holing up on the cheap?

The bitch. That's the way she thought. He was a tightwad, he never gave her enough, money was to spend and oh, boy, could she ever do it, but *no more.* It was all coming down, what he'd saved despite her, and it was going into some fast-appreciating land—as MacPherson had suggested, along the Paseo in Palm Desert?—and then he could stop running for a while, from her and after the dollar, stop. If he could stop, just for a while, if he could *think,* his life would get sorted out, he knew that.

Free from Cleo. His money safe. And then he could stop and think. He had it vaguely formulated that he didn't want to do any more buildings. They were difficult to get and they took forever and there was too much interference and although he was very good he wasn't great. He wasn't going to be Le Corbusier. Or a Niemeyer or a Saarinen. Or even an Owings or a Mies.

What he had to do was lower his sight. Like Hemingway, who (and this he imagined) shot himself because he couldn't be Shakespeare, St. Pierre had once aspired to greatness. What architecture did, it proclaimed the existence of civilization, and to be a great architect, what that meant, essentially, was to be in charge of your time.

Who was in command down the ages? The pyramids said the Pharaohs and Babylon said Nebuchadnezzar. The Forum said Caesar, and Europe's cathedrals said the Church, and then its palaces and chateaus proclaimed the arrogant opulence of the age of kings.

For a while, St. Pierre thought he'd like to be in charge of his time—not directly, of course, but essentially—leaving the master's mark (which the master would think was his own, but which actually would be his, St. Pierre's). For a while he thought he might work in concert with the new masters, the large corporations glorifying themselves—Lever, Seagram, John Hancock, Transamerica—but he wasn't Le Corbusier, or Owings, either. And like Hemingway must have felt, opening the pages of Shakespeare, he knew that however much he aspired, he'd never build the Parthenon.

The Palatine Chapel? St. Peter's Basilica, Notre Dame, Versailles? No, little man with your pushed-in face, lower your sights and find your place, go build the houses which of all things you are best at, and go build them in the sun. Remember Le Corbusier's definition: "Architecture is the play of forms under the light, the play of forms correct, wise, magnificent."

The play of forms under the light, St. Pierre remembered, thinking that one day he must build houses again, and build them here—in the sun.

"Good morning."

"Huh?" the guard said, caught by surprise. There were but a handful of residents this time of year, and when any of them moved, they didn't walk. He peered out at St. Pierre, his legs a strange white color, sticking out of shorts that hadn't been worn before.

"Good morning."

"Yes," the guard said. He came and stood at the door.

"I'm St. Pierre," St. Pierre told him, showing the keys. "A guest in the MacPherson condo, and what I came to say, my wife isn't."

"Your wife?"

"No."

The guard thought for a moment. He was an old man, a pensioner, paid the minimum wage, and he said hello and waved good-bye, and checked names on a clipboard and asked polite questions and wrote down license numbers and sometimes made a telephone call, just checking to make sure, but that's all. "Where is your wife?"

"Coming, I think," St. Pierre said. "Possibly this afternoon. There's a plane then." He pointed dramatically. "When and if she arrives—I don't want her past that gate."

The guard looked at the flimsy barrier. It was a single arm of wood, meant as an obstacle, not a true gate, and he'd often wondered what would happen if there was any real trouble. He'd spoken to the security chief about it, as a matter of fact, and the security chief, a former policeman, had said there wouldn't be any real trouble.

"We're separated," St. Pierre said. "I'm a guest, a live-in guest, deserving of the same consideration and protection as any other tenant or resident, and I am officially and for the record stating at this time that my wife is not to be permitted within the walls of Five Lakes."

Oh, boy, the guard thought. He wished the security chief was around to hear this guy.

"Do you understand?"

"If your wife shows up, we tell her you're not here?"

"No. She knows I'm here. If my wife shows up, you tell her to go away."

"To go away," the guard repeated, feeling the adrenaline start. Come November, he'd have three years on the job, and this was the first real trouble, gate wise. "What's the lady look like?"

"Who said she was a lady?" St. Pierre asked. He produced a photograph, brought especially for the purpose. "I'll thank you to post this and inform the other shifts."

"Yes, sir."

"Any other questions?"

"What's her name?"

"Cleo."

"All right," the guard said. He tacked up the photograph, a wanted poster. She didn't look dangerous—a small, dowdy woman with eyes too close together, a pinched nose—but then appearances could be deceptive.

Satisfied, St. Pierre nodded and stalked away, thinking he'd been a bit brusque, perhaps, but at least he'd made an impression. The first line of defense had been established.

The guard stood studying the photograph. The security chief couldn't help. He was on vacation, in Sacramento, he always took August, didn't come back till after Labor Day. No, the guard thought. Like it or not, he was on his own.

Suzy Braverman listened to the telephone, counting the number of rings, wondering why Dex wouldn't answer.

"Dex!" she called, spreading her nails to dry. "Honey? Would you get that?"

"*Mom*," Dex complained. "They're out there." To illustrate, she left the door open. "'Bye!"

"Where are you going?"

"Tennis."

Suzy got up to close the door, watching Dex fly down the sidewalk, Milo Chermak waiting in his Morgan, the other boy in the Corvette, what was his name, Fred?

Well, keep your pants on, Suzy thought. She waited to make sure Dex got into the Morgan before she closed the door.

The phone was still ringing.

"Coming," Suzy sang. She hoped it wasn't a hot prospect. She wanted the whole day off to get ready. Blowing on her nails, she picked the phone up gingerly, tucking the receiver under her ear, taking it into the living room that way. "Hello?"

Em was on the line. "Suzy?"

"Oh, hi, darling," Suzy said, relieved. "I was going to call you. Dex just gave me the message." She paused, checking herself in a mirror, thinking that she really did look like Vanessa Redgrave. "What's happening?"

"I'm in trouble."

Suzy laughed. Em was the Rock. "You?"

"Remember me mentioning my nephew?"

"Uh, huh. The flake. Corporal Sargent."

"He's here."

Oh, no, Suzy thought. Not this afternoon. She'd promised, but not this afternoon. "Darling. I know I promised. But not this afternoon."

"How about tomorrow?"

"Tomorrow? You sound frantic."

"I am."

"Just a minute," Suzy said. She took the phone back to the hall, getting her appointment book off the sideboard, wetting a finger and flipping through the pages. The morning was free. "The morning's free."

"What time?"

Suzy thought for a moment. The party probably would run late. "Ten?"

Em sighed. "Okay."

Suzy found a pen, writing a reminder, Corporal Sargent. He sounded like somebody in *Catch-22*. "What else is happening?"

"That's all."

"Well, don't worry," Suzy said. "We'll have him fixed up in no time." She looked at herself in the sideboard mirror, seeing Vanessa Redgrave. "Has he got any preferences?"

"Yes, a dinosaur."

"Say again?"

"A dinosaur."

"Okay. A dinosaur. Any second choices?"

"A water tower."

"He sounds difficult."

"That's the trouble."

"Don't worry," Suzy said, laughing. "Fixed up in no time. Love ya, gotta go."

"I hope," Em said, sounding doubtful.

Suzy rang off, taking the phone down the hall, untangling the long cord as she went. There was just the one for the whole house. She didn't want any extensions to encourage eavesdropping. What Dex did was her own business. As long as she kept her pants on.

In the bathroom, sitting on the throne, she dialed Gwen's unlisted number, keeping her fingers crossed. Four former husbands watched from identical frames, married, in order displayed, for love, money, convenience and—finally—out of desperation. Only Hank's picture—Hank was Number Two, Dex's father—had any sentimental value. He still paid child support. Norman, Larry and H. Mickey Rose, they were just reminders to never, ever, try it again.

There was no answer. Suzy hung up, swearing softly, wondering if she ought to try Louise, and deciding no, she was such a bitch, she'd want to split the commission. Money, money, money. That made her think of the party, which made her think of the Chermaks, which made her think of Dex and Milo. Fantasy: Her golden girl—married into the Chermak wealth.

Gawd, Suzy thought, trying to think of something else, that almost gave her a coronary. Money, lots of it, that was the key. If you had money, you had it all, and if you didn't have it, you were nothing.

Tonight's party. Let's be honest. She wouldn't have been invited if Dex wasn't dating Milo. Oh, sure, she had achieved recognition of sorts, the big hello in public places, but that was still just surface stuff, she wasn't *in*. How could she be?

No. It wasn't going to happen. Bust your ass for the Desert Circus, kissy-kissy all over the Racquet Club, tramp through Melvyn's in ermine for a month—none of that got you invitations to *the* parties.

Tonight was a fluke, Dex. The rest of the year? Zilch. Hal Wallis wasn't going to have her over, and she'd never get her

picture taken with Bob Hope, and Gerald Ford was a total absolute loss.

Suzy sighed, taking the phone into her bedroom, trying to
cheer herself up by picking out what to wear. She had already
decided to overdress. A long, flowing gown, that was definite,
and loads of jewelry, and maybe just one really stunning feather.

Feathers were her trademark. One night she put a boa in
Sonny Bono's soup, which was quite a feat really, considering he
was at the next table.

Suzy dialed again, trying one last time, examining herself in the wardrobe mirror, a tall, striking, ageless divorcee.
Though something of a phony—too vibrant, too gushy, too
kissy-kissy—she nevertheless was a real pro and turned a big
volume. Her pose was that she did it only to keep busy, that
it was better than boozing the day away, the biggest decision
which belt to wear, but the truth was she desperately wanted
and needed the bucks.

"Darryl? Darryl, darling, do me a favor, you know that dinosaur out on the interstate, the one by the Texaco Truck Stop?"

"The museum?"

"Yes, but it's a gift shop, actually. Darling, do me a favor, find
out if it's for sale, and if it is, how much?"

"You got a client?"

"I might have," Suzy said, still looking at herself in the mirror. It was amazing, really, the resemblance, and no matter how
hot it got she always seemed cool, perfectly coiffured, spotless.
Opinion was divided as to whether she was without sweat glands
or carried an air conditioner between her legs.

Mallory toyed with the breakfast that he had wanted so
badly. He had been playing a stupid game, pretending not to have
guessed that the real estate office was established for him, but
now the question of who was supposed to sit behind the antique
desk couldn't conceivably be put off any longer.

"Do you have someone in mind?" he asked, thinking that it obviously wasn't going to be her, she hadn't done a day's work in her life.

Lois forced herself to look at him. Sensing defeat, trying to blot it from her mind, she had been going along with the charade, discussing the new enterprise in very general terms, carefully avoiding any direct reference to his possible involvement.

"Yes," she said slowly, "but it is apparently a difficult decision—I knew it would be, actually—and the party needs some time to decide."

The party, Mallory thought. Why hadn't he thought of that? It helped to have a party to put the blame on. "And if the party says no?"

"Well. I'd be sorely disappointed, of course."

"You could get someone else, though," Mallory told her, wanting that established.

"I suppose so," Lois admitted. "There must be others. Someone I could hire. Go into partnership with…" She looked away. "Don't worry. It won't mean financial disaster."

"Good," Mallory said, a bit inanely, but he wanted that established, too. "You always had a good business head."

"Did I?"

"Yes."

"Well, I'm glad to hear."

Mallory eased away, the worst part over, the rest put off for later. He didn't have to kill and bury all in one day. "More coffee?"

"No, thank you."

"Would you mind if I…?"

"Go ahead."

Mallory showed his cup to the girl and they sat in silence while she came over and refilled it. There were four years to catch up, but why bother now?

"Actually, maybe I should just leave you here," Lois said finally, barely able to keep up appearances. In her heart, she knew his decision, that the answer was no. She also knew she'd been a fool to have hoped otherwise. "Spisak's office is just a couple of blocks—and I've got some errands to do."

"Sure."

She got her purse and the gloves she carried though didn't wear. "I could pick you up later."

"No. I'll find my way."

She stood up. "Any idea of when?"

"When?" He got up belatedly, too late to move her chair.

"How long do you think you'll be?"

"I'm not sure."

"Oh." She looked at him, thinking that this was when she was going to mention the Bollinger party, when he was going to agree to that, too, but now she couldn't even ask if he'd be home for dinner because "home" didn't sound right and everything was in tatters. "Good-bye, then."

"Good-bye," Mallory said. He stood watching her leave, wondering what the hell had got into her, she had always been smarter than that.

The man with the golden hair came up.

"You do that very well," Jody said after a while. "I don't want to embarrass you—can you take a compliment?—but you just might be the best cunt eater in the whole world."

"The second best," the man said, laughing. "Everybody's the best."

"Mmmm, a modest man, I don't believe it." She twisted her fingers in his golden hair.

"You all right?"

"Yes."

She kissed him, brushing his lips, tasting herself. "Thank you."

"You're welcome."

"Mmmm." She slipped off the bed, impossibly beautiful, perfect.

He ached as he watched her go, thinking that her skin was the most incredible thing, so goddamn soft.

"When your eyes are closed, you look like a princess, you know that?"

"Do I?"

"Yes."

"Which one?"

Anne, he was going to say, but that wouldn't explain it properly, because she didn't look like her at all, except for the regal part. Lying down, head back, eyes closed, she looked very regal then. The rest of the time she didn't. Not particularly, anyway.

Jody was waiting at the bathroom door. "Well?"

"Anne."

"Fuck you," Jody said.

The man laughed. "What do you want to do?"

"You mean next?"

"Today," the man said.

"I don't know. It's awfully hot out, isn't it?"

"Yes."

"What is there to do?"

"Nothing. My kind of town."

"You've got a car?"

"Yes."

The telephone rang.

"Get that, will you?" Jody called.

The man reached for it a bit reluctantly. This wasn't his room. "Hello?"

"Jody?"

"No," the man said, "but she's here." He put the phone down. "It's for you."

Jody came out, a towel wrapped around her, giving him a look, *Who?*

"A woman," the man said, barely audible, mouthing the words. He eased off the bed and went into the bathroom and carefully closed the door.

Jody got a cigarette going before she answered. "Yes?"

"Jody?"

"Yes. Who is this?"

"Mary Alice. Remember?"

"Oh, it's you," Jody said, relaxing. "I was wondering…" I put the cigarette down. "How are you, anyway?"

"Fine. And you?"

"Good."

"Settling in?"

"Yes."

"The reason I called," Mary Alice said, "there's a party tonight, and if anybody ought to attend, it's you."

"Me?"

"The perfect place to get you acquainted. Normally, no one's in town, but if anybody is here, they're going to be there, plus a lot of people coming up from the beach, just for the evening. Am I making sense?"

Jody laughed. "Not exactly."

"It's social."

"Oh."

"I've got to go," Mary Alice said. "Everybody wants to see Billy, and I want them to see you, too. I lied to Stu. Told him you were family. You'll knock him on his ear."

"Stu?"

"Bollinger."

"Oh," Jody said again, the name meaning nothing.

"You'll love him. He's fabulously rich."

"Isn't everybody?"

"It's something to do," Mary Alice counseled, "and you can bring your young man if you want to, the more the merrier."

Jody hesitated. It sounded like gate-crashing. "You're sure it would be all right?"

"Of course. It's settled, you're coming. We'll pick you up at six. There'll be dinner, and dress casual. Smashing—but casual."

Jody still wasn't sure.

"It's a deal?"

"Sure," she decided, thinking, why not? "It's a deal. Six o'clock, and thank you."

"Wonderful. We'll see you then."

"Uh, huh. 'Bye."

"'Bye."

Jody hung up and retrieved her cigarette, taking just one puff, then stubbing it out. That way it wouldn't count.

The man came out of the bathroom. "Who was that?"

"Family."

The man frowned. It hadn't sounded like family.

"Distant," Jody explained, making it jibe with what she'd told him before. "A great-aunt I'd forgotten about."

The man didn't say anything. He got his clothes and started to dress.

"Somebody must have told her," Jody said, wondering why she was lying. "She used to come to visit us when I was a little girl. A really wonderful person. She wore teddies, long after they were out of style, and she also dyed her hair, so she wouldn't have to confess she had taken ten years off her age."

The man continued dressing, pulling his pants on, the anger starting to show.

"She could still put her foot behind her head when she was in her early sixties," Jody said, "and played a mean game of canasta. She never married, and I never wondered why."

❧ ❧ ❧

Stu Bollinger stood before a massive picture window overlooking an Olympic-size pool. Where did they get such ideas? he wondered. His son, Chip, was trying to get up on water skis, being pulled by a girl on a golf cart.

Behind him, Benson coughed discreetly, the other emissary from the Ford camp.

"Yeah, go on," Bollinger said absently.

"Betty wanted to stress that they were sorry, that's all," Benson said. "As you can guess, Jerry's got a pretty heavy schedule."

Bollinger thought that he didn't have to guess, he could read the newspapers, and what was this all about, anyway? He didn't recall the invitations being RSVP.

"I'm sure she'd have called," Benson said. "That's the kind of lady she is, and she did ask for a number, as a matter of fact."

"Did you give it to her?"

"No. I said I'd tell you myself."

Bollinger kept watching Chip. He was still trying to get up. "Okay, you did. But what's it all about?"

Benson shrugged. "I dunno. Just keeping the door open, I guess."

"The door is closed," Bollinger said, "if that's what you're talking about." He swore under his breath. "Get up, damn you. *Get up!*"

"The boys could change their minds."

"I won't."

Benson shrugged again, thinking what the hell, why stick his neck out?

The "Bollinger Boys," or parts thereof, got together frequently, for golf or tennis, for cards or boozing. It was an informal, loose-knit association, and it was also a disciplined, tight little club. Membership was not offered to just anyone. When President Ford moved to Rancho Mirage, to build his $600,000 retirement home at Thunderbird Country Club, he was considered, of course, but he didn't get enough votes.

Nor, Benson thought now, wondering how to exit gracefully, was he going to get them. He, Benson, wasn't going to try anymore, and Howard Chermak—who had put him up to this—had better wise up, too. Chermak could find himself on the outside looking in.

Bollinger, as the name implied, was the undisputed leader, they were his boys. Benson, Chermak, the rest of them, each was a big name in his own right, but they all catered to him and it wasn't just because of his fabulous wealth, a reputed billionaire. He had something more than that, a style, a kind of magic, an irresistible attraction. He made things happen.

And, another factor, equally important, he looked like a god. A man from a myth, tall, muscular, Adonis handsome, he was born to lead, a mandate he exercised covertly, especially in politics. There, he always preferred chamberlain.

Together the Bollinger Boys constituted the ruling elite of Palm Springs, which, in its broader sense, encompassed the several smaller adjoining cities, including Rancho Mirage and Palm Desert. They couldn't be bothered with the actual process—getting elected, serving—but they still effectively ran things in the twenty-mile length of the Coachella Valley. Nothing really important was done without their approval.

Like Benson, most were retired, former captains of business and industry, and the behind-the-scenes power play helped give reason to their lives. None was fool enough to think that golf and bridge and booze alone could ever replace a board room. They needed something going. Twist an arm here. Kick an ass there.

Keep busy.

Bollinger kept the busiest of all. Nominally retired, he couldn't resist a deal, the lure of the numbers game. Promoters were constantly coming to him with proposals and projects and schemes, and his blessing, when given, was sorcery. With

Bollinger in, the project became viable, the banks and other moneylenders got interested, the whole thing pulled together. It was his nature, however, to remain in the background, not get actively involved. He had a private saying, not original, that there was no sense having a dog and barking, too.

With so much money, the deals were hardly more than games, amusements, and he quickly tired of them, restlessly moving on to the next. He was like a man who buys a mechanical toy and winds it up and sets it loose but then doesn't stay to watch it work, because he's already left to buy another. Or a man who bets on a race but doesn't wait to see the horses come in, he's too busy figuring the next race.

Stu Bollinger, who looked like a god, who had so much money he didn't know what to do with it, and who was so busy looking for new worlds to conquer he barely knew what was happening on this one, stood before a massive picture window overlooking an Olympic-size swimming pool and wondered why, having been so blessed, he couldn't also have a son with balls.

Marion came in, looking more like a receptionist than a secretary, too good to waste in some back office, a tall, lithe, handsome woman stepping from the pages of a fashion magazine, but it was her brain you noticed. "It's getting late. Do you want to make that call now?"

Bollinger considered for a moment. "No, just send them a telex. 'Fuck off. Strong letter follows.'"

Marion nodded and went out.

"Tenneco," Bollinger explained. "Somebody else who wants me to change my mind." He left the window, going over to the bar, making himself another drink. "I'm worried about Chip."

Benson followed. "Why?"

"He doesn't do anything."

"Neither do we."

"I'm serious," Bollinger said. He took Benson's glass, tossing out the dregs. "What was in there?"

"Scotch."

"The special?"

"Please."

Bollinger poured it, his anger growing. "You think that's right? His whole life, one ambition, to water-ski in a swimming pool?"

"Kids," Benson said.

"If he'd *get up*," Bollinger said, "and he's not a kid, he's a man, he's thirty years old. Do you know what I was doing when I was thirty?"

Benson took the drink. "Making the money that now indulges that, I suppose."

"Working," Bollinger told him. "It is part of the cycle. It is required." He looked back at the window, shaking his head. "That boy..."

"Man."

Bollinger laughed. "Man," he repeated, accepting the correction, and then he was serious again. "Joe. What the hell am I going to do with him?"

Benson thought for a moment, he didn't appreciate questions like that, they provoked the wrong answers. "What happened to his solar energy enthusiasm?"

"It's been reduced to acquiring a tan."

"Well. Perhaps he needs motivation."

"Jesus."

"He does," Benson said, telling himself, see? He took his drink to the window. Chip was on the golf cart now, the girl trying to ski, both of them laughing, the thing hopeless. "Who's the girl?"

"Who cares?"

"You should," Benson said, taking a chance. "The right girl? Then he'll have it. Motivation."

Bullshit, Bollinger was going to say, but he changed his mind, wondering if the answer might really be that simple. He sipped thoughtfully at his drink.

Normally, money solved any problem, but in Chip's case money *was* the problem. He knew it was there and that he was going to get it. In the inheritance business, you sat on your ass.

Marion came in again. "Now it's Jurgensen's. The question of the day—'Do you really want baloney?'"

Bollinger frowned, then saw her look, reminding him that he'd promised. "Where's Blodgett?"

"Locked in her room. Two hours, no interruptions, absolute rest. Otherwise, she won't be able to function."

"Well, I guess it's up to me," Bollinger said. "Tell them yes, and I'll get to that other thing shortly." He watched her leave, then joined Benson at the window. Down at the pool, Chip crashed the golf cart into an umbrella, knocking it over and falling into it. "The right young lady, huh? You wouldn't happen to have one in mind?"

Benson shook his head.

"But you do know what qualities you'd look for?"

"Yes. First off, she'd have to be hungry."

Hungry, Bollinger mused, forgiving Benson his trespasses, he liked that idea, he liked it very much.

A hungry girl.

Cohz, Massa and Spisak were above a poodle boutique, so that dogs always could be heard faintly barking, a strange thing for a lawyer's office. There was just Spisak left. Cohz had retired, and Massa, Spisak was fond of saying, Massa was in the cold, cold ground.

Mallory climbed the stairs, the doggy smell (Spisak would never admit to it) bringing back a flood of memories. The late nights. The boozing and the card games, and the women. B.C., Before Cissy.

Spisak was waiting at the top, a small, spare man, a baseball mitt for a face, that kind of leathery, stitched, oiled, spit-on and rubbed-in look, and with an owl's eyeglasses and the expression of having to take a piss, which he had to do quite often. And he wore a suit when nobody else did.

"Did she show you?" was his first question.

"What?" Mallory asked.

"The real estate office."

"Yes," Mallory said, wondering how he knew, and then thinking it would be a surprise if he didn't. Spisak heard all, saw all, knew all.

"What did you say?"

"I said I was seeking legal advice."

Spisak laughed. "How are you, you sonofabitch?"

"Fine," Mallory said, laughing, too.

They shook hands, admiring themselves, glad to see the other in worse shape.

"You haven't changed. Paler, that's all."

"No. Nor you. Except more wizened."

"It's the sun."

"It's the rain."

Spisak led the way inside, limping slightly, an affectation. He thought it brought him sympathy.

Ivy wasn't there.

"The morning off," Spisak said, noting Mallory looking around. "Just you and me. The door locked. The phone off the hook." He paused to accomplish those things. "Right?"

"Right," Mallory said.

They went into Spisak's inner office where the same procedure was followed, Spisak grinning like a small boy, legal counsel in a tree house, pulling up the rope ladder.

"Right?"

"Right."

Spisak fitted into the recliner behind his desk. Mallory took the couch, hands behind his head, feet up.

"Now," Spisak said, fingering a stack of file folders. "Where do we begin? The Krawitz property…?"

Mallory winced. That had been his all-time worst deal. Other people bought up land in front of a railway. He had tried to do it in front of a wind tunnel.

Spisak was waiting.

"Tell me the bad news first," Mallory said. "If I cashed out now, what would I be worth?"

"Altogether?"

"Yes."

"Ballpark figure?"

"Close as you can."

"One hundred thousand dollars," Spisak said, asking to be contradicted.

Mallory winced again. "That's all?"

"That's generous."

"You're sure?"

"Positive."

God, Mallory thought, wondering where he'd gone wrong. Other men, the same start, the same path, they were millionaires now, their heaviest burden a golf club. And he was broke with the world on his shoulders.

"You can always go to work," Spisak suggested.

"Thanks," Mallory said. He had thought he was worth more than a hundred thousand. Not much more, maybe. But more.

"How long would it take, do you think?"

"To do what?"

"To cash out."

Spisak looked at him. "That's what you're thinking of doing?"

"Yes."

"And then...?"

Mallory shrugged, his whole body moving.

"How should I know?" Spisak asked. "You're the one selling. It depends on your price." He selected a file and opened it. "The Deepwell lot, you've got it listed at forty, and that's too high. The

Lady Patmore says the sign is rotting. Thirty-five and she'll sell it tomorrow."

"What do I still owe?"

Spisak checked. "Four ... no, say fifteen. And you've got five in it."

"Fifteen profit?"

"Well. You remember your arithmetic."

Mallory considered. "Okay. Tell her to come down."

"Ninety-five thousand," Spisak said, adjusting Mallory's total worth by that amount. He selected another file. "The Racquet Club Road lots. You're asking five and ..."

"Wait a minute," Mallory complained. "The hundred thousand is figured on asking prices?"

"They're going to blow away first," Spisak finished. "Three thousand, eight hundred, you've got a chance. Meltzer, across the wash, he's been getting three-five." He looked over his glasses. "Of course it's on asking. Tell me if I missed something. You previously mentioned a fire sale?"

"I assumed fair value," Mallory said, still complaining.

Spisak closed the file. "What's fair?" he wanted to know.

Mallory leaned back. He never had an answer for those kinds of questions.

"Fair is what makes the other guy happy," Spisak told him. "You want to make the other guy happy, figure eighty, eighty-five." He waited for that to sink in. "On the other hand, you don't have to sell, do you?"

"What do you think I'm down here for?"

"To put things in order," Spisak said. "Four years, I've heard from you twice. I'm an attorney, not a mother. How do you think ..." He stopped, taking off his glasses, cleaning them on his shirttail. "To sell, yes, that you mentioned, but I would have thought selectively. Some things. Not others."

Mallory stared at the ceiling for a while, shaken by the revised figure, unwilling to accept it. "You've got some suggestions?"

"Yes. Keep Deepwell. Five years from now, it's eighty thousand, easy."

"Then how come I can't get forty now?"

"Because it's not the last one."

"Oh."

"Listen," Spisak said, "it's none of my business, I'm just your best friend in the whole world, why do you need the money?" He waited, holding his glasses at a distance, checking them for spots. "You don't want to say, you don't have to. I resign, and fuck you, too."

Mallory hesitated. "I don't know. I guess I just want to hold it in my hand, that's all. I thought…"

"It might make you feel better?"

"Maybe."

"It would," Spisak assured him. "But then you'd have to put it somewhere. The bank. Under the mattress. A beaver farm."

Mallory wasn't listening. The question was like a lament. "What the hell is wrong with me?"

"Your propensity for the spectacular," Spisak said immediately. He put his glasses back on, smiling. That was an easy one. "It's a disease. You can't think small."

Mallory almost laughed—with three piddily lots on Racquet Club Road?—and then he remembered that they had come into his possession as part of a larger tract, and that the larger tract had been part of an even larger deal, and that Kaiser Aetna had been involved, almost, except…

"And for spreading too thin," Spisak added, more kindly. "Your propensity for trying to do it all." He made a motion that seemed to encompass his version of creation. "You really expected to build this place, and to build a fortune, too?"

This time Mallory did laugh. It was true.

"You should have made up your mind, one or the other. The sharpies are reading the ads, 'Business Opportunities,' and you're in a city council meeting till midnight, arguing whether some sign should be red or beige."

"Beige," Mallory said, laughing some more, remembering the vote. A national chain had to change its colors or it couldn't build a hotel.

"What did that whore say?" Spisak demanded, warming to the subject. "The one who didn't have time for dinner?"

"Uh," Mallory said. "'If I don't fuck, I don't eat. Who's got time to eat?'"

Spisak pointed. "That's you!"

Mallory didn't see how it was, but he wasn't inclined to argue. The Spisak logic was convoluted.

"And the distraught mother. Remember her? The daughter being gang-banged, every boy in class, what can she do?, she asks, and you suggest Father McIntyre."

"Not being a Catholic."

"Next thing, Father Mac and the girl, they're in the Virgin Islands..."

"Canary."

"...and the distraught mother's suing you. How can she sue the Church?"

How indeed? Mallory thought. He'd settled out of court. Spisak's advice. It was election time and wouldn't look good in the papers.

"Oh, oh," Spisak said, "speaking of fucking, remember Nora and Crazy Daisy? There's just the couch and it's my office and all you've got is the Sunday funnies so Crazy Daisy goes home with Dick Tracy on her ass? I can still hear her yelling. 'Don't call me Fly Face!'" He took a deep breath, coming back, suddenly saddened. "What do you want it for?"

Mallory was lost. "Where are we?"

"The money."

Yes, the money, Mallory thought. It was true what he'd said, he wasn't certain. He just wanted it out, all the disasters put aside, forgotten (was that possible?), and he wanted one last go at something solid. He wanted to be respectable in his old age.

"It's not to go in with her?"

Mallory came up slowly, thinking that the question sounded familiar, like it had been in the room since the beginning, hanging between them. "Lois?"

Spisak nodded.

"I'd have said so." He sat up properly, putting his feet on the floor. "She wants a broker, that's all. It's a job, not a partnership, and I've as much as told her no."

Spisak still wasn't satisfied. "What am I supposed to think? All summer long, she's running around here, ordering rugs when she's supposed to be in Laguna—'What's this about?' I'm asking—and when the thing is finally ready, flash, you're here—'Where's my money?'"

Mallory snorted. "Jesus Christ. They're two different things."

"And I'm supposed to know?"

"*I* didn't," Mallory said, becoming angry. "It was a complete surprise. She just went ahead and did it."

"As soon as she knew you were coming?"

"Yes."

"Three months ago," Spisak reminded him, pouncing triumphantly, "and when did I find out? Last night."

Mallory didn't have any real answer for that. Lois had kept after him, that's all. Letters even when he didn't answer, and phone calls on special occasions, the one person who really seemed to care, and finally he had promised to make a quick visit. No definite date, just sometime in the summer, and she had said fine, she'd be here the whole time, she had a project going, just as long was he promised. She made him swear—laughing, "Cross your heart?"—but he wasn't certain he'd keep his word until he actually got on the plane.

Project? How was he to know? He thought she meant some charity, and come to think of it, it was.

"When did I find out, last night, wasn't it?"

"Yes."

"And you're her house guest?"

"Yes."

"Well," Spisak persisted. "What did you expect? I put two and two together."

"And came up with a hundred thousand," Mallory said. "Excuse me, eighty-five, and you don't want me to do anything foolish, right?"

"Right."

Mallory sighed. "Rest assured."

"I've your word on that?"

"Yes."

"It's no business for you now, been taken over by women, every matron in town with time to kill, and there aren't enough houses, and condos are overbuilt, et cetera, et cetera."

"*Yes.*"

"It's not like you never," Spisak mentioned, fingering the Krawitz file. "This lizard pasture, for example."

"Spare me."

"Why should I?"

Mallory didn't know. "Whatever happened to that wind tunnel, anyway?" he asked, changing the subject.

"The government," Spisak said, as if that explained everything, and maybe it did.

Normally, Jacobi wouldn't have gotten involved, but nobody had been murdered for three weeks—a record during the summer—and he was going crazy figuring ways to waste time and still stay sober. The other thing was that they were both rookies and weren't handling things very well. They could use the help. A favor to be repaid.

He swung off the highway, bouncing across the desert, a huge cloud of dust rooster-tailing in his wake, and he hit the siren—just one short, screaming *Wowoooo*—as he skidded to a stop in front of Five Lakes.

Grand entrance. Everybody stared.

"What seems to be the trouble?" Jacobi asked, unfolding from his car. He already knew—it had been on the air for half an hour, the dispatcher laughing, having a grand time—but there was a form to be followed.

"This lady," Novick, the older deputy, told him with a look of relief. "Her husband, he's in there, he won't come out, and she says she's going to camp here until he does."

This was in reference to Cleo, who was sitting cross-legged under the gatehouse barrier, bagged as she ever got, refusing to budge. Mouse, a ratty Jack Russell terrier, was spread out on the pavement beside her, still groggy from a tranquilizer and not happy with the unaccustomed heat. She looked as if she'd like to throw up.

Jacobi tilted his Stetson. He was supposed to be in plain-clothes, but he wore a kind of uniform all the same, it never varied. The broad-brimmed hat, a plaid shirt, western-cut jacket and pants, cowboy boots with pointed toes and lots of scrollwork, and a huge solid-silver buckle on the tooled-leather belt that held him together.

"Bowden," Novick said, meaning the dispatcher, "he says she's not camping, she hasn't got a tent, but we've got a complaint here all the same." He looked at the guard, who had retreated to the gatehouse, his door locked and staying that way. "He says she's blocking traffic."

"Is she?" Jacobi asked, leaning against his car. It was supposed to be unmarked, but it had a large and very official-looking decal displayed on the driver's door. Speeding motorists invariably slowed down sharply as they came up alongside and spotted it. Upon this closer examination they saw that it identified an Official American Taxpayer.

"Will be—if a car shows up."

"That's what you're doing, huh?" Jacobi asked, getting out a cigar. "Waiting for a car to show up?"

"Yeah," Primo, the other deputy, said, moving in alongside Novick. They were a team.

"Well," Jacobi said. He tore the cellophane off the cigar and put his mouth around it, not planning on lighting the thing, he never did. "You got a car. Why don't you show up?"

"You mean drive inside?"

"Uh, huh. You want to talk to the husband, don't you? Get his side of the story. Find out why he's been being so mean to this nice lady."

"Sure. But what if she don't move?"

"Then I'll just have to arrest her for obstructing traffic."

Primo and Novick looked at each other and promptly clambered into their patrol car.

"You gonna move, lady?" Jacobi called.

Cleo stuck out her jaw. "No!"

Jacobi waved a gorilla's hand. "Okay. Run her over."

Primo hit the starter. The Dodge heaved, its motor roaring. "Go!"

Primo carefully drove to within about two feet of Cleo's outthrust jaw.

Jacobi shook his head. Rookies, they had no style. He pushed off his car and walked over to Cleo, moving like a cowboy, rolling on his heels.

"I'm not budging," Cleo said.

Jacobi reached down and got hold of one of her ankles. He gave it a jerk, pulling her leg out, knocking her on her back, and then he turned and walked back to his car, dragging her behind him on the pavement, ignoring her kicks and screams. Mouse just stared.

"Jesus," Primo said softly.

Novick closed his eyes.

Jacobi muscled Cleo into the back seat of his car, pushing her head down on the seat, holding her there.

"Lady," he grunted, "if you don't shut up, I'll have to sit on your face." He pushed harder to muffle another scream. "Well? What's it going to be?"

"All right," Cleo gasped.

Jacobi let her up, a hand still on her arm, making sure she didn't go anywhere.

"You're going to shut up?"

Cleo nodded, suddenly sober and staring at him hatefully, unable to believe what had happened.

"Good, then we can talk," Jacobi said. He took the cigar out of his mouth, the other requirement. "You got some kind of identification?"

Cleo kept staring, thinking, the sonofabitch, how could he do it, there were witnesses. "My purse."

Jacobi untangled it, a shoulder-strap job, taking possession and opening it up, removing a fat wallet the size of a bun. He got settled up front and thumbed through and found her driver's license. "Cleopatra?"

"Yes."

"You must have had lovely parents," Jacobi said, checking her against the photograph. In both cases, the eyes were too close together, pinching the nose. "What was it? Their idea of a joke?"

"No. They just had high hopes, that's all."

Jacobi became aware of the patrol car making a slow turn, coming around toward him. He rolled down his window, calling, "You guys can go now."

Primo nodded and took off.

"I assume you're a police officer?" Cleo said.

"Uh, huh," Jacobi told her, flipping plastic inserts. "A sergeant, Homicide, the Riverside Sheriff's Office. They've got a regular form for citizens' complaints. You just fill it out and sign your name and nobody believes you. Is that your dog?"

"Yes."

"The reason I could tell, she's in this picture with you," Jacobi said, showing her. "What we call in police work a deduction."

"You're not funny."

"No, but I'm not pitiful, either. You know what you smell like? A gin mill. What's her name?"

"Mouse."

Jacobi rolled the window down some more. "Hey, Mouse! You want to get your butt over here?"

Mouse just stared.

"What's it take?" Jacobi asked.

Cleo took her wallet back, and her purse, too. "She's had a tranquilizer. For the plane trip."

Jacobi thought for a moment. "You going to stay put?"

Cleo nodded.

Jacobi got out of the car and went back to pick up Mouse.

Cleo watched, putting her wallet in her purse, thinking that he was still a goddamn gorilla.

The guard came out of the gatehouse. He made a motion, to somewhere over the rooftops. "Her husband's in there. He won't come out."

"A wise man," Jacobi said. He let Mouse smell him, then scratched an ear, making friends.

The guard ventured closer. "Listen. The way you handled it. I didn't see a thing."

"You bet your ass," Jacobi said. He picked up Mouse and took her to the car and stuffed her in with Cleo.

The guard couldn't believe it. This was like the old days. A real cop.

Jacobi roared away, bumping across the desert, retracing his shortcut from the highway.

"You taking me to jail?" Cleo asked.

"No," Jacobi said, "but I know a nice little motel in Oregon."

He made the highway, headed for Palm Springs, thinking that he probably could get her in at the StarBrite.

Cleo nuzzled Mouse. How could you stay mad at a man like that?

Mallory waved a dollar at the bartender. "Can you give me some dimes? I've got to make a call."

The bartender found one in the change on the bar. He held it up. "If it's local, that's all she takes."

"Not the way I dial," Mallory said, but he took the one dime anyway, retiring to the pay phone. Never argue with the help.

"You okay?" the bartender wanted to know.

"Yeah," Mallory assured him.

Tina, the "day lady," answered first, and Theo came on right after, talking over her.

"I've got it, Theo," Tina said.

"Who's it for?"

"Lois."

Theo hung up. It was never for him, and that must be hard, Mallory thought. He used to be a star.

"Hello?"

"Is she there?"

"Oh, it's you," Tina said. "Do you know what time it is?"

Mallory frankly didn't. He had stopped looking at his watch several hours ago.

"It's almost five o'clock."

"What happened, I got tied up," Mallory said, wondering where he might get some rope burns. "I suppose she wanted to know about dinner?"

"I think so."

Mallory considered the alternatives. The best, it occurred to him, was to have her not there. He tried that, tentatively. "It sounds like she's not there."

"No, she isn't."

"Well, tell her I called," Mallory said, and he hung up and went back to the bar, being careful about the peanut shells on the floor.

The bartender had been watching. He came over, making sure.

"Problems?"

"Yeah," Mallory said. He got off his stool, retrieving his drink, swirling the dregs. Dinner hadn't been settled on anyway. That was the trouble with Lois. She *assumed*.

"You want another?"

Mallory shook his head. "No. I'm a little shit-faced already."

"Ehhh," the bartender said, wiggling a hand. He went back to his own perch at the other end of the bar. He wished they were all that easy.

Mallory looked around. There were just the two of them, and a waitress who had disappeared somewhere. The fag in the booth had gone.

"It's slow."

The bartender glanced up from his newspaper. "Summer."

Yeah, Mallory thought. It was summer, and the town wasn't the same, they were building warehouses and calling them restaurants, and that sonofabitch wouldn't have got past him. What color should a sign be?—laugh, sure, but little things added up, and how's that for arithmetic, Spisak? "The town's not the same."

The bartender glanced up again. "What town's that?"

"Palm Springs."

"No, I guess not," the bartender said. He put the newspaper away. "What is?"

"What is what?"

"What is the same?"

"Not Palm Springs," Mallory said.

The bartender thought about that for a while and then got his paper again.

Why should it be? Mallory mused, looking at the bartender not looking at him, the only constant was change. He should know that better than anyone.

Unbidden, the memories flooded, Palm Springs a path to the post office. A dozen year-round families. Maybe three hundred people showing up come winter.

Primitive, no telephones, and you were rich if you had electric lights, but they made do, Mallory thought. As Doris, his mother, was fond of saying, she *preferred* candles at the dinner table, and there was nothing like a good kerosene lamp for fireside reading. A handful of hardy pioneers challenging the empty desert—Spisak's lizard pasture—and fifty years later it rivals Palm Beach?

Mallory sighed, having been one of them, having spanned that half century, and having so very, very little to show for it. He wanted to go home, but he didn't have a home. Like Mike, his father, fifty years before him, he had worked so hard, and he had so little to show.

The fates. Blame them. Old Mike, he was lucky, he could blame Congress, possibly with more justification. It took the homestead away and gave it back to the Indians. The first time, Mike said, writing to the *Guinness Book of Records*, that such a thing had happened.

The Agua Calientes didn't have a reservation and there were newspaper articles and other pressures. Finally, it got all the way to Congress, where they decided they ought to rectify that oversight, and in the final resolution of that continuing process they canceled Mike Mallory's grazing leases, one argument being that he wasn't grazing anything anyway.

Empty, desolate desert, so they gave it to the Indians, along with half of Palm Springs, every other section, the other half, naturally, having gone to the railroad. Largesse which, when it ran its ultimate course, would make the Agua Calientes, then among the poorest, the richest Indians per capita in the United

States. The beginning of a glorious fuck-up, because the city couldn't zone, or tax, the Indian land. Every other section was beyond its authority. Two councils trying to run one town. And they were still arguing. The Golden Checkerboard.

The Calientes, there were only a hundred and twenty or so, just a band, not a tribe, they wanted individual holdings, arguing that joint ownership was impractical. So the reservation was officially divided up. Everybody got a piece. Man, woman and child. Fifty acres each. The same amount. Regardless of location.

Which put kindly was dumb, Mallory thought, remembering. Those shitpies in Washington, they'd ignored the maxim, the three most important things in real estate. Location, location and location. After the war, things getting better, no boom yet but things getting better, an Indian with a centrally located parcel, he was sitting pretty, worth several hundred thousand. But down the road a piece there'd be a brother or a cousin with the same amount of land and it was practically worthless.

Unfair? Yes, it was, it made for hard feelings, which aren't nice, so the shitpies dreamed up equalization. Downtown, the six richest Indians, their holdings were valued at $335,000, and the only way to make everybody happy was to make everybody worth $335,000, right? Right.

And it was easily done. They simply gave away some more land. Why not? They had the whole fucking desert, and it belonged to the Indians in the first place, didn't it? No quarrel. They owned it. Give it back to them. Downtown, it didn't take much, a couple more parcels, you've got a rich Indian, just like his brother. Out in the lizard pastures? It takes a bit more. Debra Sue, to make her rich, they had to give her two thousand acres, and Angel Patino...?

Mallory caught himself, wondering if, as Bluestone once suggested, he'd run for Congress just to get even?

Angel Patino, who, as his allotment, had taken all of Sun Devil Canyon.

Fuck, Mallory thought. He pushed his glass aside, collecting his scattered change, leaving a barely adequate tip.

"Thanks for listening," he said. A little unsteady on his feet, he headed for the door.

CHAPTER THREE

The party swirled, Bollinger thought. It was amazing what a truckload of booze and caviar could do. People came for miles, like flies. Half of them he couldn't recognize.

Marion came in. "Are you going to go down?"

"In a while," Bollinger said, staring at the swarm. "Have the Sinatras arrived?"

"Just. Larry called. They're at the gate."

"Did they bring anyone?"

"Jilly."

"Good," Bollinger said. He liked Jilly. "How about Kirk Douglas?"

"He's down there somewhere."

"George Hamilton?"

"Uh, huh."

"Good," Bollinger said again. No party could be a success without its quota of stars. "Incidentally, who invited Harry Guardino?"

"I did. Is that all right?"

"Sure."

Marion went to the bar, mixing herself a light drink, Campari and soda.

"How's Blodgett holding out?"

"Fine. But I think she'd like you down there."

"In a while. What happened to Chip?"

"He had to take his girl home."

Oh, yes, the girl, Bollinger thought. "Who is she, anyway?"

"Rita Prost."

"Prost?"

"General Telephone."

Bollinger paused, craning to see, wondering if that had really been Oscar Levant. "I guess you couldn't call her hungry, huh?"

Marion shook her head. "No, I wouldn't think so."

The picture window was one-way glass and there were hidden microphones everywhere, permitting Bollinger to watch and listen without being seen, present at the party, at least for the moment, in spirit only. The house was off limits, his guests restricted to the patio, the surrounding grounds, the various cottages and the other facilities. Dinner, when it was served, would be buffet style, eaten on tables set up on the lawn, and there would be dancing later on the tennis courts. Still later, when it finally cooled off, there might be some discreet humping out on the greens, and perhaps a little cocaine-sniffing behind the stable. Like Annenberg's estate, Sunnylands, which was spread over 240 acres, the property took up more than a quarter section of prime Rancho Mirage real estate. There was room and opportunity to do your own thing.

"I'm becoming insulated," Bollinger complained. "Benson and I were talking this afternoon. Do you know what conclusion we came to?—that we don't know any hungry girls." He paused, waiting for her reaction, but there wasn't any. "Do you?"

Marion shook her head. For five years, ever since taking the job, she had lived in a world of picky eaters. Guinea hens and hearts of palm. "No, I'm sorry, but I'm afraid I don't."

"Well, keep your eye open, will you?"

"All right."

"You know who for?"

"Yes."

It was for Chip, of course. The Constant Concern.

"Hey! There's Stanley Kramer."

"I know. You really ought to go down there."

"In a while," Bollinger said, searching for more celebrities. Zsa Zsa making a grand entrance, and Harry Guardino again, on the other side of the pool now, and Kirk Douglas talking to Connie Considine. "You didn't happen to invite Oscar Levant?"

"No."

"Why not?"

"He's dead."

Bollinger laughed. He really was getting insulted. "Here's Frank now..."

Despite herself, Marion came to look, arriving as Blodgett greeted Barbara.

Bollinger switched off all the channels except the receiving line.

Sinatra's voice: "Where's Stu?"

Blodgett: "He was here a moment ago. Have you met the Chermaks?"

Barbara: "Hi."

Chermak: "Hello."

Marion turned it off, keeping her hand on the switch. "Not when I'm here, okay?"

Bollinger frowned. "What's wrong?"

"I just don't like it."

Below, Blodgett stared at the Sinatras, thinking that was great, Bollinger hadn't even been down for them. "You had enough?" she wondered aloud.

Howard Chermak shrugged, looking at Ruth, the other end of the receiving line. "What do you think?"

"I really couldn't care less," Ruth said.

Chermak squeezed his wife's hand. "Now, now..."

Ruth pulled away angrily.

"She's right," Blodgett said, missing nothing. She was a sturdy, no-nonsense woman who had come home from the hospital with baby Chip, a surrogate mother until his own got better, a temporary position entering its thirty-first year.

The Sinatra limousine pulled away, another stopping in its place, and Theo got out, one of the attendants hurrying to help him.

Chermak mouthed the question. Are you crazy?

Ruth replied the same way. Bugger you.

"We've had enough," Blodgett decided. She started down the stairs to get Theo. "Where's Lois?"

Theo stopped to get his breath. "Sick. Where's Stu?"

Ruth turned and walked away, wishing she wasn't so angry, she'd feel better if she could cry.

Chermak called after her. "Where do you think you're going?"

"To get a drink!"

Jesus, Chermak thought, hurrying to catch up, let's not spoil the evening.

Involuntarily, he glanced back at the main house, to the greenish black rectangle that was Bollinger's one-way window.

Watching, Bollinger handed Marion his glass. "I think I'll go down now," he said casually.

Marion followed Ruth's angry course for a moment longer. "You're devious, you know that?"

Bollinger smiled, patting her on the bum. "I'll see you later."

"You don't ever do that to me, do you?"

"What?"

"Listen in."

"No," Bollinger lied.

The sign said *Sun Devil Canyon, 4 Miles.* Under it was an Indian arrow, pointing. The cab left the pavement and went that way, following a rough gravel road twisting along the side of the mountain. Around the first bend, the point of no return, there was a small weathered billboard with additional information: *Picnic Grounds, Public Welcome, Admission $1 Per Car.*

The cab driver glanced back at Mallory's provisions, which included a bag of potato chips, a bottle of whiskey and four six-packs of beer. "That's what you're planning on?"

Mallory looked at him.

"A picnic?"

"No, a reunion," Mallory confessed. "The guy who owns the joint ... I haven't seen him for a while."

"An Indian?"

"He thinks he is."

The driver was confused again. "You mean he isn't?"

"Yes and no," Mallory said. "Nothing is as it seems. What you've got to remember, the Spanish brought the first cattle to California, and the mission padres taught the Indians how to herd and graze 'em. One of history's little ironies—the first cowboys in this country were the Indians."

The driver laughed. "You sure about that?"

"Positive," Mallory told him, opening another beer. "I am an expert on Indians. You may ask me anything. Anything at all."

The driver couldn't think of anything, concentrating on his driving. The road was very narrow and poorly maintained.

Ask me where all Palm Springs' Indians live, and I will tell you, Orange County, Mallory thought. Except the exceptions. Take it from an expert, you can't generalize. *Some* live in Orange County, not all. Some live in Palos Verdes, while others live in Pacific Palisades. Others, of course, live in Palm Springs, holding the fort, so to speak. "If I sound bitter, I am."

Good, the driver thought, not laughing anymore. The road was too narrow for him to turn around and he had come too far to try backing up. All he could do was keep on going. He switched on his lights, it was getting dark.

Mallory sipped at his beer, wondering why it hurt so much, Miguel Patino, alias Bluestone, ungrateful little bastard. Because he cared? Had tried and failed? He had a talent for that. No, a disease. Spisak's diagnosis: your propensity for trying to do it all.

But what Spisak forgot was that sometimes a man didn't have much choice. He just had to go out there and do it. His duty— even though it got his ass kicked.

His duty, Mallory thought, remembering all the times he'd come up this same road, playing the harmonica, "One Meat Ball." His duty to Angel Patino and to Miguel alias Bluestone and to Sun Devil Canyon itself.

Angel, a renegade Caliente, had claimed the canyon during equalization, when the Indian Bureau, as directed by Congress, handed out additional lands so that all band members might have holdings valued at $335,000. Shown a map, Angel stabbed a crooked finger into the middle of the canyon, and no amount of argument, threats or coercion could change his mind.

The canyon was remote, completely arid, utterly worthless. There was no access. Nothing, they told him—but the crooked finger kept stabbing.

Finally, in desperation, they gave it to him, thinking good riddance. He'd always been a loner, a dangerous troublemaker, right out of *Tom Sawyer*, another Indian Joe. Let him rot there if that's what he wanted.

In truth, though, Angel hadn't struck a bad bargain, a whole canyon that was his and his alone. Four thousand, one hundred and forty-six acres to do with as he pleased. To keep and to cherish—and to let somebody else worry about.

The Allotment Act required guardians for minors and adults in need of assistance in handling their affairs and nobody needed more help than Angel. The judge overseeing the process tapped young Jack Mallory. He'd been a fool to accept, Mallory was to admit later, but he was a comer than, only thirty and already being noticed, the boy wonder desert developer, and it was a kind of public-spirited thing, like serving on the hospital board. How was he to know what was actually involved? Trustee, conservator, those were the titles, but they ought to have been nursemaid and psychiatrist.

The main problem with being Angel's conservator was that there was nothing to conserve. At the time, the canyon wasn't worth a pinch of coyote shit, to quote the judge. The most Mallory could do to satisfy his trust was build Angel a shack and keep him in flour and beans.

Mallory had expected Angel to sit out there and drink himself to death while he, Mallory, closed his eyes to the whole goddamn disaster, a nice, easy, harmless solution, but it hadn't worked that way. The shack was a big mistake. In those days, if a man had a shack, he could get himself a woman, even Angel Patino. Carol, white trash, the worst kind, a slut and a scold, she deserved all she got, the Saturday-night punching bag, Carol, God Almighty, what a bitch, she showed up one night and stayed for three years and provided both of them with a lifetime of hell.

The genes were surprisingly good, though, everyone had to admit that, when the bastard child came it was a fine strapping boy, everything one could want or expect, a pleasure to behold. Mallory was surprised, proud, and he wasn't sorry that Carol was dead, it was the only nice word he ever had for her, she had the decency to expire and save the little man from knowing his mother.

Denied a son, Mallory would have taken Miguel into his own home, but Cissy's health was poor even then. The doctor had said no. Even with help; there'd be the psychological strain.

Miguel should have gone to an Indian family. The obvious alternative and there were lots of offers. But Angel had been dead against it, he wanted nothing to do with the band, and he did have some say, the natural father, after all.

Inevitably, there was a succession of white foster homes, the constant change Angel's fault, not Miguel's. Angel had a bad habit of visiting at odd hours, whenever the whim struck. Suddenly, there'd be a drunken Indian at the front door, screaming like a banshee, "White son'bitch, fuck' bastards, steal boy, I kill!"

Mallory spent many a red dawn going to the canyon instead of the police, retrieving Miguel from an immediately repentant Angel, but by then the damage was done. As Cissy, feeling guilty, often said, that kind of experience had to be hard on foster parents, and on the boy, too.

Especially foster parents, apparently. One drunken raid was all it ever took. By the time he was ten, Miguel, like Angel, was an outcast. No one wanted him. The word had gotten around, embroidered in the telling.

Fortunately, Mallory had pull then—mayor, in his second term—or the Indian Bureau would have taken over long before, packing Miguel off to some reservation boarding school in another jurisdiction. Instead, they looked the other way, effectively giving him custody, and Mallory enrolled Miguel at Xavier. Angel could mount all the assaults he wanted on that Jesuit stronghold. He'd have more luck invading West Point.

It was the right decision, the only one possible, really, for the boy's best interests, but it harvested worse trauma in the end. With ready access denied, the father-son relationship, already strained and tenuous, slowly ceased to exist. Home from Los Angeles—holiday weekends, the Christmas and Easter vacations, the long, hot summer—Miguel ventured less and less to Sun Devil Canyon. Angel and his peculiar ways were alien to him and each year the gap widened. They became strangers, ill at ease in each other's company, Angel baffled and in awe of what his loins had wrought, and Miguel ashamed that this primitive should be his father. He didn't want him, wouldn't accept him, and when he turned away, looked elsewhere, he found Mallory.

It was inevitable. Angel had reverted and lived in another world. He was the complete aboriginal, prehistoric man, hunting with crude weapons, and making strange drawings, wild and beautiful, on the canyon's rock outcroppings, leaving a crazed, indecipherable record of his passing. Mallory hadn't planned it, didn't want it. He wasn't a son'bitch, fuck' bastard who would steal another man's son. It just happened, that's all.

An act of God? Maybe, Mallory thought sometimes. Like Angel, he could blame/credit Him, too. The rock outcroppings had burst forth with a pure rushing spring in one of the frequent shifts along the San Andreas Fault. Where once there was nothing, stone daggers thrust heavenward, water flowed. Angel proclaimed it a miracle—and began to draw.

Alone, he made his strange drawings, wild and beautiful, and the years passed and he died alone, half eaten by buzzards when Mallory finally found him, a silly old man no one cared for.

It was a mean funeral. Besides the priest, there were just two of them, Mallory and Miguel, and there was no loss, no sorrow. Mallory cried, but that was out of frustration, for his own failure, his defeat. The tears were for a dry-eyed son at his father's grave.

Later, enraged, Mallory decided he'd make something of the canyon, prove that Angel hadn't been completely wrong to choose it. The new spring was providing a good supply of fresh water, so he bulldozed a road in, dug a pond, planted palm trees. Miguel, old enough, strong for his age, helped him all one summer, every weekend with a borrowed bulldozer. Miguel singing while Mallory accompanied him on the harmonica. The songs from camp. "One Meat Ball" and "About a Mile."

By October, when the season started, they had tables and fire pits and rest rooms, a picnic ground that proved fairly successful in those less sophisticated times. There wasn't the aerial tramway yet. No museum or leisure center. Just the one movie house.

People were willing to go out of their way and they didn't mind rough roads and they also had a certain innocence. The transplanted palm trees and the pond with its phony waterfall weren't the main attraction. The lure, as it happened, was Angel's strange drawings, wild and beautiful. Someone decided they were ancient—and Mallory saw no good reason to disabuse them of that.

The Garden of Mystery? What do the strange markings mean? Mallory actually turned a few dollars on that intriguing question with nothing for an answer. Not all that much—a caretaker had to be paid, and there were other expenses—but at least it helped. Miguel got his education, graduating from Xavier, going on to Berkeley.

Salad days. Mallory felt pretty good then, everything finally together and functioning, maybe he hadn't failed his obligations after all, and then—without warning—down the crapper.

Third year, working to a law degree, and then abruptly, suddenly and without warning, Miguel was a campus radical, at the storm center of the violence, everything else tossed aside. One cataclysmic upheaval and it was all over. Down the crapper. Gone.

He dropped out and he went away—"To find my identity!" the shout—and when he came back he was a stranger. He wasn't Miguel Patino, prospective lawyer, not anymore. No. he was Bluestone, more Indian than the rest of the Calientes put together, brave warrior fighting the white man's injustices.

Fighting me, Mallory raged, a silent scream. Abruptly, the world was upside down and twisted, a stranger in the body of the boy he loved, a stranger asking awful lies. Who dug the chasm between me and my father? Who robbed me of my heritage?

Abruptly, it was over, done. The petition to the court. The dismissal as conservator. These are enlightened times, Congressman. Surely two years of college means a young man is capable of managing his own affairs, even if he is an Indian?

Yes, Your Honor. But...

The driver slowed, coming around the last bend, the canyon wide and flat below, the palms black clumps but the water glistening.

Mallory looked. There was a light in the shack, the old truck out back, a small car—Bluestone's?—in the front yard.

"Stop here," Mallory ordered, finishing his beer, "and put out your lights."

The driver complied. Mallory paid him, passing crumpled bills, adding two dollars for a tip. He got his provisions, easing out of the cab, closing the door softly.

The driver watched him, wondering what he was supposed to do, and Mallory slapped the side of the cab, pointing to where there was room to turn, signaling as to how it should be done.

Laboriously, the driver followed instructions, finally getting the cab around, facing back the way he'd come. When Mallory slapped the side again, he pulled away slowly, waiting until he was certain of escape, then picking up speed as he turned on his lights and fled.

Mallory waited for a long moment. Nothing had changed below. The shack looked the same, no sign of activity, just the thump-thump-thump of the generator, drowning out everything else.

It probably was true what he'd heard somewhere, that sound carried up, Mallory decided. He got his packages arranged and started down into the canyon.

The party swirled, a judicious mix of money, fame and achievement, the Chermaks' anniversary only a camouflage for the real intent, which was mutual admiration. Even Suzy Braverman—sneaking in the back door, as it were—had come to be admired. Bringing her feather for the mass preening.

George Spector found her floating detached, a recurring question in her wake—Is that Vanessa Redgrave?

"What are you doing here?" George asked, demonstrating the lack of tact which had ensured his success.

"I was invited," Suzy told him, not saying why. George wasn't one of her favorite people. She'd have left his employ long ago if George Spector Realty wasn't *the* firm. It had the carriage trade. All the best listings.

George stared foolishly for a moment. Being one of the exceptions himself, he knew it was unusual, even rare, to work up to the charmed circle. One was either accepted immediately or not at all.

"You don't mind?"

"No, no. Of course not."

Suzy smiled, waving to Noah Dietrich, whom she had shown several houses when Noah, after publication of his book on Howard Hughes, had decided to move to Palm Springs.

"Actually, nothing could please me more," George said. "Welcome aboard. You're going to find it marvelous for contacts."

Suzy smiled again, blowing a kiss to Ingrid Margellos, the wife of the producer. "I suppose it could help."

"Business with pleasure," George said. Initially, he had been jealous, this was his private turf, but now he was prepared to take advantage. "Can I get you a drink?"

Suzy hadn't been aware that her glass was empty. "Oh. Please."

"What is it?"

"Champagne."

Ingrid came over, radiant in her beauty, still the fashion model. "Suzy. You look marvelous."

"So do you."

George waited to be introduced.

Suzy pretended not to notice. This one night, this *first night*, she was not going to talk, not even think, business. "Where's Jim?"

"Turkey," Ingrid told her, adding as explanation, "Pepsi money."

Marion remained at the window, finishing her Campari and soda, waiting for Bollinger to make his delayed appearance. She didn't want to show up with him. People might get ideas.

To amuse herself, she played with the switches, making quick cuts to various locations, thinking that she was creating—if that was possible—a montage of sounds.

"*David!* It's been forever!"

"Abbey Rents? You're not serious?"

"Darling, don't talk politics. I can't even *spell* Califano."

"So there I am, in the middle of the goddamn jungle, and I've got diarrhea, and my back is out, and I've got to vomit standing up."

Marion laughed. That had been Arthur Lyons, Chip's novelist friend, holding forth in one of the guest cottages, and she was tempted to find out who with.

"Yes, I know exactly what he makes. Two hundred thousand dollars a year. But he spends his *whole life* looking up assholes."

"Listen, I'd give my right arm. As far as I'm concerned, she's got a standing invitation to lie down."

Marion kept switching, testing herself—who was *that,* for example?—and wondering if, in a few select places, Bollinger had hidden cameras, too. There was no reason for him to tell her everything. Yet.

In the greenhouse, someone was crying, a woman.

Ruth? Probably, Marion thought, Bollinger really was a sonofabitch, what did she see in him?

She laughed again. What a stupid question.

Bollinger was outside now, working his way across the patio, belatedly greeting his guests.

Marion switched off the monitors and left.

Mallory stood in the yard. Inside the shack, a woman laughed, a little drunk. She had been laughing like that on and off, a beacon directing him across the desert, substituting for the light, which had blinked out when he reached the canyon floor.

Caught, Mallory had feared then, sure he'd been heard, but she had laughed right away, guileless and soaring. No danger in that.

He stood in the yard, wondering what he was interrupting, and thinking, yes, that's what it probably was. He could imagine them keeping time to the generator. Thump-thump-thump.

Maybe he ought to wait?

Inside, the woman laughed.

Well, there was lots of time, Mallory decided. He made his way to the porch, piling his provisions there, and then sitting on the step, leaning against the post. He could hear their voices now, slurred, teasing.

"One thing, he's got ambition."

"Sure. When he gets out of the Army, he's going to join the Navy."

"Blue!"

"It's true."

And more laughter.

What pissed him, Mallory thought, the worst saved to the last, what pissed him was the campaigning for Ellis. Coming out for the enemy. The other side. The ungrateful bastard—how could he do that?

"Can I put it in your ear?"

"No!"

Silence. Giggles. The sound of a struggle.

Mallory sat remembering, wishing they'd get it on. Miguel— no, Bluestone—he was Bluestone then—Miguel came to all the meetings, following him around, booing and heckling. "Pie in the sky promises? Hey, who you kidding, King? You gotta whole bakery up there."

"Lucy. Come on."

"I'm not *Lucy*."

Jesus, Mallory thought. That was gratitude. He got out his harmonica, banging it into his palm, wondering what would be appropriate.

"Uhhh."

"You..."

Mallory started playing. "About a Mile." The words danced in his head: I knew a man/His name was Ford/Took a tin can/A piece o'board/A rusty nail/Which was goin' too far/Put 'em all together and he made a

Bluestone heaved, rolling off Millie, right off the pool table.

Millie stayed sprawled there, frozen. "Jesus Christ. Who's that?"

Bluestone pulled up his pants, scrambling for the door, yanking it open.

"Bastard!" Mallory said, hitting him.

There was an explosion of blood. Bluestone sagged, face contorted, eyes rolled back.

Millie screamed, still frozen, and Bluestone kept slowly falling, already unconscious, crashing into a chair, breaking it apart. He rolled into the shambles and stayed there very still.

Mallory stared down at him, feeling cleansed, sorry. He was glad to have done it at last. But it hardly seemed enough.

"Blue," Millie cried, coming off the table. "Oh, God. Blue…"

Mallory went back outside, returning to his place on the step, getting out his harmonica. He started to play again. "One Meat Ball."

In the open doorway, Millie was cradling the bloodied head. She was naked and she didn't care. The word was a sob. "Why?"

"I love him, too," Mallory told her. He started over. One meat ball/Without the gravy/One meat ball/No french fries/The waiter's voice could be heard by all/This gentleman here wants one meat ball

Bollinger kept moving, dispensing his favors by rank. Some received an embrace, others a handshake, still others only a wave.

"Eva! How the hell are you?"

"Sharon, let me look at you."

"Sonny! I'll talk to you later."

Billy Segundo left the bar, holding three drinks in a triangle, suddenly realizing that he was lost. Mary Alice was gone, swallowed up by the crowd, and there was no sign of Jody, either.

He stood frozen for a moment, what had been discomfort turning to fear, fighting the urge to cry out for help.

A woman stopped. "Are you giving those away?"

Before he could answer, she had the scotch, taking a sample sip. "Good. You're a godsend. And I need a gin and tonic."

Billy looked at her unsurely.

"Please?"

Oh, Billy thought, wanting it to be the rented tuxedo, but knowing that it was him. *He* was the one who didn't fit.

The woman flushed, realizing her mistake, "I beg your pardon. I thought…" She offered to return the drink, but the glass was splotched with her lipstick. "Now what?"

"Keep it," Billy said finally.

"You're sure?"

"Yes."

"I could get you another…?"

"No."

The woman kept the drink, turning away awkwardly, gone as quickly as she had appeared.

Billy stood staring at the empty space between his outstretched fingers. Another slight, however unintentional, and it would keep on happening as long as he was… what?

Mary Alice's voice sounded above the babble. "There you are!"

An appendage, Billy decided.

Mary Alice pushed through to him, followed by another woman, almost a carbon copy of the one who had taken the drink, so many of them seemed to look the same.

"Well? What do you think of him?"

"I think he's marvelous."

Billy smiled inanely, not paying attention to the introduction, the names all seemed the same, too. Hadn't he already met a Gloria?

"I'm *so* glad to meet you," Gloria said. "Mary Alice has been telling me everything, of course. But..." She took hold of Mary Alice. "We're going to have to get a picture. Where's Justin?"

"Here."

Justin, Gloria's personal photographer, was already getting into position checking the wattage in his strobe pack.

Gloria arranged them, herself in the middle, linking arms with Billy and Mary Alice, standing with one leg forward.

"Everybody smile."

The strobe flashed.

"One more," Gloria said. She put Billy in the middle this time, standing the same way, one leg forward. "Everybody smile."

There was another flash.

"Good," Gloria said. She released Billy, patting him on the arm, as if to say he'd been a good boy, too. "Oh, oh. There's Fred Apollo."

Justin looked, getting out a notebook.

"William Morris," Gloria said, taking Mary Alice. "Fred could be *so* helpful to Graham."

Justin stayed behind with pen poised. "I'm sorry. You're, uh...?"

"An appendage," Billy said.

Bollinger put a big arm around Lady Weinerbaum, stealing her drink for a taste, making sure it was weak enough. The bar had strict orders. One ounce.

"How's it going, darling?"

Lady Weinerbaum sniffed. "A bunch of rich people, standing around looking at each other."

Bollinger laughed. "You still love Palm Springs?"

"Sure. Half the population in walkers."

"Lew," Bollinger called, returning a wave. "Glad you could make it." He gave her a squeeze. "Cheer up. You could still be in Russia."

"Romania," Lady Weinerbaum said.

Bollinger moved on—he'd have to remember that—reaching for an outstretched hand.

"Jerry. How's my boy?"

Jody purposely lost herself in the crowd, glad to be rid of Billy and Mary Alice for the moment, it was like being part of a circus, the hawker at the freak show. Hey, ya. Hey, ya. Come see the wrinkled lady and her smooth brown husband. The sensational, the incredible, the taboo-breaking, the society defying... Segundos!

The worst part was that everyone was so insincere. They said one thing and they meant another. You could see that in their eyes, and, when they thought you weren't looking, the way they smiled.

If this was high society you could have it. Billy and Mary Alice, they wouldn't last, they didn't have a chance, and Billy already knew it, you could see that in his eyes, too. He was already sorry, embarrassed for both of them, and if Mary Alice hadn't come to realize it—she was so secure in her position?—it wouldn't take much longer. They'd drag her down soon enough. Fit the mold. Or else.

It was the one thing she would never do, Jody decided, marry someone a lot older than herself, no matter what he had to offer. The man older, that was accepted, it was supposed to be different, but it really wasn't, not as far as she was concerned. It was the same thing.

Inside, she'd feel like Billy, and she'd never put herself in that position, no matter what was offered.

"Say. Haven't I met you someplace before...?"

Jody kept moving, thinking the nice thing was, unlike Billy, she'd never be tempted to sell out or compromise, she was the Empress.

Perfect.

Bollinger excused himself, easing through the crowd, going over to collect Theo. He took him by the arm and walked him for a way. "At least you came. Good."

Theo nodded glumly. "Smashing party. Who are these people?"

"Half of them, I don't know myself," Bollinger admitted, laughing. Theo's idea of a celebrity was Theda Bara. "It's nothing serious with Lois?"

"No. She's just in the dumps."

Bollinger raised an eyebrow.

"A man," Theo said, never able to keep more than half a secret. "I left her thinking positive thoughts. Make a list of your ten best qualities, I told her, and I'll bet she's still at Number One, 'I'm not bald.'"

"It's that bad?"

"It's worse."

"Well," Bollinger said, moving on, "give her my love, will you?" He smiled and waved to Mickey Proxmire. "How's my favorite dope peddler?"

Theo called after him with half another secret. "Blodgett's mad at you."

No doubt, Bollinger thought. "Shirley! Glad you could make it."

George Spector got Suzy, taking her away from David McDonald, confidant of Presidents, dragging her over to meet Max Guttman and his wife, Riva.

"Max is looking for a house," George said, coming right to the point.

"I did mention," Guttman admitted. He looked at Suzy, not saying hello. "Who's this? One of your salesladies?"

George didn't blink. "The best."

"Which is why you're here, huh?" Guttman asked Suzy, smiling. He stopped a passing waiter, giving him his empty glass, searching the tray for another martini, settling for a rye and water instead. It was all liquor.

Suzy gave George a look.

"I was thinking of the Lutz house," George said, pretending not to notice. "I was telling Max, it would be perfect for him—and for Riva, too, of course."

"It's for weekends," Guttman told Suzy. "We come down every Friday, the nature of the business, and have you seen what the Ingleside is charging lately? A hundred a night, and it's old furniture."

Riva smiled. "Antiques."

"Don't listen to her," Guttman said. "I make all the decisions. Believe me, it's old furniture."

"Well, if you'll be here this weekend," Suzy offered.

"Are you kidding?"

"Max means in the season," George said. "He's just here for the party, driving back tomorrow morning, so what I thought ..." He appealed to Guttman. "You'll love it. It's perfect for you."

Guttman motioned with his glass. "Convince your saleslady."

"Would you like to see it?"

"Convince her."

"Then it's settled," George said. "You'd be happy to show it, wouldn't you, Suzy?"

Suzy couldn't believe it. "Now?"

"Time is of the essence," George said, looking at his watch. "You can be back in an hour. I'll save you a lobster."

Guttman finished his drink and gave the empty glass to Riva.

"Don't you want me to come?"

"Naw, stay," Guttman told her. "Enjoy yourself." He smiled, looking at Suzy. "I make all the decisions anyway."

Bollinger couldn't pretend any longer that he hadn't seen Chermak. He went over to him, giving a hopeless little shrug, the kind meant to be an apology.

"Howard. Jesus, I'm sorry. Cardew called from London with a fuck-up on an oleo deal…" He waved. "Charlie!"

"That's all right," Chermak said.

"I should have come down but it was one of those minute-to-minute things. I'm still not sure what happened. Either I made or lost a million dollars. Lucy! Good to see you!"

"Really. It's all right."

"Well, it's your party, anyway," Bollinger said, smiling in agreement. He put a big arm around Chermak, friends together. "What the hell do you need me for?"

Chermak smiled wanly. It wasn't a question he was prepared to answer.

"Incidentally, where's Ruth?"

"I'm not sure."

Bollinger waved, smiling at someone, giving no indication that the reply registered. "There's Simpson, for Christ's sake. Who let him in?" He moved away. "I'll check you later."

"Right."

"And cheer up, will you? You look like someone who's been married for twenty-five years."

Jody slipped into the greenhouse, standing quietly for a moment, listening to herself breathe. The other sounds weren't apparent yet, she thought. Condensation and flowers growing.

Quite apart from the Segundos, she wasn't enjoying the party, and she had to get away for a while, just be alone with time to think.

Disappointing? No, that wasn't the right word. Frightening? No, too strong. Worrisome…? Yes, that was it.

The party was worrisome.

Like Sargent, a note pinned to his shirt, the party was showing signs of insanity, it hadn't noticed her.

It really hadn't, Jody thought. Not enough, anyway. There was too much competition. The Segundos weren't the only freaks. In a way, *everybody* was, that's why they were here, wasn't it?

You weren't invited without reason. You had to be somebody. A socialite or a personality. Rich, famous. Talented. Somebody or something, an *attraction,* anyway, and when everyone was so busy looking at everyone else...?

So busy looking at *themselves,* Jody thought, relieved. That was the trouble. She had met her own kind, that's all. The party was all mirrors.

"Marion, I've tried to commit suicide five times!"

Shocked, Jody stood frozen, unable to believe she wasn't alone, it had been so utterly silent when she entered.

"Jesus Christ, I wish I was German."

A sob, broken laughter, both mixed together, a clatter of approaching footsteps, and still Jody couldn't move.

Ruth Chermak, her face streaked with tears, came running from the rear of the greenhouse, Marion giving chase grimly.

"Don't let her out!"

Jody couldn't do otherwise. Ruth stopped, trapped, and Marion grabbed hold of her. "Ruth. Listen to me..."

Ruth twisted free. "No!"

"You're not getting out," Marion said, moving over beside Jody. "You're not getting out until you listen."

Ruth picked up an empty pot, breaking it against another, keeping a jagged shard.

"It's all right," Marion told Jody, sounding like a nanny lecturing. "She's not going to make a fool of herself. She knows he's not worth it."

Ruth stiffened. "Do I?"

"Ruth," Marion said. "Do you want to know why? Do you or do you not want to know why? It's got nothing to do with *you.* He was punishing Howard, not you, it was all to punish Howard, and it had nothing whatsoever to do with *you.*"

"Howard ...?"

"Yes. Howard's been insistent, he wants Jerry Ford in the club, and you know what Stu is like, he can't be Number Two—they're the Bollinger Boys, remember?—and so what happened out there was just Stu's way of showing Howard and it had nothing to do with you."

"Howard?"

"Howard," Marion repeated, wondering how many times it would be required. "He's putting down your husband, not you, and if you think it's going to help, throwing a tantrum ... well, that's exactly what Stu would like, isn't it? So why don't you go out there and show all your many friends just how easy it is for Stu Bollinger to belittle Howard Chermak. React. Show it hurts. Make Stu that important—and Howard that small."

"I ... I didn't know."

"No, you didn't know, and you didn't want to know, either. You wouldn't listen. You had to ..." Marion stopped, as if giving up. "Ruth, I'm sorry, I know you've had a couple of drinks, and I've had a couple, too, I guess."

Ruth shook her head. "No. You're right. I did have a couple of drinks. Otherwise ..." She put the shard aside, wiping at her eyes, trying to laugh. "Jesus Christ. Howard?"

Marion nodded, moving aside, taking Jody.

"I'll be all right," Ruth said. "Just let me get to a can." She brushed past them, face averted. "Excuse me."

Marion closed the door after her, slumping against it. She was a byzantine bitch, but it had worked, she thought. Stu could treat Ruth like dirt forever and she'd take it. She'd grovel and keep coming back for more. But if she thought Stu was kicking Howard ...

Women, Marion sighed. One less in Stu's bed?

Jody finally found her voice. "Uh, maybe I'd better get going, too."

"Sure," Marion said, not moving. "Thanks for the help. That could have been ..." She smiled tiredly, one problem solved, now there was another. "I'm Marion. Mr. Bollinger's executive secretary. And you are?"

"Jody Walsh."

Marion tried to remember. That wasn't on the list. "I'm sorry. Walsh?"

"With the Segundos," Jody explained. "Mary Alice asked me. She said ..."

"Oh, yes. Mr. Bollinger mentioned it. You're related, aren't you?"

"Not really," Jody said, uncomfortable with the idea, not the lie. "I'm afraid she made that up."

Marion smiled, thinking that was obvious, beauty and the beast. "I understand. It happens all the time."

"Does it?"

"Yes."

"Well," Jody said, suddenly and unaccountably angry, "I'm really quite sorry, I'm sure that must be very hard on you, the lower class come to drool, and now ... would you mind getting out of my way?"

"Honey ..."

"Jody," Jody said, "and if you're worried—what happened in here?—don't be. I wouldn't repeat it because I don't believe it. That was just as unreal as what's going on out there."

Marion stepped aside, pulling the door open. She made a gesture, thanks and good-bye.

Jody was still spoiling. "This is one time I don't care to be the belle of the ball."

Oh, yeah? Marion thought, watching her march away. That's what they all said. Yon pouting beauty was just another hungry young lady and ...

Just what the boss ordered?

Marion hurried to catch up. It would be quite an accomplishment, she decided, not only to bust up a romance, but also to start one, all in the same evening.

Mallory opened his bottle of whiskey, throwing the cork as far as he could, a ritual. They were going to drink it all.

Bluestone watched, trying to smile, but his jaw hurt too much for that. He was still dressed only in his pants, a tall, muscular, warrior specimen, blessed with the Cahuilla's darkly handsome big head, his jet black hair cut in long bangs.

Millie, a pale, wasted thing by comparison, waited in the doorway.

"You feeling better now?" Bluestone asked, finally saying something.

"I guess," Mallory admitted. He took a drink and passed the bottle.

Bluestone washed his mouth with the liquor and offered it to Millie.

Disappointed, Millie shook her head and went back into the shack, thinking both of them were crazy, that's all there was to it. Half an hour to revive him, she thought he was dead, and the bozo sitting on the porch the whole time, playing his goddamn mouth organ. Maybe Blue's honor wasn't important. But what about hers?

"Where'd you get her?" Mallory wanted to know.

"Bob's Big Boy," Bluestone said, spitting over the porch.

Mallory took back the bottle. "A waitress?"

"She ain't the manager."

Mallory didn't say anything.

"She's married," Bluestone said, a plus. That kept him from a similar tragedy. He might get drunk and do something foolish.

Mallory considered, then nodded solemnly, agreeing that it did make a difference. He took another drink and passed the bottle.

Millie came back out, smoothing her dress, not so much disappointed now, but angry instead.

"I hope you gentlemen have a nice time," she said, not looking at either of them.

Bluestone didn't see why she should be mad. "You going somewhere?"

"Home." She started down the stairs, walking very erect.

"When am I going to see you again?"

"That depends."

"On what?"

Millie kept on going, throwing her head back.

Bluestone called after her. "He's my guardian."

Millie slammed into her car.

"Women," Bluestone said. He washed his mouth out some more, spitting over the porch, feeling for loose teeth. "When did you get back?"

"Last night," Mallory told him.

"Staying?"

"Hell, no."

Bluestone drank some of the whiskey this time, watching Millie drive away, grinding gears and throwing sand. "You never were a forgiving man, were you?"

Mallory was watching him, bigger than he remembered, filling out finally, and better-looking, too. The years had added what ... character?

"Were you?"

"No."

Bluestone took another drink, aware of the scrutiny, waiting for a verdict. He wondered why he should care now. He hadn't before.

"What I've come to say, though," Mallory said, "I've mellowed."

Bluestone looked at him, glad his face was swollen, he couldn't laugh.

"It's true," Mallory complained. He paused, examining his shoes, thinking this was going to sound awfully fucking ponderous. "What I came out to say—I can rationalize your rebellion and the form it took."

Quietly, Bluestone claimed a part of the steps, keeping possession of the bottle, he was going to need it.

The question took a while coming. "What couldn't you forgive?"

"Ellis. Going over to a shitpie. What did you do that for?"

"I wanted attention."

Mallory looked at him.

Bluestone nodded. The truth.

"Well," Mallory said after a while, "you got it."

"Yeah," Bluestone said. He laughed and drank some whiskey.

Mallory sighed. He wondered what the rich people were doing.

Suzy was furious. The Lutz house was in Deep Well, which meant a drive all the way to Palm Springs, and there was no way she could get there and back in an hour and show the place, too. The whole evening was ruined. She could kill George Spector.

Guttman couldn't care less that she was angry. He didn't get where he was, one of Hollywood's top agents, four big stars as personal clients, by worrying about other people's feelings. Fuck her, it was her job, wasn't it?

Which wouldn't be a bad idea, Guttman thought. Despite her age, she was still a pretty good-looking broad, she took care of herself, and she dressed nicely, too. He especially liked the feather boa. That was class.

"What are they asking for this place?"

Suzy looked at him, her eyes leaving the road for just a moment, she was doing close to seventy.

"You mean George didn't tell you?"

"No."

"One-sixty," Suzy said, holding her breath. If it was out of his bracket . . . well, she'd kill George, that's all.

Guttman whistled. "This is just for weekends."

She'd kill him, Suzy thought. She'd very definitely kill him. "You're not going to find anything for much less. Not in a house, anyway. You'd be better to look at a condo."

"Naw, I don't like condos. Listen, if I wanted to live in a tenement, I could have stayed in New York."

"There's some nice condos . . ."

"Sure. There are some nice rhinoceroses. You want to dance with one?"

"It depends on your bracket."

"So what's my bracket?"

Suzy didn't say anything.

"I should tell you my bracket?" Guttman said. "Then you know how much I can afford? Listen, I only look stupid, how much do they want?"

"I told you. One-sixty."

"That's what they're asking. Now tell me what they want."

"They want one-sixty. It's firm."

"They're not open to offers?"

"Not according to the listing."

"Listen," Guttman said. "Listen to what we both know already. Everybody's open to offers."

Suzy sighed. Normally, they saw a house, *then* they haggled. "Maybe you'd like to see it first?"

Yeah, let me see it, baby, Guttman thought. Open your legs and let me see it.

Marion introduced Jody to Bollinger, making it clear she had come as a guest, not a relative, of Mary Alice, and asking—almost in the same breath—if he had seen Chip.

"Chip?" Bollinger said. "No, I thought . . ." He stopped, catching on immediately, which was one of the things Marion had come to respect. He didn't have to have maps drawn for him. "No, he's among the missing, I'm afraid. Do you think we ought to send a search party?"

Marion shrugged, leaving it for him to decide, and Bollinger, taking Jody into a better light, made up his mind immediately. He personally wasn't attracted to exceptionally beautiful women, they were more interested in themselves than him, but he still could appreciate their beauty. An admirer's, not a collector's, eye. His own tastes were eccentric.

"I'm glad you could join us. New York, isn't it?"

"No. Baltimore."

"Baltimore. Do you know the Comptons?"

"No, I'm afraid not."

"Well, you're not missing anything," Bollinger said, looking for Blodgett. "Did you go to school there? In the East, I mean."

"Hood College."

"Hood? Oh, yes. I had a friend whose daughter ... I'm sure it was Hood. Nancy Marwell?"

"That doesn't strike a bell."

"She'd be about your age. Twenty-two?"

"Five."

"Not that it matters," Bollinger said. He motioned to Marion. "Find Blodgett for me, will you? Is your family still there?"

"My mother."

Marion nodded, giving Jody's arm a reassuring touch. "I'll see you later."

Bollinger waited for the rest.

"My father's dead," Jody said. She had the strange feeling of being interviewed for a job.

Guttman bounced on the bed, watching Suzy's reaction, smiling.

Another invitation, Suzy thought. He'd also done a routine with the lock box.

"Hard, the way I like it," Guttman said. "How about you?"

"It's a four-piece bathroom," Suzy told him, ignoring the question. She pushed open the bathroom door, so he could look if he wished. "Tub with a separate shower."

Guttman got off the bed and peered inside. "Yeah."

Suzy was already back in the hall, the tour of the house finished, anxious to get outside again. She'd feel safer there. Someone might hear her scream.

Guttman followed, looking disappointed.

"There's just the yard," Suzy said, leading the way. "It's small, but very private, and you don't want a lot of upkeep, anyway." She flicked several switches, lighting the patio and the pool, too.

Guttman whistled, impressed.

"Lovely, isn't it?"

"It's okay."

His disappointment forgotten, Guttman circled the azure pool, making a careful inspection, taking note of everything. Suzy wondered if by a miracle she might have a sale.

"The patio furniture. Does it come?"

"We might be able to do something."

Guttman paused, checking an umbrella, making sure the lift mechanism worked.

Even if it comes out of my commission, Suzy thought.

"It's good quality."

"Yes."

Guttman lowered the umbrella, looking around the yard once more, seriously considering.

Suzy waited.

"I don't know…"

"You won't find better."

"It's the first I've looked at."

"It's why you looked at it first."

Guttman smiled, a con man being conned. He started back for the house. "I'll have to think on it, okay?"

"Don't you want to see the men's room?" Suzy blurted, suddenly remembering. She should at least be *trying*, she thought, but being so angry at George Spector, and then letting Guttman rattle her?

Guttman stopped. "The what?"

"The men's room," Suzy said, which was Gwen's name for it. On the first showing, held for realtors, the men had spent the whole time there, like children with a new toy.

Suzy went back around the pool, to a grating hidden in a flower bed. In every home she'd ever shown, it was the entrance to a dirty, jerry-built hole, but this one was different. "Look..."

Fluorescent lights blinked on below the grate, revealing a concrete bunker filled with glistening machinery, the pump, filter, heater and fittings all much more elaborate than required, a mechanical engineer's showplace.

Guttman came and stood at the edge, reminded of the engine room of an expensive yacht. He stared, fascinated.

"You want to go down?"

Guttman shook his head.

"Oh, come on," Suzy said, realizing that he was afraid. She lifted the grate and went first. "You talk about quality. Look at these fittings. They're all brass."

Guttman was still peering over the edge.

"Don't be a sissy."

Mustering his courage, Guttman followed her down the ladder, both feet to each step, making Suzy think of Dex's first visit to a playground. When he reached the bottom, he took a deep breath.

"See? Wasn't that easy...?"

"Yeah," Guttman admitted, looking around, getting his confidence back. "This is really something, hunh?" He touched a pipe, then a valve. His fingers lingered, lovingly. "This guy Lutz. What was he—an engineer?"

"No. There was a previous owner."

"He do the plumbing the same way?"

"Apparently."

Guttman whistled, looking around.

Suzy couldn't believe that she'd almost forgotten. This was the clincher. A marvelous, ridiculous macho toy.

"What do you think it cost?"

"I don't know, but I could find out."

Guttman nodded. "I'd be interested."

Sold, Suzy thought. Impulsively, she started for the ladder, then changed her mind.

Guttman had noticed. His smile was a leer. "Ladies first."

Suzy stood aside, waiting for him, thinking, like hell. That would be too grand an opportunity for a hand up her dress.

"What's the matter?"

"Nothing."

"Then go ahead."

"No."

Guttman gave her a look, pretending to be offended, but amused and emboldened. He moved toward her.

Oh, God, Suzy thought. She steeled herself, wondering how she could have been so stupid, there had been enough warnings.

"Don't..."

"What?" Guttman asked. He eased around the ladder, backing her into a corner, shoving with his body.

Suzy pushed desperately. "Get *away* from me!"

"Why? You wanted to play in the men's room, didn't you? Isn't that why you brought me down here?"

"No!"

"A little pinch and tickle. That's always good for business, hunh?"

"*No!*"

"Terrific," Guttman said. "I'd like that. But don't change your mind now..." Surprisingly strong, he grabbed her hand, pulling it down to rub against his penis. "You get a guy all worked up. You don't want to leave him frustrated."

Suzy was helpless against his weight. "Let … me … go …"

"Come on," Guttman said. "What're you complaining? You gotta sale." He unzipped his fly, taking out his stiffening penis, rubbing it against her hand. "Feel that? You gotta sale."

Suzy couldn't move, barely able to breathe. "Please …"

"Pull it." Guttman kept rubbing against her hand, harder now, masturbating. "Just bring me, okay? Just bring me—and you gotta sale."

"*No!*"

Guttman released her, backing away. He gulped for air, his face glistening with sweat. "Goddamn …"

Suzy turned into the wall. For a moment, she thought she was going to vomit, the nausea hitting like a wave.

"Cock tease," Guttman complained. "You get me down here …" He held himself, pounding a fat fist against a pipe. "Goddamn!"

Suzy kept facing the wall, wiping her hand on the concrete, trying to clean it. She couldn't believe what had happened. The drunken animal, he almost raped her.

"Cock tease," Guttman repeated, holding himself. His anger at not being gratified had given way to the fear of what she might do. "It's your fault, you led me on, and don't think I won't tell them that …" He tried to laugh. "Listen. No damage. It never happened, okay? Why make a big thing out of nothing?"

Nothing? Suzy shuddered, feeling dirtied, defiled. He was an animal and she had been assaulted and now he was trying to make it her fault?

"Let's leave it that way, nothing happened. You just keep your mouth shut, and I will, too. Forgive and forget. How's that?"

Never, Suzy thought. He wasn't going to laugh and say it was nothing. She'd call the police and have him arrested. He was an animal and he was going to be punished.

"Let's not be stupid. Show me the damage."

Suzy slowly turned to face him, thinking that was probably true, without some physical evidence, her word wasn't enough to support a charge. He could make a story that put the blame on her. Or just simply deny that it had happened. There wasn't anything she could do. He'd get away with it.

"Show me the damage."

"If you were patient, you might get what you want," Suzy told him. She smiled, straightening her dress, the panic and revulsion gone, purged by the anger. She felt very calm and deliberate and she knew exactly what she was going to do. "You don't have to push. I like it better in my mouth."

Guttman stared in disbelief.

"Give me that big thing," Suzy said. She hunkered down, taking hold of his penis, putting it to her lips.

Guttman moaned as he pushed it into her. Yeah.

Suzy took him out, wiping the swollen head, getting her breath, and then very quickly, with a surgeon's deft precision, she took it back and bit as hard as she could.

Guttman reeled backwards, clutching his crotch, the blood spurting. He looked down at himself, horrified, and first he vomited, and then he fainted. He crashed down heavily against a tangle of pipes.

Suzy scrambled up the ladder, pulling it out of the pit, then slamming down the grate. Safe, she slumped onto the grass, her heart pounding madly. She'd gotten even for so many things. For Guttman and George Spector and four lousy husbands and the invitations that didn't come and the photographs that weren't taken and *everything*.

Blodgett steered Chip across the lawn, disregarding the protestations which, as surrogate mother, she'd heard a thousand times before. He didn't like parties and celebrities bored him and he particularly wasn't interested in meeting "somebody new."

Chip wished he had Milo Chermak's guts. Milo had passed, and the party was for his parents.

"How do you know if you haven't met her?" Blodgett asked. She had a grip like a vise, lowered over the years. First an ear, then the scruff of the neck and now the soft flesh at the back of the arm, fastened just above the elbow. "It's the least you can do for your father. He doesn't ask that much."

Chip looked at her, letting himself be pushed. Blodgett was the only one he had any use for. The only one who could "handle him," the household saying went, and so he continued to allow her that distinction, a way of showing his appreciation and because it simplified things. He only had to deal with the one combatant. All attacks were channeled through her.

"Well, does he?"

"No. I guess not."

"You guess?"

"All right, for God's sake. He doesn't ask much."

Blodgett beamed—she was surprised to hear him admit it—and gave a final push, propelling him toward the waiting semicircle which had now grown to include the Chermaks and Benson.

Bollinger professed surprise to see him. "Chip! There you are!"

"Yes," Chip admitted, rubbing his arm.

"Come here. I want you to meet someone."

"All right."

Reluctantly, he went to join them, wishing he'd had the sense to get a drink first, the girl probably would be a crashing bore. Remember the last one? Her hair done like a unicorn?

"Jody," Bollinger said, taking her away from Benson. "Here's that son of mine I've been promising you." He turned her around, motioning impatiently. Chip had stopped. "Come *here*."

Chip stood looking at her.

"What's wrong?"

"Nothing," Chip said. "I'm just...surprised, that's all." He moved closer, making sure. "Hello."

Jody decided that he was talking to her. He wasn't looking at anyone else. "Hi."

Bollinger was confused. "Do you know each other?"

Chip shook his head.

"Well," Bollinger said. "Jody Walsh...Chip Bollinger..." He waited a moment. "Is there something wrong?"

Marion smiled, thinking that he must be getting old, had he actually forgotten what it was like to fall in love at first sight?

"Lady, let me get this straight. He can't get out of the pit?"

"I told you. There's no ladder."

"Jesus. And he could be bleeding to death...?"

"Yes."

"Okay. I need your name."

Suzy hung up, her first anonymous telephone call, wondering if Guttman might really die, and deciding no, he wouldn't. He had his fist for a tourniquet.

Initially, she had tried calling from the Lutz house, but the phone had been disconnected, and then she had wasted more time, frantically trying to find a pay phone. Anyway, it didn't matter. She had left him bawling like a wounded bull.

Sighing heavily—all she could do now was wait—Suzy sank down onto the sofa, kicking her shoes off, wiping her brow. But whatever happened she knew she was right. She'd do it again.

The front door opened and Dex's voice drifted in. "Milo. You can't."

"How do you know she's home?"

"Her car."

Suzy thought she ought to turn on a light, but she didn't have the strength. Instead, she'd simply lie there, not even bothering to call out.

"Maybe she left it? Somebody could've taken her."

"Milo, *good night*."

The door closed.

"Hi, honey," Suzy said.

Dex came into the living room, switching on the chandelier, dimming it immediately.

"When did you get in?" she asked.

"Just now," Suzy told her.

"You're early."

"Yes."

Dex slumped into an easy chair, the golden girl, a goddess. Or, as her father called her, a happy combination. She had his eyes, which were like almonds, and the same full-lipped mouth, and that's all.

"Are you feeling all right?"

"Sure. Why?"

"You look awful. A bundle of frayed nerve endings."

"I'm fine," Suzy lied. She had made up her mind, she wasn't going to tell anyone. She was just going to wait—and whatever happened, happened.

"Then why leave the party early? You were so looking forward to it."

"I don't know. It just wasn't as much fun as I expected, I guess."

"Did you see the Chermaks?"

"Only in the receiving line. Then Ruth disappeared somewhere."

"Oh."

"How about you?" Suzy asked, sensing Dex's disappointment. "The whole day with Milo? Where did you go?"

"Gilman Hot Springs. To watch Kenny Norton work out."

"Oh? I didn't know Milo was interested in boxing."

"Actually, he's more interested in wrestling," Dex said, smoothing her dress. "It's a good thing you were home. I don't know how long I can keep fighting him off."

Suzy thought for a moment, all of her own failures with men, the good ones so few and far between. Dex was damn lucky to have the attentions of the town's most eligible young stud. "Well, don't make him too unhappy."

Dex looked at her, surprised, wondering if she should interpret that as permission, if she needed it, to do all that was necessary to keep Milo.

Chip stood silently studying Jody, still too taken aback to join in the conversation, he'd never been "fixed up" by his father in this fashion before, they were always horses, but this one was stunning. And what astounded him more—an even more radical departure from the norm—she was a nobody.

Walsh? That was potato Irish. And Hood College? For God's sake, what had she majored in, baton twirling? Chip couldn't believe it. Over all the years, he'd been presented with horses, Miss Penelope Huntington Libby Bellflower Hartford DuPont Jones, and they had graduated, with difficulty, from Vassar, and they had speech impediments and dry cunts, but *this one?*

She'd be wet, Chip decided, undressing her in his mind, and himself, too. He was like his father, too handsome, another god, but a smaller, more compact version. To make up for it, he lifted weights, trained faithfully every day, his one discipline. He had a good body and he liked to show it.

Behind him, Billy worked his way closer, hoping that Jody would notice him, so that he wouldn't have to interrupt. He remembered the Chermaks from the receiving line and the others in the group looked equally important. It wouldn't be polite to go barging in.

"In my day, nice girls couldn't do that," Ruth Chermak was complaining.

Jody didn't blink. "When was that?"

Bob Vickers, "The Conduit," a frog-like man through whom the very rich made their wishes known at City Hall, squeezed past, jostling. "Sorry…" He kept on going. "Stu? Have you got a moment?"

Stu? That would be Bollinger, Billy thought, picking him over Benson, even before he frowned.

Vickers took Bollinger out of earshot. He spoke in a whisper.

Billy tried to catch Jody's eye. He was being polite, not barging in, he told himself, but he was very much aware that the new arrival had had no qualms about interrupting. How long was he supposed to wait? Did the girl want a ride back to her hotel or not?

"The police?" Bollinger said.

Vickers nodded, moving farther away, keeping his voice very low.

Bollinger was becoming angry. "Max? That's bullshit!"

Everyone turned. Billy waved, rising up on his toes, but Jody still didn't notice him.

Vickers was insistent.

"Well, Jesus Christ," Bollinger said, finally convinced. He returned to the group. "I'm sorry, something's come up." He squeezed Howard's arm and planted a quick kiss on Ruth's cheek. "You'll just have to get along without me. And Chip…?"

"Yes?"

"You'll take care of Jody?"

"Sure."

Billy moved out of the way, giving Bollinger room. When he turned back, Jody was looking at him. Briefly, she smiled in recognition, then said something to the Chermaks. She made no effort to look his way again.

Well, that settles that, Billy thought. He left to find Mary Alice.

Driving home, Billy didn't use Jody as an example, he took her snub as personal. Instead, he told the story of the woman who had mistaken him for a waiter.

"It could happen to anyone," Mary Alice said.

Billy doubted that. "To Stu Bollinger?"

"Of course not. Don't be ridiculous, everyone knows Stu."

Not everyone, Billy thought. He didn't, since Bollinger wasn't in the receiving line, but when he saw him later, even at a distance, there was no mistaking that he was someone important, not an appendage. His own man.

"Well, you'll be known soon enough," Mary Alice counseled. "A few more parties, your picture in the paper. The one Gloria's photographer took…? I bet they'll use it. The first fresh face this year."

Billy wondered how he could explain. "I'll be known as your husband."

"That's who you are."

"Yes, but I want to be a person, too. My own man."

Mary Alice looked at him. In their brief courtship, one of the things that attracted her, the quality of which she took special note, was that he did not aspire.

"Is that so much to ask?" Billy demanded.

"That all depends," Mary Alice said carefully. What was his complaint? That he'd been sent for drinks?

Billy tried to contain himself, thinking that he shouldn't ask now, just lay the groundwork. She had very definite ideas on the way things should be between them. And they had been married so briefly, she might suspect, which wasn't true, that he never intended to keep their bargain. Yet surely she would understand? After all, for someone so rich—and she was far, far wealthier than he had ever imagined—it really wasn't that much to ask. He'd always had his heart set on a restaurant. At the very least, a bar. And it would be an investment, not a gift. She'd be the owner and he'd simply manage the place.

"I want a business," he said, blurting it out.

"A business?"

"Yes."

Mary Alice wanted to laugh, he looked so serious. "Whatever for?"

"It would be an investment, not a gift," Billy said. "You would own it and..." He stopped, not content with what he had rehearsed. Manager wasn't enough to bring him recognition. It would be better if he was a proprietor. "I would own only a very small part."

Mary Alice stared at him, thinking he couldn't be serious.

"What I had in mind is a restaurant," he told her. "When I was a young man, I worked in one, a busboy, and I always dreamed..."

"No," Mary Alice said at last.

Billy blinked, surprised at the vehemence of her answer. "Why not? You have the money, and as I said..."

"No!"

"...it would be an investment," Billy said, stopping the car. They were at a red light, opposite the Ocotillo. "I don't hear any better when you scream."

"It wasn't our arrangement," Mary Alice reminded him, trying to control her anger. "You were to be my husband, and you were to be taken care of... and that's all."

"Yes, but..."

"I said no."

Billy looked at the light, waiting for it to change. He wasn't asking that much, he thought. She had so much money. Why deny him such a small thing? To be respectable.

"I just want something to do."

"And you have it," Mary Alice said. "With you running a restaurant, where would I be, sitting at home alone? Is that your idea of companionship?"

"Other men have to work."

"And wish they didn't. You don't know how fortunate you are."

Fortunate? Yes, he had thought so. A life of ease, and not having to worry where the next meal came from. To be taken care of—and that's all.

The light changed. Behind, a car honked.

"Are you going to drive?" Mary Alice asked. "Or shall I?" If you want, Billy thought. He got out, closing the door and walking away.

Bollinger paced the small alcove that was the waiting room in Desert Hospital Emergency. Marion sat in a corner, wondering why he had brought her, trying to hide in a back issue of *Reader's Digest.*

"You're sure you can keep this out of the papers?" Bollinger asked.

"Yeah," Vickers assured him. "If he lives."

"He'll live," Bollinger decided, equally certain. He got out his cigarettes, fitting one into a gold holder. "Did you ever hear of anything like this?"

Vickers thought for a moment. "Does it fall into the category of having a Coca-Cola bottle shoved up your ass?"

Bollinger looked at him, thinking that wasn't very funny.

"It's the closest I can come," Vickers said. "Some poor goddamn fag. He got it up there and then he couldn't get it out."

Marion sighed. "Do we have to?"

"No," Vickers said.

Bollinger lit his cigarette, wondering why he suffered Vickers, and knowing damn well why. He needed him. As Benson was fond of saying, "Nobody does it better than Bob." Part of Vickers' job was handing out favors. The other part was collecting on them.

"How about the woman. This ... Suzy?"

"Braverman," Vickers said, referring to the investigating officer's report.

Bollinger made a mental note of the name. For one thing, she wasn't coming to any more parties.

Wojek, the urologist, put his head in the door, not sure who to tell.

"I think I'll join the ladies," Marion said.

Bollinger made a motion, indicating that she should stay. Marion sank back into her chair.

"He, uh, ought to be okay," Wojek said. "There's an artery that runs along the top of the penis and she managed to cut that, but we got it patched together all right. I'm not promising there won't be complications. Human bites…?" He made a helpless gesture. "And it's not the best place, either."

"He's not mutilated?" Bollinger asked.

Wojek shook his head. "Not in the true sense. There'll be a scar, though, and he'll have trouble taking a leak for a while, and he, uh, won't be thumping anybody right away, either." The rest was for Vickers. "Incidentally, I was holding three aces."

"Can we see him now?"

"Sure."

Bollinger looked at Marion. "You'd better tell Riva."

"Tell her what?" Marion asked, but it was all settled. Guttman had fallen into the swimming-pool pit and hurt himself "there." She went to find a telephone.

Vickers shredded the investigating officer's report, putting the pieces in his pocket. That was also settled. There'd be no record of the incident. Officially, it never happened.

The officer, a candidate for sergeant, had called Vickers as soon as Guttman mentioned the magic name, Bollinger. Vickers had taken it from there: Admission under an alias. Wojek and two other specialists hustled in to assess the damage. Bollinger summoned, not because he was really needed, but rather to be shown that his house guest and business associate was being given every consideration that a grateful city could bestow.

On his way home, Vickers stopped at a pay telephone, tying up the last loose end.

Suzy answered, groggy from a sleeping pill. "Yes ...?"

"About this evening," Vickers said. "The gentleman has decided not to lay charges. May I assume a similar reticence on your part?"

"Who is this?"

"Is that important?"

No, Suzy decided. Actually, it was the kind of call she had hoped for. Anonymous, like her own. If he gave his name—a face to the voice—she'd be embarrassed if she ever met him later.

"It's ... going to be kept quiet?"

"As far as possible," Vickers said. "The gentleman certainly isn't going to tell anyone. But you know what nurses are like? Ambulance attendants ...?"

Suzy waited.

"Well, it's the kind of story they're going to pass around, of course. It will be all over town by tomorrow. No names. The gentleman was admitted under an alias. And he's the only one who knows who you are." A pause. "Unless someone else knows you were showing him the house?"

"George Spector."

"Won't be a problem," Vickers said. "I'm not in real estate, but it seems to me, this isn't something you'd advertise?"

"No," Suzy said. She hesitated. "How is he?"

"The gentleman?" Vickers asked. "Let's put it this way—he was a six—and now he's five and seven-eighths."

Suzy laughed—cut down to size?—and Vickers hung up, the night's work done. If there was trouble, it wouldn't be his fault. Nobody did it better than Bob.

Billy closed the bar at Lyons English Grille, celebrating what, he was certain, was his elevation to restaurant proprietor. When last he'd seen her, Mary Alice had the Bentley up on the sidewalk, threatening to send private detectives after him, and that—when you thought about it—was a good sign. She must really want him, to pay a fee.

Initially, he hadn't been so sure. After he'd left her at the light, the cars behind honking, he had walked a full block, afraid to look back to see if she was following. If he showed any interest she might think he wasn't serious.

Finally she had caught up, ordering him to get in, but he had paid no attention then, of course. He just kept on walking, letting her plead and threaten.

What was he doing? Running away. And when she tried to cut him off, he simply walked into the desert.

Talk? They'd do that later. First she had to find him.

Humming to himself, Billy thumbed through the telephone directory, looking for detective agencies in the Yellow Pages, and finally locating them under "Investigators." There were about a dozen listings, most of them in Palm Springs, but one as far away as San Diego.

Trying to imagine what Mary Alice would do, he picked the three with display ads, all of which promised "24-Hour Service." He'd call them immediately, advising that Mary Alice might hire them to find him, and if so he was prepared to split the finder's fee.

"Do you want a cab?" the bartender asked.

"No, just a detective," Billy said. "As a child, I occasionally picked up a few pesos this way." He slipped off the stool, looking for the phone. "I'd purposely lose my younger brother ... tie him to a fire hydrant several blocks from home ... then get a reward for 'finding' him."

The bartender considered for a moment. "Listen, maybe I better get a you a cab."

"Not necessary," Billy told him. "I'm hiding just up the street. The Westward Ho." Unsurely, he started for the phone. "A funny thing about my brother. He was four years old before he discovered he wasn't a dog."

"Oh, yeah?" the bartender said. "Listen ..."

Billy ignored him, deciding to make the first call to Heisig Investigative Services. "Discreet—Ethical—Effective," their ad said. "Worldwide Capabilities."

Lois lay awake. Her pills wouldn't work, and she heard every sound, Theo going to his wing, the television set turned on before he thought to close the door, and Mallory still not back even though it was after midnight.

Where was he?

On his way to Oregon? Lois wondered, hating herself. She'd scared him off, so thoroughly a lady with her cap set, and the real estate office unfairly presented as a *fait accompli*. If he did feel anything for her, a regard that could, with time, become love, it would be snuffed out now, bludgeoned.

She closed her eyes, trying to contain the tears, unable to believe she was so inept, a grown woman, would someone please help her, she wanted him so desperately.

CHAPTER FOUR

Sargent squinted into the sun, trying to think of where, other than a dinosaur or a water tower, he might want to live. The dinosaur, as it turned out, wasn't large enough for a family of five, quite apart from the unrealistic price being asked, and there were no water towers on the market at the moment.

Or so Suzy said.

Was she telling the truth? Sargent wondered, going along for the ride, taking a look—you will excuse the expression—at the lay of the land. One of Suzy's standard operating procedures was to give prospective home buyers what she called the grand tour before showing them specific houses. The grand tour was exactly that—a sight-seeing trip through not only the better districts of Palm Springs, but also to the neighboring communities of Cathedral City, Rancho Mirage, Palm Desert, Indian Wells and La Quinta.

Within this twenty-mile stretch of mountain-ringed desert, there were, at last count, forty golf courses, two hundred and eighty tennis facilities, and some ten thousand swimming pools. There were also—in "The Season"—an estimated seven hundred resident millionaires.

Wherever man's hand decreed, the barren sands had been transformed, as if by magic, into verdant oasis. Palm trees towered amid a patchwork profusion of luxuriant lawns and flowering shrubs. Blossoms clustered in dazzling overabundance.

The secret was a plentiful water supply, pumped from deep underground wells and replenished, through vast spreading grounds, from the Colorado River Aqueduct. Palm Springs alone used almost fifty million gallons a day.

This morning, the temperature climbing to 120 degrees, an average day for August, the whirr of sprinklers were everywhere, keeping the summer's hell reasonably at bay, and maintaining what would be, in another month, the winter's paradise.

When the weather broke, there'd be a mass influx, part-time residents coming in from all over the United States and Canada. The steady stream would continue and by the height of the season the valley's population would quadruple.

Except for Cathedral City. Cat City, like comfortably distant Indio, the disdained East End, hardly constituted anyone's idea of heaven. Suzy was simply driving through it in order to get from Palm Springs to Rancho Mirage. Cat City, unfortunately, was unavoidable, and even Sargent—well acquainted with the drearier side of life—had occasion to wince as he squinted.

The place seemed purposely erected to offend the eye. The buildings fronting the highway were small and tacky, and on the streets behind, narrow and crooked, the pinched houses had gone to slum. The massage parlors were here, and the crummy cafes and bars, and the used-car lots, and the drive-in theater that doubled as a swap meet.

The only things of note were the Desert Auction Gallery and an interesting old brick storage shed with a greenhouse attached. The rest? Blah.

"They had to put it somewhere," Suzy remarked, seeing Sargent's look.

Sargent grunted. "Sure. But why here?"

"It's between cities. Under county jurisdiction, so the zoning isn't as strict..."

"What zoning?"

"... and you're right, there isn't much indication of it, is there? I'll rephrase that answer—Because they could get away with it."

Exactly, Sargent thought, feeling like an argument, but not knowing how to start one. Em had warned that Suzy was feisty but she seemed rather subdued this morning.

"It's the same thing that made television a wasteland."

"What?"

"Lack of zoning, only there it's called an infringement on free speech, of course. Or the lack thereof, rather. Briefly, you see here, as you see there, the results of unbridled freedom of expression which is to say that we get dragged down by the company we keep and even Neil Simon finally saw the light and why aren't you more feisty?"

"Feisty…?"

"Yes. I was promised feisty."

Suzy smiled wanly, thinking wasn't it like Em, to list that among her credentials, and, God, if she only knew! The previous night's calamity weighed heavily and so did the nagging question; Would it—as promised—be kept quiet?

"Well…?"

"Well what?"

Sargent wasn't sure, and anyway now they were in Rancho Mirage, the city hall looking like a Chinese Stetson, the streets named after Frank Sinatra and Bob Hope. Back to the *real world*?

"You see what I mean?" Suzy said, falling into her standard spiel. "He could live anywhere."

"Who?"

"Frank Sinatra."

Sargent nodded, that much remembered. The tour had opened with the recitation of a long list of celebrities who presumably could afford to domicile wherever and who unaccountably had not chosen dinosaurs, they had chosen Palm Springs. The fact that this was Rancho Mirage, not Palm Springs, was not grounds for argument as Rancho Mirage was another Palm Springs, part of it, really, too close and too similar to make any valid distinction, as were—coming up down the sun-baked highway—Palm Desert and Indian Wells. You lumped them all together and you excluded Cathedral City.

Yes, my friend, think about it, these people could live *anywhere,* but they have chosen Palm Springs—P.S., I Love You—and there must be a reason and the reason, according to the Gospel of Suzy, is that Palm Springs—even on a subdued morning—is the finest place in the world (excluding Cathedral City, of course).

The perpetual sunshine. The clean air. The desert's golden beauty. The stars bright at night. The small-town atmosphere with the big-city ways—and all within a two-hour drive of Sodom and Gomorrah.

Yes, let's not forget that, Sargent thought, wondering if it might provoke an argument and deciding no, it was an argument for. They could live anywhere but they didn't want to stray too far. P.S., I Love You, and S & G, Too.

"I remember once, a friend living in Hawaii, she said that the only nice thing about Toronto, it was close to London."

Suzy looked at him. Which was apropos of...?

"Relatively speaking, of course," Sargent said, giving up. Feisty she was not. He might as well relax and enjoy himself. "Em mentioned my, uh, problem?"

"She said you were battier than the Dodgers."

A way with words, Sargent thought, squinting.

Bollinger walked Guttman to his car, Marion a couple of paces behind, taking shorthand notes.

"You still haven't told me," Guttman complained. "Did you like the script or not?"

Bollinger didn't see how that mattered. He had pledged the six million, provided they got Bronson. "You're the expert."

"Sure," Guttman lied. Actually, he had no taste, relying solely on the opinion of others, he had readers who told him what was good or bad. "Still, I'd appreciate your opinion."

Bollinger looked over his shoulder. "You had some comments, didn't you, Marion?"

Marion flipped back through her notebook. "Page twenty-four, I thought the head in the toilet was a bit much. Page forty-two, the Japanese official—where he says, 'Now crap'—that's a BJ."

"What's a BJ?"

"Bad joke."

"Anything else?"

"No."

"Jesus Christ," Guttman said impatiently, stopping at the car, his cock aching, "did you like it or not?"

Marion shrugged. "It's not a woman's picture."

"What's that supposed to mean?"

"What I said."

"Get Bronson," Bollinger told him. "Then, who cares?" He offered his hand, a dismissal. "Drive carefully."

Guttman went around to the passenger's side. Riva was at the wheel, having brought the car from the garage.

"Good-bye again," she said.

Marion wondered how much Riva believed of the story. Falling into a swimming-pool pit? Really.

Bollinger waved, watching them drive off. "What did you think?"

"I thought it stunk."

"You did?"

Marion closed her notebook. "Yes. Whoever heard of a cop shooting off a woman's breast?"

"It's not her real breast."

"It's the idea."

Possibly, Bollinger thought, but he wasn't inclined to tinker. He didn't have a clue what appealed to the masses, and he doubted if Marion did, either. She'd crossed over.

"Frankly, after what happened …" She let it hang there.

"What happened," Bollinger told her, starting back up the stairs, "has nothing to do with whether or not it's a lousy script. The script hangs by itself."

"All right. On its merits alone, then. If you're going to make a movie, you have a responsibility, don't you?"

"I'm not making a movie. I'm making an investment. It's the other fellow—what's his name, the director?—Brokowski?"

"Zukowski," Marion said, giving up.

Bollinger didn't pursue it. The disputed scenario, however bizarre, paled beside life's real drama, he thought. Guttman had told him everything—he had insisted upon that, the price of their continued association—and now he couldn't put Suzy Braverman out of his mind.

After the fact, that's what was so intriguing. It wasn't self-defense, she'd been safe enough then, practically being apologized to, Guttman desperately wanting it kept quiet, of course. Most women, any he knew, they'd have run for their lives, yet she had chosen to attack, and what an incredible act of retaliation and revenge. It was so basic, *so animal,* and yet, from all reports, she was an intelligent, beautiful woman. There must be something inside that made her different. Inner fires ... that raged for what?

He couldn't know, Bollinger thought, except that she must be very strong, determined and strong like himself, and he would like to meet her. Without being obvious—don't make her feel like a curiosity—he should like to meet, and, perhaps, know her.

Chip came out of the house, whistling. "Good morning!"

Bollinger looked at his watch. It was hardly eleven. "Well, young man. This *is* an occasion. Would you like to join us for lunch?"

"Can't. I've got a date." He swept past them, smelling of after shave. "Catch you later."

"Jody ...?"

"Who else?"

Bollinger turned to watch him go. The other miracle took a moment to register. Instead of the usual, a grubby tank top and frayed cut-offs, he was wearing a shirt and slacks, even shoes.

"Mmmm. I guess I'm not such a bad matchmaker after all?"

Marion shook her head.

"Let's hope, anyway," Bollinger said, starting for the house again. "And incidentally—if there is trouble, we should know who we're dealing with. You'd better run a check on that Braverman woman. What's her name? Suzy?"

Marion nodded, asking herself a familiar question: What did she find attractive about him?

Normally, Suzy wouldn't have ventured into the neighborhood. It was tract housing, beneath the dignity of George Spector Realtor. But Sargent had seen a jewel from afar—a small green oasis in a sea of gravel lawns—and he had insisted and she had come out of her way to indulge him.

"Satisfied?"

"I love it."

Sargent piled out of her Oldsmobile, wondering if he had actually said that, it was so out of character, but then the house was, too.

A heavy shake roof, an addition by a previous owner, and an incredibly overgrown yard—no gardener all summer, automatic sprinklers run amuck?—effectively hid its common origin. Elsewhere in Sunshine Estates—the subdivision's name, according to a sign—four models were repeated with singular regularity, the exterior styling apparently influenced by Spanish, French, Far Eastern and Ranch architecture. They went on and on that way, one, two, three, four, variations on an identical floor plan, no doubt, cactus gardens and colored gravel substituting for grass, smugly content in their anonymous sameness, but this one rebel dared to explode. It was different, part design, part accident. A mess. And, best of all, for sale.

"What do you think?"

"Well…"

Suzy had to admit the place possessed a certain charming distinction. You had to look closely to discover its French brothers, in the unadorned plywood mansards. The yard, a wayward nursery, positively luxuriant, was all the more inviting for its stark surroundings. But as for location?

Em would have a fit. This was a *housing development,* a slice of middle-class suburbia, a world unto itself, light-years from the glitter and glamour. Open desert on all sides, that probably meant it was Indian land, leasehold, not fee, you couldn't actually own it. And the postage-stamp park and those two tacky tennis courts? They'd be "private," for the use of residents and their guests only, you'd need a key to get on the courts, there'd be a rule against lending it to "outsiders," and…

"Be honest."

"It's not Las Palmas," Suzy said, a wail.

Sargent laughed. Was that such a tragedy? Angie could be happy here, it erased the greatest fear of her impending move, that she might not have a garden, and the children would be more likely to make new friends their own age in a subdivision. Las Palmas would be full of rich old crocks, their children, if any, long gone.

"Let's take a look," Sargent said, already making further changes. The picture window, it ought to be a bay, a bench inside, leaded glass, shutters. Some more of those shakes on the overhang? "It's probably worse in back."

It was. Even more overgrown, the shrubbery a tangle, the grass a foot high, and the swimming pool half full of dead water, the bottom streaked with black algae. The pump was silent, burned out, probably, from sucking air. No one had been around for a while. An abandoned ship?

Suzy shook her head, ready to call it quits, but Sargent persisted, moving from window to window, peering through breaks in the venetian blinds.

Inside it was the same story, let go. The carpets worn, the wallpaper peeling, the plaster chipped. The ceiling around the air ducts streaked with black soot and the rest could be imagined. Cracked mirrors and stained sinks. Leaky faucets.

"It wouldn't take much," Sargent said, talking to himself. "A few trips to the dump and a couple tubs of chlorine." That was the yard. The house? It required closer inspection. "Could you get a key?"

"You're not serious?"

"Uh, huh."

Suzy stared at him, still holding her dress up. "For God's sake. *Why?*"

"I like it," Sargent said.

Good, Suzy thought. He would, and he'd probably buy it, too, and Em would never recommend another prospect, her own nephew in this disaster area?

The clincher was waiting on the sidewalk out front. A hunched figure—from not standing up straight—dressed in a sailor cap two hours from the ocean and khaki shorts and battered running shoes and steel-rimmed glasses and that's all.

"You thinking of buying?" he asked, hands in his pockets and looking someplace else.

"Maybe," Sargent admitted. He let Suzy through the side gate, hanging on one twisted hinge. "You live around here?"

"Yes."

"What's it like?"

"Hot."

Sargent smiled in agreement, glancing both ways on the shimmering street, which was deserted. "And dead?"

"No. Murdered."

Suzy rolled her eyes, going to the car, and Sargent followed reluctantly. "Any kids?"

"Who, me?"

"In the neighborhood."

"Watching TV."

Suzy got into the car.

The hunched figure ventured closer. "What do you do?"

Sargent told him. "Nothing."

"Mmmmm," the hunched figure said, impressed. "Me? I'm a writer. 'The Desert Fox.'" He came closer still, lowering his voice. "Subtitled, in my drunken moments, 'But Palm Springs Sucks.'"

"Let's go, shall we?" Suzy suggested, starting up.

Sargent got in, thinking that he'd stay if he had other transportation. It was unusual to establish immediate empathy.

There was a shout as the Olds pulled away. "Make an offer. They're desperate!"

Sargent, as he was to learn later, had just met Norman Chaney, who was looking for himself in the desert, surrounded, as he was fond of saying, by sand.

Billy awoke with a start. For a moment, he thought someone was trying to break in, hammering against the door with a club.

"Billy? Open up! I know you're in there."

Oh, God, Billy thought. Mary Alice, with her cane. How had she found him? He got out of bed, surprised to find he was still in his clothes.

"*Billy!*"

"Who is it?" he said, trying to remember. He'd made all those telephone calls, leaving recorded messages. None of the detective agencies had been open.

"Billy. This instant!"

"All right."

Feeling his way, he made it to the door, opening it on the chain. "Yes?"

"Let me in."

Billy considered, wondering if there was a back way out. What had he said in the messages? That he'd split the reward?

The cane became a pry. "Let…me…*in!*"

"Holy Mary, Mother of Mercy," Billy whispered. He crossed himself and unhooked the chain and got out of the way.

Mary Alice pushed in, almost falling. She had to grab the dresser for support.

Involuntarily, Billy started toward her, stopping when he saw that she was all right.

Mary Alice waited, catching her breath. She had dropped the cane, which was now on the floor between them.

Billy bent to retrieve it, aware that this was a kind of reflex, too. She didn't need the stupid thing.

She extended her hand. "May I have it, please?"

What for? Billy wondered. To wave? The cane was a symbol of what was wrong between them. He wasn't a husband, he was a servant. Did she think she could beat him into submission? Before he could change his mind, he snapped it across his knee, tossing the pieces aside.

Mary Alice stared, too shocked to speak, and Billy turned away, immediately sorry. If he was going to quit, he thought, at the very least, he ought to do it in dignity. He must look a mess—and she had made a special effort to fix herself up.

"I . . . came to tell you something," Mary Alice said, suddenly subdued. It took her a moment. "I'm a stupid old woman."

Billy shook his head. "You're not."

"I am," Mary Alice said. She moved away from the dresser, sitting in the only chair, finding it difficult to keep her composure. "It isn't going to work, is it?"

"No," Billy told her. He wasn't sure what she was talking about, but it didn't matter. Anything that involved them, the verdict applied.

She looked at him. "Knowing that . . . I don't suppose you'd want to try again?"

He shrugged. "What would be the purpose?"

"I don't know."

"Neither do I."

There was a long silence.

Abruptly, Billy went into the bathroom, splashing water in his face. He couldn't understand what was happening. Was it over?

The question didn't help. "What are your plans?"

Plans? What plans? He didn't have any. "Go back, I suppose."

"Mexico City?"

"Yes."

Billy looked at himself in the mirror. He'd had too much to drink. It was his reflection, not him, having this conversation, saying words without bidding.

A small round brown man who had spent a lifetime pointing out things of value to others—and who had nothing of value that was his own. A small brown man who led the way—and who was lost.

"A stupid old woman," Mary Alice said, more loudly now. "If you got your restaurant ... would you stay?"

Billy put his hand on his reflection, covering the mouth.

"Well ...?"

"Perhaps."

"What was that?"

"I said yes."

Suzy hung up the phone for the last time. As often happened, the deal had made itself, almost independent of her own efforts to influence matters either way. A call to Em, who surprisingly had only two criteria, did he, Sargent, like the place and did it made sense financially, and if so why waste time looking elsewhere? A call to Angie, who, after a lengthy discussion of other matters, confessed that it was difficult if not impossible to form an opinion at such a distance so why didn't he, Sargent, make the decision, which was what he had gone ahead to do, and which he had to start doing again. A call to Mr. Baker, the absentee owner in Chicago, who, after very little discussion, had agreed to come down from $89,500 to $83,000 and was now expecting the papers in the mail.

"Done?" Sargent wanted to know.

"If the bank approves the loan," Suzy said darkly, her last hope that sanity might prevail and which wasn't any hope at all. Em was loaded, even if Sargent wasn't. She got a form out of her desk and stuffed it into her typewriter. "What day is it?"

"The twenty-eighth."

"One o'clock," Suzy said, checking her watch, reminded they hadn't even stopped for lunch. "Do you realize that all of this has been done in three hours—and that two of them were spent just driving around?"

"Yes."

Suzy typed in the date and time. "I, for one, a stranger in town, would not buy the first house I looked at."

Sargent smiled. "Not even if advised by an experienced real estate person who came highly recommended by a close relative?"

"My advice," Suzy began, but she really didn't have any. It was a good buy, well worth the money, an ideal investment as a fixer-upper, *but.* "If I may express a personal preference, I wouldn't live there on a bet."

"It can be repaired."

"Not *the area.*"

Up front, the door opened, someone coming in. Suzy rose to look out of her cubicle. George Spector.

"Excuse me," Suzy said, moving around the desk.

Sargent got out of the way. "Sure."

"Where is she?" Spector demanded, talking to Gwen.

"In her office."

Suzy left, looking angry, and Sargent was mildly puzzled, because the inquiry had been angry, too. He leaned back to wait.

"You're fired!"

"I'm *what?*"

"Pack your things."

"Now, just a minute…"

"And *get out!*"

Sargent looked over the cubicle. Suzy and Spector were standing in the middle of the front office, Suzy's face drained white, Spector's shimmering with rage.

"If this is about last night…"

"You're goddamn right it is," Spector shouted, pushing past her. "How you had the nerve to come in…" Before Sargent could move, he was in the cubicle. "Who in the hell are you?"

Suzy was on his heels. "A client. If there are to be any apologies…"

"Not any more," Spector told Sargent. He took the form out of the typewriter, ripping it in half, throwing it on the floor. "You can leave, too."

"I *deserve* one," Suzy said, close to angry tears. "It was your fault, forcing a drunk on me, and…"

"You deserve a kick in the ass," Spector shouted. "The story is going to get out—there's no way something like that will be kept quiet—and then what will this firm look like? I've spent a lifetime building my good reputation. I'm not going to let some sex maniac ruin it."

"I beg your pardon?"

"You heard me."

Suzy slapped him across the face, a hard, stinging blow.

Spector staggered back. "You… bitch!"

"Hey," Sargent said, stepping between them. "If you keep swearing at the lady…"

"Get out, both of you," Spector said. "Get out or I'm call-ing the police." He backed out of the cubicle, holding his cheek. "Gwen, get the police on the line."

Sargent took Suzy by the arm. "Don't worry. We're leaving."

"But what about my things?" Suzy protested.

"You can get them later."

"But…"

"Later," Sargent said, escorting her to the front door. He paused for just a moment before Gwen. "She'll call you about her things. Okay?"

"And stay out!" Spector shouted.

Sargent steered Suzy through the door, not releasing her arm until they were on the sidewalk. "Are you all right?"

She nodded, the reaction starting.

"How about a coffee or something?"

"No, I'll be okay."

Sargent looked back into the real estate office. Through the window, he could see Spector at Gwen's telephone, angrily punching out a number.

"Well, let's get out of here anyway."

Quickening his pace, Sargent led the way to the parking lot, putting Suzy in the passenger's side of her car, getting behind the wheel himself.

"The keys?"

"In my purse."

Sargent got them, starting the car and backing up. As he drove out of the lot, Spector came out of his office, shouting abuse.

"That, I take it, was Mr. George Spector, realtor?"

Suzy didn't reply and they drove in silence for several blocks, Sargent simply staying with the flow of traffic, not caring where they were going, just as long as it was away. It frightened him to think that he had almost interceded. He was here to start anew, he reminded himself, and that required, among other things, that he avoid public scenes. He looked for a landmark. He wanted the safety of Las Palmas—and Em.

Suzy was trying to accept the fact that she had been fired. Five years with the same firm. The only job she had ever had. And suddenly—out! There were other real estate companies, of course. Lots of them. But if George started bad-mouthing her ...?

That could hurt, Suzy thought, grimacing. If he spread the story, twisting it all around, making her the aggressor—that could hurt.

Sargent's aimless driving had taken them around the switchback onto Palm Canyon Drive. Suzy saw Lois Sills' new office and made up her mind the next instant. "Turn here."

"What for?"

"Please," Suzy said, pointing, and Sargent did as instructed, pulling in front of the converted house with the big front window waiting for a sign.

Jacobi kicked at the door, both arms full of groceries. The lazy slut. Wasn't she up yet?

Cleo called hoarsely, "Who is it ...?"

"The police," Jacobi answered, kicking some more.

Finally, the door opened, Cleo buttoning a yellow housecoat, her eyes puffy and her hair looking slept on. She yawned, not saying hello. "Gawd. What time is it?"

"Time you were out of bed," Jacobi told her. He pushed past, going into the kitchen, a tiny closet of a place with the stove, sink and refrigerator all combined in one unit.

Cleo followed, watching from the threshold. There wasn't room for both inside. "What do you think you're doing?"

"What does it look like?" Jacobi unpacked a supply of basics. He stopped when he came to the coffee. "Have you got a pot?"

"I haven't even washed yet," Cleo complained. She went away.

Jacobi found a chipped enamel tureen, rinsing it out. The search confirmed what he suspected would be the case. Her only purchase, hidden under the sink, had been a bottle of gin, now half empty. A crumpled cellophane bag—it once contained Cheezies—was insufficient evidence of nutritional intake. Knowing the StarBrite, that probably came with a previous tenant.

"How about cups?"

For answer, there was the sound of the shower.

Jacobi found one, the handle broken off, and a bent spoon, rescued from a garbage disposal. There wasn't any sign of a can opener.

"Can ...?" he started to say, but she wouldn't hear him. The water was pounding. He used his knife instead, punching holes in the coffee-tin lid, then sawing them together, making a slit he could turn up.

Belatedly, Mouse came in, sniffing at his cowboy boots.

"You're a fine fucking watchdog," Jacobi said, wondering what next. He'd bought the plastic cone and filters but the cone wasn't going to fit on the tureen. Surely there was another container?

Mouse went back into the room, curling up beside the unmade bed, a fold-out sofa.

Jacobi swore, remembering the stove. Only one switch was intact. He turned it on, then filled the tureen, pouring some out while waiting for a burner to glow.

"You're like your old lady? Too fucking lazy to bark?"

Mouse put her head on her paws and closed her eyes.

Well, company anyway, Jacobi thought. He set the tureen down and returned to his first problem, which was another container. There had to be something.

He was still looking—slamming things around—when Cleo came out of the bathroom. She had the yellow housecoat on again, drying herself with it. She watched him for a while.

"Haven't you got anything?"

"What are you looking for?"

"A pot."

"You've got a pot," Cleo told him, thinking that he really was a goddamn gorilla. Even squatting down he seemed as tall as Elliott.

"That's a tureen."

Tureen? She hadn't heard the word for years. Not since her mother. "Listen, the groceries and everything, how come you're being so nice?"

Wait till she saw her newly acquired car, Jacobi thought. He'd bought her a cream puff, an ancient, battered, stupendously finned Cadillac, incapable of any great speed or distance, he didn't want her going fast or far, yet still sufficient to track and besiege her husband. He liked to help ladies in distress. It made them grateful.

"I was hoping to get laid," Jacobi said.

Cleo laughed, glad she'd showered, because there wasn't going to be time for it now.

Suzy took a moment to compose herself. Before leaving Bollinger's party, she had heard the gossip that Lois Sills, all on her own, had set up a real estate office and was now in trouble. One version of the story had her failing the exam for a broker's license, and still another, dismissed as too outrageous, had her trying to lure back Jack Mallory. In any event, the office had been ready for weeks, yet still hadn't opened for business.

Sargent stared at the expanse of window that was still lacking any kind of identifying sign.

"What's this?"

"Another real estate office, I think."

"You think...?"

"Let's find out, shall we?" Suzy said, getting out of the car. If she was going to outwit George Spector, she had to get another job immediately, before he could spread the word on her, and it ought to be with a firm that really needed help, so that she would be safely entrenched when the barrage started.

Sargent followed, puzzled. "Why not go someplace where you're sure?"

"Because this could be the best bet," Suzy said, answering for her own benefit. Normally, she didn't wish trouble on anyone, but now she hoped that there was some truth to the party gossip. If she could rescue Lois and make herself indispensable? George Spector could tell all the lies he wanted then. He couldn't hurt her.

"Listen. Maybe we should just pass."

"You want the house, don't you?"

"Sure, but ..."

"Then come on."

Suzy led the way in, literally dragging Sargent. "Hello?"

Lois came out of the back office, looking both relieved and angry, expecting it to be Mallory. She stopped short.

"Your first customer," Suzy said. With a flourish, she presented Sargent.

Lois had to come closer to make sure it was Suzy. She had been crying and had removed her contact lenses. "Oh. It's you."

"He wants to buy a house," Suzy said, wading right in. "He's picked it out and made an offer and the owner has accepted. Now all we have to do is write up the deal." She looked at the row of empty desks. "Where do you want to enact this historic occasion?"

Lois didn't know what to say. She knew Suzy only slightly, from their work together on the Desert Circus, and this was the first indication that anyone, apart from Theo and Mallory, was aware of what kind of activity she intended for the office. All questions had been parried with the same answer, which she had thought was rather clever: That's my business.

"I've left George Spector," Suzy said, still looking at the row of empty desks. "And you do need salespeople, don't you?"

"Well, yes," Lois admitted. "And I'd very much like to take you on. The only trouble is ..." She stopped, wondering how much Suzy knew, who she had heard it from. Surely not Mallory? "I'm afraid there's a problem—I don't have a broker."

"You don't?" Suzy turned back slowly, thinking this was too good to be true, it was more than luck—divine guidance?—that had brought her here. "If you're really stuck ... well, if you need a broker, I can handle that, too. I got my license last year. Haven't used it, of course. It was just something to have. You know— In case, one day ..." She laughed. What was wrong with her? Talking a mile a minute and acting like a fool. But what a perfect opportunity! "Frankly, I don't have the money for this kind of setup, and, as you obviously know, it is the only way to go in this town. First-class."

Lois brightened. "Well, I did want to make an impression."

Suzy took an admiring look around the office. "Lois, this isn't an impression. It's a *dent!*"

Sargent began to feel ignored. He told himself he should walk out, the whole thing was ridiculous, all he wanted to do was buy a house, but Suzy wasn't just a real estate agent, she was a friend of Em's.

"You really think so?"

"Honestly. It's smashing."

Yes, Lois thought. It was, she didn't need someone to tell her that. Yet all morning she had been mooning around, cursing herself for a stupid fool, just because she hadn't heard from Mallory.

"You had a designer in?"

"Leonard."

"Yes, it's his touch."

Lois wondered if she should change her mind. Until now, she had been prepared to throw in the towel, to take her losses and walk away. Without Mallory, it was no good, it wouldn't work— that's what she had been telling herself. But was it really true? If someone with Suzy's experience and drive took over ...?

"I'd like to talk about it," Lois said, not having to explain what.

Suzy smiled. "So would I."

"Have you got a moment now?"

"Of course."

Jesus, Sargent thought. He stared in disbelief as the two women started for the back office, a quick, helpless little shrug from Suzy the only apology for leaving him abandoned.

"When did you quit George Spector?"

"This was my last day."

"So you could take over immediately?"

"Yes."

To hell, not even for Em's sake, Sargent thought, but he made no move to leave. He wanted the house and he couldn't properly take the deal to someone else. That would be unfair, the owner would be confused and eventually there'd be a squabble over the commission. Trouble.

"You're going to think me awfully stupid, but the truth of the matter is, I don't know the first thing about real estate."

"Listen, I admire your courage…"

The office door closed. Sargent sat down to wait.

You left it out.
I'm not about
To pick up after you.
Put it away
Or
Here it will stay
If you don't pick it up when you're through.

Chaney smiled, reading the poem, which he really didn't have to do, he'd memorized it a long, long time ago. Then, an act of defiance, he dropped his sailor cap on the floor.

"You ever hear from her?" Picot asked, meaning the author, the former Win Chaney nee Wallquist, who had printed the immortal words on a Booby Box.

Chaney shook his head.

"Too bad," Picot said. "She was nice people."

Chaney nodded, being polite. Actually, she wasn't, he thought. She was a bitch. And a nag and a poor sport and a bad Scrabble player and a lousy lay. Briefly, he tried to remember what she looked like, lying there like a dead fish, and smelling like one, too.

"Why weren't you at Rotary?"

"I dunno. I just didn't have the heart for it, I guess."

"You didn't miss anything," Picot assured him. "They didn't even have a speaker, his radiator boiled over in Riverside. Panski substituted, telling more than we needed to know about the undertaking business."

"Panski? Shit, he substituted last year."

"A perennial," Picot agreed. Chaney straightened the poem's frame, making it the only thing that wasn't out of kilter in *The Sandbox*'s entire editorial office. "How about the lunch?"

"Rubber chicken and hand-painted peas."

"Ugh," Chaney said, immediately sorry. He kept forgetting that Picot was an Indian, which was easy to do. Picot wore Stuard of Sahara clothes and drove a white Cadillac and belonged to the Racquet Club. One of the chosen. "How long have you been waiting?"

A plump, pleasant man, seemingly forever smiling, Picot uncrossed his fat legs, the movement revealing a gold chain. He pulled on it and revealed a gold watch. "Oh, maybe half an hour."

Chaney picked his way through the litter to his desk.

"The door was open," Picot added, explaining his presence.

Chaney sat down, trying to reconstruct the previous night's events. Somewhere in the shambles, McClatchie, under threat of dismissal, had permitted him to finger a distressingly large vagina *but that's all*. And it didn't explain why they'd left without locking the door.

"McClatchie wasn't here?"

"No."

Chaney tried to remember. Had he perhaps actually fired her? The thought made him shudder. He hated pasting up, a job which McClatchie, after several uneven months, had just finally mastered. For a while *The Sandbox* had taken on the appearance of the office from which it was produced.

"Something you might want to check out," Picot said, putting the watch away, "is who's backing Refalo at the Boom Boom Room. There's talk that it's Mafia money."

Chaney looked at him, suddenly interested. "Oh? Where did you hear this?"

"From an unimpeachable source."

"Not Soliz?"

"Something else," Picot said, ignoring the question, "is that Jack Mallory is in town."

"Hold it," Chaney complained. He found a pencil, thinking that he had half his column written. "Any idea why?"

"No. But start with Lois Sills."

Jesus, all of it, Chaney decided. He scribbled some quick notes. "That's one I owe you."

"Yeah," Picot agreed. He stood up, taller than expected. "You going to the Chamber meeting tomorrow?"

"Maybe."

"Try. It might be interesting. Conroy's going to recommend taking over the Desert Circus."

"That klutz." Chaney finished reading his notes, underlining a final word, *romance,* and then drawing a large question mark. The idea intrigued him so much that he felt obligated to ask. "Incidentally, what's happening with City Hall?"

Picot paused at the door. "Nothing. The bastards won't budge."

Doodling, Chaney made the question mark larger, completely fascinated now, prepared to pay any price. "You think I should write another editorial?"

"It wouldn't hurt," Picot said, leaving it at that. He went out, a big diamond flashing as he waved.

Before the door closed, Chaney was already reaching for the telephone, pulling a battered typewriter into positon as he did so. When he finished dialing, he stuffed it with a sheet of yellow paper, typing with the phone cradled under his chin.

chaney THE DESERT FOX 1

Ex-Mayor Jack "King" Mallory has set tongues wagging with a surprise visit to Palm Springs. Anyone wondering what he's doing back is advised to ask socialite Lois Sills...

Local law enforcement officers fear Mafia money may have built a new Palm Springs disco joint. If so, expect its city license to be lifted...

The Agua Caliente Tribal Council is getting nowhere in zoning pow-wows with Palm Springs City Council. Civic nabobs seem to have forgotten that the Calientes were here first (see Editorial)...

"Hello?" McClatchie said, answering on the sixth ring.
"What the hell happened to you?" Chaney demanded.
"Huh?"
"Why aren't you here?"
McClatchie made a sniffing sound. "Don't you remember? You gave me the day off."
"Oh," Chaney said, the night a complete blank. The last thing he remembered, he'd been standing in the back yard, staring up at the tram light and waiting for his scotch and water buzz to pass so he could go back inside and face the Turks without making a drunken fool of himself. Or was that the previous night?

Embarrassed, he hung up, pulling the typewriter closer, checking his notes. He started typing again.

What the wagging tongues are asking:
Could a romance be in the offing?

An old pickup truck stopped at the curb, Mallory getting out with difficulty. He looked like he had been up all night, which was the case.

"You're sure you'll be all right?" Bluestone asked.

"Yes," Mallory assured him.

Bluestone pulled away, Mallory slapping at the side of the truck, a last good-bye.

Sargent watched through the office window. He recognized him from the limousine. The man behind the newspaper. Mr. Mysterious.

Mallory made his way up the walk, a little unsteady on his feet. He wasn't drunk, not anymore, but he had a terrible, pounding hangover. They'd run out of liquor at dawn and he'd fallen asleep on the shack's porch and he had awakened broiling in the sun.

Sargent waited apprehensively. He didn't like coincidences, they were somehow unnatural. Suzy was still in the back office with Lois. Their "moment" together had dragged on and on. It had been at least twenty minutes.

Mallory pushed inside, smelling stale. "Hullo."

"Hello," Sargent said.

"Where's the boss lady?"

"In the back."

"Is she alone?"

"No."

"Fuck," Mallory said softly. He just wanted to tell her and go.

Lois had heard him earlier. She came out, peering over glasses that she hadn't been wearing before. "King...?"

Mallory drew himself up, unshaven, rumpled, bleary-eyed.

"For God's sake. Where have you been?"

"Getting drunk."

Lois came closer, staring in disbelief.

"I went out to see Bluestone," Mallory told her, looking to Sargent. "Old times."

"Drunk," Lois said. Her voice had an oddly plaintive quality, as if she had been falsely accused of something. "Do you think that...was called for?"

Mallory shrugged, looking at the ceiling now.

"It wasn't," Lois said, "and you didn't telephone, and you're a very, very rude man. Look at you, *you smell.*"

Sargent eased away, going over to Suzy, who had emerged from the back office. "Listen, I think I'm going to pass, okay?"

Suzy shook her head. "Sit down."

"After all I've done?" Lois demanded, oddly plaintive again.

"Nobody asked you to," Mallory said.

Sargent sat at one of the desks, thinking that if things got too out of hand, he could always crawl under it.

"No, they didn't, did they?"

"No, they didn't."

Lois brushed by, close to tears, and Mallory shambled after her, catching the office door as she tried to slam it shut.

"Just leave, will you? That's what you want to do."

Mallory shouldered his way in and closed the door behind him.

"Just go, damn you. Just...*go.*"

Suzy took a chair across the desk from Sargent. She opened her purse and removed a compact and examined herself in the mirror. In the next few minutes, a choice would be made, either herself or Mallory as broker, and she wasn't too worried about the outcome. Lois had explained the situation and said the job was hers if Mallory didn't want it. Suzy was certain Mallory would never come back to Palm Springs on a rich widow's skirts. After what Mallory had been, after what had happened, his pride wouldn't let him. Lois didn't know her man.

"Do you know what you're doing?" Sargent asked.

Suzy nodded. "Waiting."

In the office, the argument continued, louder than before.

"The least you could have done was telephone."

"From Sun Devil Canyon?"

"You didn't have to spend the night."

"What's it to you where I spend the night?"

Satisfied, Suzy closed her compact, putting it back in her purse. Wait, that's all she had to do. And then pick up the pieces.

Sargent almost laughed. This reminded him of his manic period. Madness.

"Where's Sun Devil Canyon?" he asked, not really caring. It was just another voice to listen to.

"Back of Cathedral City."

"Oh. My slum town?"

"Yes. It ruins it."

In the office, the argument was still audible, the door no barrier to anger.

"For all I knew, you could have gone back to Oregon."

"And it's where I'm going, just as soon as I can."

"Then *go*."

"Ruins what?" Sargent asked.

"The canyon," Suzy told him. "That's where you should be wanting to live. The perfect site. Remote. Beautiful..."

"Are there houses there?"

"No. They'll never develop it. You have to drive through all those dreary slums."

Sargent tried to picture the canyon, a substitute for other images, Mr. Mysterious returning to Oregon, hidden behind the

Los Angeles *Times.* "That's the only way in? Through Cathedral City?"

Suzy nodded, listening to Mallory.

"And I'm not feeling guilty. There's a proper way of doing things, speaking of courtesy. Throwing your money around ... Why didn't you ask me first?"

"And why don't you just *go*?"

"How big is it?" Sargent asked. He waited a moment. "The canyon?"

Suzy frowned, listening. "Fair-sized ..."

"Big enough for a housing development?"

"Oh, God, yes. You could put a whole town in it."

"Then why don't you?"

Suzy looked at him, annoyed at the interruption, this was important to her.

"Then why don't you?" Sargent repeated. He made a motion, encompassing the office and its row of empty desks. "When you take this place over, that would be a good project, wouldn't it?"

Suzy smiled unsurely, wondering if this was another of his jokes, or if, as it seemed, he was being rude.

"Cathedral City isn't a problem," Sargent said, used to thinking big in his manic state. "All you have to do is buy it and tear it down."

Mallory opened the office door, backing out.

Lois was crying. "... and I don't want to see you again."

Wait, Suzy thought, that's all she had to do, and then pick up the pieces, but Sargent's crazy idea made a mere broker's job look so piddling.

But Cathedral City. Level the damn thing. Then start all over.

Crazy, but it *was* possible, Suzy thought. The slum houses could be picked up pretty cheaply, and when they were torn down, *when all of them were torn down,* the raw land would be extremely valuable. There was nothing wrong with the site itself.

It was in a protected cove. And much closer to Palm Springs than Rancho Mirage and Palm Desert. And...

God. With the slums gone? With a glorious new entrance to Sun Devil Canyon?

Suzy jumped up, grabbing Mallory. She couldn't let him go now. He was the key. "Wait a minute!"

Mallory pulled free, not even looking at her.

Desperately, Suzy ran ahead of him, bracing herself against the door, blocking his exit. "Please! Will you listen?"

Mallory stopped, shaking his head, wondering if there was another way out.

"One minute," Suzy said, taking a deep breath. "I'm Suzy Braverman, and that idiot over there, he's my partner, Mr. James Sargent, and we've got the hottest idea since toilet paper, which is..." She took another breath. "Which is—buy Cathedral City."

Mallory kept shaking his head, reaching out to physically remove her.

Suzy closed her eyes. "Buy it, tear it down, get rid of the slums. Do you know what Sun Devil Canyon would be worth then? Do you realize what you could *do* there?"

"Will you get out of my way?" Mallory demanded, but he dropped his hand, the rush of words finally registering.

There was a long moment of silence. Suzy opened her eyes, to find Mallory staring into them.

"You could build your own town," Suzy said, "and that's the only way you can ever come back."

Mallory kept staring. He wanted to leave. Every fiber in his body was aching to get through the door. Get out, that's all, he'd told Lois, and now he could go, he was free—and he couldn't move.

Suzy looked away, waiting.

Fuck, Mallory thought. Fuck, fuck, fuck, fuck, fuck. Why hadn't it come to him twenty years ago? It would have been easier then, and cheaper.

"You can be the broker," Suzy said. "It really doesn't make that much difference to me."

Mallory shook his head. "No, that's okay. You take it."

Suzy laughed. "How about we both take it?"

"If you insist," Mallory said, laughing too. He motioned with a big thumb. "But what's wrong with him?"

"He hasn't got a license."

"Is he a salesman?"

"No. He's just buying a house."

"Do you think we can get rid of him?"

"I don't see how."

"His idea?"

"Yes. And he's Em's nephew, and you don't want to cross her."

Mallory sat down, putting his head between his knees, holding it there for a while.

Suzy stayed at the door, not trusting herself to move.

"Mrs. Sills!" Mallory roared. He lifted his head, looking at Suzy. "I think I'm still drunk." And then another roar. *"Mrs. Sills!"*

Lois came out of the back office.

"You've got two brokers," Mallory announced, "me and her, and that fellow over there, you've got him, too, in some capacity."

"I beg your pardon?"

"I'm *staying*, Mrs. Sills," Mallory told her, putting his head back between his knees. "Do you understand that part?"

Suzy mouthed the words. Say yes.

"Yes," Lois said, barely audible. She stood watching Mallory, impossibly happy that he changed his mind, and completely baffled by all the rest.

...and they put me away? Sargent thought.

The crowded aerial tramway car pitched sickeningly as it passed another tower on its journey up Mount San Jacinto. Chip brushed against Jody, accidentally touching her breast, and he quickly put the offending hand in his pocket, as if God might cut it off.

It had happened to him twice before, Chip thought, remembering. The first time, in Grade Three, in Miss Christie's class, during the year known as The Public School Experiment. Her name was Hildegard Rudi and she was the most beautiful girl in the world and when Kenny Winters said fuck right out loud in front of her, he, Chip, who said it all the time, just as often as Kenny Winters (but *never* in front of Hildegard Rudi), he, Chip, clamped his hand over his mouth, absolutely aghast. That instinctive reaction—clamping his hand over his mouth, absolutely aghast—was the talk of the class for about three weeks, until Gordon Cooney ate a whole box of Dodd's Kidney Pills and pissed blue and Jack Lamaroux came into the school yard kicking a pair of girl's pants along in front of him (taken from a clothesline, of course) which, coming both on the same day, provided sufficient diversion. Saved, he'd been very careful after that, Chip remembered, not to clamp his hand over his mouth when anybody said anything, but Hildegard Rudi, the most beautiful girl in the world, was nevertheless kept on a pedestal by Stuart (Chip) Bollinger III all through Grade Three.

The second time it happened was when Armand Bell, his roommate at Duke, introduced him to Susan Sahulka, a classmate of Armand's "fiancee," Cheryl Fisher, on the first weekend they went to New York (actually, it was Bronxville). Susan Sahulka had Hildegard Rudi all beat to hell. In the first place, she was at least four times as beautiful, and in the second place, she wouldn't say shit if she stepped in it (this being at a time, you must understand, when all the girls were saying it, or at least all the girls he knew).

Susan Sahulka was a lady. She didn't say shit, and she didn't kiss on the first date, and after that she only kissed, she didn't neck, and she only let you touch her breasts accidentally, and although she had the same stirrings and desires as any other young woman (they discussed this, in rather vague terms) she wasn't going to go to bed with a boy unless she was engaged to him and she wasn't going to get engaged to Stuart (Chip) Bollinger III, who put her on a pedestal once reserved for Hildegard Rudi, where she remained, virginal, throughout the winter of '68. Cheryl confided later that Susan probably would have remained that way several more winters except that Chip was the first boy ever who didn't try to drag her behind a bush the moment he laid eyes upon her and it was for this reason and this reason alone that Susan Sahulka surrendered her body somewhat earlier than planned in the back seat of a restored Hudson Hornet parked behind the Dixie Hotel following, among other things, a performance of *Blume in Love,* 1:32 A.M., January 16, 1969.

The third time it happened, Chip thought, looking at Jody Walsh, was right now, and though he had missed getting into Hildegard Rudi (they were separated, perhaps, she to Grade Four, and he to the coats and ties of Stony Brook?), he wasn't going to fail with Jody, having been so fortunate as to have had that long-ago post-insertion critique from Cheryl Fisher, namely that all good things came to those who were patient and took their time. Helpless in the presence of such stunning beauty, he had placed the young lady on a pedestal, but he knew from experience, advice received and taken, that he'd take her off and bang her—if only he was patient.

The tramway car shuddered, passing another tower, and the recorded announcement informed them they were now entering the arctic zone, the fifth climatic change since they'd left the valley, the weather now corresponding to that of Alaska. They'd soon be at the 8,516-foot-high Mountain Station.

Jody shivered, not from the cold, there'd been a thirty-degree change during the tram's fifteen-minute climb up the face of Chino Canyon, but at the sight of the desert floor so far below, as if seen from a high-flying jet, Palm Springs a toy city, and, on the far side of the valley, the patch of blue that was the Salton Sea. Planes made her nervous. And this was worse.

"Don't worry," Chip said, taking her arm, not her hand. "We'll soon be off."

Jody did her best to smile. By now, most men would have her in bed, but Chip professed to be a nature lover, and they were going to walk among the pines, breathing deeply instead of heavily.

Using Lois' second car, the Cadillac Eldorado that had been preferred by Jock, Mallory drove out to Sun Devil Canyon, brimming with an enthusiasm that he hadn't felt for years. The idea would work. He knew it.

With Cathedral City's slums bulldozed away, the canyon was the perfect place for a new community, near all the facilities and conveniences of Palm Springs, yet offering complete privacy. The twisting road he was driving through the narrow pass was the only way in and easily guarded. There'd be no need for the high walls and constant patrols that maintained security in the open desert. Here impassable mountains did a better job, and they looked better, too.

High Desert—he had already picked the name, appropriating a generic term—promised what everybody wanted and hardly ever got. It was like an island, the privacy and security a natural thing, an integral part of the setting. You didn't have to sacrifice beauty for safety. Beauty was the safety.

Mallory wondered. Might that be the slogan? "High Desert—Where the Scenery Is Your Security."

Corny. But it might work. Something like that. Those were the two things that were going to sell: privacy and security without having to live in a goddamn prison. The only walls were the canyon walls, as wild and beautiful as Angel's drawings, put there by the Creator.

And convenience. Don't forget that, either. It was like an island but it didn't have an island's drawback. Once the road was paved, access would be quick and easy. Ten minutes in the convenience of your car.

Talk about having your cake and eating it, too, Mallory thought. Safe and sound in your own little world, everything serene and perfect, but when you wanted, *if* you wanted, the other world only a few short miles away.

Two worlds. Keep that distinction. High Desert serene. The hustle and clamor below. Make that a rule: *nothing intrudes.*

No business of any kind. No supermarket, no service station, no restaurant, no liquor store, not a goddamn thing.

Leave all that crap in Rancho Mirage and Palm Springs. In the canyon, there would be homes, that's all. Beautiful homes. Castles...

Yes, that's the way he'd go, Mallory decided. Homes, and that's all. No golf course, no tennis center, no clubhouse. Nothing like that. Just superb homes in a natural setting. A very special residential community, and very, very exclusive. The canyon walls decreed that. They were a built-in "no growth" factor.

Goddamn. He had paradise by the tail. Developed properly, High Desert could become the supreme place to live, overshadowing Palm Springs.

What a marvelous way for him to come back, Mallory enthused. There was no reason why he had to crawl. Not when he could burst on the scene as the driving force behind a rival community.

The idea would work. With the slums gone, the canyon was invaluable, the absolutely perfect setting. All it needed was money—and there was a millionaire under every rock.

Em was delighted. Outlandish or not, the scheme at least had gotten Sargent moving. For an hour now, he had paced the patio, protesting that he had agreed to nothing. Suzy had announced him as her partner and Mallory had included him—and they were actually going ahead with the thing!

"Good," Em said, which had become a standard response. "It's exactly what you need. Ever since I've known you—your whole life—you've been an observer, Jim. A watcher. A note-taker. Here, finally and at last, you're going to be a *do*-er, and it's about time, isn't it?"

Sargent didn't think that an accurate appraisal. A note-taker, yes. But Em forgot that the notes had to be translated and put in order, and he did that, too. They had to be presented to the public so they could be understood. From the start, his first job, a cub on the old *World,* he never felt the real work started until he rolled the paper into the typewriter. In all the positions that followed—correspondent, editorial writer, the first column that had earned his reputation—he never found reason to change his mind.

The real work started with words on paper. Everybody watched, the world was full of observers, but how many fashioned their findings into readable copy? He refined and interpreted the awful facts and he presented them in palatable form, the only way they could be accepted, with laughter. He was a historian, damn it—or at least he had been.

Now? Sargent wasn't sure. A mess, his career ruined, so busy trying to figure out what went wrong that he didn't have time to pick up the pieces. In a long dark tunnel and the hole at the end kept getting smaller.

"I have done things."

"Then do some more," Em said, her logic resolute. "Here's your chance to do something different. Get involved, for God's sake. Take a chance."

On a joke? Sargent grimaced. That's what finally brought him tumbling down. The rights to the *real* Barbie Doll. It had been a funny column, one of his best. Washington's foremost political humorist strikes again. And then Ross had said, "What if...?"

"It's a crazy idea," Sargent protested.

"Of course it is, dear," Em said, patting his hand. "What's wrong with that? Lots of crazy ideas have succeeded. Take peanut butter, for example."

"Leave me alone. I came here for a rest."

"You came here to start over, so why don't you?"

Em went into the house to make some lemonade. She wasn't going to let him back out, she decided. The man needed help. Something, anything, to keep his mind occupied. Shopping, gardening—that wasn't going to do it. Wielding a paint brush—that didn't stop the mind from churning.

Like a war, it had to be something that swept you up. Terrible odds, and danger. Pack you off in irons if you don't win. That kind of stuff.

Besides, she trusted Mallory.

Bluestone spit, watching it dry, the rock like a stove. Then he looked at Mallory, back immediately after leaving forever, bloodshot eyes burning with a vision that didn't make any sense at all.

"I don't get you," he said at last. "Yesterday, the place is practically worthless. Today, it's worth a million dollars?"

"Potentially, yes," Mallory said, not explaining why. He'd submitted his offer and it was a fair one. In return for the long-term lease, Bluestone would become an instant millionaire, getting $500,000 up front and another $500,000 worth of shares in the development company. In addition, there'd be annual payments, 10 per cent of whatever moneys were collected from the individual home owners who took subleases.

"Potentially?" Bluestone snorted. "Listen, there's a big desert down there, room for another fifty years of growth, probably more. So what makes somebody want to come up here and build?"

Mallory used the same arguments he had used on himself. "The setting. It's beautiful and it's private."

"It always was."

"Yes, but now we're going to share the secret. We're going to widen the road, pave it, and we're going to advertise, full page spreads in the *Times*."

"And what about Cathedral City?" Bluestone demanded, the obvious objection. "You're talking crazy. Nobody in his right mind is going to build a big expensive house up here if he has to drive through that mess to get to it."

Mallory wanted to tell him. The solution, so simple. But if Bluestone accepted it—believed as strongly as he, Mallory, did—then a million dollars might not be enough. "They do in other places," he said instead. Difficult in the past, the boy could be again, he had it within him. And the offer was fair, goddamn it. Fair and square. "Have you ever been to Rolling Hills? You go through Torrance."

Bluestone still wasn't convinced. "They've got limited choices there. People drive through Torrance for the same reason they drive around Watts. They *have to* to get to the other side. Here, there's a whole fucking desert. You can go in any direction and you'll always find the same thing. If you're protected from the wind, the sand isn't any better one place over another, and the sun isn't, either. Whatever else the canyon's got—and you think I don't know it's pretty, it's quiet?—whatever else, that's still not worth two trips, twice daily, through the scum end of Cathedral City. Me? I don't give a shit. But some lard ass and his blue rinse? Tooling through in their Cadillac ...?"

Mallory pushed off his rock. "You finished your speech?"

"Yes."

"One question. You had any better offers lately?"

Bluestone grinned, shaking his head. "No, I guess not."

"You expecting any?"

"That's two questions."

"Yes or no," Mallory said, staring down at him.

Bluestone thought for a while. "Where you going to get the money?"

"Raise it."

"You haven't got it now?"

"Ha, ha."

Bluestone thought some more. "How do I know you can get it?"

"You don't," Mallory said. "You take a chance. You give me a three-month option. If you haven't got your half million by then ..."

"I'll see you in Oregon?"

"If you can find me."

"All right," Bluestone said. He stood up, offering his hand.

Mallory took it, thinking that he was committed now, starting down that long road which went in only two directions, forward and back. There weren't any turnoffs. You either arrived or you didn't.

"Something made of this place, at last, huh?" he said hoarsely.

Bluestone shrugged, still not that sure.

"I've always tried to do the right thing by you, you know that?"

"Yes."

"I have," Mallory insisted. His grip tightened.

Bluestone looked at him, wanting to believe. He did, he thought. There couldn't, unaccountably, be anything wrong. That was just his own dark nature, the devil within, never quite suppressed.

CHAPTER FIVE

Outside, a painter had started on the empty window. Ǝ ꓘИIꓭ HT —he had gotten that far.

Watching, Sargent wondered if they were doing it on purpose, another puzzle to confound him. He had been led to understand that Sun Devil Canyon was owned by an Indian named Bluestone. Yet the option was signed by a Miguel Patino.

Ought he ask why? Or, better yet, now that Em had left, why didn't he just get up and walk out? Suzy he barely knew, Mallory and Lois not at all. How could he possibly consider forming a syndicate with them? Seriously—and it was time to get serious—he had been put away for just this kind of idiocy.

"Next," Mallory said, taking the option back. In return, he gave them single sheets of paper, headed PROPOSAL. "I worked the figures out with Spisak. He's more up to date on values, but if you think he's off base anywhere, don't hesitate to quarrel."

Suzy shook her head. "No, he's good."

Sargent started reading. Mallory wanted $2,500,000 in seed money. He proposed to raise it by offering shares at $100,000 each, the minimum buy-in $100,000, the maximum $500,000: As the syndicate's founding members, each was personally to commit $100,000, and to take on the obligation of raising $400,000 more.

"You'll have difficulty," Mallory said, anticipating Sargent's objection. "I realize you're a virtual stranger here. But I took the liberty of talking to Em, and she's agreed to help."

"Has she?"

"Yes."

That was nice, Sargent thought. One hundred thousand dollars. Angie would never agree to it. Half of her precious "cushion"—and no guarantee of when he would be functioning again. If ever.

The inheritance was the glue that held them together. Uncle Bill's surprise contribution to marital stability, it allowed, for the moment, co-existence. It promised, however vaguely, the possibility of a future. To Angie, still in shock, it was the only thing left, and she wanted it spent slowly, prudently. How could Em in her wisdom lead him to a gaming table?

Mallory looked at Suzy. "Anyone else...?"

"I'll manage," Suzy said.

"Then let's assume it's done."

Before Sargent could protest, another sheet of paper came around, this one headed CONFIDENTIAL. It swam with figures. The bottom line said $50,000,000 (est.). The sum, apparently, that would be required to buy Cathedral City, although nowhere was that specifically mentioned.

Lois paused in her reading. "Where did you get the figures?"

"From the county," Mallory told her. "Based on residential/commercial values in similar neighborhoods in Indio."

"They compare?"

"Close enough."

"How about the industrial area?"

"I'd leave that alone. It's far enough away."

Lois was dubious. "You'll still need a green belt."

"Then let's put one in."

"This item—'Escalation Factor,'" Suzy said. "That's to cover any price increases spurred by our buying activity?"

Mallory nodded. "Too high, probably, but better safe than sorry."

"What's it based on?"

"It's out of thin air."

Lois hesitated. "Is that wise?"

"I don't know of any scientific basis," Mallory told her, "but I can assure you of this, by the time we're through, we'll be paying prices comparable to Rancho Mirage."

"For sure," Suzy agreed. "I don't think it's too high. This item—'Vacant Land.' I assume we're talking here about open desert. That's surely not for a subdivided lot?"

"Which reminds me," Mallory said. "The four of us. And Bluestone, Spisak, Em..." He looked at Lois. "Theo?"

Lois shook her head.

"Okay. Let's keep it that way. Quiet. I'm sorry, Suzy. What was the question?"

"Never mind. I've got it here. Open desert."

Mallory looked at Sargent. "How about you? Anything that needs explaining?"

"Yes. Who's Miguel Patino?"

"Oh, I'm sorry. That's Bluestone."

Mallory waited, ready for the next question, but Sargent made a motion, indicating that he should get on with the meeting.

"You're sure?"

"Yes," Sargent said. The discussion resumed, excluding him, and the sheet of paper kept on swimming with figures, none of which he really understood. He didn't even know who was ƆИI Ж ƎHT

The meeting over, Mallory went into his office, sitting at the antique desk. *His* office, and *his* desk, he thought. They'd all agreed—everyone but Sargent, who hadn't said no, either. Which meant they were going ahead.

Lois looked in. "I've got to run. I just want you to know..." For a moment, it appeared she might cry. "I'm so happy."

"Go," Mallory said. She had an appointment with her hairdresser.

The door closed and then opened again. "You'll be home for dinner?"

He nodded. This time, yes. "When?"

"Seven o'clock."

"Okay."

"We'll celebrate."

"Yes."

"'Bye."

Mallory looked at his watch. Home, she had said, and that was something else he had to do, he decided. Get one of his own, a small apartment somewhere. And rent a car. He couldn't bunk at Lois' place forever. Tina had been looking at him funny, especially since he'd taken to driving around in Jock's old Eldorado. It wouldn't be long before the gossip started.

But first things first. They were going ahead. He found a phone book, turning to the listings for architects. Spisak had recommended Bailey, but Mallory didn't want him, he specialized in condos, and this wasn't that.

Carter? No, he was a tyrant. Feeny? Hardly. He'd botched the shopping center, remember? Palomino & Associates ...?

Well, Mallory thought, smiling faintly. Joe had moved up in the world. Tighman, he could do it, he'd done the Swan house, that was spectacular. Or maybe too spectacular? He'd want an arm and a leg now, and he was uneven.

Before he knew it, Mallory was through the list, not having found anyone who really appealed to him. So now what? Los Angeles?

Actually, it might be best to go out of town, he thought. It would be easier to keep the thing under wraps that way. Unless ...

The self-proclaimed genius in the limousine. What had been his name, St. Pierre? He was here, new in town, nobody knew him—and if he was half as good as he said he was ...?

Mallory flipped through the pages, looking for "Limousine Service," finding "Libraries—Public."

He smiled. Fate's hand, making sure he did things right? Maybe, this time, finally and at last, he'd put something together that would hold.

Em picked Sargent up on the corner, twenty minutes later than promised, the back seat piled with groceries.

"Sorry. I had to go to Jurgensen's."

Sargent got in, his annoyance giving way to apprehension. There was enough to feed an army.

"How did it go?"

"As expected," he told her. "They're deranged, just like me. The only difference is—aren't I lucky?—I know it."

"Don't be too sure," Em counseled, pulling back into the traffic. "Mallory's no fool. He built this town, remember. And Suzy isn't, either."

Sargent scoffed. "They're crackers, I tell you. This was the proposal—we each throw a hundred grand in the pot, then find four others who'll do the same."

Em looked at him. "What's wrong with that?"

"Everything. First off, I can't afford the risk. Secondly, I don't know…"

"What risk?"

"The risk, very real, I suspect, that there isn't a financial institution in the country willing to spend fifty million dollars buying Cathedral City."

"Well, that's not the way I understood it," Em said, having been briefed by Mallory. "It would be a consortium. That's how all these things are put together. Everybody in for a piece and nobody gets hurt too badly."

"Oh, good. We're not looking for just one dippy bank? It's dozens of 'em…?"

"Yes, and you've got three months, and if you haven't the financing lined up by then, you let the canyon option lapse, that's all. You get your money out. No harm done."

"Sure. Except that it's been tied up when it should have been earning interest."

"It'll be earning interest."

"How do you know?"

"It'll be in a bank."

Sargent sighed. "Sorry. I didn't know you attended the meeting."

"And I didn't know you didn't," Em said serenely. "Now, your second objection? You don't know...?"

"Anybody."

"Nonsense. You know me, and I know everybody. Mary Alice, for example. I've got dibs on her."

God, Sargent thought. What had they done? Conspired with Em and divided up the town? Everybody with a list of suckers?

"Which is what that stuff is all about," Em confirmed, nodding toward the back seat. "The old girl is coming to dinner. I'll get her drunk and you make the pitch."

Sargent couldn't believe it. He was going to protest, but Em shushed him. "Think of it as a favor. That new husband of hers, he's going to get everything that isn't nailed down. Wait till you hear the latest."

"Em. Listen..."

"No, you. He ran away—and to get him back she promised to buy a restaurant."

"A what?"

"You heard me, and what does she know about running one, I ask you? It'll fold in a month."

Well, Sargent thought, amused by the idea. So the Gingerbread Man was a fortune hunter, after all? And fast, too?

"As I said, think of it as a favor," Em repeated. "It's the least we can do, tie up her money until she comes to her senses." The smile intruded. "What's so funny?"

For one thing, Mary Alice running a restaurant, but she wasn't so silly as to try, Sargent decided. That would be Billy's job—she was buying it for him, wasn't she?—and he might know enough to make a go of it. If it was honestly Mexican and had a good location and ...

"I don't see what's so funny," Em complained.

Sargent ignored her, getting another of his crazy ideas.

Mallory went to the new main library, a low, slanted, dung-colored concrete bunker, another of the grotesque edifices which had sprung up in his absence. Inside a fountain rose and fell noisily, a constant disturbance, and—as he expected—there were pitifully few books. Like the new museum, another fortress, all structure, he thought. The powers who had replaced him were dedicated to outward show. When would they put something worthy *inside?*

For a while, searching the shelves, he was afraid he would find nothing, but finally he came across a reference in the index of a slim volume titled *The New Architect.* St. Pierre, Elliott Louis. That had to be him.

Mallory flipped back through the pages, finding St. Pierre briefly mentioned as one of Canada's foremost architects, equated with Moshe Safdie, designer of Habitat. It called him a "complex blend of poet, artist and engineer" and had photographs of two samples of his work, Greensward, an office building in Montreal, and the Franklin house in Rosedale, a suburb of Toronto.

So he does houses, too? Mallory thought, impressed. The house was marvelous, uniquely its own self, old and new at the same time, an integral part of its riverside setting and yet boldly assertive. A home—and also a kind of monument.

Mallory closed the book. He had his man, he decided. All he had to do was find him, and get him to agree.

Millie tensed.

"What is it?" Bluestone asked, holding in her.

Millie didn't answer, straining to hear the sound again, her expression telling him to be silent.

There was nothing.

"I thought I heard a car," Millie said after a while. She tried to relax, lifting her buttocks, resuming the circular motion.

Bluestone held in her, not reacting.

Millie kept the circle going. "Maybe your guardian's back…"

Jesus, Bluestone thought. He could feel himself starting to soften. Reluctantly, he eased out, kissing her as he did so, a gentle good-bye and thank you. "I will be."

"What?"

"Back," he promised, smiling. Shifting his weight, he carefully rolled off the pool table, doing it just like Burt Reynolds.

Millie closed her eyes and waited, hoping she was wrong, that it hadn't been a car. They were just getting started.

Bluestone found his pants and pulled them on and went out on the porch. He stood listening.

The sound came again, the distant purr of a finely tuned engine, released momentarily on the rise of a hill.

"Is that him?" Millie asked.

"No," Bluestone said. He came back in, leaving the door open. He found his shirt and started putting it on. "It's Picot."

Millie let her breath out in a long sigh. "Shit."

"Don't worry, I'll get rid of him," Bluestone told her. He finished dressing, pulling on sneakers and tying the laces, something he normally didn't do for company. "It's probably about the option."

"What option?"

"Uh, just an option, that's all."

"On what?"

"A piece of land I own in town," Bluestone lied, remembering Mallory's insistence that it be kept secret. He checked his appearance in the mirror over the sink, wondering how Picot had found out about it so quickly, but then there wasn't much that Picot missed hearing. Or telling, when it suited him. "Maybe you'd better get dressed, huh?"

"I thought you said you were going to get rid of him?"

"Don't worry, I will." Bluestone rubbed his mouth, removing the faint traces of lipstick. "But he might want to come in for a while ..." He looked at her, then at the shack's one room, the pool table the only piece of furniture. "Be a sport, huh?"

Millie responded with another sigh. She didn't move.

Bluestone shrugged and went outside and stood waiting on the porch. The sound of the approaching car was much louder now. Picot's Cadillac, very definitely, Bluestone decided, and then the generator cut in, the thump, thump, thump drowning it out.

Sneaking away from Five Lakes, St. Pierre wondered if he was being followed, a white Eldorado had been parked across the street, and now there was another, two cars back on the highway as he headed for Palm Desert.

The same one? There were so goddamn many, a multitude of white Eldorados, it probably was just a coincidence, but there was no sense taking chances. Cleo's drunken threat to have him roughed up couldn't be dismissed out of hand. Down here, the bars were full of gangsters. She had all day to meet them.

To ease his mind, St. Pierre slowed and pulled over, stopping on the shoulder of the road. He caught just a glimpse of the driver as the Eldorado swept by. The craggy profile seemed familiar.

Yes, too familiar, St. Pierre thought. He *was* being followed, and it was fortunate he had noticed and stopped. The man wouldn't try anything here in the middle of traffic.

Fifty yards ahead, the Eldorado also pulled off, sending up a spray of gravel. Mallory got out and started walking back. Impulsively, St. Pierre opened the glove compartment, removing the small automatic he'd found hidden in a closet in MacPherson's condo. He released the safety and held it ready in his jacket pocket. The crazy bitch, he thought.

Mallory trudged back, hoping he'd be remembered. He smiled tentatively.

Not here, in the middle of traffic, St. Pierre told himself. The gun was just a precaution. He wouldn't need it.

"You remember me?" Mallory called, smiling. He moved around to the passenger side, out of the way of whizzing cars.

St. Pierre sat frozen. He hadn't expected that side, the door wasn't locked.

Mallory opened it and extended a huge hand. "Jack Mallory. We met in the limousine."

The limousine, St. Pierre thought, everything coming back in a rush: the guy in the rear seat, dropped off at Canyon Country Club, sneaking in some lady's back door … and anyway, nothing to do with Cleo.

"Mallory?"

"That's right."

Belatedly, St. Pierre released the gun, wiping his sweaty palm on his pants leg. It was too late to shake hands. Mallory had pulled back, staring at the telltale bulge.

"I thought it was Brown."

"An alias. I'm a kind of celebrity."

"Oh. Well, I'm St. Pierre."

"Yeah, I know," Mallory said, still staring at the bulge. "What's that thing for?"

The gun? St. Pierre wished he knew. A lot of good it was, he'd been scared silly, unable to move. Drive away, that should have been his first reaction. Or lock the door, for Christ's sake. But to just sit—*frozen?* "I've, uh, been getting threats," he said at last, feeling even more stupid. "My wife."

Mallory looked at him.

"To have me beat up … and I thought you might be someone she hired."

"Me?"

"Yes."

"I'm sorry," Mallory said, laughing. "All I want is your money." He relaxed, leaning on the open door. "No wonder I've been having so much trouble. Your phone always busy—off the hook, I suppose?—and the guard claimed you'd gone back to Canada."

St. Pierre nodded. "Yes, not that it's convinced her. How did you know where I was staying?"

"Lewis, the limousine driver," Mallory said. "And when I couldn't reach you, I just sat out front, waiting."

"That was you?"

"Yeah. Half asleep. You'd gone by before I realized. So ..." He laughed again. "I chased you down. Now, is there somewhere we can talk?"

"What about?"

"All that money burning a hole in your pocket."

Money? He didn't have any, St. Pierre was going to say, but then he remembered, he'd blabbed all.

"He's got Joe with him," Bluestone told Millie, who had finally decided to put on her dress.

Picot parked in the scant shade of a scraggly piñon pine. He got out pushing his passenger before him.

"I brought a present for you."

Joe Patino grinned foolishly, unsteady on his feet.

"Thanks," Bluestone said. Joe Patino was blood, his father's brother, and another disgrace to the Agua Calientes. He usually was drunk, as he was now.

"Keep him for a while," Picot ordered, shoving Joe forward. "I'm sick of looking at him."

"What's he done now?"

"Offended me."

No doubt, Bluestone thought. He took hold of his swaying uncle, offended himself. "All right, I'll dry him out." The rest was for Joe. "Jesus. *Why*?"

Joe Patino grinned foolishly.

"It's a sickness," Picot said, answering for him. The burden transferred, his voice was gentler now. "A plague ... to which we are especially susceptible."

Bluestone wondered. Did that really explain it? He knew when to stop, and Picot did too. None of the other Agua Calientes were drunks. So why Joe? "Do you want to come in for a while?"

Picot looked at Millie, standing in the shack's doorway, blocking it. "No. I'd better be getting back."

"You're sure?"

"Yes." He took another quick look at Millie. "I hope I didn't interrupt anything."

"No," Bluestone lied, wondering what to do with Joe, and then remembering that he had a full shithouse.

Mallory took St. Pierre to the back booth at Tito's, hoping that the picture still would be there. Fortunately, it was, showing him with Tito and Alan Ladd at the restaurant's opening, and despite the years he hadn't changed all that much. As ugly as ever.

St. Pierre noticed it.

"Yeah, I used to be mayor," Mallory said, taking the seat facing the front, "but that's not why I brought you here. They make the best breakfast in town and this is my table, or at least it used to be. I hope you're hungry."

A waitress came with menus.

"Coffee," Mallory told her, ordering right away, it was noon and he still hadn't eaten, nobody did at Lois' house till the arrival of Tina. "Eggs over easy and sausages and rye toast." He looked at St. Pierre. "You want something else?"

St. Pierre shook his head. It didn't matter, his stomach was churning, he was just going to pick. He still didn't know why he'd agreed to come. Because he couldn't run from everybody?

"Twice," Mallory said. He waited for the waitress to write that down and leave. "Now—where was I?—what made me look you up? The money, yes. That impressed me very much. Lots of money and looking for a place to invest it. It's not a combination one runs across too often. Usually, the money is already invested, huh? Tied up, so they have to sell or borrow ..." He paused, as if a terrible thought had just crossed his mind. "You, uh, haven't done anything foolish, have you?"

Again, St. Pierre shook his head. Mallory sounded like a con artist. A former mayor, and he snuck into town?

"Good. You're still ripe for plucking, then. And what else impressed me, providing that wasn't all hot air—a respected architect-engineer."

"It wasn't."

"I didn't think so."

The waitress came back. "Sorry. Did you want hash browns with that?"

"Yeah, but coffee first," Mallory said, annoyed at the interruption. "Is Tito around?"

"Tito?" She shook her head. "No, he's dead."

"The mayor, were you?" St. Pierre asked. He smiled, feeling in control of the situation for the first time.

"Uh, huh. Six years. And then a term as congressman."

"But I take it you have been away for a while?"

"Yeah," Mallory admitted. "I ran away, the same as you're trying to do now." He waited briefly for an argument. "Different demons, but at least they didn't follow me. Maybe that's why I got homesick?"

St. Pierre shrugged, the advantage suddenly gone.

"Actually, I refused to admit it," Mallory said, continuing with his confession. "I got burned. Defeated in an election. Other problems ..." He glanced at the photograph. "Me, before the fall. And if I come back, it's got to be with that kind of smile. I used to *own* this fucking town."

The waitress came with the coffee, saving St. Pierre the need to reply.

"I did," Mallory said, "and now the waitress doesn't know me." He looked at her. "You don't know me, do you, honey?"

She shook her head.

"See?" Mallory demanded. He sipped at his coffee, waiting for her to leave. "Like you, I've got to start over. Build anew. You interested?"

"In what?"

"Recognition," Mallory said, lowering his voice. "You were somebody in Canada, right? You mentioned Greensward, Crofton Place—and what was the third one?"

"Century Towers."

"Yeah. Well, don't try to impress some architect at a cocktail party here. He'll probably have designed Century City."

St. Pierre felt himself redden. "I wasn't trying to impress anyone."

"Of course not." Mallory laughed. "You're just telling it like it is, which is bad enough. But wait till you start telling it like it *was*. I'm reminded of old Tom Higgins. He's always relating how he elected the President. Saved the day, he says, got labor united, and the President called him in and admitted it, right in front of all his aides. 'Wasn't it nice of the President to say that?' he asks—and he's talking about Truman."

Despite his embarrassment, St. Pierre had to laugh, too. He knew the type, resting on withered laurels. Still, it hardly applied to him.

"Don't be too sure," Mallory said, reading his mind. "You come down here, tail between your legs, bleating about how badly you've been done by. That's boring."

"Is it?"

"Yes, it's within you. The stuff to bore. And if you buy some frontage in Palm Desert and wait until another fag wants to open another boutique, thereby turning a tidy profit ...?"

"That's also boring?"

"It's deadening."

Yes, it would be, St. Pierre had to admit, and he could picture himself in exactly such a role. Wasn't that the haven he sought? Once rid of Cleo, just to sit in the sun, watching his sand increase in value. He'd built enough castles. Let someone else have a turn. "For a while," he said, almost to himself. "I need a rest. Time to glue the pieces back together. Later ... who knows?"

Mallory scoffed. "Later? Bullshit. I've seen it happen too often. Once you quit, something dies inside. When you finally realize it, that you're boring, then it's too late. The momentum is lost and however you try it's only make-work. It's never the real thing again. So aren't you glad of this favor? I've caught you just in time. Your avalanche of life, almost grinding to a halt, and here I am to kick your ass, to keep you rolling."

St. Pierre looked at the photograph. Mallory had hold of Alan Ladd, telling him something he ought to hear, and he wasn't going to let go until he finished. "All right. What are you selling?"

"God, I thought you'd never ask," Mallory said, drawing closer. "I've got a canyon. Private, beautiful, the nicest place within a hundred miles—and there's only one thing wrong with it."

St. Pierre waited. What was that?

"It's empty."

The waitress came with their food, bringing everything at the same time, the cutlery rolled up in napkins, ketchup and steak sauce. She made a production of getting it all laid out.

They both sat silently watching.

"More coffee?"

"Please."

"Raw land?" St. Pierre said then. He started to eat, hungrier than he had realized. "No, I don't think so. The long haul doesn't interest me. What I'm looking for ..."

"... is a fast turnover."

St. Pierre glanced up, nodding. The waitress was pouring the coffee.

"No, you're not," Mallory told him. The question was for the waitress: "Why do I waste my time with idiots?"

She shrugged and left.

"You're looking for a challenge," Mallory said loudly. "What have I been telling you all this time? You're in danger of becoming a bore!"

St. Pierre looked around. People were staring.

"Yes, yes," Mallory said more quietly. "It's supposed to be a secret, so why am I yelling? Can you keep your mouth shut?"

Can you? St. Pierre wondered, becoming angry. For the second time, he could feel himself getting red in the face.

"Your performance in the limousine, if that's any indication, no," Mallory continued. "But then I'm desperate. I need an architect."

"I'm sure there are plenty," St. Pierre said stiffly.

Mallory shook his head. "Of your caliber? Temporarily unemployed? With money to invest? Willing—no, anxious—to work in secrecy?"

St. Pierre started to slide out of the booth. "If this is your idea..."

"No, it's Sargent's," Mallory said, holding him back. "Like yourself, I was invited later, uniquely qualified. The plan—listen to this, now—the plan is to fill that empty canyon with a new community designed, start to finish, every stick and brick, totally and completely—listen to this—by one man's hand."

St. Pierre looked at him.

"Why not?" Mallory demanded. "You can do it, can't you? Crofton Place, you said it was a landmark. More innovative than Habitat. And Greensward? How many awards?"

Yes, he is talking about me, St. Pierre decided. For some reason, despite his apprehension, the fear that Mallory wasn't quite all right, he felt oddly flattered by the offer. The first time, since arriving, that his skills had been recognized by other than himself.

"You could design the whole thing?"

"Yes, I suppose so. But ..."

"Shit, I know you can. You think your own word was enough? I looked you up in the library."

"Did you?"

Mallory nodded, smiling. "And made a few telephone calls. Your last client? She sends her love." He waited a moment. "Now, would you like to hear more about my canyon?"

"No."

"Good," Mallory said. "The setting is perfect. Whatever goes in, I want it to fit, you understand? Every home contributing to the complete whole. If we can do that—while still allowing individual expression—we'll rival anything anywhere in the country."

Was there no shutting him up? St. Pierre wondered, returning to his breakfast. "I don't do subdivisions."

"Is that what you think this is?"

"Isn't it?"

"No, nothing like it. These would be very, very exclusive residential properties. Five acres, minimum. Top quality homes costing hundreds of thousands, every one different, custom built for the owner, but blending in or it wouldn't be allowed, and you as the architect to have the final say. Instead of a pattern—what is the word I want?—a theme?"

Well, there was no escape, he'd have to discuss it, St. Pierre decided. He continued to eat. "All right. I know what you mean. But is there enough money around, willing to submit?"

Mallory laughed. "Are you serious? Women here, they can spend that much redecorating, and they don't know what they want, either. An interior designer has to tell them."

"Houses can be a bit different."

"Maybe, but that's your problem, and it won't be that difficult, I promise. The attraction we'll offer, almost irresistible, is that guarantee of uniformity and high standard, hitherto not achieved in our desert paradise."

St. Pierre really didn't know. Thus far, his movements restricted, he certainly hadn't seen any one neighborhood of truly quality housing, except—from a distance—the small mountain-side enclave that was Southridge. "Surely there are a few places?"

"Las Palmas?" Mallory shook his head. "It's a mish-mash. Canyon Country Club? That *is* a subdivision. And even Thunderbird, what is it really, a high-priced trailer court. No, believe me, there's a ready market, extremely wealthy people looking for a second Bel-Air, another Holmby Hills. They don't willingly set jewels on this trash heap. It just happens that the trash got here first and now there is too much to clean away. So they band together in small clearings and spend most of the time looking up, the one view that never offends. But if you offered a viable alternative?"

Not me, St. Pierre thought. He was in no condition to design a dog house. Yet, damn it, Mallory's enthusiasm was contagious, he could feel the juices flowing.

"There's a ready market," Mallory repeated. "Every year, more of them come, the puzzled rich, congregating."

"Puzzled?"

"Yes, shaking their heads, what's wrong with the world? It used to be their oyster. They could go anywhere, chasing the sun. They lived abroad and loved it. But now?

"First, you get hijacked, just going there. If you make it, then you're kidnaped, held for ransom. Or, if you prefer, you can be beaten and raped by restless natives, killed in a political upheaval, arrested for smuggling…"

St. Pierre laughed. "Yes, it is getting that bad, isn't it?"

"Worse. Before, no matter how you suffered, at least you had an excuse, it was cheaper, but it isn't anymore. The puzzled, restless rich, all they ask is a place in the sun but where the hell is it now, and they're looking inward and they're coming here. The sun, that's the attraction, and in this whole blessed country, name the one place where it shines longest and hottest, every goddamn day, practically guaranteed?"

"Death Valley?"

"Okay, laugh, but it's true, goddamn it. This isn't just a show biz hideaway anymore. The super-rich have discovered it, and they're choosing it as a place to live, to put down roots. This is their new home. More than any other spot—Palm Beach to Newport—here's where they're settling—the desert has become fashionable—here is the chosen sand."

St. Pierre sat eating his day's second breakfast. He wasn't laughing, he thought. Who could, at the chosen sand?

"Let me think on it," he said, chewing thoughtfully.

The phone was ringing when Suzy got home. She answered it, looking at her watch, wondering why Dex was late, school had been out more than an hour. "Hello?"

"Mrs. Braverman?"

"Yes?"

"One moment for Mr. Stuart Bollinger."

Oh, God, *no!* Suzy thought, wanting to hang up, but she was too frozen with fear. Bollinger meant the party, and the party meant Guttman. It meant changing his mind, filing some sort of damage suit, a public trial, the scandal.

"Hello, Suzy?"

"Yes..."

"It's Stu Bollinger."

"Yes," Suzy said again, conjuring up the worst. Her whole world was going to come smashing down. Just when things looked so good.

"I hope I'm not catching you at a bad time," Bollinger said. "Are you free to talk...?"

See? She sat down, going dead inside, all the hope draining out. "About what?"

"Well, first off, I want to apologize. I should have telephoned earlier, or called personally, actually. As your host, I feel responsible, of course—Mr. Guttman was present at my bidding—and needless to say I very much regret bringing you into contact with that kind of person."

First the windup, Suzy thought. Then the pitch. She waited.

"Hello?"

"I'm listening."

"Well," Bollinger said. "I do apologize, and I do hope you accept that, and without wishing to pry into your private business—if this is an intrusion, tell me—it has come to my attention that you're no longer with George Spector Realtor."

The last part, the intrusion, was what registered, and Suzy thought that it was one. Her being fired was none of his concern.

"Hello?"

"That's right, I'm not," Suzy said curtly. She wondered why she was angry, she ought to be relieved.

"Yes, and the other reason I'm calling, if you want the position back, rest assured that you may have it."

After the way Spector acted? "That's hardly likely."

"With George Spector's apologies," Bollinger hastened to add. "Or, if you prefer to locate with a new firm, I would be happy to assist you. I have some considerable influence with several of the larger..."

"Mr. Bollinger," Suzy said. "I appreciate your call, but I've already joined another firm, thank you."

"Oh. Well, that is good news."

"Yes."

"Anyway," Bollinger said, sounding flustered. "My apologies. And if there is anything else I can do...you won't hesitate to ask?"

"No, and thank you. Good-bye."

Suzy hung up, still wondering why she was so angry. He probably had the very best intentions. Yet it wasn't his concern, damn it. Why didn't he mind his own business?

Dex came bounding in. "Hi!"

"Where have you been?"

"Milo gave me a ride."

"And that takes longer than the bus?"

"We talked," Dex said, dumping her books on a chair. "What's wrong with you?"

The great Stu Bollinger, that's what, Suzy decided. He had so much money, he thought he could buy anything.

Later, in the kitchen, making a much-needed martini, it occurred to her that she had very stupidly passed up a potential investor.

She went back to get the phone, trailing it by its long cord, taking it into the bathroom with her drink. Bollinger certainly could come in for a hundred thousand, she thought. Heck, for him, that was loose change, wasn't it?

She wondered if she should go whole hog and pitch him for half a million. The amount made her shiver. Only in Palm Springs, Suzy thought, dialing Information. Only in Palm Springs.

Benson, the dealer, was the last to look at his cards, thinking that it was about time he got a little luck. Three aces.

Chermak bet, throwing in a white chip. "I guess I'm worth a hundred."

Rex Wills, who always raised, put in two, not saying anything.

"Two," Sommerset confirmed, dropping his carefully, one at a time.

McGregor hesitated.

Benson called to Bollinger. "Are you in?"

"Yeah, put me in," Bollinger said from the galley. "What is it?"

Sommerset put him in, not answering, and McGregor, unable to stall any longer, reluctantly added two more chips to the pot.

"Trying to buy it again, are you?" Benson asked Rex Wills. He looked at his hand, pretending to be appalled. "Well..." He waited until Rex Wills thought he was out. "Fuck you."

The others laughed.

"Coming 'round," Benson said. He met the bet and picked up the deck, looking at Chermak. "How many?"

"Two good ones," Chermak pleaded, discarding.

Benson dealt them, waiting for Rex Wills, smiling at his discomfort.

Rex Wills tried to make up his mind. He had four diamonds, and he had two queens, too.

"What'll it be?" Benson said, smiling.

Rex Wills discarded the spade queen.

"An inside straight, who's he kidding?" Benson said, flipping him a card and waiting for Sommerset.

Sommerset smiled back serenely. "I'm fine."

"He's fine, another kidder," Benson said. He called again to Bollinger. "Are you going to look at your cards?"

"Yes," Bollinger grumbled. He came out of the gallery, holding a half-made sandwich. "What's the bet?"

"There isn't any."

Bollinger wiped his free hand, lifting his cards awkwardly. "Where are we?"

"How many cards do you want?"

Bollinger considered for a moment. "Can I take four?"

Benson shook his head.

"Okay, three, then," Bollinger told him. He put the cards back on the table, fanning three off the top.

Benson silently put three more in their place. "Next?"

"Two," McGregor said.

Benson gave him two and took two for himself and carefully lifted the corners. His luck had changed, all right, he thought. He'd added kings. Full house, aces up.

"Bets?" Benson said, looking around.

Chermak threw in a white chip, watching Sommerset's expression. "Another hundred."

"And up," Rex Wills said. He put in two.

"Nonbelievers," Sommerset mourned. "And up again ..." He carefully counted out four chips.

Benson called to Bollinger. "Are you in?"

"Yeah," Bollinger told him. "Put me in."

Benson hesitated. "You haven't looked at your cards."

"Put me in," Bollinger repeated.

Benson shrugged and did so.

"I fold," McGregor said, looking relieved.

Benson examined his cards again, confirming that he did indeed have a full house, the best one possible, beaten only by four of a kind or a straight flush.

"I'm raising," Benson decided. He got a blue chip. "Is it okay if we make it an even thousand?"

No one said anything.

"It's a thousand," Benson said, putting in the blue.

Wordlessly, Chermak and Rex Wills met him, and Sommerset, smiling serenely, raised.

Benson called to Bollinger. "Do you want me to fold you? It's two thousand."

"Naw," Bollinger told him, still busy with his sandwich. "Put me in."

"You haven't looked at your cards."

"So? Put me in."

Benson shrugged, thinking what the hell, he was a billionaire, wasn't he?

"Okay, he's in, and I'm raising. Now it's four thousand. Let's separate the men from the boys."

The phone rang in the galley. Bollinger answered it. "Yes?"

"Mr. Bollinger?" Suzy said, close to stammering. "I'm sorry, I didn't mean to bother you. I called this number, trying to find out how one *did* contact you, and the switchboard transferred me."

"That's all right," Bollinger assured her. "Hold on a moment." He put a hand over the mouthpiece. "Keep putting me in, will you?" He closed the shutters and pushed the door shut with his foot. "Now, what can I do for you?"

Suzy took a deep breath. "Well, you remember when you called, you said if there was anything you could do, you wanted me to ask...?"

"Yes?"

"Well, this new firm I'm with, we're in real estate development, and we're looking for investors, and I wondered—if you had the time—if I might explain it to you. It's really quite an unusual opportunity."

Bollinger hesitated. This wasn't exactly what he had in mind. "Now?"

"No. This call, I was just trying to find out, you know, how to make an appointment?" She laughed nervously. "I'm sorry, I'm making you sound like a dentist, aren't I?"

Benson was complaining on the other side of the shutter. "Stu! We're going crazy here. You'd better look at your hand."

Bollinger opened the shutter briefly. "I said, *put me in.*"

Suzy was confused. "Hello...?"

"It's all right," Bollinger told her, wondering why he should hesitate, after all, he did want to meet her. Why not do it over business, the first time, anyway? "What kind of development?"

"Housing. An exclusive residential community. Are you familiar with Sun Devil Canyon?"

"You mean behind Cathedral City?"

"Yes," Suzy said, immediately sorry, she could tell he wasn't interested. She should have waited and explained it all properly. "I know what you're thinking..."

Bollinger had to laugh. "Do you?"

"You're thinking Cathedral City, ugh," Suzy said, plunging ahead. "But listen to this. Have you got a moment? What if you could make Cathedral City go away?"

"I'm afraid," Bollinger said, laughing again, "that it would take me a little longer than that. Is your firm developing property anyplace else?"

"No, just the canyon." She paused, worried that he should be laughing, he had the reputation of being a very shrewd investor. "You don't think that's a good idea? Getting rid of Cathedral City, I mean?"

"I think it's a marvelous idea. I just can't imagine how you expect to do it."

"The plan—and all of this is confidential, of course—is to have a consortium buy it up, as much as possible, for renewal."

"My dear lady, have you any idea of how much that would cost?"

"Yes. We're estimating fifty million."

"Mmmm. At least."

Now Sommerset was paging. "Stu, I think you'd better get out here."

Bollinger ignored him, wondering where the hell that crazy idea came from, there were miles and miles of empty desert, if they wanted to start a community, why not do it somewhere fresh and clean?

"Are you interested?" Suzy asked.

"In what?"

"In discussing it."

No, he wasn't, Bollinger thought, but he had maneuvered her this far, he might as well arrange something. Later in the morning, and then, if she was interesting, he could suggest lunch? "Well, there's no harm in that, I suppose."

"Say when."

"Tomorrow, eleven. You know the place?"

"Of course."

"Then it's settled."

"Eleven," Suzy said, her excitement rising, "and oh, I can bring my associates?"

Bollinger frowned, trapped. "If you wish."

"Thanks. We'll see you then. Good-bye."

"Good-bye," Bollinger said, hanging up. He stared at the phone, thinking he had fouled that up nicely. A simple tête-à-tête, that's all he wanted, and she was bringing "associates," and they wanted to fit him into a fifty million dollar crackpot deal? That was the trouble with having money. People thought you were rich.

"Stu!"

Angry, he ignored the plea, completing the sandwich he'd been making, cheese and onion because it was poker night, Marion away for the evening, gone to a movie with Blodgett. Then he got himself a beer, another normally shunned item, bad for the waistline. He stood drinking it.

McGregor came in.

"Who won?" Bollinger asked, knowing it couldn't be him. McGregor never stayed long enough. Strictly a donor.

"They're still playing it," McGregor told him.

"The same hand?"

"Yes."

Bollinger whistled. "What's in the pot?"

McGregor shrugged. "I dunno. Fifty, sixty thousand."

"You're kidding."

"Uh, uh," McGregor said. "Benson and Sommerset, they're taking a run at each other." He opened the freezer, getting a handful of ice. "You want me to look at your cards?"

Bollinger almost choked on his beer. "I'm still in …?"

"Yeah," McGregor said innocently. He got a glass, depositing the ice in it. "You wanted to be, didn't you?"

Bollinger took a moment. "Sure."

Putting down his sandwich, Bollinger returned to the game room, trying to appear casual about it. Benson and Sommerset were glaring at each other across a table heaped with chips.

"You kept me in, huh?"

Benson nodded grimly.

"Where are we?"

"I've raised, another five thousand, and now we're waiting on the kidder, who, incidentally, didn't draw."

Bollinger sat down, looking at his cards. He didn't have anything.

"I'll see you," Sommerset said finally.

Bollinger quietly folded, watching Benson and Sommerset play their drama out, Benson turning his aces one at a time, slowly, deliberately. There was a sizable amount of money involved.

High stakes for them, Bollinger thought, but not for him, his part in it was meaningless, and they knew it and that's why they left him in, when you compared resources, he played for pennies against their dollars, what he won or lost didn't matter, it was meaningless.

Bollinger sat watching, feeling left out, which he didn't like, these were his Boys. He could drop twenty thousand dollars because he was making a sandwich and they didn't even blink. He sat watching, feeling left out, which was unusual for him, and wondering what would impress them.

Spisak listened to the one-sided conversation with mounting skepticism. Suzy had caught Mallory going out the door, yet another example, Spisak thought, of rushing things. High Desert was literally being thrown together and he was being consulted after the fact. This St. Pierre, for example. Was he really the architect they needed? Photographs in a book weren't good enough. They ought to have one of his houses at hand. Be able to see it, touch it. *Live* in it.

"Bollinger, huh?" he said when Mallory hung up.

"How about that?" Mallory grinned. "Suzy thinks we've got a chance. Anyway, she's made an appointment." That reminded him of his own and he looked at his watch. "Listen, I've got to run. If I miss dinner again I'm really in the doghouse."

"Oh, you've got a chance, all right," Spisak said, thinking that Mallory was beginning to sound married, a deviation he normally would remark upon, but this new development concerned him more. "Duck soup, I'd say. Bollinger's kind of deal. A silent partner while you folks do all the work."

"So what's wrong with that?"

"Nothing."

Exactly, Mallory thought, he didn't want interference, but Bollinger's name could be very helpful in putting together the consortium to buy up Cathedral City. The man was legend. He made things happen. When he came in, others did, too.

"Did you ever wonder," Spisak asked, leaning back in his chair, looking Mallory in the eye, "how Stu Bollinger managed to get so rich? They say he's a billionaire."

"He's smart, I guess," Mallory said after a moment. "And he worked at it." He thought some more. "And he got lucky?"

"I don't know the man," Spisak said, "never met him in my life, too big a cheese for my plate, but what I think is, show me a billionaire and I'm looking at a crook."

Mallory laughed. "Bollinger?"

"What do you know about him?"

"Good-bye," Mallory said, getting up. Fate's hand was at work and the deal was going to hold together this time and he wasn't going to listen to Spisak's baseless alarums. He'd heard all he wanted to hear, that it would be duck soup.

❧   ❧   ❧

Em refilled Mary Alice's glass, giving Sargent a black look, then marching into the kitchen.

"No more for me," Mary Alice said belatedly. She turned back to Sargent. "Do you really think so?"

"Absolutely," Sargent told her. He took a careful sip of his own wine, nursing it.

"Well, I'm glad," Mary Alice said. "Most of my friends … they think it's silly." She looked for Em. "Em? Did you know you had a very intelligent nephew?"

Em called from the kitchen. "Jim. Can you help me with something?"

"Excuse me," Sargent said. He got up, taking his glass with him.

Mary Alice looked at Billy, as if to say I told you so, and Billy smiled and shrugged, admitting he'd been wrong. Initially, he had suspected the worst, the dinner another attempt to get Mary Alice to renege on her promise.

Sargent went into the kitchen.

"Are you daft?" Em asked in an angry whisper, not even waiting for the door to close. "What did you tell her that for? An absolutely marvelous idea? You're *supposed* to be pitching High Desert."

Sargent eased by her, not attempting to explain. It was too complicated and she wouldn't approve anyway. There wasn't a devious bone in her, the dinner notwithstanding.

"The woman's not made of money," Em complained, following him. "She's not going to buy a restaurant and buy into the syndicate, too. It's one or the other—and look out, that's Martin Ray, for God's sake!"

"And of excellent quality," Sargent said. He shook the glass, a last drop joining the rest in the sink.

"What are you doing?"

"Keeping up. Have I helped you with what I'm supposed to be helping you with?"

Em gave up. "You *are* daft."

Sargent nodded, going back into the dining room, the empty glass at his lips, pretending to be finishing it off.

"...family operation," Mary Alice was saying to Billy. She paused, waiting for Sargent to join them. "I was telling him about Las Casuelas Nuevas. Do you know it?"

"I don't think so."

"It's on Restaurant Row in Rancho Mirage, and very, very, elegant."

"Oh, yes," Sargent remembered. The Mexican place with the stunning architecture. Suzy had pointed it out as one of the better bets. "Is that what you're thinking of buying?"

"If they'd sell," Mary Alice said, her expression indicating that there wasn't a chance. "But that's the competition. So we'll have to get something similar."

"Well, you're going first-class."

"Don't you think we have to?"

Billy half rose from his chair, signaling Em's return.

"I think you ought to be authentic," Sargent said, conscious of her anger. The instructions had been to ridicule the restaurant and offer High Desert as an alternative. "I don't think that necessarily means Restaurant Row, or some equally expensive site in Palm Springs. If it were me..." He paused, as if suddenly aware that his glass was empty. "Would you like some more wine?"

"No thank you."

"Just a touch," Sargent told her, pouring more than that. "You can't refuse Martin Ray." Smiling at Em's look, he also topped off Billy's glass, leaving just the dregs for himself. "Where was I?"

"If it were you," Billy prompted.

"Oh, yes. Myself, I'd want something authentic. Have you considered Cathedral City?"

Mary Alice spluttered. "That awful place?"

"What's wrong with it?"

"Well, my God, it's a terrible dump. Have you seen the restaurants there? They're shacks, some of them, and the taverns…" She appealed to Em. "Isn't that where they raided the massage parlor?"

"Yes," Em admitted, wondering what was going on.

"Local color," Sargent said. He looked at Billy. "What do you think? I mean, what the hell, that would give the place a little flavor, wouldn't it? Like going to Chinatown."

Billy hesitated. He didn't want to quarrel with an ally, especially not the first encountered.

"People want atmosphere," Sargent lectured. "It gives eating out some oomph, makes it an adventure. They love offbeat places, and that's what is missing here, it's too goddamn sterile, sand in every direction. Where's your fish dock? Your farmer's market?"

Billy shrugged helplessly.

"You haven't got any."

Em cleared her throat. "Jim. Don't you think you should warn…"

"There's the cost to consider, too," Sargent told Mary Alice. "Like Las Casuelas, you could spend a fortune creating the right mood, but then what have you got? You're stamped from the same elegant cookie cutter and they were here first." He looked at Billy. "I know just the place for you. It's an old brick storage shed, a cavernous thing begging for some easy remodeling, and the back half is a greenhouse, most of the glass intact. You could put a million tables in there alone. I was going to buy it for myself, turn it into a house, Casa Verde—but you know what wives are like?"

"Jim."

Sargent frowned, pretending annoyance. "Yes?"

"I think it's only fair that you should warn them."

"That's confidential," Sargent said. "Besides, if it actually were to happen, it could only be to their great benefit." He turned back to Mary Alice. "She's defeating my argument, but what I'm saying is, the way Cathedral City is now, the locale provides the atmosphere. It may not be elegant, but at least it's authentic, it's where you'd expect to find a Mexican restaurant, and the nice part, all that color and romance, you get it for nothing."

"Warn me about what?" Mary Alice asked.

"That all that is subject to change," Em told her. "Like you, Jim is thinking of taking a flyer. If it works... Well, I suppose you're right, there is no way they could get hurt, is there? If it works, they'd be part of the renewal, in on the ground floor?"

"I wouldn't have mentioned it otherwise," Sargent said.

"Whatever are you talking about?" Mary Alice demanded.

"You tell them."

"No, you."

He was wrong, Sargent thought. She was devious. Unbeknownst to this poor lunatic, the con artist lurked in her soul, summoned forth by what—his need?

"This *is* confidential," Em said. "I must have your word. You won't tell anyone?" Not looking at them, she turned over a fork, wondering where to begin. "You knew Jack Mallory was back, and that he's gone into the real estate business with Lois Sills, and that Suzy Braverman left George Spector to join them? Well..."

After dinner, Lois took Mallory to the patio for their coffee. They were finally alone, Tina busy with the dishes, Theo watching one of his old movies, *Nightbird*, on his own television set. He preferred being an audience of one, the only saving grace in his preoccupation with his celluloid self. Conversation distracted.

"You were good today."

Mallory looked at her.

"The meeting," Lois said, even though he knew what she meant. "The man I used to know. Full of beans."

"Yeah."

"Really. It's where you shine, you know. Showing the way."

Mallory laughed, imagining himself with a flashlight. Usher at the Bijou.

"I mean it. Not that many people are leaders. And you are."

"Thank you."

"You're welcome."

Mallory sipped at his coffee, not inclined to argue. It had been a good meeting. The only question mark was Sargent, who barely seemed to comprehend.

"Strong enough?"

"Sure."

Lois sat down, feeling very housewifely. That was the kind of question asked of a husband, she thought. And if he said no, would she brew another pot?

"This is nice."

"What …?"

"I don't know. Being in business together, and being friends, too. It …"

Mallory waited.

"Makes me feel confident," Lois said. She tucked her legs under, smoothing her dress. "Ever since Jock died, I've needed something like this, a project. But who with?" She smiled. "I guess I don't trust that many people."

Mallory still didn't say anything. For him, being friends was a complication, raising the specter of emotional decisions.

"Anyway, I'm glad it worked out," Lois continued. "For a while, it was all a big bust, wasn't it? Screaming at each other, and you going back to Oregon." Again, she smoothed her dress. "Saved by the bell."

"Sargent."

"Yes, Sargent. Our crackpot savior. Bolt from the blue. Do you think he'll actually come in?"

Mallory shrugged. "Em says so."

"He's got the money?"

"Yes."

"And Suzy?"

"Let's hope."

"You don't sound worried."

"Because I'm not," Mallory said, knowing what she didn't know, that St. Pierre would be calling tonight, and that tomorrow morning there was a meeting with Stu Bollinger. He hadn't told her because he didn't want to raise false hopes, and he had another reason, she might attempt to interfere, there was that inclination. "On something this good, there'll be lots of others, Mrs. Sills. Standing in line."

Lois laughed. "Full of beans. But that's one of the things I wanted to ask you. Why make it so high?"

"The buy-in?"

"Yes. If it's just to give them a piece, why not fifty thousand or even twenty-five? I'm sure that's a lot of money for Suzy. A woman on her own...?"

"It's called a sweat guarantee," Mallory told her. "If they're in, I want them all the way, buying their dedication with their own money. They'll be working just as hard as me if they've got just as much to lose."

"I suppose. But what about you?"

He looked at her questioningly.

"Doesn't it overextend you?" she asked, deciding to be blunt about it. After all, they were partners.

"A bit," Mallory admitted. He had the impression of being maneuvered.

"Is that wise?"

"It isn't unwise."

She wasn't satisfied, and Mallory remembered that Spisak wasn't, either. His net worth in a fire sale was $85,000. And he had to live.

"Just barely, I'll scrape it up," he assured her. "There's three months, and we'll be going blazes by then. I've already got a line on some listings."

"King…"

Mallory wished he hadn't put it into words. That obviously wasn't enough. "There's always the bank."

"King," she said, starting again. "Why not let me lend it to you?"

"No."

"Why not?"

"Because it isn't necessary," he said, annoyed. He had been maneuvered.

"Come on, don't be silly. I insist."

You what? he thought. Now he was angry, even though it was irrational. The remark was innocent and he ought to be grateful.

"We'll call it an advance on your broker earnings. We are in business, aren't we? What's wrong with an advance?"

Nothing, he told himself. In any other firm he would take it. So why make a fuss because it was her? "We'll see."

Lois regarded that as acceptance. "Now you're being sensible."

Was he? Mallory wondered. He couldn't quite get rid of the feeling that Lois was buying him, much as she might purchase some piece of furniture she coveted.

Bluestone came out of the shower, drying himself with an enormous fluffy towel, one of his few luxuries. Another was the shower itself.

"You shouldn't take so many showers," Millie told him.

He paused. "Why?"

"If you shower too much, you remove all the natural body oils, and your skin ages a lot more rapidly than it should."

"Oh, yeah?"

"It's true. I read that somewhere, that if you shower a lot, your skin can get twenty years older than the rest of you."

"From showering?"

"It's true."

Bluestone looked at Millie, lying dirty on the pool table, a believer. "I like to keep my private parts clean."

"Then just wash your private parts," she told him. "You don't have to wash your whole body. Just your private parts."

Bluestone climbed aboard the pool table.

"If I did that," he said, pulling her head down, "you know what would happen, don't you? When I'm eighty years old, I'd have a hundred-year-old prick."

Outside, Joe Patino paused in his labors, wondering what the hell was so funny, he could hear them laughing all the way to the shithouse.

The call came very late. Mallory, waiting up, took it on the first ring, hoping Lois wouldn't be awakened, she had an extension at her bedside.

The first question was the answer he wanted. "Where is this canyon of yours?"

"Ours," Mallory said, reaching for his drink. "Ten minutes from where you're sitting."

"How big is it?"

"Four thousand acres."

"Divided by five? That's just a few hundred homesites?"

"I told you it would be exclusive."

"What's it called?"

"Sun Devil, but we're changing the name. High Desert."

High Desert, St. Pierre thought, trying to picture it. A small canyon with a flat floor. Somewhere close in the mountains.

"The road's in," Mallory said. "Gravel. We'll have to pave that, and the utilities can go in at the same time. What you've got to do …"

"I know," St. Pierre told him. "The gate, first of all. Something grand, but not too imposing. Reminiscent of an old Spanish mission, and there ought to be a bell tower. What's left of the church that never existed."

Mallory was going to protest—Christ, St. Pierre hadn't even seen the place yet—but then quickly changed his mind.

"The first house, that same flavor," St. Pierre said. "As if it had been restored, and lovingly, sparing no expense. It's got to be magnificent. The standard for all the rest. Right?"

Mallory nodded wordlessly.

"That's just inside the gate. You catch glimpses of it as you enter, the original house on the property, dating back—what would be realistic?—to the twenties?"

Christ, Mallory thought again, but still he nodded, it wasn't a bad idea. "Yes."

"This is an old estate. Formerly, one man held it all, the whole four thousand acres, he had it in orange trees. Is that possible?"

"Date palms."

"Okay, date palms. It doesn't matter. That's just rumor. Everybody makes up their own story. He fell on hard times, the estate had to be broken up, but isn't it wonderful what they're doing? The lots are large enough, there's still that feeling of living on an estate, everyone has his own. It's been saved, not destroyed. Winding country roads, very narrow, poorly paved. Just enough to keep the dust down. Horse trails alongside and between various properties. How am I doing?"

"Fine."

"Wait till you see the second house. It's across from the original, again just as you enter, and the people are horse lovers, they keep them to look at. There are always a couple grazing near the fence. And the stable? Mother of Jesus, can I do a stable?"

Mallory laughed. "What made up your mind?"

"What does it matter?" St. Pierre asked, but it was Cleo. If she was to give him no rest, perhaps work was the answer. People around, there'd be that protection, an office to escape to, and Mallory had mentioned he wanted it done in secrecy. Maybe they'd assign a guard and he could put MacPherson's gun back in the closet. "How are you working it—selling shares?"

"Yes. There's a minimum buy-in, one hundred thousand."

"What's the maximum?"

"Half a million."

"And the total capitalization?"

"Two and a half. It gets you a fifth."

"Where's the other money come from?"

"We borrow as we go."

St. Pierre considered briefly. If it was good, and he'd soon know, that would solve his biggest problem. His money moved and tied up, safe from Cleo's grasping hands, and Ottawa's, too. "Okay. Tentatively, I'm a full partner. How does the other part work?"

"Initially, like the rest of us, you work for nothing. We're trying to keep the nut down. The general layout ... the lot plan ... the roads ..."

"The first two spec houses?"

"No compensation," Mallory said. "but after that, it's monopoly time. No one can build a house that hasn't been designed by Elliott St. Pierre. Or, if you wish, that hasn't been designed in association with you, subject to your final approval. In any case you get a fat fee."

"And the kickback?"

"Nominal."

More than fair, St. Pierre had to admit, he'd have his half million back in no time, his own firm established to handle all the business, ten draftsmen working overtime. "I trust you're taken care of, too?"

"Adequately," Mallory said. "If that's a concern ..." He paused, aware of Lois, watching from the stairs, pulling her robe about her. "I take it you're in?"

"Tentatively," St. Pierre repeated. "Subject to site inspection. Can we do that tomorrow?"

Then you're in, Mallory thought. He put his drink aside, motioning to Lois, indicating that she should come down. "Yes. I'll call you."

"Right," St. Pierre said. He hung up.

Lois stopped at the foot of the stairs. "What's going on ...?"

Before Mallory could answer, the telephone rang again. He picked it up, thinking it was St. Pierre wanting to settle on a time, but it was Em, sounding like a schoolgirl.

"I had to tell you," she whispered, not even waiting for him to say hello. "We've got Mary Alice, full partner."

Immediately, the phone went dead, leaving Mallory looking blank, taking a moment to comprehend. Full partner? That's what St. Pierre was considering.

He put the phone back. God Almighty, were they going to do it all in one fell swoop? There was only Bollinger to go, and he'd be duck soup, easy.

Lois came closer. "Is something wrong?"

"Hello, no!" Mallory said. Impulsively, he grabbed her up, taking her by the waist, lifting and twirling.

"King!" she screamed.

He put her down, wondering what was wrong with him, he shouldn't have had those drinks, it was no way to treat a lady, and he had to get his own place, familiarity bred ... what?

"That was Em," he said, flushed. "We've got Mary Alice, and a couple other prospects ..." He stopped, telling too much. "Well, I've got a busy day, I'd better say good night." He looked at her. "Good night, huh?"

"Good night," Lois said, her sides aching where he'd held her, and her heart, too. It was going to happen, she thought. Given time, one of these nights, it was going to happen.

Sargent sat out watching the stars. Over and over, endless, the events of the evening kept running through his mind, every detail remembered with the same awful clarity that marked his manic state. Em turning over the fork, preparatory to laying out the grand scheme, and Mary Alice's eyes bright with interest, despite the wine.

Billy had been no problem, of course. He would have agreed to any location, and bought, built or remodeled, what did he care? He was getting his own restaurant. For a poor tourist guide—and he'd been a busboy, didn't he say?—the mind boggled.

Mary Alice, though. She took her time and she asked all the right questions. Nobody's fool except Billy's, and that was okay, he gave her pleasure. She asked all the right questions and she knew what she was doing despite the wine. When she agreed to do both—Em had said she wouldn't, remember?—when Mary Alice agreed to do both, that had been a cool, calculated decision.

Her kind of gamble, she said. The restaurant in Cathedral City and buy into the syndicate, a major shareholder, $500,000. Her kind of gamble because she couldn't lose.

Then what was wrong?

Nothing, Sargent thought, except that he was trapped, a spider who had fashioned a web and caught himself. He had tasted blood and he couldn't back out now.

Joe Patino exchanged a pick for a shovel, using it to pry at the broken shale, sweating and cursing as he strained. He had to get the new pit dug tonight—when the sun came up, it would be too hot to work—and Bluestone wouldn't drive him back to Palm Springs until the job was finished.

He heaved, almost breaking the shovel handle, and finally a slab of shale lifted free. He turned it over and then put the shovel aside and picked up the loose rock with his hands. With an effort, he threw it out of the pit, cringing against the wall for a moment, fearful that it might fall back and hit him.

It was hard, dangerous work, especially at night, but he *had* to get it finished, he thought. He wouldn't get a drink till he did. And he couldn't live without a drink.

Hands trembling, he got the lantern, holding it next to the hole he'd just made, trying to see if it was down to sandstone yet. It would be a lot easier when he got to the sandstone.

The lantern's feeble light fell upon an exposed vein of ore, grayish black and a greenish caste, its surface oddly greasy.

Joe sighed with relief. The ore meant nothing to him. All he saw was the sandstone which bore it. He put the lantern down and reached for the pick. By morning, he'd have the pit dug, the shithouse moved over it.

What he was digging now, the last to come out, tossed atop what had been dug before, naturally would be the first to go into the old pit, which meant that no one else was going to see the strange-looking ore.

CHAPTER SIX

Bollinger studied the map that Mallory had spread out on his desk. If he got involved—and he still hadn't made up his mind—they wouldn't have to buy the whole goddamn place, he thought. Just most of it.

He studied the map, careful not to look at Suzy, who had come to the meeting wearing a gown, who'd ever heard of that, a real estate saleswoman wearing a gown, a long white gown, in the middle of the morning?

"There are precedents for this kind of thing," Mallory told him.

"Yes, Zeckendorf in New York," Bollinger said. "He bought all around the stockyard, and then he bought the stockyard, and then he tore the stockyard down." He smiled faintly. "Incidentally, what's he doing now?"

Mallory didn't say anything—his example, more to the point, was going to be Kaiser—and Bollinger resumed his contemplation of the map, careful not to look at Suzy. The entire commercial district, including Midway. All the slum housing clustered in and around it. Both sides, every piece of property, no exceptions whatsoever, on whatever road they picked for access through the cove.

"I've been here once, to the church," Bollinger said, tapping a finger on the cove area. "As I recall, some of it wasn't too bad."

Mallory nodded agreement. "The worst is downtown. We'd want to clear that all out. To the south, in the actual cove, starting about here, it becomes a mix, some of it quite acceptable. There's no reason why much of it shouldn't remain as is—just as long as it isn't on the access road."

"Selected on an individual basis?"

"Yes. If it's decent, we pass, and if it's a dump, we make an offer."

Bollinger thought for a moment. That presented a problem. "If the house stays, so do the occupants."

"Not if we don't want them. Let's be realistic. Unless we upgrade, we're going to take a bath. It isn't only houses that have to go. It's people, too. The whole makeup of the community has to be drastically altered."

"I agree. But if we come upon—what shall I say?—an undesirable? What if we find an undesirable in a perfectly acceptable house?"

"We make him an offer he can't refuse."

"And the house stays?"

"Yes."

Bollinger frowned. "HUD would have a fit."

"I doubt it," Mallory said. "Mainly, we'll be moving white trash, the unrepresented minority. I spent a term in Washington as a congressman. When they screamed—nobody listened."

Bollinger still wasn't convinced. "I'm sure you're more familiar with what is in here than I am," he said, a finger tapping the map again. "But as I recall we'll be dealing with a lot of Chicano families."

"Yes," Mallory admitted, "but on the same basis as everyone else. The slums go, period. That's basic, and it solves most of our problem. Next, we move over here, the south side, and it's on an individual basis. It doesn't matter if he's white, brown or purple. If his house doesn't meet a certain standard, we buy it and tear it down. If he personally doesn't measure up—he's a drunk, he's a wife beater, he's got six wrecked cars parked out front?—then he can be living in the Taj Mahal, we've still got to buy it, get rid of him."

"That sounds too complicated. Individual social judgments?"

"Actually, it's easy. Drive down any street. They stick out like sore thumbs."

Bollinger still didn't like the idea. It would be easier to buy everything, raze it all, start anew. That way, everyone treated the same, no one could complain of being discriminated against.

"Frankly, I find the Zeckendorf approach more appealing. Everything goes."

"If it was necessary, yes," Mallory said. "If it was financially feasible, but it isn't." He stopped, thinking that argument probably didn't faze a billionaire. "Yes, if you've got money to waste, clear the whole thing away, but it's not the kind of project I'd want to be associated with. The point is—there are some good houses in there, and a lot of good people, too. I was hoping to upgrade, not destroy."

Bollinger smiled. The celebrated Mallory temper?

"I don't want a massive uprooting just because we haven't got the time or inclination to be selective."

"Well, I suppose that is a point," Bollinger said mildly. "But it strikes me that your definition of 'good people' equates with the well-to-do. What I mean … you don't have any objection to uprooting the poor?"

"No," Mallory said, smiling himself. "They'll just have to be poor someplace else." Again, he stopped, thinking that he was handling this very badly, rusty from his long banishment in the boondocks. "However, if it will salve your conscience, you might want to provide some alternative housing."

"Keep them in the community …?"

"Not if there's room at your country club."

Bollinger laughed. Besides the temper, there was spirit, which he found easier to indulge. "All right. Let's do it your way. On a selective basis." He went back to the map. "If I get involved, of course. What are your thoughts on the industrial area?"

"Leave it."

"This squiggle here?"

"Buffer zone. North of it, I wouldn't concern myself at all. Stay south—the highway ... the commercial district ... the cove ..."

"And we've already spent the fifty million?"

"Maybe more. That's a rough estimate."

Bollinger spent a few moments considering, careful not to look at Suzy, which meant he also had to avoid looking at Sargent, the dead-eyed genius who had spawned the scheme. It really was quite a brilliant idea, he thought. There was an enormous amount of traffic between Palm Springs and Rancho Mirage/Palm Desert. Highway 111, slicing through the middle of Cathedral City, was essentially the only route, unless one went far over north to Ramon Road. Few bothered to do so. It was inconvenient and perhaps even less inviting, going through a large industrial area, past the airport and low-flying planes.

For whatever reason—simply because of the central slums?—Cathedral City had been leapfrogged by the better class of commercial and residential development. When it couldn't find room in Palm Springs, it went beyond, bringing a building boom to Rancho Mirage and Palm Desert. Yet the irony was that Cathedral City was actually a far better site. Rancho Mirage had to contend with high winds, Palm Desert with floods.

If a developer was starting from scratch, if all three locations were still open land, no previous hands at work, there could be no question but that he'd choose Cathedral City.

Actually, that's what had happened, what had gone wrong, Bollinger mused. Cathedral City had been developed first, when the valley was initially being settled, when the county exercised very little control. Any free spirit who didn't cotton to Palm Springs' big-city standards, all he had to do was drive down the highway a bit, put up any old kind of shack. It must have been a haven then—they sure let a man do his own thing—the evidence was still there—and that's what had gone wrong.

Too many free spirits. The place was a mess, an abomination, irreversible. You drove through with blinkers on.

"Do you think anyone ever thought of it before?" Bollinger asked, staring at the map.

Mallory shrugged. "If they did, they didn't do anything about it. Too big for them to handle."

Yes, Bollinger thought, and he wondered about even a consortium, it was in the big real estate deals that the strongest crumbled, and fifty million dollars was not an inconsiderable sum, and renewal could be very, very risky.

"This consortium you envisage—how long before it starts getting a return on investment?"

"Immediately, if it wants," Mallory told him. "That's the beauty of it." He moved a thick finger along the map. "This strip, more than a mile, both sides of the highway, the center of town. It's all shit, cracker boxes, one-story. Buy 'em all and take a bulldozer and run it from one end to the other and then what have you got?"

"A wider highway."

"No neighbors," Mallory said, "and overnight, you've made a fortune, this one-mile stretch alone. You've bought it at distress prices and suddenly it's worth as much as anything on Paseo." He chose a spot at random. "Here, for example, say it's vacant now, room to build a sizable store. Put up a *For Sale* sign and who's going to buy? I. Magnin? Not in a million years. You'll be lucky to get a thrift shop interested. But take away the beanery on this side and the mattress store on the other and all the rest of this mess ...?"

Bollinger listened, enjoying the pitch, the tantalizing discipline of not looking at Suzy. It *might* work, all right, providing you cleared to the rear, too. Providing enough sold at reasonable prices and there weren't too many holdouts in crucial places.

"You'll have a Miracle Mile," Mallory promised. "Instantly. The big stores, they'll come flocking, waving checks. The highway is the key. You should have stood out there with me this morning. How many Rolls Royces I counted? How many Mercedes?" He shook his head, still not believing it. "Not one of them stopped. Not a goddamn one!"

"Yes, I had considered that," Bollinger said. "There's an incredible amount of the *right kind* of traffic, isn't there? Immensely wealthy people, constantly traveling back and forth, and right now they have to wear blinkers. But if instead of a wasteland, we offered them an oasis?"

"They'd stop!"

Bollinger wondered. Would they? That was the gamble. Mallory was too enthusiastic. There were no miracles, let alone instant ones. The commercial district razed, the consortium would have to put up the first new shops itself, prove that people—the *right kind* of people—would stop.

If they did? Well, then it would be as Mallory suggested, Bollinger thought. Waltah Clarke would come running, and could Saks be far behind?

"You sorely tempt me."

"Here," Mallory said, making a concession. "Make this the access road, down the middle of the cove, into the center of town. Then you've got everything from High Desert, coming and going, east or west."

"Yes, you sorely tempt me."

Presentation over, Mallory decided. He looked at Suzy, wondering if she had anything to add, Bollinger was her prospect, after all. If not, perhaps they ought to take off, let him think on it for a while. Bollinger was intrigued, that was obvious, he'd asked so many questions, more interested in Cathedral City than High Desert, which is what any shrewd investor would be, because if renewal wasn't feasible, nothing was.

Mallory got his map, folding it up, wishing Suzy would say something, Bollinger was her prospect and he was the key. If he bought into High Desert, even a minimum share, it would be an enormous help in forming a consortium, just being able to use the magic name, Bollinger.

There was a long silence.

Bollinger checked his watch. They'd gone ten minutes over. It was almost twenty to twelve. He pretended that it had just occurred to him. "Are you doing anything for lunch?"

Duck soup, Mallory thought, and Suzy felt her pulse quicken, and Sargent sat staring with dead eyes, thinking—as always—that he'd been put away for less.

While Mary Alice waited in the Bentley, placating Graham, Billy inspected the empty storage shed and greenhouse that Sargent had suggested for his restaurant. He'd been disappointed initially—afraid, really—the shed was so huge and dark and empty—but as his eyes adjusted he saw the potential.

There was room, that was good, he'd have a big place, not some hole in the wall, and with the cheap paneling removed and the old brick walls showing it would have substance, a solid place, looking as if it had been around for a while, as indeed it had, not some Johnny-come-lately. By virtue of time spent, that sense of *belonging*, which was what he, Billy Segundo, wanted. More than anything else, he wanted to belong, to be somebody.

Billy walked the shed, changing it as he went, baring the old brick walls and putting tiles on the concrete floor and restoring the beams and timbers. The bar would be here, the main dining area there, and there'd be a balcony, of course, a huge fireplace, and the greenhouse, which was going to give the restaurant its name, Casa Verde, that would be a very special and grand kind of solarium where, in season, on cool, pleasant nights, his guests would dance to violins.

He imagined it all and it took form and he grew with it. Billy Segundo, proprietor.

In the Bentley, where Graham insisted upon staying, there was air conditioning, Mary Alice wondered what else might appease her pouting nephew. The piano, which he loved, she'd given him that, and he had the promise—written down—that when she died he'd get the car.

A curious man, she thought, he didn't want money, only possessions, and he saw value in them only when they belonged to someone else—especially her, it seemed.

"You're losing weight," she said, paying him a compliment. "You'll soon be able to get into Jarvis' pants."

"I already have," Graham said.

Mary Alice reddened. There was talk, which she tried not to hear, that Jarvis, the slim, beautiful youth who shared Graham's apartment, was—what did they call them these days?—a fairy queen? No, one or the other. Surely not both.

Billy came back out onto the sidewalk, padlocking the shed door, pocketing the key they'd picked up at Yolanda of the Desert, Inc., the salesman hadn't even come with them, that's how much hope he had of moving the place. It could be had cheap. Another plus.

Mary Alice waited until Billy had rejoined her in the Bentley's back seat. "Well, what do you think of it?"

Billy didn't want to sound too enthusiastic. "It's all right."

"Will it do or not?"

"It will do."

"Good," Mary Alice said. "That's settled, then. We'll get it." There was no need for an inspection on her part, she wouldn't know what to look for, and Mallory had promised, welcoming her into the High Desert project, that he'd quietly oversee Billy's little adventure. She already had his word the building was solid. "To celebrate, we'll make the rounds tonight, all the better places, stealing their ideas. How does that sound?"

Billy smiled in agreement, taking hold of her knee, and Graham, watching in the rearview mirror, pouted.

Marion joined the lunch. Bollinger let her entertain while he took several business calls on the patio extension phone, talking to New York and London.

At first, Mallory thought the calls were meant to impress them with Bollinger's importance—after all, couldn't they be made some other time?—but that idea soon passed. He was obviously dealing with urgent matters involving huge sums of money.

"Anyway, that is Arthur's version of the starving artist," Marion was saying, picking at her potato salad. "I had to agree. What doctor would do it?"

Mallory hoped that was a rhetorical question. He hadn't been listening, unable to tune out Bollinger. To be safe, he smiled.

"Do you have children?"

"No." He hesitated. "Not really."

Marion looked at him. "What does that mean?"

"Well, I've an adopted son—sort of," Mallory explained. "Bluestone."

"That's the Indian boy who owns Sun Devil Canyon?"

"Yes."

"Which I want to hear more about," Marion said, "if His Nibs ever gets off the phone. It sounds interesting." She examined his plate, which he had barely touched. "How are you doing?"

"Fine," Mallory told her, still eavesdropping. Bollinger was telling someone named Stella to track down someone named Lou Ferzacca. If he wasn't in Zurich, try Rome.

"Everything Stu—Mr. Bollinger—does, it always seems to be on the other side of the world. It would be nice to have something close by. We could go over and watch it grow."

"Yes." Mallory wondered if the slip had been intentional, and if so, for whose benefit? Suzy's, probably. Marion would want Suzy to know that as his personal secretary, Mr. Bollinger, sometimes, was Stu. Suzy was competition. She had an in. Somehow, she'd arranged this, and what was so strange, Bollinger had looked at her just the once, when they had met for what was obviously the first time.

"Other than this place," Marion said, a wave of the hand taking in the whole estate, "and he really wasn't involved—he did it all from Dallas—this would be his first project here. It seems like forever, but I guess we're relative newcomers. And you go way back, don't you?"

"Yes."

She smiled. "Another legend."

"Yes," Mallory said again, smiling too. Marion wouldn't look at Suzy, either.

"Well, I'm glad you're back. I've heard so much."

"It's good to be back."

Bollinger hung up, putting the phone aside.

"All done...?"

"Except for Lou."

Marion shrugged.

"A mechanic," Bollinger told Mallory, oddly vehement. "He knows one thing—cars."

"Don't listen. He's a great guy."

"As he never tires of telling me," Bollinger said. He got his plate. "Okay. Let's talk. If I did buy Cathedral City... what's in it for you, apart from making High Desert feasible, of course?"

Mallory stared at him, stunned. "If *you* bought it...?"

Bollinger nodded. "Why not?"

"Well," Mallory said, trying to think what it would mean, if it would make any difference, "I never contemplated... just one individual..." He stopped, remembering Spisak's warning: "Something that ambitious, it requires a group."

"Why?"

Mallory had no answer. It didn't, of course. Bollinger could do it alone, if he wished and if he had the resources to divert, it was just that ... what? He looked at Suzy, who was no help, mouth agape.

"I can manage it, I assure you," Bollinger said, smiling, "and it's the only way to go, really. I was just thinking there, talking on the phone, a consortium could be cumbersome, too slow and cautious. You've got a good idea, but if it's going to succeed, it's got to be carried off quickly, boldly." The smile widened. "You ask me dancing—and you don't want to go to bed?"

Mallory spread his hands in a helpless gesture. Jesus Christ, it was perfect, the whole thing done, how could he object?—and yet there was something wrong, too. It gave Bollinger total control. They'd be at his mercy.

"Well ...?"

"It's your money," Mallory said finally, deciding to take that gamble. They'd also be at the mercy of any consortium that might be formed.

"Good," Bollinger said. He reached for his plate. "We've got a deal, then. I'm to transform Cathedral City, make it a shopping and dining mecca, and you're to build High Desert, which is going to be *the* residential community, and all along the way we complement each other. You make it good, you hear? I want only millionaires in that canyon. Captive customers for my town."

Mallory nodded, thinking oh, so that was it? My town. Wasn't that familiar? What he, Mallory, used to say about Palm Springs, and what he would be saying again, if this goddamn thing worked, about High Desert. My town.

"Now, the details," Bollinger said, enjoying himself. "We've got to keep my role secret or prices will skyrocket." He looked at Sargent, sitting there dead-eyed, wanting no part of his brainchild. "Why don't we have this gentleman act on my behalf?"

Sargent stirred uneasily. "Me ...?"

"Why not? Suzy here, Mrs. Braverman, she can be the agent, and you can be the mysterious Mr. Big, huh?" Bollinger studied

Sargent for a moment. "What would be your motive? You'll have to have some sort of explanation that will keep the lid on things... or maybe, which would be simpler, we could pretend you're an eccentric, perhaps a bit daft?"

Me? Sargent thought again, but he didn't say no. It wasn't a bad idea. He pretended so well.

Bollinger turned back to Mallory. "What do you think?"

"It's one way, and we'd like to act as your agent, of course," Mallory said. "We could use the commission." He glanced briefly at Sargent, giving him the chance, just barely, to object. "Yes, we'll do it, and thank you."

"Good. What do you think would be fair?"

"The commission?"

"Yes, how much?"

"Well, that's up to you..." Mallory stopped, trying to organize himself, thinking once more that he was awfully rusty, streaked yellow by the rains of Oregon. What the hell was he saying? "You want to talk specifics now?"

"What have we been doing till this point?"

"Well... two per cent?"

"That's a million dollars."

"It is?" Mallory asked, feeling like a fool, he was totally unprepared. "I don't think it's out of line, though. There'll be a lot of work."

"Not that much. Let's split the difference, say one, all right?"

Marion got her notebook, writing that down, not waiting for Mallory's reply.

"What else?" Bollinger asked.

Mallory tried to recoup. "Your agent for all resales."

"Exclusively?"

"Yes, it's cleaner."

"No. Open it up. Split with brokers bringing in buyers."

Marion wrote that down.

"What else?"

What was there? "First refusal on some key property fronting the highway."

Bollinger considered. "All right. But only after I've reserved for myself."

"How much will you be taking?"

"Three, four blocks."

"Okay. Give us one block."

"Give it?"

"Sell it, at your cost."

"Plus the cost of clearing?"

Mallory shrugged. "All right."

"Anything else?"

"No, except as I mentioned, Mary Alice has the key corner, which she won't be giving up."

"Budget for fifty million," Bollinger told Marion, "plus ten million for reserve." He looked at Mallory. "And you'll want what ... a three-month call?"

"Yes."

Marion wrote that down, closing her notebook, and Bollinger started to eat, frowning when he noticed the potato salad. "Oh. I almost forgot. I'm still not in your syndicate. What was the maximum buy? Half a million?"

"Yes."

"Put me in for that," Bollinger told Marion. He dumped the potato salad, glancing at Suzy as he did so, grinning like a bad boy.

Chip took Jody into the gym, the last stop on the tour of the estate, and it was as unreal as all the rest, Jody thought, because it didn't smell of sweat.

She stood looking around, searching for some sign, if only a scuff mark, that it served a purpose. "Who uses it?"

"Me," Chip said.

Just you, huh? Jody mused, thinking no wonder he was lonely, a whole gym to rattle around in by himself, a huge estate with no friends, just staff. It wasn't a home. It was an institution.

"Dad was going to use it," Chip said, apologizing. "He thought he'd get his pals over, pickup basketball games, that kind of stuff, but they're too old for that, of course. Golf is about the most they can manage."

Jody nodded, indicating that she understood, even though she didn't. Someone as smart as Bollinger—and he had to be smart, or he wouldn't be a billionaire, would he?—you'd think he'd ask his friends whether they'd use a gym or not and if they said yes *then* he'd build it. Or maybe it was a surprise ...?

She could picture it. The Bollinger Boys assembled before a circus tent—the tent being used as a tarpaulin—covering the gym like a statue at a dedication ceremony—and then the tent is whisked away and there it is, your own gym, duh-dah! And everybody yawns and goes home. Poor Stu, he made a mistake, but better luck next time, and gosh it must be tough being rich.

Chip leaped, grabbing a swing bar, chinning himself with one hand, doing it ten times before it became an effort.

Jody watched, not the bulging arm muscles, which was what he wanted, she thought, but the tight crotch. He didn't look very big there.

Chip dropped, bouncing as he landed, smiling at her. "Want to try?"

Jody shook her head. "I can't do that." She paused, remembering Hawaii and Phil, who didn't have a gym, just a chinning bar. "But I can swing, though."

Chip laughed. "Oh ...?"

"Lift me," she told him.

He hesitated, thinking he shouldn't have laughed, she hadn't meant that as a double entendre, she wasn't that kind of girl.

She was waiting under the bar. "Please ...?"

He took her waist, lifting her, watching, releasing as soon as she took hold, then quickly standing back. It was the first time that he had touched her. All he could think was that she was heavier than he had expected.

Jody got a better grip, starting to swing, backward and forward, her body stretched, long legs together, remembering Phil—and George, too—that summer in Hawaii. Whose idea was it? Hers…?

Anyway, she didn't have any pants on, she never did, and Phil had been watching, standing where Chip was now, and he started moving closer, seeing how close he could come without being hit—like Mickey Rooney daring the carrier catapult in *The Bridges at Toko-ri*—and she was afraid of kicking him in that freckled marzipan face so she opened her legs and he kept moving between them and closer and she kept swinging and somehow they got it just right. Perfect, they marked the spot later, and Phil would stand there, his head back and his tongue sticking out, licking as she came by, and George, who was taller, he had to stand back two inches, and that's how she came to be christened "the Swinger" that summer in Hawaii.

Swinging forward, Jody parted her legs, holding for an instant, then dropping back and hanging loosely, waiting to catch her breath. She looked at Chip. "It's a good thing I've got pants on…"

He nodded. "Yeah."

Jody hung from the bar, her arms tired, she hadn't done that for a while, looking at Chip and wondering, what the hell did it take?

Bollinger stood at the window, watching them leave. He had committed to spend a huge amount of money, even for him, and he wondered about his motives. The sheer audacity of the project—to demolish a small city and build it anew—was that what had compelled him to get involved? Yes, he kept telling himself, that was the reason, the sheer audacity, something that people would talk about for years. Another chapter in the Bollinger legend. He didn't like a city. So he rebuilt it.

"I hope you know what you're doing," Marion said.

"Don't worry," Bollinger told her. "I do."

On the steps below, Suzy gave Sargent a playful shove, reacting to something he'd said. They both laughed, jubilant.

The sheer audacity, Bollinger thought, trying to hold on to that idea, a project to impress the boys, but Suzy's laughter was calling him a liar. His motive, from the start, had been to get to know her. That's why he had telephoned, wasn't it? And wasn't it why he bought in, all the way?

"If I didn't know you better, I'd say the whole exercise was to get Chip a job."

"No, it wasn't that."

Sargent stumbled, almost falling, and Suzy ran ahead, looking like a nymph in her flowing gown.

Bollinger decided that was ridiculous. No one wore a gown during the day. Still, she got away with it, didn't she? It looked good on her. She *belonged* in a gown.

"Then why, for God's sake?"

"Does it matter?"

"Yes."

Bollinger turned, surprised. "Why?"

"I'm trying to learn the business," Marion said. "When you die, I'm going to take over."

He smiled. "Really?"

"Sure. Who else is there?"

Who else indeed? Certainly not Chip, who couldn't keep a checkbook balanced, let alone juggle millions, but at least he had a job again, however temporarily. Fitted into still another deal— and how long would he last?

"You learn by watching, not asking questions," Bollinger said, getting out of that nicely.

Still laughing, Suzy ran to her car, fumbling for her keys, trying to get inside before Sargent caught up.

Motive, Bollinger thought. What, precisely, was his motive, and don't say it was to get to know a lady who bit off cocks. That wasn't worth fifty million.

Suzy scrambled into the car and locked herself in. Belatedly, Sargent caught up, pounding on the window, and then—when she wouldn't let him in—kicking at the wheels in mock anger. He knocked off a hubcap and it went spinning away.

For some reason, Suzy thought that was hilarious. She started laughing again.

"They're both crazy," Marion said.

"Mmmmm," Bollinger answered, imagining that he could see the tears.

"And that doesn't worry you?"

"No."

Marion shrugged and left the window. It didn't matter, she decided. There was lots of money. Too much, really. And Mallory—desperate for this chance, last grab at the gold ring?— Mallory would keep those two in line.

As always, Bollinger could safely move into the background, the silent partner, the gamesman. Pulling strings from afar, dropping enticing little hints to his millionaire cronies, but not getting directly and personally involved. He'd stay out. He always did.

"What about Lasky?" Marion asked, looking at her watch. "You were going to call him before the market closed."

"Mmmmm," Bollinger said again.

Suzy was driving off, Sargent running after her with the retrieved hubcap. After a moment, Sargent gave up, turning back to join Mallory, who by now had reached his own car and was standing at the door watching. They said something to each other and Mallory got in and Sargent went around to the other side. There, Sargent hesitated, looking oddly apprehensive, and then—suddenly and unexpectedly—he sent the hubcap sailing off into the bushes.

Bollinger blurted the question. "What in the hell did he do that for?"

"What?" Marion asked, worried about Lasky. The market closed in less than ten minutes.

"He threw away her hubcap."

Marion returned to the window. Suzy's car was gone and Mallory's was just pulling away. "What do you mean?"

"He threw away her hubcap," Bollinger repeated, sounding even more astounded.

"Where?"

"In the bushes."

"Well," Marion said. She wondered what she was supposed to do. "I'll ask the gardener to look for it." She checked her watch again. "Let's not forget Lasky."

"Never mind, I'll handle it myself," Bollinger told her. He stood staring into the empty driveway. "Get him for me, will you?"

Marion nodded and picked up the phone. Not Suzy, she thought, starting to dial. For God's sake, not Suzy?

They regrouped down the road from Bollinger's walled estate. Suzy was waiting, pulled over, and Mallory parked behind her, so that Sargent could switch cars.

As Sargent got out, Suzy did, too. Mallory rolled down his window.

"Conference?" Suzy asked him, grinning at Sargent. She hadn't seen the hubcap go sailing.

"I guess so," Mallory said. Bollinger's unexpected decision—it was still hard to believe, especially how quickly made—had him both exhilarated and wary. If the man made snap judgments, he might change his mind just as abruptly. "But what's left to talk about?"

"I don't know," Suzy admitted. Like Mallory, she was cloud-walking, but without the concern of falling. She felt as if she had been in the presence of a god. Bollinger looked like one, and when he wanted to, he acted like one, controlling everything.

Mallory shook his head. "Stu Bollinger, and he says he'll do it all. Someday, if you don't mind, I'd like to hear how you made *that* connection."

My secret, Suzy thought, already flushed, another rush of blood apparent only to her. She had made it by doing something outrageous. An excessive, irrational act. But *justified*, damn it, and Stu Bollinger, who looked like a god, understood and respected her for that. It was why he called and why he agreed to the meeting and, perhaps (she wasn't certain), why he decided to become so deeply involved. He had established a link—"Suzy here, Mrs. Braverman, she can be agent"—and he might try to establish something more, the mischief in his eyes when he finally looked at her, and that could lead ... where?

It was possible, Suzy thought. Even gods got bored, and Stu Bollinger, mixing only with the upper crust, meeting only perfect ladies, how many women did he know who were—as she had become—outrageous?

"In the meantime," Mallory said, tired of waiting for an answer, "why don't you two get to work? Try Stu's idea—just be yourself, will you, Sargent?—and see what happens. If it goes over, run with it. The more money we spend, the less chance of him backing off."

Suzy came out of her reverie. "You think he might?"

"No, I can't think, but the day's young, so let's use it."

Suzy was going to ask where he'd be, in case they ran into a problem, but Mallory already had Jock's Eldorado in reverse, the window coming up to muffle his parting words. She returned his wave, deciding there wasn't going to be a problem, and if there was, she'd handle it. She was the agent.

"Well," she said turning back to Sargent, "do you think you're crazy enough to buy Cathedral City?"

"Whatever," Sargent said, suddenly down. He'd been up—first time in a long time—and now he was suddenly down.

They headed for her car. Mallory was gone, a distant speck on the road, before she thought to ask. "Oh, no! You didn't bring my hubcap?"

Sargent shook his head.

"You goose," Suzy complained, looking at the unadorned wheel, then to the speck that was Mallory. "Damn." She frowned, on the verge of being angry. "Well, I can always get it later."

Sargent decided to let her think that. Throwing the hubcap away didn't seem quite so funny now and getting back through the gate could be a hassle. What if the guard insisted on calling the house? And how to explain if someone found him searching the bushes? It would be a lot simpler to buy a new one.

St. Pierre was sitting on the front step when Mallory got back to the office. He had a leather case in his lap, newly purchased by the shiny look of it, and another mark of his trade, a large T-square, was propped by the door.

Mallory smiled, thinking that a drafting board probably was being delivered. He got out of the Eldorado. "Ready to go to work, are you?"

St. Pierre nodded.

"I thought we were going to look at the site first?"

"I took the liberty," St. Pierre explained, pushing to his feet. "I was up early. Couldn't sleep…" He extended a hand. "So, I went out alone. You don't mind?"

Mallory shook hands. "No, of course not." He paused, admiring the leather case. "And anyway, I didn't have to be there. The place sold itself, I take it?"

"Yes."

Good, Mallory thought. Having St. Pierre's quick decision made Bollinger's more firm. "Well, that's all of us, then."

St. Pierre looked at him. "Bollinger, too?"

"That's right. Full partner, and you're not going to believe this, but there's no need looking for a consortium, he's buying Cathedral City."

"By himself…?"

"Yes."

"Jesus Christ," St. Pierre said. "Why aren't you dancing?"

Mallory shrugged. He didn't know why. Dancing? Hell, he ought to be on the first rooftop, shouting hooray. "Next question. What are we standing out here for?"

"That, I know," St. Pierre said, getting his T-square. "The door's locked." He stood aside. "There was a woman leaving when I came. An attractive lady with a Rolls Royce. One of our partners, I hope?"

"Lois Sills. You should have said something. She'd have let you in."

"Actually, I said I'd come back," St. Pierre said. "I didn't feel like explaining myself. All this stuff…" He laughed. "And I didn't know how much you might have told her."

"Nothing," Mallory said. He found his keys and unlocked the door. "Despite the name, it's her firm."

St. Pierre looked at him, easing past.

"In what amounts to a separate venture," Mallory hastened to explain. "The firm is one thing, the project quite another. Lois just happens to be in both." He stopped himself. "Well, not 'just happens.' She's an old and dear friend, who really got me started on this in the first place."

"Did she?" St. Pierre stood for a moment, examining the office with a professional eye. "While we've got the chance, I'd like to hear about the others, too." He turned, smiling. "For something so ambitious, we really don't know that much about each other, do we?"

No, Mallory thought, and perhaps that's why he wasn't shouting hooray. Bollinger, he didn't know him at all, hardly knew the legend. And he knew barely more about Sargent and Suzy and St. Pierre himself. The one undoubted partner was Lois. His old and *dear* friend. Had he said that?

Actually, it was a shack, not a house. A small square box baking in the sun, the roof curling and the paint peeling, a window cracked and fixed with washers. The sign stuck in the screen door, a crudely lettered K-DES—in response to some radio promotion?—was the only indication that it might be occupied.

"What do you think?"

"Why not?"

Suzy had chosen it for no good reason, just because it was there, she said, and Sargent didn't have any better suggestion. They had to start somewhere.

"Do you want to come with me?"

"No, I'll just sit here and look glazed."

"All right," Suzy said. She got out of the car, picking her way gingerly, holding her dress up as she walked.

My partner, Sargent thought. He wondered why she persisted in wearing long gowns. It couldn't be bad legs. She had beautiful feet.

Suzy looked back. "You're supposed to be glazed."

"I am."

"Try harder."

"Okay."

Satisfied, she continued up the walk, rehearsing what she was going to say: Hello, my name is Suzy Braverman, and I'm conducting a survey on behalf of the The King Mallory Company, a new real estate firm in Palm Springs, and ...

Someone had seen her coming. A dark figure appeared behind the screen, silently waiting, suspicious.

Suzy stopped. "Hello?"

There was no answer.

"Are you the owner?" Suzy asked, shading her eyes.

"Who wants to know?"

"I do."

"Why?"

Oh, good, she thought, moving closer. The shadow took a form, becoming an undershirt and then the man inside it. He wore thick glasses and he needed a shave.

"I'm a real estate agent."

"So...?"

"Would you consider selling?" Suzy asked, her speech forgotten.

The man laughed, showing crooked, yellow teeth. "This place?"

"Yes."

"No."

Suzy hesitated, hating to give up, defeated before she even started, but there really didn't seem to be much hope. The man was staring at her belligerently.

"Well, then I'm sorry to have bothered you."

She waited another moment. The screen door was latched and seemed likely to stay that way.

"Have you got a buyer?" the man asked, just as she turned to go.

"Yes. This is a legitimate offer. I'm not trying to get a listing."

The man moved, trying for a better look at Sargent. "Is that him?"

"Yes."

The window down, Sargent could hear them. He stared ahead blankly, trying to appear properly glazed.

"What's he want with the place?"

"Speculation."

The man laughed again. "In Cathedral City?"

"That's what he says."

"Huh."

Suzy again turned to go. "Well, I'll try the neighbors, anyway."

"Wait a minute. What do you mean…he's just buying anything?"

"Yes. It's not something we'll be able to keep secret. There'll be substantial purchases."

"Hold on," the man said, interested now. "What the hell is going on? You discover oil or something?"

"No, it's speculation, pure and simple. He's got the money and he's willing to take the risk, that's all."

"Huh."

"Well," Suzy told him, smiling, "I'll talk to the neighbors. Thank you." She opened her purse. "And I'll leave you my card. Just in case you change your mind."

The man unlatched the door, looking at Sargent. "Who do you think you're kidding?"

Suzy gave him the card. "You can call me anytime."

Lifting her dress, she returned to the car, listening for the screen door to close. She got to the sidewalk and still it hadn't.

"Do I look glazed?" Sargent wanted to know.

"Yes, and make sure you stay that way."

Without pausing, she went to the next house, another forlorn shack in similar disrepair. It appeared to be vacant and she hoped it was. The man was watching from his porch.

"Do you know the name of these people?" she called.

"Ferguson," the man answered. "But I don't think she's home." He came along the porch, getting as close as he could. "Sometimes she works."

Suzy knocked anyway.

"That guy," the man said, lowering his voice. "What's wrong with him?"

"What do you mean?"

"He looks kinda funny."

"Maybe he's crazy," Suzy said, knocking again. "That's what the boss says. Buying all of Cathedral City…?" She waited, but obviously no one was coming. "Anyway, it's his money."

The man looked back at Sargent. "*All* of it?"

"So far, two blocks. That's what is taking so long. If there are holdouts, he won't exercise the option."

"You gotta be kidding."

Suzy shook her head, getting out another card, writing a note on the back.

"Listen," the man said. "Just out of interest. What would this place of mine be worth."

"How many square feet?"

"The house?"

"No, the lot," Suzy told him. She finished the note and stuck it in the doorjamb. "It's the land, not the house, that he's interested in, and you could probably go on living in it."

"There's a fifty-foot frontage."

"How deep?"

"I dunno. I think a hundred."

"Okay. That's easy. Five thousand square feet. How does twenty thousand dollars sound?"

The man considered. "Sure. But these days… where do I go for that?"

"I'm sure I don't know," Suzy said, shrugging. "But I'll tell you one thing. You won't get a better offer."

"Yeah," the man admitted. He looked at Sargent. "Let me think on it. Cash?"

"Uh, huh. And don't think on it too long. You can never tell with these flakes. Sooner or later, the money runs out—and then?"

The man nodded, and Suzy started down the steps.

"Hey, lady," the man said then. "Where do I sign?"

Jacobi, stiffening, rocking forward, his whole weight momentarily on her, only for a moment because he didn't want to squash her, marveled again at how he'd lucked out. For an older woman, just into menopause, two months without a period and it wasn't a baby, Cleo was really something, it had been a long time—Lassie, the showgirl?—since he'd gotten it up twice in one afternoon.

The thing was, *she* was having a good time, or pretending to anyway, moaning like tires in a too tight turn (how's that for a simile?), squeezing the life out of his weary but valiant fifty-four-year-old hard-on.

He was going to come again, Jacobi thought, rocking forward, and when he did, he'd pretend, too. He'd moan and groan and shudder and shake and kick the fucking wall out.

"Ohhhh," Cleo cried, squeezing. "Ohhhh. Ohhhh. *Ohhhh!*"

Jacobi came to her, not exploding, but pretty good for an old crock, twice in one afternoon.

"Hello, my lady," he said softly, and he held her for a moment, as in love as he'd ever get again, and then he carefully got off. He fell beside her and he took her hand.

Cleo sighed, exhausted, happy.

"We're pretty good together, aren't we?" she said after a while.

"Yes," Jacobi admitted.

"Why?"

"I don't know."

"Yes you do."

He really didn't. And what he suspected, that she thought every time was her last time, which made her put her all into it—he certainly wasn't going to tell her that.

"It's because it's all we do."

Jacobi didn't answer, wondering where this was leading, she could be like a puppy sometimes, she'd get hold of something and worry it to bits.

"Make love, and that's all," Cleo said, squeezing his hand, "nothing intrudes, and that's why we're so good. And why we can only get better. Because nothing intrudes."

Jacobi relaxed. For a moment he thought he'd have to take her to a show or something.

"With Elliott," Cleo said, "there was always something—his work, and entertaining clients, and keeping that big house up, and all the bills and everything..." She stopped. "It just...got in the way."

Again, he didn't answer, letting himself drift, content that there weren't going to be any complications. They'd just fuck, that's all.

Cleo pushed up, looking at him. "Have you any idea what I'm talking about?"

"Mmmm," Jacobi said.

Cleo fell back, smiling and squeezing his hand, thinking that it didn't matter, and what did she expect, anyway? A goddamn gorilla.

"Speaking of Elliott," she said after a while, "I tried to talk to him this morning, but he got away."

Jacobi stirred. "Don't worry. I know where he's hiding."

"Oh? Where...?"

In a minute, Jacobi thought, letting himself drift, a careful man for all his bravado, he wanted to know where the husband was, and he also wanted to be as helpful as he could, she had a nice way of showing her gratefulness.

Suzy came out of the C.C. Thrift Shop, looking as if she had just dropped off a bundle, which—in a sense—she had.

"How did it go?" Sargent asked, even though he knew. She'd looked the same on her other definite deal.

"He signed," Suzy confirmed. She got in the car, handing him the option. "The only reason it took so long, he had to call his mother." She laughed, sliding down in the seat, a balloon slowly deflating. "God, I'm exhausted. How many is that now?"

Sargent consulted his list. Two definites, two pretty sures, a think about, a maybe and a flat no. "Seven, and we could have six of them. Do you want to call it a day?"

"Well, maybe one more," Suzy said. "I may have just perfected my technique. Not only are you looney, but I'm working my way through college."

"With a sick mother to support?"

"No. He has the sick mother."

"That's why he sold?"

"Yes. He wants to spend more time with her."

Sargent wondered what was funny. Goldman, the other definite, had sold because he had three daughters, none of whom wanted to go into the second-hand business, and that was funny. But a sick mother wasn't.

"She's got athlete's hand," Suzy said, seeing his expression.

Ha, ha, Sargent thought.

"That's what he told me," Suzy insisted. "She's got cracks between her fingers, and they're itchy."

"Athlete's hand?"

"Yes."

Jesus, Sargent thought. It was very hot, the peak of the afternoon heat, and he hadn't been using the air conditioning, afraid of being asphyxiated. His role as looney required that he stay in the car. Shopkeepers came to their windows to stare at him.

"Just The Animal Kingdom, then we'll go home," Suzy promised. "You know what I think? We're going to need more than the two of us, or at least, a follow-up team. How long was I in that carpet place? It seemed like hours."

Sargent answered in order. "No, a good idea, and I don't know, but it sure seemed like it, all right."

She turned to look at him.

"Do you want me to repeat that?"

"No."

"If we've time to do another, let's skip the pet shop," Sargent said. "I don't want monkeys coming to the window. And anyway, I'm tired of being the looney. How about taking turns?"

"No," Suzy said again. Before he could stop her, she was out of the car. laughing as she went.

Well, I insist, Sargent decided. There was an auto wreckers in the next block, he could see part of the sign, *Ace Auto Wrec,* and he'd been thinking about it all the time she'd been in the thrift shop. Fair was fair.

When she went into The Animal Kingdom, he got out of the car, prying off a hubcap with a punch opener he'd found in the glove compartment. He hurried up the street with it, passing the pet shop while she was still introducing herself to the proprietor.

At the auto wreckers, he almost changed his mind, there was so much stock it could be a problem, but then a man came in from the rear yard and it was too late.

"Yeah?" the man grunted. He wore a name patch, "Si," but he didn't look like one, and Sargent imagined that the patch, like everything else in the place, had been salvaged from some broken body.

A nice beginning.

"I need a hubcap," Sargent said, showing the one he had. "An Oldsmobile Ninety-eight, a '78, I think."

"You think?"

"Yes," Sargent said, relieved. He could have asked which.

The man went away for several minutes—stealing one, possibly?—and then returned with a marred but acceptable replica.

"That'll be twenty bucks."

"*Twenty?*"

The man started to move away.

"All right," Sargent told him. It beat beating the bushes at Bollinger's. And what had possessed him, anyway? Sending the stupid thing flying like that. Was he cracking again?

The man took the twenty, which he put in a pocket, not the till. He didn't offer a receipt.

Sargent stood looking at him for a moment. It was now or never.

"Are you the proprietor?"

The man nodded. "Yeah."

"Would you be interested in selling?"

"What? The business?"

"The land, actually," Sargent said. "Do you own it?"

Another nod.

"How big a lot?"

"There's two of them."

"Fine. But how big?"

The man found a ballpoint and piece of scrap paper. Laboriously, he drew an odd-shaped triangle, one corner squared off. divided down the middle. Then he wrote the lengths for each side. They were all uneven, to the first decimal point.

Sargent could figure it only very roughly in his head. Twelve thousand square feet, give or take a few hundred. At their starting bid for commercial property, $3.25 per square foot, that came to—what?—$39,000?

"I could give you forty thousand," Sargent said, a nice round figure, "and three months to sell or move your stock."

"Forty, huh?" the man said, not looking very pleased, but he didn't say no. He considered.

Sargent wondered if he should point out that a few blocks north, away from the main street, where his junk ought to be anyway, the same amount of space could be readily purchased for half the price. Twenty thousand in his pocket and no loss of business. He didn't subsist on impulse buying. But that's probably what was being considered.

"Would you go to fifty?"

Sargent started to move away.

"Fifty," the man repeated.

Suzy was at the door, trying to catch her breath.

"We had an agreement," she said angrily. "You were to stay in the car, and I was to negotiate."

The man looked at her, and then back to Sargent. "Who's she?"

Sargent shrugged. "Some looney."

"I mean it!" Suzy said, her anger mounting. "You're not licensed, and you're *not* the buyer."

"Okay," the man said. "Make it forty." He came around the counter, taking Sargent by the arm. "You said forty thousand."

Suzy's face was chalk white. "For how much land?"

Sargent gave her the scrap paper and its crude drawing of the odd-shaped triangle. With an effort, she managed to compute the square footage, gradually relaxing when she saw that it was the same offer, within a matter of dollars, that she herself would have made.

"Well," she said, looking at the man. "You say this is acceptable?"

Sargent went outside, not hearing the rest of it. He put the two hubcaps on her car, making it whole again, and then he went into the pet shop, the last place he expected her to look for him.

He was right. Later, puzzled, she drove off alone, and he telephoned Em to come and get him. As a gift, he gave Em a goldfish, which was on a special for a dime.

As he left The King Mallory Company, St. Pierre was feeling very pleased with himself, the first day having gone well, better than expected. Mallory had fixed him up with an "office" in what, prior to the house's conversion, had been the kitchen and was now unused. It was at the rear, which gave him privacy, but the best feature was the natural light, diffused but in abundance. Working in it, he imagined that he was more creative, and it struck him that God probably made the sun first, so He could see what He was doing. Was there mention of that in the Bible?

Something to look up, St. Pierre thought. For a builder—and that's what he was, primarily—he wasn't at all well versed on the various theories of creation. His father, a fallen Catholic, had early implanted the idea that all faith was false, give a man something he could hold, such as a hammer. It seemed like good advice at the time—the repetition, perhaps?—and anyway, in his orderly fashion, in his single-mindedness, St. Pierre had avoided theology's clutter until well past middle life. Now, occasionally, he tripped over it, always vaguely surprised that it should be there.

Cleo was parked across the street.

Damn, St. Pierre said to himself, the day's pleasure gone. That morning, she had been waiting outside Five Lakes. Driving into town, he'd thought he had lost her, he was sure of it, but obviously he'd been wrong.

"I want to talk to you!" Cleo called.

St. Pierre pretended not to hear. He got into MacPherson's car, starting it up. That was the only way to handle the situation, he thought. Act as if she didn't exist. Just drive away.

Before he could back out of his parking spot, Cleo's stupendously finned Cadillac came roaring across the street, bumping into the lot with a terrible clank. She swung in behind and trapped him.

St. Pierre looked at her in the rearview mirror. Well, that was smart, but she could sit there forever, he wasn't going to pay any attention. He turned off the ignition and made sure the doors were locked.

Cleo emerged from the Cadillac and came to pound on his window. "Get out! I want to talk to you."

St. Pierre stared ahead stolidly, telling himself that she didn't exist. Ignore her, and eventually she'd go away.

"You're not moving till I do," Cleo warned him. "I'll keep you here as long as necessary. I don't know about you, but there's nowhere I've got to be."

St. Pierre kept staring ahead.

"Do you know who this is?" Cleo demanded of a passer-by. "My husband ... and he won't talk to me." She raised her voice. "Hey! Come here! Do you want to see a trapped rat?"

St. Pierre told himself that she didn't exist. Like some ancient theologian, he had simply invented her, his own personal devil, and he could exorcise her as well. She didn't exist ...

"Everybody! I've got a trapped rat!"

St. Pierre looked longingly at the glove compartment where MacPherson's gun rested. He wondered if—pushed far enough— he'd ever have the guts to use it.

Jody accepted Chip's chaste kiss, which wasn't really a kiss at all, she thought, but the kind of peck one got from a maiden aunt, fearful of contracting some childhood disease.

Chip pulled back behind the steering wheel of his Ferrari.

"When can I see you again?"

Probably never, Jody thought, looking past him to the door of her apartment building, where on previous occasions he had formally said good-bye, not even coming into the lobby.

The first night, when she was still staying at the Riviera, she could understand his reluctance at not taking her to her room, the staff knew him and it would look obvious and in a sweet way he was protecting her reputation, had she any need or desire of it. But no one knew him at the Diplomat, and it didn't matter if they were seen going in together, and what in the world was wrong with him, anyway?

If he wasn't so damn good-looking (and rich), she'd have dropped him after the second date, and that's all that was saving him now, she thought, the fact that he was so damn good-looking (and rich).

"Is there anything wrong ... ?"

"Yes."

Chip was confused. He had been, he thought, the perfect gentleman, hands in his pockets at all times, lest God cut them off.

"I'm not," Jody said, deciding that she didn't care how rich he was, "the kind of girl you think I am."

Chip frowned. What the hell had he done? "I beg your pardon?"

Jody reached forward, putting her hand between his legs, almost surprised to find that there was a cock there, and relieved—God, was she relieved—that with patience and time it got bigger.

To try to divert his mind—it kept churning, relentlessly—Sargent borrowed Em's car and drove over to the house he'd purchased in Sunshine Estates. Escrow wouldn't close for several weeks, but since it was vacant he'd been given possession, paying rent for September. He opened it up, letting out the stale air, and checking all the things he should have done before, making sure that the furnace and air conditioning and all the rest worked.

They did—as promised, it was basically sound—but there were an awful lot of small things that needed repair, the leaky faucets that could be so time-consuming, and then a major redecorating job, of course. The physical things that he had wanted to do as therapy—and now where was he going to find the time?

Sargent looked around despairingly. Angie and the children were due by the middle of September. The way things were going, pellmell, he'd barely have it swept out by then, let alone in decent shape. Maybe he ought to hire someone?

Trying to do everything, twenty-hour days, that's what preceded the crack-up, he reminded himself. He got going too fast and hard, just like he was doing now, and would it happen again if he didn't watch out? Was he especially vulnerable now, once a victim, weakened?

He went into the back yard, surveying yet another mess, sorry now that he'd bought the house, he should have gotten something they could move straight into, and sorry too—no, dismayed—that he'd let Em talk him into High Desert. It was happening too fast, just the way it happened before, he was getting silly, peaking. That business with the hubcap? And making a buy when he wasn't supposed to? "Jesus..."

"You called?" a voice asked, an old joke, and Sargent looked up to see Chaney sitting on the fence, looking exactly as he had before. A hunched figure.

"Oh, you're back, are you?" Sargent said, remembering that he was the clincher. Another writer. Empathy.

Chaney nodded. "Yeah."

Sargent looked away, petulantly thinking that it was all Chaney's fault, he shouldn't have strayed by at a weak moment, and he'd had no business giving advice, either. Make an offer, they're desperate? Yes, and with good reason, look at this fucking mess.

"You bought it, did you?"

"Yes."

"Then we're neighbors." Without waiting for an invitation, Chaney slipped down off the fence separating their yards, landing softly, surprisingly agile. "When do you move in?"

"Anytime," Sargent said, turning to see it. An athlete, he thought at first, but then changed his mind, thinking no, a slinker. "Whenever I can get it habitable."

Chaney viewed the yard, everything at once, clucking sympathetically. "Yeah, she'd have a fit, wouldn't she? When she due?"

Sargent looked at him.

"Your wife."

"A couple weeks," Sargent said, wondering how he knew. "I look married, do I?"

"Harassed, and you asked about kids, remember? How many?"

"Three."

Chaney clucked again. "How old?"

"Four, eight and twelve."

"Ooooh."

"You?" Sargent asked, not wishing to have all the misery.

Chaney shook his head. "No, I married a schoolteacher."

Sargent thought for a moment. He really didn't see how that applied.

"Grade One," Chaney explained. "You'd have to experience it to know, but in her eyes, everyone was six years old." From behind his back, he produced a can of Schlitz, sucking on it. "The last straw was the Booby Box."

"The what...?"

"The Booby Box. The performance charts weren't enough. Our names and a list of chores and little squares to check off when they're done? No. she had to get this cardboard box, unhappy faces drawn on the sides, and if I ever left anything lying around, a sock or my shoes under the sofa, that's where they'd end up, the goddamn Booby Box."

Sargent stared at him, not knowing what to say.

"Can you imagine this? One day, I'm late for work, I can't find my glasses, I'm looking all over the place, I know they've got to be somewhere, I'm frantic, searching—and where are they?"

Sargent stared, not believing it. The Booby Box?

"Yes," Chaney confirmed, finishing his beer. "The last straw, so I burned it. I took it outside and I burned the goddamn thing." Like a bombardier, he sighted along the empty can, aiming between his battered sneakers, letting it drop. "End of marriage."

Sargent stood staring.

"Feel better?" Chaney asked, smiling, and Sargent decided yes, he did. They were going to get along famously. Another writer, another victim.

They got more beer and they sat far into the night and they told each other everything.

Norman Chaney, thirty-five, a Nam veteran, the Marines, later a war protester, in the peace marches in uniform, six years of college, no degree, a rebel in the cause of the little man, editor of a struggling, shit-disturbing, pro-ecology, anti-establishment throwaway newspaper, for free love and against the Bomb (nuclear proliferation, that's a sin), sleeping on the floor and bathing in the swimming pool, a member of Rotary and a valiant cocksman, nothing in the house to eat but cold wieners.

James Sargent, three years older but infinitely so, especially around the eyes, a high school dropout and an award-winning journalist, a draftee corporal in the Yellow Berets, a briefly brilliant, burned-out comet, former author of "Play-Doh's Republic," presently recuperating from madness, purchasing (on behalf of an anonymous client) all of Cathedral City (this is confidential, mind you), unable—it must be the depression—to raise an erection, and concerned, when his wife arrives, that she won't be.

They were going to get along famously, another writer, another victim.

Not that kind of girl. Wow, no she certainly wasn't, Chip thought, falling back exhausted, he hadn't been that acrobatic since he and Jerry, noses stuck up assholes, formed a daisy chain with those two stewardesses from Toronto.

They were silent for a long while, lying beside each other in the ravaged bed, holding hands.

Jody was mildly disappointed. He could turn her on, he knew how to do that (not that it took much, she thought), but he was a clumsy lover, rough at the wrong moments, and he couldn't pace himself. He'd come awfully quickly, both times.

And she still hadn't.

"I'd like to do that again," she said finally.

Chip laughed. "Yeah. So would I."

She didn't like the way that sounded, the laughter kind of apologetic, and the words themselves hopeless, as if he was talking about cloud-walking.

"You're not going to quit on me now?"

Chip laughed again. "For a while, yeah."

"What's a while?"

Chip got up on an elbow, reaching for her cigarettes. He didn't smoke himself, just grass sometimes. He offered the pack to her and when she shook her head he took one for himself.

"You're, uh, quite the lady, aren't you?" he said, lighting up. He lay back, one arm propped behind his head, smoking but not inhaling. He wondered what the hell he was supposed to do. Twice was his limit, and she had to be a very, very special girl, as she indeed was and had been, and when she was she drained him. He went limp and he stayed that way. Jerry, the lover, he could go all night, not one drop of juice but still a perpetual hard-on, fucking till they screamed for mercy, but he, Chip, didn't have that kind of stamina, and what the hell was he supposed to say or do when twice was not enough?

"What's a while?"

"Do you think you could live till the morning?" Chip said. If he tried, he knew what would happen, nothing. And that would be even more embarrassing.

The morning? Jody wanted to scream, she hadn't even come, for God's sake.

Chip could sense her frustration. "I'm sorry, It's just..." He stopped, rolling away, stubbing out his cigarette, thinking that he didn't have to apologize. Normally, it wasn't a problem, he satisfied most women, or at least they seemed to be satisfied. He wasn't used to getting complaints. "Let's not make a federal case, huh? Take a douche—and I'll put a head on it."

You'd better, Jody thought, thinking that would do, but normally she liked it later, after she had been properly and thoroughly laid, it was the dessert, not the salad. And she liked a lot of the other little special things that he hadn't been inclined to offer and that a girl shouldn't have to ask for if the man knew what he was doing.

"Move it," Chip ordered, feeling better. It was what he did best, so there shouldn't be any complaints.

Jody slipped off the bed and went into the bathroom, telling herself that she ought to make allowances, it was their first time together, and perhaps he could learn and improve, and he was so damn good-looking (and rich).

Later, though, when Chip was doing what he thought he did best, Jody decided that while she might make allowances she wasn't going to compromise, which is what she'd have to do with someone who wouldn't know a clitoris if it was staring him in the face.

PART II

CHAPTER SEVEN

"So," Angie said, looking around, little beads of perspiration forming at her temples, "this is it?"

Yes, Sargent thought, the promised land, and he wasn't surprised that she was disappointed, almost everybody was at first, it was the kind of place that had to grow on you, *if* it grew on you.

The constant contradictions made it difficult. Here, leaving the air terminal, starting down between the towering palms on Tahquitz-McCallum, the modest but pleasant civic buildings to either side, Mount San Jacinto looming ahead too high, wide and overpowering to possibly be real, here, at this gateway, there was hope for the legend.

But a few blocks away things would change abruptly, the houses suddenly shacks, a stark coin laundry marring the gracious boulevard, the desert open where it shouldn't be—Indian land, yet to be developed—full of weeds and wind-blown rubbish.

Like the seasons, the summer unbearable, but broken in one day, the weather perfect now, the change came abruptly, disconcertingly. And if you waited it would suddenly change again. Ugly now, in the harsh sun, but at first light the open desert would be beautiful, a marvelous place to walk and flush rabbits, a constant contradiction, which made it difficult.

The sun played tricks. It was why people came here, it gave them life, restored, prolonged. During the day, too bright, it made things ugly, but at dawn's first pale light and in the evening's first soft shadows it made things very, very beautiful.

The kind of place that had to grow on you. If it ever did.

"I don't like it," the Squish announced from the back, appropriately squeezed between Ann and Brodie. She was the middle child, her real name, Laura, used only for official purposes, such as conversations with Santa Claus.

"You will," Sargent promised. "Just wait and see." Quoting Mallory, he waxed poetic, which she sometimes enjoyed. "The sun on your back, sand in your shoes ... you'll never want to leave."

"Horseshit," the Squish said, summing it up for them all.

Sargent drove, glancing occasionally at Angie, his wife and the mother of his children. Once, she was beautiful, a college queen and a model, a fashion writer and a hostess, an intelligent woman and an accomplished athlete and—what had impressed him most?—a pilot.

Now, his fault, he'd made her wife and mother, she was too busy for all the rest, she was merely beautiful, and even that had faded, a light gone out somewhere inside, snuffed by his acts of madness. Among other things, love had died, been killed, murdered. It would and could not persist.

Yet, grant her this, she stood by. My wife, Sargent thought, standing in the wings as always, and if it wasn't for her there, he wouldn't be here.

"I bet the house is nice," Ann, the optimist, said.

"Well, maybe not as nice as in Washington," Sargent told her, "but it could be, once we get it fixed up, and finally we've got a swimming pool."

The Squish sniffed. "What's so great about that?"

Sargent glanced at her. "What's not so great about it?"

"Everybody's got one here."

"Who told you that?"

"Amy."

"Amy? You mean Amy Carter?"

"Yeah."

Sargent turned back, looking at Angie. "Where was this? School?"

Angie nodded. "Yes, they made friends. Two weeks before we had to leave."

"Well," Sargent said, trying to make amends, "I'll tell you what, maybe I can swing an invitation to Susan Ford."

There was another sniff.

"Okay, who would you like to meet?"

"The Fonz."

Sargent drove, all of them bundled in a second-hand Morris Minor convertible, the best he could afford because of his heavy investment in High Desert, headed for an unremarkable subdivision where the only personality was a throwaway newspaper editor who wrote a column called "The Desert Fox" and which was titled, in his drunken moments, "But Palm Springs Sucks."

He had, Sargent thought, come down about as low as he could get, and if he didn't feel comfortable he at least felt safe, because he couldn't fall any further. He wondered if Angie would understand that when she saw Sunshine Estates, block upon block of gravel lawns, four models of houses repeated with singular regularity, all of them smugly content in their anonymous sameness, and occupied by anonymous people.

In Washington, however briefly, they had rubbed shoulders with world figures, that came automatically for the writer of "Play-Doh's Republic," but here, like their neighbors, they would be anonymous. That was why they were here, to start over, to begin again, afresh, new.

She had agreed. She had come. But would she understand?

Finally, they were in front of the house, the small green oasis in the sea of gravel, hopelessly overgrown and desperately in need of repair.

"So," Brodie said, forever the mimic, "this is it?"

Mallory couldn't believe how easy it was. Every time he picked up the phone, the magic name, Bollinger, was immediate entree. Bank of America, City National, Wells Fargo, Crocker...they were all interested, and more. He wasn't shopping for money. He was shopping for the best price.

Elated, he made another call, to Michael Spencer at Mission Guaranty & Trust, an old friend whom he'd been saving, wanting to test the waters first. If there were deals to be had, Spencer, a project backer from his salad days, probably would offer the best of all. He was put through immediately.

"Mallory?" Spencer boomed. "You old sonofabitch, I heard you were back, how come it took you so long to call?"

Mallory smiled. "I didn't need money till now."

There was a pause. "Oh? How much?"

"I've got a project going."

Another pause. "Oh...?"

"I'm in with Stu Bollinger," Mallory said, trying to sound casual. "We're at the preliminary stage, we've got the deal together and we've got the nut, and now we're lining up the long-haul financing, determining how much is available and at what rate."

Spencer interrupted. "*The* Stu Bollinger?"

"Yes."

"Put me down as definite," Spencer said.

Doodling as he talked, Mallory wrote that down, "definite," underlining it. He couldn't believe how easy it was. "When do you want to hear the details?"

"How soon can you get down here?"

"I've got some people I want to see in Los Angeles on Friday," Mallory said, not wanting to sound too eager. "We'll be through, oh, two o'clock. Maybe I could make a circle tour? See you around four-thirty, five?"

"Four-thirty," Spencer said, "and if you're late, don't worry. Can you stay for dinner?"

"Sure."

"How about overnight?"

"Well, we'll see."

"Okay, but you're welcome, you know that."

"Yeah."

They said their good-byes and Mallory wrote "very" in front of "definite" and underlined it several times. He couldn't believe how easy it was.

Whistling, he went into the front office, looking for his appointment book. He remembered having it when he told Suzy about the Los Angeles meeting with Bank of America. A familiar perfume greeted him and he pulled up warily. The man trap was back, he thought. That was her scent. Bait.

Jody was sitting on one of the desks, talking to St. Pierre.

Mallory stood staring for a moment, thinking that she looked more beautiful than ever, and wishing he was thirty again, or even forty. This was her second unexpected visit. The first time, Chip had brought her, when he'd finally shown up to discuss the "position" Bollinger had arranged. That had been typical of a billionaire's son, mixing pleasure with business, and it had thrown the place into a tizzy.

Bluestone, when he saw her, he'd walked right into a wall, and Sargent couldn't bear to look at her (lust was a sin, Sargent said), and he, Mallory… he had just wished he was thirty again, or even forty.

St. Pierre turned, noticing him. "Kismet," he said enigmatically, returning to his own office. Kismet, it was written in the sand, that every passenger on that fateful limousine trip would end up involved in High Desert.

Mallory kept staring, wondering what that was all about.

Jody smiled for him. "I'm looking for a job."

Oh, Mallory thought, the cryptic comment explained. St. Pierre didn't like her (nor Chip either, for that matter). He didn't consider her "functional."

"What kind of job?"

"Whatever's going."

Nothing, Mallory was going to say, a sop to St. Pierre, who inclined to hysterics, but the truth was he could use her. He needed someone to keep track of things, they were happening so fast, and she was as smart as she was attractive, a rare combination. Super.

The only trouble, she distracted. Bluestone had been compelled to give her a run, putting Chip's nose out of joint, as if it wasn't out enough already, St. Pierre pissing all over the kid's solar energy suggestions.

Poor Chip. How long had he lasted? Less than a week, he didn't have any staying power, but then what the hell did you expect, everything on a platter? He'd never had to bust his ass. And it was too late to teach him.

"How about general factotum?"

"Is the pay any good?"

"It's adequate."

"All right."

Just like that? Mallory wondered about her motive. He couldn't imagine her really interested in routine typing and filing and such. Was it some kind of lark? Second thoughts about Bluestone? Or ...?

He gave up, telling himself not to ask questions, just accept and enjoy, that's all. It wasn't going to hurt to have a distraction around. He got his appointment book and took it to her.

"Would you like to start now?"

She smiled and found a pen. "Why not?"

"This is Mission Guaranty & Trust, San Diego," he told her, showing the piece of paper with *"very definite"* in the doodling. "The gentleman's name is Spencer. I'm seeing him Friday. Five o'clock."

Opening the appointment book in her lap, Jody turned the pages to that date, where there was a noon meeting entered for Bank of America. "You know you're supposed to be in Los Angeles, too?"

He nodded. "Yes."

"Busy man." She made the entry for Spencer, writing quickly and precisely, the way Marion did for Bollinger. Then she looked up, waiting. "Anything else?"

Mallory was suddenly at a loss. Somewhere in the process she'd somehow got a carbon smudge on her nose, which was very unlike Marion, and which he thought made her look even more beautiful.

"You interested in lunch?" he asked at last.

She nodded, smiling.

"And afterward," Mallory said, thinking he'd already done a full day's work, Mission Guaranty & Trust all sewed up, "maybe you could help me find an apartment. I've got to get out of the place where I'm now. The lady's father wants to know my intentions."

Jody laughed, closing the book, sliding off the desk. "I know a fabulous furnished place you could get on a short-term lease … if you don't mind orgies all over the walls."

Mallory looked at her unsurely.

"Paintings," Jody explained. "This man I met, he's an art collector, and his tastes are a bit kinky." She paused, amused by the reaction. "I'm sure you could turn them over."

"When is the place available?"

"Now. He's going to Europe for three months."

Mallory hesitated. It sounded expensive.

"Don't worry. The main thing, he wants the place baby-sat, and besides, he's a good friend. I can get you a deal."

"Then why don't you sit it?"

"Because he's afraid who I might have over," Jody said, starting for the door. "They might get excited and rape the Mona Lisa."

"He's got the Mona Lisa, has he?"

"A reasonable facsimile, and in this version, you know why she's smiling."

Mallory followed, wishing that he was thirty again, or even forty?

❧ ❧ ❧

Bluestone piled the last of his gear into his pickup truck. Rodriguez, the construction foreman, wanted the shack for an office, the preliminary road-widening had been completed and now it was time to start on the canyon floor.

Mallory was moving fast, spending money, getting it done, pushing to the point where he could only go forward, not turn back. His final dream—and it had to come true.

At last, something made of the place, Bluestone thought. And while they were at it, something made of him, which would be nice. Now that he'd stopped fighting the world, he wouldn't mind a piece of it. Like Mallory, his mentor, he aspired of late. He wanted to dine at Melvyn's instead of Bob's Big Boy. And he longed for a Jody Walsh rather than a Millie.

Maybe, someday, in exchange for this, the canyon, something made of him, and also of Mallory. He went for a walk, saying his good-byes, trying to form permanent mental pictures, an album of the mind which he could leaf through later, memories of Sun Devil Canyon before Mallory—his final dream—made it High Desert.

Without design, he came to Angel's rock drawings, wild and beautiful. He stood looking at them.

The best showed a stick man either half in or half out of a circle. Bluestone believed he was half out, on account of the arms being raised, as if the man was falling (or was he jumping?), and because of the way the feet were spread, as if vainly searching for a place to land. The circle, Bluestone thought, represented the Earth, which meant the stick man was falling/jumping off it, and which meant he was going to fall forever.

Who was the stick man? Bluestone wondered, looking at the drawing. His father? Was this possible? Was it Angel, a self-portrait, he didn't fit in this world, so he solved his problem by simply getting off?

Feeling strangely moved, he seldom thought of his father, and never in any emotional sense, Bluestone wondered if he ought to at least save the stick man.

Originally, he wanted to preserve them all, he had supposed they were ancient drawings, he hadn't known they were Angel's doing, the chasm between them had been that wide, he hadn't known.

It had come as a complete surprise when Mallory announced that the rocks had to be removed in St. Pierre's concept of High Desert. Prehistoric Indian art—blasted away?

Mallory had laughed, explaining Angel had drawn the pictures, not ancient man. Hadn't he known that...?

Embarrassed, he'd had to say no, he hadn't known, and he'd had to laugh, too. It was a joke on him and he could see the humor. Now, though, it wasn't quite so amusing. While the drawings might not be "authentic," they nevertheless had been drawn by his father's hand.

Yes. His father's hand...

Strangely moved, Bluestone reached out to touch it, thinking this was something he should keep and hold.

Angie lounged in a deck chair, trying to adjust to her new surroundings, which she found foreign. The back yard's tangle of growth, the bougainvillea run amuck, reminded her of Spain, and the huge mountain so close, rising so abruptly, recalled a similar slab in Italy. The name of the village below escaped her. It was on the sea. That's all she remembered.

Not that it mattered. She wouldn't be going back. Upon graduation from college, she'd spent an obligatory year in Europe, and later, marriage threatening, she'd done the Far East, and in both instances she'd returned unimpressed. She liked home, which was America, where there was some assurance that the toilets would flush.

In a word, security. That above all. And recently, due to Sargent, it had become an obsession.

For an intelligent, educated, multi-talented person, there was little security within. Sometimes, she wondered who she was. A tall, thin, almost translucent creature, she herself seemed foreign, almost disturbingly different, a visitor from another planet. Striking more than beautiful, which was her own summation, and, depending how viewed, her gender not immediately discernible. She wore her straw blond hair very short and no makeup or jewelry of any kind and the woman parts were so small as to escape notice.

Another thing that made her different, seem foreign, was the inability to get quotations correct, an affliction which indicated—but which wasn't the case, of course—a lack of familiarity with the language. She suffered from *lapsus linguae*, slip of the tongue, which found her issuing hilarious warnings ("Jim, you're going to cry fox once too often!") and dreadful truths ("Time wounds all heels.").

Foreign, different, with lapses, she was difficult to take seriously, and that was a mistake.

It was, Sargent thought, as close as he was ever going to get to the "right" moment. The children were occupied, seeing how much water they could splash out of the swimming pool, and Angie, whose limit was normally two, had just finished her third martini. He would tell her now.

"What do you think of the place?" he asked, settling into the hammock that had been Chaney's house-warming gift.

The rest, here and in the house, was from Abbey Rents. They weren't shipping furniture, just a few precious items, and clothes and personal things, and pictures and books.

"The house?" Angie shrugged. "It's all right, I suppose. A start…" She moved her chair, getting a clearer view of Southridge, where Bob Hope's multimillion-dollar home, delayed for so long by fire and law suits, was perched like some giant eagle, magnificent wings spread, prepared for magic flight. "Later, if we stay, I'd like to move up."

If, Sargent thought, which struck him as a lack of commitment, but then she had been here only what … three hours?

"I meant the town."

"I haven't seen the town."

"Yes. but if you did see it?"

She looked at him, confused.

"If you saw it and liked it?"

She still didn't understand. "If I saw it and liked it, what?"

"Would you consider … well, making it a permanent move, putting down roots?"

"Here?"

Which, when translated, meant ab-so-lute-ly not, Sargent thought. By staying, she meant two years, the doctor's uneasy estimate of how long it would take for him to fully emerge from his depression. Their agreement, mediated by Em, was that they would make a new beginning here, not that they would remain forever. It was a starting point, not the finish line. When he was better, *if* he got better, they would venture forth again—that was the rest of the agreement, although unstated by either side, the premise, the *if,* being so shaky.

In her mind (and he was imagining this now), they could not conceivably stay, *if* he got better, because he—get this now—showed promise. He had his list of why he married her, because she was beautiful, because she was so accomplished, because she did so many things. And she had her list, which had the one item, he showed promise.

It followed, therefore, that he must fulfill that promise, which was why he finally left the Sweet Springs *Gazette*, where he was editor and nobody, to go, finally to the Washington *Star,* where he was a columnist and somebody. Actually, the move was prompted by a bitchy remark that it must be hard for a beautiful and accomplished woman to be buried in the backwoods because her husband couldn't handle the Big Time. The exact words. Sargent never would forget them, seared into his memory: "Her face belongs on the cover of Vogue—and she's sitting on an apple box in Sweet Springs."

Anyway, he went, he ventured forth, he presumed to fulfill the promise, and for a while he did. What he had to say, thankfully, was just as meaningful in Washington as it was in Sweet Springs, we are all brothers under the Louis Roth suits, but the trouble was he had to say it more often. Once a week wasn't enough. It had to be every goddamn day.

And. after a while, he got tired, and then he got very, very tired, and then Ross, who was po'r, said, "What if...?"

Sargent sighed. In retrospect it wasn't a good idea. Had they really believed, finally and at last, once and forever, they'd avenge—with the sword of laughter—the Holocaust?

Naked Nazi and Naked Nancy.

Had they actually believed those dolls would sell?

"Here?" Angie said again.

"No," Sargent answered, trying to sound cheerful. "It's not the place for us. What would I do?"

She considered, not looking at him, watching the children instead. "I'm sure I don't know. *The Desert Sun,* it's just a small paper, isn't it?"

"Yes. Another *Gazette.*"

"How about that magazine Em sent us? It looked pretty slick. *Palm Springs Life.*"

"Not my style. It's all booster stuff."

"Then that answers the question, doesn't it?"

Yes, Sargent thought. When he got better, *if* he got better, he would have to venture forth again, to fulfill the promise.

"If you're thinking of magazines, there's *New West,*" Angie said, "and *Time* expressed an interest once, remember?"

"I wasn't thinking of magazines."

"Well, how about the Los Angeles *Times*? Beth was saying, before we left, that Los Angeles is a much-maligned city."

"I wasn't thinking of newspapers, either."

She looked at him. "Then what were you thinking of?"

Sargent turned away. It was the "right" moment, time to tell her that, upon the advice of his psychiatrist, Em, he was going to be a do-er, not an observer, and that he had committed a large sum of money, half of their savings, his half, to the deal. He was going to build with other than words, and if he succeeded he might do it again, and then again and again. He might put down roots here and, added to all her other disappointments, he might not fulfill the one item on her list, the promise he showed.

He might not try, which would kill her.

"I was thinking," Sargent began carefully, and then stopped. "Did I mention we're expected at Em's tonight?" Inside, the churning stopped, and he eased back onto the hammock, the torch passed to a fleeter runner. Em, she was so smart, she could tell her. "Last one out of the pool is a turd."

Bollinger looked at the menu, wondering why he bothered, it never varied. The soup of the day was potato (made from yesterday's boiled and you could have anything else but it would be from a can). There was a green salad with either cheese, thousand island, or oil and vinegar dressing. There was a choice of three entrees, fried chicken, baked ham and cold cuts. The vegetables were stewed zucchini and/or boiled carrots. The dessert was tapioca pudding (unless a piece of pie was kicking around). And coffee, tea or milk.

Blodgett ran a tight kitchen. Three choices, the same three choices, every Tuesday. Tomorrow, Wednesday, there would be three different choices, of course. But they would be the same choices as the previous Wednesday. It went like that. A cycle which, as she said, was life.

Trudy, the waitress, looked bored, as well she might. Besides Marion and himself, Wilkinson had been the only other person at breakfast, talking car wheels for half an hour and then rushing to catch his charter to Long Beach. Calvelli, the overnight guest, here with the first draft of Guttman's script, had slept in and then gone off to play golf with Harry Guardino. Harry had the idea they could get Eastwood if they couldn't get Bronson. Maxwell hadn't arrived from London—he'd missed his connection in New York—so now, with Marion shopping, there were just two of them for lunch. Chip and himself.

"What's good?" Bollinger asked Trudy.

She took her tongue out of her hollow tooth. "You can never go wrong with cold cuts."

"Cold cuts, then," Bollinger decided, "and skip the soup, and the tapioca, too. Have you got any pie?"

"I'll look," Trudy said, sounding like she wouldn't. She turned to Chip. "How about you?"

"The chicken."

Trudy nodded and disappeared into the kitchen, the swinging door banging back and forth, permitting snatches of her shouted orders to Raoul, the cook.

"Well," Bollinger said, wishing he'd thought to ask for coffee now, "what shall we talk about?"

Chip stuck the menu back in its holder. "It beats the shit out of me."

"Is there anything new?"

"No."

Bollinger sighed. Occasionally, when time permitted and Blodgett could find him, Bollinger summoned Chip for what he termed, not without wincing, a man-to-man talk. In his eyes, Chip would not be a man—age and physical and mental development quite aside—until he accepted manhood's responsibilities. One of these was that he make something, anything, of his life. It was unthinkable that he sit on his ass forever.

"I wish you'd have taken on the solar energy system for High Desert," Bollinger said, trying again. "When I talked to Mallory about it, he was quite enthusiastic. He thought it could be a first. The only community in the country to be totally powered by the sun."

"Sure," Chip said, "when he talked to you, but with me it was different. St. Pierre—that's the architect?—he doesn't want a central collector in the canyon, and the way he's designing the houses, he doesn't want individual roof systems, either. He says they're ugly and he can't hide them."

"What about those new solar tiles?"

Chip smiled. "On Spanish roofs?"

"Well, be inventive then," Bollinger persisted. "Put the collector in an adjacent canyon. Design a panel that goes under clay roof tiles. *Something.* My God, you studied it long enough, you know the potential."

Chip smiled again, his voice flat, quoting from a textbook: "The Sun lavishes one and a half million billion horsepower on the Earth every second..."

"Then why waste it?" Bollinger demanded, staring at him, totally unable to comprehend. "If you know that, and if you know there's an energy shortage, and if you have the expertise to harness some of this enormous, staggering, mind-boggling power... *then why waste it?*"

"I'm not wasting it," Chip said, still smiling. He opened his shirt, tensing the chest muscles of the junior god's golden brown body. "Did you ever see a better tan?"

Bollinger shook his head. The boy was hopeless, absolutely hopeless. He had no motivation. None. Despairingly, he tried to think of what might do it—kick him out, cut off his allowance?— and then he remembered Benson's solution, a hungry girl. "By the way, whatever happened to that very pretty girl, the one at the party—what was her name?—Jody?"

Chip's smile suddenly blinked off. "Nothing. It, uh, just didn't work out, that's all."

Bollinger looked at him, sensing there was more than that, knowing it. He struck instinctively. "Something else you can't handle, is that it?"

Chip felt his neck start to turn red. "I can handle her."

"Oh?" Bollinger smiled now. "Then where is she? If you can handle her, if you're man enough, where is she?"

Flushed, Chip threw down his napkin, pushing away from the table.

Bollinger shouted after him as he fled the dining room, "If you're man enough ... where is she?"

The door slammed and he was gone.

God, Bollinger thought sadly, Chip, but he wasn't off the old block. When he was that boy's age, there wasn't a girl alive he couldn't take to bed, and no billionaire father as an added attraction, either. The best stud for a hundred miles around—and he still didn't do too badly. Marion, and Ruth on the side for a while, just to fuck Howard Chermak's head, and ...

Bollinger paused, thinking that he'd been busy, he'd forgotten about Suzy Braverman.

There was a copy of the latest issue of *Sand-to-Sea* on the slab of glass that served as a coffee table. Mallory picked it up, something to divert him from the Mona Lisa, who—if Baron Philip Ronay approved—really ought to be put away.

The cover photo showed a bejeweled lady in a ruffled gown, the bodice lifting and pushing her breasts together, making them appear to be her buttocks.

Designed by some fag, no doubt, Mallory thought. He read the identification, "Maggie Cochran, who divides her time between the United States, England and the Continent..." and then his eye strayed to the list of cities the magazine covered, from Acapulco to Santa Barbara, and with stops at Beverly Hills and La Jolla and Palm Springs and Newport Beach and Paris and Rome.

Ah, when in Rome. Mallory put the magazine back on the slab of glass, wondering if Maggie Cochran, prominent socialite known for her contributions to various charities, was aware of what the fag had conspired to make of her luscious breasts. Probably not.

Baron Philip Ronay returned smiling from his private conversation with Jody. "Yes, you may have it," he announced, meaning the apartment.

Mallory had never doubted it. He took the baron's extended hand.

Jody winked from the background.

Who's she after? Mallory asked himself, another thing to wonder about, knowing it wasn't him.

Suzy answered the door to find Bollinger.

"Oh, it's you," she blurted, not because she didn't expect to find him on her doorstep someday—after the meeting, the way he looked at her, she *knew* that was going to happen—but only because he hadn't telephoned first. Besides everything else, he struck her as a very organized man, leaving nothing to chance.

"Yes," Bollinger admitted. "I was in the neighborhood..." Self-consciously, he brought forth the hubcap, which he had been holding behind his back. "I had this—and I thought I should drop it off."

"That?" For a moment, Suzy was about to deny ownership. "Oh, yes, of course. How good of you."

"It was cluttering up my garden."

"I'm sorry."

"Don't be."

Suzy took the hubcap, wondering how he knew it belonged to her. Someone must have seen Sargent throw it. "Thank you. Will you come in?"

He shook his head.

"You're sure?"

"Yes."

"Well," Suzy said. She didn't want him to leave, and she had the impression, the way he was looking at her, that he didn't want to go. "I suppose you're wondering how it got there? In the bushes, I mean."

"Boyish exuberance."

"Oh. Someone told you?"

"Actually, I was watching," Bollinger confided, smiling. He would have accepted her invitation, but that would make this all too obvious. Instead, he took back the hubcap. "What I do have time for ... would you like me to put it back on?"

Suzy hesitated. For some reason, that didn't seem proper, a billionaire stooping to manual labor, and she looked beyond to his Mercedes, half expecting to see the chauffeur changing into overalls.

"I think I can manage without the auto club," Bollinger said, smiling again. "Where is it?"

"The garage."

"My first guess, had you gotten difficult."

Still smiling, he led the way, Suzy hurrying after him, thinking that she should stop him but unable to do so. God, the *length* of the Mercedes, it must have been specially made for him, and he had a Rolls, too, and a Fleetwood limousine.

"Incidentally, how is it going?"

"Fine."

"Just fine?"

"Excellently," Suzy said. And it was, except for Sargent's bit of nonsense at the auto wreckers, and she had made up her mind not to mention that to anyone. Mallory might put someone else in charge if it came out that she couldn't handle Sargent. "We've got options on most of the key properties fronting the highway in downtown Cathedral City, and now we're doing pretty well in Midway, too."

"Good."

Suzy slipped ahead of him, bending to lift the garage door. Quickly, he grabbed hold, his hand over hers.

"Please, let me."

There was an awkward moment while they got untangled.

"You don't think me capable, is that it?" he asked. He got the door open and stood back, trying to remember which side. Right front, wasn't it? "Actually, you could be right. This, believe it or not, will be the first time in … well, I'm not going to tell you how many years."

Suzy was still trying to comprehend her reaction to his accidental touch. It had been almost like a religious experience, which was absolutely ridiculous, of course. Except that he *did* look like a god.

Bollinger squeezed along the right side of the car. There was barely enough room for him, half of the garage taken up with a solid wall of cardboard wardrobes.

"What have you got here?"

"Just old clothes. It's a failing, I can't throw anything away."

"Oh."

Bollinger hunkered down awkwardly, only to find he was wrong. The wheel had a hubcap. He stood up, looking at her. "I'm sorry. Which is it?"

Suzy tried to see. "Isn't it that one?"

"No."

Puzzled, she didn't reply, and he eased around the front of the car, walking sideways in the confined space. It *had* to be the right side, he thought. Otherwise, the way the car had been facing, toward the gate, he wouldn't have been able to see Sargent kick it off.

Suzy belatedly checked the right side herself, equally certain.

"Well, you've got one here, too," Bollinger said, becoming annoyed.

"Are you sure?"

"Yes."

"That's funny."

The way blocked, Bollinger retraced his route, thinking that it wasn't.

"I, uh, don't understand," Suzy stammered. She stood waiting for him to squeeze out, embarrassed by the garage's clutter, she'd been going to clean it up for years.

Bollinger finally extracted himself. He put the hubcap on the trunk, looking at his hands for dirt. "Anyway, you've got a spare."

"I really don't," Suzy said. "I mean, if I'd known, I wouldn't have let you..." She looked at him hopelessly. Go to all that trouble, she'd been going to say, but that was stupid, all out of proportion, was what had happened so terrible?—he'd wasted two minutes of his precious time? With anybody else she'd be laughing by now.

The explanation, she decided, was that Sargent had replaced the hubcap—that's what he was doing in the auto wreckers—and she hadn't noticed because she hadn't used her car since. For their Cathedral City forays, they'd taken to Jock's old Eldorado, which Mallory (wanting to be less beholden to Lois) considered more appropriate.

Bollinger stood looking at his hands, thinking the whole thing was ridiculous, was she that flustered in his presence, why didn't she just tell him?

"Do you want to wash?"

"No, I'll be fine." He started down the driveway, still looking at his hands.

"Well. Good-bye, then."

"Good-bye."

"And thank you."

"You're welcome."

Feeling like a fool—what was wrong with her, why hadn't she laughed?—Suzy stood staring after him, waiting until he got into the Mercedes before she closed the garage door, and not going into the house until he was out of sight.

What was wrong? Nothing and everything. Stu Bollinger, who was a billionaire and who looked like a god, and who probably could have any woman he wanted, Stu Bollinger—say it—was *interested* in her, Suzy Braverman.

She sat down, feeling weak. He was interested, she thought, he *was* interested, but after that disaster in the garage, would he be interested enough to come back?

Women, Bollinger mused, baffled by it all. If she had bought a new hubcap, why hadn't she told him, for pity's sake? Instead, she had just stood there, looking dazed and foolish, and making him look the fool, too.

Goddamn. He'd thought he was on to something really special. How she handled Guttman, now *that* was something, but it wasn't her usual flair with things, obviously. She had just stood there. A blank.

Goddamn, and to hell, also. He didn't like silly, stupid, foolish women. Fifty million dollars ... and this was what he got?

A blank?

Well, he wouldn't try again, Bollinger decided. There was no sense throwing good money after bad.

"No dice, huh?" Harry asked.

Bollinger looked at him. Normally, Harry was the perfect chauffeur, seemingly oblivious to what went on in the back seat. "I beg your pardon?"

"Nothing," Harry decided. "Excuse me, sir. I was just thinking out loud, that's all."

Oh. And had come to that conclusion? Bollinger got out his cigarettes and his gold holder. Hell, he hadn't even tried, and if he had, Mrs. Braverman would gladly have said yes. He just hadn't tried.

No dice, indeed. If ...

Hold on. Hadn't he just finished lecturing Chip on lack of persistence?

Bollinger took pause, reluctantly reminding himself that he wasn't omnipotent. He wouldn't know, absolutely for sure, until he did try, and that fluster in the garage wasn't enough—let's be fair, shall we?—to warrant a complete write-off.

There could be any number of explanations for her strange behavior. Let's say, for the sake of argument, the lady had another admirer, one who had replaced the hubcap without her knowledge, and who, that very moment, was in the house?

Yes. How's that sound? Bollinger lit up, feeling better already. He liked competition, and he'd show Harry. No dice, indeed.

Sargent had the children in Jack's old room, showing them the Big Little Books, which were peculiar to a single generation, his own. Collector's items.

"How much would they be worth?" Ann asked. She was going to be a financier, after she made it as a tennis pro.

"Oh, I don't know," Sargent told her. "Not much. The trouble is, too many kids saved them." He paused, remembering Romeo Jacobucci, who had painstakingly printed on the flyleaf of every one of his. Not for Lends. "I imagine, across America, in thousands of attics and basements, in dusty shoe boxes and at the bottoms of old trunks, there are, by very conservative estimate, a hundred million Big Little Books."

"You wouldn't collect them, huh?"

"No. I would collect something that people throw away, but which will be highly valued by the next generation."

"Such as?"

"Bullet-shaped radios."

Ann gave him a look. "People don't throw them away."

"No," Sargent admitted, "Not anymore, but they used to, and a bullet-shaped radio is, therefore, very valuable today. That is one example. Another is the ice box, which brings a pretty fancy price these days, and another is upright telephones, originals, not replicas, and another is wooden toilet seats."

"You wouldn't happen to have a more contemporary example?"

"One you could turn a buck on, you mean?"

"Yes."

Sargent considered for a moment. "Old tennis racquets."

The suggestion was met with silence. Sargent noticed that they were looking at each other, all three of them, Ann, the Squish, and even Brodie.

"Listen," he said. "Go to any Garage Sale. See if they aren't practically throwing away old tennis racquets. You can pick them up for two bits. Maybe fifty cents tops...and do you know what those old tennis racquets are going to be worth thirty years from now?"

More silence. The Squish, inclined to dramatics, rolled her eyes.

"Okay, but don't say I didn't tell you." Sargent tried to think of something else, but they had lost interest already, Ann back into Dick Tracy and the Mole Gang, and the Squish returning to the yellowed photos she'd found, and Brodie staring fascinated at the model airplanes slowly twisting out of his reach, hanging overhead from invisible wires.

Sargent slipped into the hall, ostensibly to visit the bathroom, but he wanted to see how Em was doing with Angie. The words drifted from the kitchen, said with caution, but audible.

"Let him," Em was saying, an order. "He won't write, he can't. If it isn't this, it's nothing. All he'll do is sit and stare. Is that what you want?"

"No. I want him better. But a hundred thousand dollars...?"

"Peanuts. Mere peanuts. He'll never buy into anything decent for less. And the potential...?"

No answer.

"Angie, be sensible, it's enormous, he could make a million, you'd have the security you need, it wouldn't matter if there were relapses then, you could weather anything."

A pause. "Yes, but I want him to write."

Em snorted. "He won't write. Why don't you get that into your head? He won't because he can't."

Another pause. "Not now, but I thought, with time, after he started getting better ... he might try a book."

"A book? A novel, you mean?"

"Yes."

"You nit," Em said vehemently. "That man can't write a column, he can't even write a note that's intelligible, you should have seen what he was wearing when he walked in here, and you want him to write a book?"

No answer.

"The man's empty, a shell, there are no words left inside. Don't make that demand on him. Let him do something else— something that he can do."

No answer.

"What he's into now, he's almost enjoying himself, it's a kind of game for him, a con ..."

Sargent quickly went back into Jack's old room. He'd heard enough. Em, his psychiatrist, fleeter and stronger, more determined because she thought it mattered and therefore cared, Em, persistent, relentless, was going to win.

Jody sat waiting in the bar at the Tennis Club, making a drink last and asking herself Mallory's question. Who was she after?

Not the Baron Philip Ronay. He was too kinky, even for her catholic tastes, and besides, there was a baroness somewhere.

Chip? No, that was over, the money would never compensate, she couldn't go through life permanently frustrated.

Bluestone? Hardly, he'd just been a ploy, her way of trying to arouse Chip, if only by jealousy.

So what exactly was she doing working for The King Mallory Company ...?

The easy answer was she needed the money, Jody thought, twirling her drink, making it last. The old bank account was getting low. It had been a long time between presents. The luggage was last, which predated Mac.

Behind her, she could see him in the mirror over the bar, an extremely handsome man went by, paying not the slightest bit of attention.

Hey! she thought, not liking to be ignored, and reminded of the first time Sargent had done that, he'd absolutely refused to look at her.

And he still wouldn't.

Later, in his hammock, the children asleep and Angie pretending to be, Sargent wondered why, if not happy (which of course was impossible), he could not at least be satisfied. Angie had succumbed to Em's relentless argument. She would "not fight" High Desert, which came closest, in their precarious relationship, to a statement of full and unquestioning support.

Then what nagged ... ?

The truth, of course, he decided. The terrible, horrible, awful truth. He had wanted Em to fail in her argument and he had wanted Angie to force him to withdraw, not only from High Desert, but the optioning in Cathedral City, too. He had been dragged in unwillingly and he had continued reluctantly and now he had been committed without consultation.

Notice that no one had asked his opinion?

CHAPTER EIGHT

Finally, it happened, the inevitable. Kroeger, the proprietor of Julie's, a junky five-and-dime, came out to confront Sargent while Suzy was next door trying for an option on Custom Unfinished Furniture.

As usual, Sargent was sitting in Jock's old Eldorado, staring ahead blankly, trying to look glazed.

"What if you're not a nut?" Kroeger asked.

The fatal question, Sargent thought. For three weeks, longer than he could have hoped, no one had raised that possibility. He looked at Kroeger, a small, untidy man, a schemer like himself. That's who it took.

"I'm not the only one asking," Kroeger said. "Cooney, he owns the Broasted Duck, he thinks you're faking, too. And Krinski, at Empire Motors." He smiled, a challenge. "I'd like to see you buy Empire Motors."

Sargent didn't say anything. Empire Motors he knew about. They'd been there twice and Suzy hadn't gotten anywhere. They weren't interested, they said, but unlike his present antagonist, they weren't so impolite as to say why.

"The way we figure," Kroeger said, "you know something we don't know, like some major industry is coming in, it's going to give the place a shot in the arm, you know?"

Sargent still didn't reply. He'd promised Suzy, she did all the talking, his job was to just sit. Actually, he liked it better that way, he didn't have to lie, just mislead.

"Tell your lady friend," Kroeger went on, relentless. "Don't bother coming in, she's just wasting her time, I'm not signing no option. You understand?"

"Yes," Sargent said at last.

Kroeger smiled, The fact that Sargent spoke was confirmation. As he suspected, the sonofabitch wasn't a nut. He turned and went back into his store, more determined than ever to hold out, they weren't getting him and that was final.

Sargent watched him go, thinking he was a brassy little bugger. The whole morning, Julie's had enjoyed one customer, and if she purchased anything it had been small, something that fit in her purse, there'd been no parcel. With business that bad, how could Kroeger say no to a fair if not generous offer?

Other income? Perhaps, Sargent thought, but he doubted it, the pants had a shine. More likely, Kroeger was what he purported to be, a suspicious holdout, and it was interesting that he was talking to others. If they ever got together prices really would go up.

Impulsively, Sargent got out of the car, crossing the street and walking back toward the center of town, where Billy was cleaning out the storage shed.

There was an old truck parked in front. Two Mexicans were loading it with wall paneling. They smiled and looked away when Sargent said hello.

Illegals, he thought immediately, they were afraid to answer in Spanish, making themselves all the more obvious. And one was wearing rough sandals with the soles cut from old rubber tires. Another sure sign of recent arrival.

Sargent wondered why Billy would take a chance on them, he himself was still being processed by Immigration, but then they were his own kind, weren't they? He must get homesick, and it was doubtful if Mary Alice, so late a liberal, had many Chicanos in her circle of friends.

Billy came out, carrying another sheet of paneling, which he dumped on the sidewalk.

"Hello," Sargent said again.

Billy smiled. *"Buenos dias."*

The difference, Sargent thought. He waited for the Mexicans to get the sheet Billy had thrown down for them, then moved closer, shaking hands. "What's this? Salvage?"

Billy nodded, still smiling. Sargent was his ally, confidant, friend. "Yes. What I thought, why waste it?"

"Well, you going to show me?"

"Sure."

Billy took him inside, the place down to mostly bare studs, the outer brick wall showing. When refinished, the brick would be inner wall, too.

"You've done a lot."

"Not really. This way, it's slower than I thought, but I ought to be finished tomorrow, Thursday for sure."

"Who's buying the stuff?"

"Grenby's Cut-Rate."

Sargent nodded, satisfied. He'd been thinking of Saturday's paper. Though the season hadn't officially started, that wasn't until mid-October, he'd noticed that Palm Springs had been filling up on the weekends, devotees making the trek from Los Angeles.

"Pocket money," Billy added, feeling obliged to explain. "Besides, it gets me out of the house."

While Sargent watched, he started removing another panel, pulling the nails out with a small pair of cutting pliers. He worked slowly, careful not to mar the finish.

"People are getting suspicious," Sargent said after a while. "Kroeger, he owns Julie's, he doesn't think I'm crazy, and he says that's why Empire Motors won't talk to Suzy."

Billy paused, looking at him. "Time for Phase Two?"

"If you're ready."

There was just a flicker of hesitation. He was going to have his picture taken. "Sure."

"Okay," Sargent said. "I'll write the press release. May I bring it around tonight?"

Billy nodded, going back to work, and Sargent spent a moment looking around, thinking that at best—even with the tiles—there could be only a few hundred dollars in it. Why would Billy bother? He had a roof over his head, three meals a day, a credit card, and ... no money?

Sargent smiled. The credit card had been a major victory. Billy, telling him about it, had been ecstatic, even though there was a limit, of course. But no money at all? Mary Alice, the old fox, she'd given him everything but loose change, the money for those little things. Such as a woman.

Yes, that was probably it. Billy confided a lot, but not everything. Come to think of it, how did he get laid?

Salvaging wall panels, Sargent decided. Desperate men did desperate things. He went outside, stopping to watch two more desperadoes, the Mexican illegals sweating in the sun.

"*Adios,*" he said, but they didn't answer.

Suzy was leaving the furniture store as Sargent was slipping back into the Eldorado. Unsmiling, she shook her head, as she always did when she'd been turned down.

"Come on, let's get back to the office," Sargent told her.

"Why?"

"Well, the word's out, isn't it?"

"I guess so," Suzy admitted, wondering how he knew. Of all the things she found annoying in him, and there were starting to be quite a few, it was his knack for presentiment that was hardest to accept. At first, she thought it was because he spent so much time thinking, he struck upon the most likely eventualities by sheer process of elimination, but lately she had come to suspect that he was simply a bungling catalyst. Without apparent effort, he caused things to happen, while he himself remained unchanged.

In the furniture store's display window, a man appeared, watching.

"What happened exactly?" Sargent asked.

As if you didn't know, Suzy thought. She got behind the wheel, changed more than she cared to admit, a helpless hostage to casually manipulated fates.

Thus far, it had been all Sargent's blind doing. High Desert. Cathedral City. Stu Bollinger. *Everything*. No matter how she tried to direct events, Sargent somehow always intervened, as when Bollinger, thanks to his shenanigans, had come calling with an unneeded hubcap.

It was time she seized the initiative and regained control of her destiny. The optioning was in trouble, buyer resistance suddenly stiffening, and she didn't know which worried her the most. That she'd botch the job? Or Stu's reaction if she did?

She also didn't know what to do.

"Let's go, shall we?" Sargent suggested, and Suzy started the car, wondering what the hell had happened to her, she used to be her own woman.

On the way back to the office, Sargent suggested that they have lunch at the Big Yellow House, a detour which took them onto the north side, far afield of their usual haunts.

There was a ravaged Volkswagen convertible in the parking lot, which Suzy immediately recognized as belonging to Jimmy Chaplin, one of Dex's former beaus.

Suzy had a premonition. Was Dex here with Jimmy, seeing him on the sly? Milo hadn't been around the house for a while, which meant she might be dating someone else, and she knew better than to bring home Jimmy, who was as worthless as his awful car. During the blessedly brief romance, he'd been under orders to park several doors away, so that he would appear to be visiting a neighbor.

If it was on again—God, a disc jockey—she'd disown Dex, Suzy decided. For a moment, she considered suggesting going someplace else, a way of avoiding the unacceptable, but she couldn't think of any good reason to do so, and besides, Sargent was already out of the car. She followed him into the restaurant feeling at his mercy again.

Dex was here, she told herself. Rather than at Shakey's or the Mall, where the other students congregated, her Golden Girl was here, in a noontime tryst with an absolute nobody who was lucky if he made a hundred and fifty dollars a week. And, unwittingly, which was his way, Sargent was forcing her, Suzy, to be a witness.

There was no sign of them in the first section. Relieved, Suzy asked to be seated there, then quickly excused herself, ostensibly going to the washroom. She made a hurried check of the other maze-like rows and alcoves. Her intention was to show herself and pretend not to see them. It would permit Dex to exit via the back and avoid a confrontation in Sargent's presence. Later, though. Boy...

Again, there was no sign of them. Puzzled—at least Jimmy had to be here, that *was* his awful car—Suzy rejoined Sargent. He'd ordered in her absence, the chicken salad, and she said she'd have the same, unable to concentrate on the menu. It was like sitting on a time bomb. Momentarily, they'd appear, she was sure of that, and how would she handle it?

The apprehension stayed with her all through lunch and nothing happened. It wasn't until they were leaving, driving out of the parking lot, that Suzy saw Dex and Jimmy across the street, leaving the Riviera Hotel.

With an effort, Suzy choked back her anger and shock, silently cursing both of them, and Sargent for bringing her, and herself for coming. Sargent was innocent of it all, aware only that, for a brief instant, the car had been out of control.

❧ ❧ ❧

Sargent spent the afternoon writing two press releases. The first, an announcement by Mary Alice, disclosed her plans to build a Mexican restaurant, Casa Verde, in Cathedral City. Most of it was about Billy, who was to manage the place, and there was a reference to their recent marriage, all of which left the distinct impression—as Sargent fully intended—that Mary Alice's only purpose was to give Billy something to do.

The Desert Sun would give it a splash, Sargent was sure. The paper was very supportive that way, often devoting a whole page to real estate blurbs, direct from the developer's typewriter, or so it seemed. Mary Alice had the added advantage of actually being newsworthy. She, after all, was a pioneer, and the marriage was the talk of the town.

Sargent wasn't quite as sure about the second press release. It congratulated Mary Alice and Billy on the restaurant and wished them every success in their new endeavor. The news didn't start until the second paragraph and a jaded editor might not read that far. Still, to succeed, it had to be amateurish, and he took the chance and left it that way.

Through fortunate circumstances, the release went on to confide, Sargent had gained advance knowledge of Mary Alice's plans for Casa Verde, a restaurant which—in Sargent's expert opinion—marked the first step toward a total revitalization of the Cathedral City commercial district. Sargent and a number of associates who preferred to remain anonymous felt certain that Cathedral City would soon experience a land boom similar to that in Rancho Mirage and Palm Desert. As a consequence, and this was common knowledge now in Cathedral City, Sargent and his associates had been optioning property in anticipation of just such a boom. Substantial holdings had been amassed and negotiations were continuing for additional acquisitions.

Was that ridiculous enough?

Yes, Sargent decided, laughing himself. It was hilarious.

Kroeger, the schemer, and the boys at Empire Motors, keeping their counsel—they were about to learn that they were wrong. He was very definitely a nut case if it said so in the paper. Only a fool would amass huge land holdings on the basis of an old storage shed and greenhouse being renovated as a restaurant.

Once they stopped laughing, the holdouts would rush to offer their property, anxious to make a deal before the dummy's magic purse was emptied. The bloom would be off, though. He'd be more selective, driving harder bargains—after all, he could be wrong, hadn't people laughed?—and the average sales price would drop surprisingly in the clamor.

Now, Sargent thought, checking for spelling errors, how to conspire to get both releases published the same day, one beside the other?

As Sargent labored, Bluestone was in St. Pierre's back office, vainly trying—one last time—to save Angel's rock drawings. He knew they had no real value—how many times had Mallory and St. Pierre both told him that?—but he still felt they should be preserved.

Moved, all right, that was necessary, they were in the way, but that didn't mean they had to be destroyed. Some of them were very good. The stick man, falling off the Earth?—that was a beautiful work of art, "authentic" or not. And the woman giving birth, if that's what she was doing, that was ... well, that might be his mother, the only picture he would ever have of her.

"Moved?" St. Pierre said, only half listening, trying to visualize what half a bell tower should look like, what parts were necessary to make it instantly recognizable for what it once, but never, was. "To where ...?"

"To some other place in the canyon."

St. Pierre considered.

Bluestone waited, thinking that perhaps, finally and at last, he'd gotten through to the puffed-up bastard.

"The bell," St. Pierre said softly, talking to himself. "You'd have to see the bell."

"What?"

St. Pierre looked at Bluestone. "Move them? No, that would be expensive, we're trying to keep the nut down, and I frankly don't want them in the canyon. They don't fit in with what I'm trying to achieve."

"They don't, huh?"

"No, they don't."

St. Pierre turned back to his drawing board, starting to draw a bell tower, half of one, and starting, as his requirements dictated, with the bell itself. He sketched it quickly and he put a crack in it.

"What are you going to do?" Bluestone demanded, barely able to speak. "Just bulldoze them out of the way?"

"Mmm," St. Pierre said. He paused, examining his bell, wondering if the crack was too obvious. "That would be easiest, I imagine. And we'll probably have to blast first. Why don't you talk to Rodriguez? He's got the timetable, and if you ask nicely, maybe he'll save something for you."

Bluestone swore. Rodriguez, the foreman, cared even less than St. Pierre, he was interested in only one thing, and that was level ground.

"Do you mind?" St. Pierre said, frowning. "I'm trying to work."

Mallory put aside Sargent's first press release. "That, they'll run," he promised, "word for word." He got the second one, aware of voices raised in St. Pierre's kitchen office, Bluestone at it again. He wished the boy had something constructive to do. "You made your living this way?"

"Writing, yes," Sargent told him. Mallory's term as congressman had been before he, Sargent, enjoyed his brief, brilliant passage at the *Star*. Mallory knew him only as an ex-newspaperman, not as a promising columnist, and as a former mental patient, not too sure (Sargent suspected) about the former part.

"You're good."

"Fair."

"Why did you stop?"

"I've nothing more to say."

Mallory smiled, wishing that also applied to Bluestone, he was yelling now, madder than a new-cut cat, calling poor St. Pierre dirty names.

"Let me see here." He began reading the second release, not quite sure what to make of it at first, but then the purpose gradually dawning, the con apparent. The smile became a laugh. "You sonofabitch."

"Think it will work?"

"Why not? You know what they say?"

Yes, Sargent thought, there's one born every minute, and there was something else they said, that all men were born equal. He considered that for a while and he decided that both could be true.

Bluestone came out of St. Pierre's office, his handsome face contorted, livid with rage.

"Angel's drawings again, huh?" Mallory asked, looking at him.

Bluestone nodded curtly. "The prick. He won't listen. He's just going to plow them under."

Mallory sighed. Bluestone's concern was of recent origin. Upon learning they were Angel's drawings, not the work of prehistoric man, the little bugger had laughed. And now, because he didn't have anything constructive to do, or was it out of frustration at being bounced by Jody, he was bound and determined to make an issue of them, wasn't he? "Did you talk to Rodriguez?"

"Why should I?" Bluestone demanded. "You're in charge."

"Yes," Mallory said, turning back to Sargent, "and I've better things to worry about. Talk to Rodriguez, he'll save something for you, tell him I said so. And for God's sake, leave St. Pierre alone."

"Sure," Bluestone said bitterly. "It's up to him, he's saying they've got to go, and I'm supposed to leave him alone, and I notice that you do, too."

"Talk to Rodriguez," Mallory repeated. He made a neat pile of the two press releases, thinking that it was too bad about Bluestone, the only malcontent on a tight and a happy ship, but he couldn't indulge the boy's whims, he had to keep his eye on the big picture, he was going to put this deal together properly and it was going to stay stuck. "Nice," he told Sargent. "Very, very nice."

Bluestone went slamming out.

Sargent put his package together and called across the office to Jody. "Want to give me that lift now?"

Jody took a moment to answer. "Sure."

Suzy was waiting for Dex when she got home from school.

"I saw you," she said simply.

Dex looked at her, knowing what she meant, and glad in a way that it was out in the open.

"How long has it been going on?"

"I've seen him twice."

"*Seen* him?"

"Dated, sort of."

"He picks you up in that awful car, in front of the school?"

Dex nodded. "Is there something wrong with that?"

"Yes," Suzy said, trying to control her anger, "and then he takes you … where?"

"I thought you said you saw us?"

"That's right. In the middle of the day. Coming out of a hotel."

"From lunch," Dex said. God, was that what she thought?

"I'm sure it was," Suzy told her, "but it's appearances that count, and what are people supposed to think?"

"I don't care!"

"Obviously."

Dex put her books down, collapsing into a chair. "Mother ..."

"Yes, I am," Suzy said, "your mother, and I absolutely forbid you to see that young man again."

"Why? Because he's a disc jockey?"

"Because he's a nobody, and because he's older than you are, and because—what's the matter with you?—you already have a perfectly nice boy in Milo Chermak."

Sure, Dex thought. If she only knew.

"Well, haven't you?"

Dex turned away.

"I'm asking a question, young lady! *Haven't you?*"

"Mother," Dex said softly, "the only thing Milo is interested in, is taking me to bed."

Suzy couldn't help herself. She blurted the words, immediately sorry, it wasn't the way to counsel your daughter. "Better that, than going out with a *nobody!*"

Silently, Dex got up and went to her room. She threw herself on the bed, burying her face in a pillow. All right, she thought, if that's what the bitch wants, I'll do it.

Mary Alice read the press releases with difficulty, it was hard for her to concentrate, she was trying to read Graham's mind at the same time. He was a constant visitor of late, and what she found disturbing, it wasn't to see her, it was Billy.

"They're fine," she said at last, passing the releases back to Sargent. "And you approve, don't you, dear?"

"Uh, yes," Billy said quickly. Graham had his hand on his knee, put there to get attention, he was telling a joke.

Sargent returned the releases to their folder and stood up to leave.

"There's just one thing," Mary Alice said. "The date. Instead of 'opening early next year,' it should say, 'opening soon.'"

Billy looked at her. The question was an echo. "Soon...?"

"Yes," Mary Alice said firmly. "I don't see why we shouldn't make a crash project out of this, if we continue to dilly-dally, we'll miss the season."

"Yes, but..."

"No arguments," Mary Alice said, her mind made up, "do you want the restaurant or not?"

A little stunned, Billy looked to Sargent for direction, and Sargent, finally aware of what was happening, decided it would be wise to humor Mary Alice. He got out his pen and did so. "Anything else?"

"No."

Sargent again stood up to leave.

"Let me finish this," Graham protested, his hand returning to Billy's knee. "Finally, he takes off his shorts, and she takes one look and she says, 'Don't tell me, when you were a kid, you had small-cox.'"

"*Graham*," Mary Alice said.

He looked at her innocently. "Yes, auntie?"

Sargent smiled, not at the joke, which he had heard before, but at the thought of knees as launching pads for seductions. He recalled Billy using one, coming in on the limousine, and now, full circle, Graham's busy hand at work.

Fortune hunters, both of them, working up from the knee, after the family jewels.

"I think," Jody said, back behind the wheel of her rented Mustang, "that Mary Alice suspects."

"*Knows*," Sargent corrected. "Crash project? Opening soon?" He leaned back, still amused. Billy was going to be installed in the Casa Verde just as soon as humanly possible. Where Mary

Alice would be able to keep an eye on him. And where he'd be too busy to be tempted.

Jody started the engine, waving good-bye. "Well, you do notice things after all?"

Sargent nodded, thinking oh, yes. He was a professional observer. A man with a trained eye. He noticed many things. In fact, he took notes, once upon a time.

"Then how come you've never noticed me?"

He didn't answer. The question had been asked so quickly, he wasn't certain he had heard correctly, the edge of complaint in her voice?

She turned out of the driveway and headed down the hill, back toward town and their last stop, *The Desert Sun.*

Sargent still said nothing, holding his folder more closely, watching the road. He wished the question would go away. For something asked so quickly, it seemed to hang between them for a long time.

Jody also was silent, braking before a curve, being especially careful. What was the matter with her? She had planned to wait until the right moment. So why ask so impulsively now?

"I have," he said finally.

She slowed again. "When?"

"Yesterday," he said, trying to turn it into a joke. "I noticed that you returned from lunch with your blouse on inside out. I noticed it before you noticed it."

There was another long silence.

"That," she said then. "I was…" Unaccountably embarrassed, her affairs were hardly secret, she tried to look at him but couldn't. "I was saying good-bye to the Baron."

"Oh. He's left, has he?"

"Yes."

Permission granted, Sargent took a moment to study the perfect profile, thinking that this was another thing he noticed, she said good-bye to them all. To Chip and to Bluestone and to the Baron—and now hello to the N-n-nut Farm?

"Why?"

"You, you mean?"

"Yes. I mean me."

"I don't know," she admitted. "Because I can't stand being ignored, I suppose. And because... well, you're different."

Yeah. Diana's reason, Sargent remembered. She'd never had a lover in a manic state. She wanted to experience all that incredible energy inside her.

"You are, aren't you?"

Different? He didn't answer. He didn't, wouldn't, answer.

Finally, she looked at him, chancing to see, the first time, the agony which the blank stare usually kept hidden. She stopped, pulling off to the side of the road. She bowed her head, ashamed.

Different? Yes, he was, Sargent thought, feeling strangely akin to Billy. Like the Gingerbread Man, he had come full circle. Where the rage to live was once too much, now he was a dead man. And a beauty was reaching for his own knobby knee, intent on awakening him? She saw him as a challenge, did she? Or perhaps just a curiosity?

Anyway, different.

Jody's voice was barely audible. "I'm sorry. I just wanted to know... what it would be like."

Sargent turned away. How could he make her understand? He didn't care. He could have Getty's money and Redford's looks and be making love to Wonder Woman and he still wouldn't care. He didn't give a sweet fuck, or want one, either.

"We can try if you want," he said, "but I know I won't enjoy it, and I don't think you will."

He waited, in a kind of panic, and what he was grateful for, she didn't answer.

❧ ❧ ❧

Bluestone drove out to the canyon in the dead of the night. St. Pierre's abrupt dismissal of his pleas, coupled with Mallory's uninterest, the preoccupation with other matters considered more important, had him seething. If Angel's drawings were to be saved, he had to do it himself, literally taking them from harm's way.

So what if they weren't "authentic"? Angel had spent half his life creating them, and they were as striking, as intriguing, as any of the other petroglyphs in the valley. And perhaps they said more.

That stick man falling out of a circle—*falling off the Earth?*—and with his arms raised to the heavens where, incongruously, there were three globes—sun, moon *and what else?*

Bluestone thought he would preserve that puzzle over anything St. Pierre might create with bricks and mortar and mirrors and shag rugs.

The stick man—falling off the Earth?—he'd dig that out first, a headstone for Angel's unmarked grave, and then the woman giving birth, if that's what it was, he'd get that next, for presentation to the Desert Museum in Angel's name. They wouldn't know there that it wasn't "authentic." Along with the Sinatra Sculpture Court and the Donald S. Stralem Grand Staircase and the Marjorie Edris Chandeleir there'd be the Angel Patino Woman-Giving-Birth Rock.

Angel, who deserved it, that much at least, would have the last laugh on a world where he never fitted. Right in there with all the big shots.

Bluestone laughed himself, sure it would happen. The museum, built on donations, all the various parts named for someone, had commemorative notices on everything but the bathroom fixtures.

The joke made him feel better, more secure, as he wound down into the canyon, the only movement in the eerie, almost deathly stillness. The moon's uneven light found only the desert floor and the canyon's serrated walls were wrapped in a thousand different shades of darkness. He could never quite get used to how incredibly silent the place could be when come upon at night. He imagined that the creatures of the canyon heard his approach from afar and waited like statues frozen in time. After a while, having accepted his presence, the first rabbit would stir, and then another, and finally he would feel welcome in what was also his home.

That thought changed his mood again. Home, the only real one he'd ever known, and now he was giving it up. It was moving time, he remembered, and not just for him, but for Stick Man Falling/Jumping Off the Earth, and for Woman Giving Birth.

And for others too, he decided.

Bluestone wasn't sure how, he didn't have a plan fully formulated, but the rest of the drawings, those he could get out, whole rocks or sheared off, they were going to be preserved, too. Right now, the first thing, the important thing, was to get them out and get them stored safely.

He parked his pickup and walked across the moonlit sand to the row of heavy equipment being used to widen and level the road and which would be at work soon on the canyon floor. He swung aboard a bulldozer, firing it up, working the levers, the right moves coming back easily, remembered from that long ago summer with Mallory. He practiced, back and forth, cutting, lifting.

One meatball/Without the gravy/One meatball/No french fries

By first light, he was ready. He swung the bulldozer around, pointing it toward the rock outcroppings, a mechanical beast come to save, and he dug the blade in and cut his first swath. The stick man—falling off the Earth?—he wanted that whole rock intact, he was going to dig it out, as deep as necessary to do so, a headstone for Angel's unmarked grave.

Immediately, under a foot of sand, he hit loose shale, fractured from the quake, and he laboriously cleared that away, several more feet to a sandstone stratum, digging a pit to take the stick-man rock. He'd upend it in there, the base cleared on one side, and then he'd lift it out with the scoop, put it—if it fit—in the pickup. The dozer's blade banged against the sandstone.

Bluestone stopped, swinging down to check, to see if he was deep enough. The side of the rock he could clear with a shovel. He didn't want it marred.

What the hell...?

Slowly, carefully, Bluestone slid down into the pit, reaching out to touch the ore deposit in the sandstone fissure he had bared. He had never seen anything like it before, grayish black with a greenish caste, appearing in rounded, irregular masses. He picked up a loose sample, finding it heavy, like iron, and equally hard, the surface oddly greasy.

His heart suddenly pounding, Bluestone scrambled out of the pit, firing up the dozer again, digging the blade harder and deeper, revealing more of the fissure and the strange ore. He didn't know what it was and he was afraid to guess, he refused even to think about that, barely able to deal with what he did know, there was an awful lot of it, possibly a major deposit, and it looked important and valuable. It could be worth a lot of money. A fortune.

And if it was...?

Bluestone backed off, the dozer stilled, his jubilation tempered by the realization that he no longer held sole claim to the canyon. Under the terms of the lease, he'd given up mineral rights, signed them over to Mallory's syndicate. The percentage he retained was what... ten per cent?

Doubt and suspicion swept him. Had he been tricked into selling? Mallory back unexpectedly, recruited by the others, they knew about the ore, the plans for a new community just a hoax, was that it? When the blasting crews moved in, would they supposedly "discover" the deposit, making the appropriate apologies—sorry, you dumb fucking Indian—and would they abandon Mallory's precious dream and St. Pierre's masterful concept and would they start mining instead?

Was that it?

Working feverishly, Bluestone filled in the pit, pushing back the fractured slate, returning a thick cover of sand. He kept only the one small sample of ore. If he needed more, he'd get it later, but not now, he had to hide the find, leave everything as it was and get away.

After all, he reasoned, this could be the initial discovery, and if so he had to keep it secret as long as possible. He needed time— to think, to get help, to determine the ore's value, to somehow devise a way of regaining full ownership of the canyon.

Driving away, Bluestone's mind was in a turmoil, torn by the suspicion that Mallory had tricked him, yet unable to accept that of the man who had raised him, educated him, forgiven him his ingratitude. He had to confide in someone, and if not Mallory, who?

The question pounded at him: Who would he go to for help?

CHAPTER NINE

For Em, there were many signs that the season had begun in Palm Springs. New lawns were being put in—twenty years away from Maine, she still marveled that it was done in October—and there was the usual financial flap at Desert Hospital, and Louise Stone had an announcement in the paper saying she was no longer engaged to Alan Bloomingdale (she never was), and a star-studded pro-am charity tournament was under way at Mission Hills, and Gordon Prettyman was suing Miriam Grosvenor for putting saltpeter in his drinks so that she, Miriam, could steal Gordon's wife, Blossom. Yet it was this party, the season opener at the Racquet Club, which made it official. The Racquet Club party was a desert classic. *Everybody* went.

It was a tradition, the last Friday in October, going all the way back to 1934 (which was pretty far by Palm Springs' standards), when Charlie Farrell and Ralph Bellamy, tired of being kicked off the tennis court at El Mirador, had bought up eighty acres of blow sand and started their own club.

For any number of reasons, but mainly on account of Charlie, who had style and still did, it was the "in" place in no time, attracting not only fellow stars from Hollywood but the rich and famous from all over the world, and the passage of years had only served to enhance its reputation as the town's most exclusive watering hole. You simply hadn't arrived if you weren't numbered in the membership's magic one thousand.

Some of the love affairs of the century, some of the biggest film deals of all time, even some pretty fair tennis games—a lot had gone on at the club and in the private condo cottages clustered about its sprawling grounds, and a lot more would occur. Like its principal founder, it persisted. The romance and the business and the game, played best here.

There might be grander places now, more than one, Canyon Country Club, and Eldorado and Thunderbird and La Quinta, but the Racquet Club's low-key elegance, its understated opulence, made it the smartest. There was something very reassuring about the whitewashed cottages and their heavy shake roofs, the geranium-ringed palms and the tall, timeless tamarisk. They had a permanence about them which came from not having to keep up with the times. The Racquet Club set the standard, its own, and nothing ever changed much, not even the staff, most of whom—like Joe, the maitre d', and Julie Copeland, the tennis hostess—were part of the tradition.

As always, there'd been a cocktail party at the Farrell House, and then everybody—the whole membership, it seemed—had moved across to the main clubhouse, for more drinks in the Bamboo Bar, and buffet dinner in the Garden Room, and then dancing in the Terrace Room.

And *everybody* was there, from Greg Bautzer to Gloria Greer, from Ty Cullen to Molly Berns.

Em waved to the Gabors, four of them at one table, and steered Sargent and Angie to meet the Gullingsruds, where an introduction might prove more helpful in the long run. Dee was a sweetheart.

Sargent was better, almost, and now Em had to work on Angie, get her mind off Sargent's involvement in the High Desert project. Angie had to meet people and get involved with a project of her own. Dee always had something going.

Stu Bollinger called to her, motioning imperiously, and Em veered that way, pulling Angie along. "Later," she told the Gullingsruds. Bollinger wasn't to be ignored, but she hoped he wouldn't talk business. He was sitting with Mallory and Lois.

"Is this the little woman?" Bollinger demanded of Sargent.

"Yes," Sargent admitted.

Suzy watched from another table. She'd come with friends, the Strykers, who were off somewhere dancing, and now she wished she had joined a larger group. Every time they danced—and Vivian seemed determined to monopolize Tim—she was left sitting alone and feeling oddly vulnerable. She couldn't very well go table-hopping on her own. Like Em, she needed an excuse, someone to drag around being introduced, or else it would look like she was being pushy.

Funny, but she *was* pushy, Suzy thought, that's how she survived. Normally she would be swirling around in her feathers and damn the excuse for it. What kept her glued in her chair, alone and vulnerable, was the fear—God, was it really fear?—of not appearing properly subdued should Bollinger happen to look her way. He hadn't looked yet. He was making an effort not to.

"Suzy," Dampier said. "What's this I hear?"

Suzy turned, grateful to have him stop, even though he was a desperate little fag. "Bo, how are you?"

On the other side of the dance floor, at a ringside table, Billy squeezed Mary Alice's knee, surprised that he was enjoying himself. The newspaper story seemed to have turned everything around. Unlike his experience at the Bollinger party, where he had been ignored and mistaken for a waiter, people seemed to know him by sight—they recognized him from the photograph, no doubt—and they stopped to talk to him as much as to Mary Alice.

Maury Adler, who wrote "Dining Out," had said he would do a column about him, even before the restaurant opened.

"Happy?" Mary Alice asked, as pleased as he was.

Billy smiled for answer. Adler had said there'd be a lot of human interest. That was the magic word. *Human.* At last, he was somebody. He belonged.

Jody swirled by, in the arms of her new passing fancy, Joseph Owens, a major producer of television cartoons. She winked at

Billy, a further confirmation, and then they disappeared among the other dancers, Owens holding her close.

Tonight, Jody thought, feeling him hard against her. This was the third time she had gone out with him. The two previous occasions, they had been with other couples, older like himself, and he had been circumspect to a fault. Saying good night, he shook hands, and he left her in the lobby, not taking her to the apartment door. For a while she'd been worried. God, not another Chip. But this was more like it.

Mallory wished he hadn't come. He was pleasing Lois, his only reason, and he had the feeling, which he knew was absurd, that she was somehow showing him off. See? she seemed to be saying, I got him to come back!—and what was he supposed to be, some kind of trophy?

But what really bothered him, if only he'd admit it, was that no one was all that agog about High Desert. Everybody mentioned it, of course. It was common knowledge and a favorite topic of conversation. But they weren't impressed, which was what he wanted them to be, and which was why he was annoyed at the absurd notion of Lois showing him off, because he wasn't returning as a conquering hero—not by a long shot.

Forsythe, who went back, a councilman when Mallory was first elected mayor, came closest to standing in awe: "Many suspect, Mallory, that you are intent on revenge, planning a fabulous spa meant to compete with and eventually overshadow Palm Springs." Then he'd spoiled it by adding: "Something both Rancho Mirage and Palm Desert, for all their posturing, have failed to achieve."

Suzy's heavy optioning activity in Cathedral City, supposedly on behalf of Sargent, was also common knowledge and the subject of much talk and speculation. But again, even though the grand scheme was partially apparent—they foresaw Cathedral

City being "prettied up" for the benefit of High Desert—it was just something to talk about, that's all.

Under the tra la la, this was a secure group, Mallory thought, entrenched, satisfied, superior. They'd seen grand schemes come and grand schemes go. They weren't about to grant him his old standing until he actually accomplished something. Didn't Lois realize that?

"Don't look now," Lois said. "Here comes Vickers, I knew he'd get up first."

No, she didn't realize, Mallory decided. Vickers, otherwise known as the Conduit, the man through whom the idle rich made their wishes known, would be coming mainly to pay his respects to Bollinger.

Lois' whispered admonition caused Bollinger to turn. As he did so, his eyes met Suzy's, watching from across the room.

"King," Vickers said, extending a fat hand. "Welcome home."

Mallory took it, half rising. "Hello, Vickers."

Abruptly, Bollinger stood up, slapping Vickers on the shoulder and moving away, making his apology to Lois. "Excuse me. I'll be back."

"Sure," Vickers said, wondering what he'd done wrong. He looked at Mallory. "Well, what's this I hear?"

"It's true," Lois said.

Bollinger crossed the room, exchanging pleasantries as he went, refusing invitations to stop. He'd made the rounds once already. That was enough.

Suzy waited, staring ahead blankly—like Sargent, was she glazed? she wondered—and absolutely unable to move.

Finally Bollinger was standing over her. "Are you alone?" he asked.

"For the moment," Suzy said. "Would you like to sit down?"

"I thought we might dance," Bollinger told her, which surprised even him.

✤ ✤ ✤

St. Pierre opened the venetian blinds a crack, revealing the blurred outline of Cleo's monstrous Cadillac, parked across the street from The King Mallory Company.

"Damn," he said softly, as if fearful she might hear. Briefly, he considered making a run for it, but the thought of being trapped quickly changed his mind. He'd wait her out, that's all.

His stomach grumbling, he returned to his office in what used to be the kitchen, wishing that he'd had the sense to stock some food. The fridge still worked, and probably the stove, too. He found a match and proved that to his satisfaction. Suddenly, a ring of blue fire.

"Damn," he said again, turning it off. But that was a good idea. Tomorrow, he'd go shopping, get some...

The telephone rang, making him jump. He ignored it, but counted the rings, which got to eight before the caller gave up.

Soup, St. Pierre decided. He went to his drawing board and got a pencil and started making a list. Soup. Bread. Butter. Cheese.

Who'd been calling all day? Not Cleo, she was in her car. He had checked several times, peering through the blinds as he counted the rings, and—like now—she was always behind the wheel.

Spiced ham.

Unless...?

St. Pierre shuddered, imagining that it was a dummy, not Cleo, sitting in the monstrous Cadillac, and that if he answered the phone, he'd hear her screeching voice: "Ha! Fooled you, cringing rat!"

Was that why he didn't answer the phone?

No, of course not. He didn't answer because it wasn't for him, no one knew he was working today, apart from the maniac loose in the street, and because it always rang eight times.

St. Pierre sighed, snapping the tip of his pencil. Where did it end? Spiced ham, mustard, catsup, bacon and eggs, pork chops, a roast, God Almighty—what was the wretched woman doing to him?

The phone stopped ringing.

Eight, he decided, even though he had lost track. Earlier, he had made an agreement with himself. Fewer than eight, he'd answer the next time. He found another pencil and resumed work on the Old Hartford Place, the name he'd given what would be, if all went well, the first house built in High Desert.

The Hartfords, Anglo and rich, were his imaginary pioneers, and John Hartford (overruling his wife, Clara, who wanted Cape Cod?) had the good sense to order a Spanish castle. It had a timeless quality. A few years hence, laced with pyracantha, glimpsed through the tamarisk, the myth would be legend.

It set the tone, St. Pierre thought.

He continued drawing, deft and sure, the house becoming an organic thing, dictating its own shape and form. It grew, guiding his pencil, and he lost all sense of time and place, Cleo happily forgotten, and the telephone, too.

"Elliott...?"

St. Pierre whirled.

Bluestone was standing in the doorway, looking apologetic.

"I'm sorry. I didn't mean to frighten you."

"God," St. Pierre said, barely able to speak. He sagged against his board. "What's the bloody idea, sneaking up on a man?"

"I saw your car," Bluestone told him. "I thought we could talk..." He made a show of putting away his office key, which Mallory had presented him. He was a shareholder, wasn't he?

"About what?"

"Angel's drawings."

"Them again?"

"Yes."

St. Pierre pushed past him, going into the front office, making sure that the street door was closed.

"I locked it," Bluestone said. "I saw her."

"Who?"

"Your wife."

Yes, of course, St. Pierre thought. They all knew. It was the talk of the office, no doubt. Look! A trapped rat! Without comment, he went back to his board, putting his things away.

Bluestone stood watching, thinking that it had been a mistake to come. Showing too much concern for the drawings, that could arouse suspicion. Yet somehow he had to buy more time.

"I don't know why you're here," St. Pierre said finally. "I'm not changing my mind. How many times must I tell you? They make the canyon look like some old Indian encampment and that's not the atmosphere I'm trying to achieve."

"I know. I just wanted ..."

"This is to be a quality development, and I don't want the rocks scribbled on, looking like a goddamn ghetto."

"... to ask if you could hold off a while," Bluestone continued, arguing as he'd agreed to do, even though it was no use. "I've found a place to store the rocks. I just need time to move them."

St. Pierre shook his head. "No."

"Why not?"

"Because."

See? Bluestone thought. He shouldn't have come. It was hopeless. "Aren't you being a bit unreasonable?"

St. Pierre whirled on him. "And aren't you being a bit ridiculous? They're some silly drawings, that's all, nothing more, and of absolutely no significance, historical or otherwise. Why persist with the sham that they're something they're not?"

"Sham? To you, perhaps," Bluestone said bitterly, trying to keep his temper, "but not to my father. To him, they were real, his whole life. You don't destroy a man's life work just because it isn't significant to you." It was all he could do to stop from grabbing

St. Pierre and shaking the truth out of him. Whose was the real sham? Did he know about the ore? Was that why he was being so unreasonable? "I'm just asking for a little time, that's all. A little time to save something important to me."

St. Pierre didn't answer. He had enough problems without being harassed by something this trivial.

"He was my father," Bluestone said, becoming angry. "Don't you understand? My father!"

"I don't have to listen to this," St. Pierre told him. Abruptly, he turned away, thinking that he didn't have to listen to Cleo, either. If she got in his way, he'd move her, bodily. Enough was enough.

Bluestone started after him. "I think you do."

You think wrong, St. Pierre thought. He went outside, hoping that Cleo would try something, he was just in the mood for a proper showdown. She wasn't the only one who could jump up and down and scream.

Bluestone followed him out. On cue, the Cadillac came screeching from across the street, blocking his exit from the parking lot. At the sight of her—face contorted in anticipation—St. Pierre changed his mind, starting back for the sanctuary of the office, but Bluestone was standing in front of the door with no intention of letting him inside.

"Let me past!"

"No. Not until you listen."

St. Pierre turned back. Cleo was getting out of the Cadillac. He was trapped between them.

"Got you at last!" Cleo shouted. In an instant, she was upon him, grabbing hold of his shirt sleeve. "All right, I want to talk to you, mister!"

St. Pierre twisted free. "Leave me alone, damn you."

Cursing, she grabbed again, tearing the front of his shirt, and when he saw the rip something exploded inside his head. Enraged, he struck out blindly, slapping her across the face, the blow so hard it knocked her to the pavement.

Cleo was too shocked to scream. In disbelief, she put her hand to her mouth, bringing it away red with blood.

Equally shocked, St. Pierre was going to assist her, but Bluestone had hold of him before he could take a step, spinning him around and trying to hit him at the same time. Overanxious, he barely reached him, his fist thudding ineffectively against St. Pierre's shoulder.

St. Pierre wasn't a fighter. Normally, he would have backed away, refusing to defend himself. But he had the taste now and his anger hadn't been appeased and Bluestone's desperate punch had been like a schoolgirl's. He got himself ready, his left hand up as a guard, the right doubled and pulled back.

Jesus, Bluestone thought. He had to watch his temper. Even though the bastard deserved it, he shouldn't be pounding on him, this was a family dispute and something for the police to settle.

"All right," he said, meaning it was over. He turned to help Cleo.

St. Pierre closed his eyes and swung. He'd have missed if his target hadn't moved but instead he caught Bluestone square on the ear. Off balance, Bluestone staggered back awkwardly, trying not to step on Cleo, and St. Pierre got in two more wild punches to the head before he could finally dodge clear.

"You fucking idiot!" Bluestone complained. "I said it was *over.*" He put a hand over his left eye, which St. Pierre had thumbed. "Why don't you get out of here?"

For answer, St. Pierre hit him again, a glancing blow off the hand protecting the eye.

All right, Bluestone thought, half blinded and not caring anymore. With his free right hand, he punched St. Pierre in the chest, knocking the breath out of him.

St. Pierre went reeling back. He tried to speak but couldn't.

Bluestone kept hitting him, alternating heavy blows to the chest with sharp, cruel jabs to the face.

St. Pierre backed into his car, a defenseless punching bag, gasping for breath.

Bluestone kept at it, not hard enough to knock him down, but bruising and drawing blood.

"Stop it!" Cleo screamed.

One last time, for pleasure, Bluestone thought. His fist dug deep into St. Pierre's soft belly.

With a moan, St. Pierre crumpled, falling to his hands and knees.

"Stop it," Cleo repeated.

Bluestone stepped back, holding his eye. He had to turn around to look at her. I'm sorry, he was going to say, but Cleo's face was shimmering with pleasure, glad to have her husband beaten and humbled, she just didn't want him killed, that's all.

"He's all yours," Bluestone told her. He headed for his truck.

Cleo stood staring at St. Pierre, who remained on his hands and knees, dripping blood.

The truck's motor roared.

After a moment, Cleo realized she was in Bluestone's way. She got into the Cadillac, backing into the street, making room for him, and after he'd driven off she decided she ought to leave, too.

St. Pierre was still on his knees.

Bollinger took Suzy back to her table, staying on to talk, and Suzy imagined that every woman in the club was watching, half of them not knowing who she was. And the other half? Livid with jealousy.

"I haven't danced for years," Bollinger confessed, which was unnecessary. He'd stepped on her twice.

"Well, you should do it more often," Suzy told him. "You're an excellent dancer."

"Haw."

"I mean it."

Like hell, Bollinger thought. He'd always had three feet. In part, that accounted for his style at parties, moving through the crowd, touching all bases. If he kept talking he kept off the floor.

The music started up again. Bollinger looked at Suzy, remembering the easy intimacy, their bodies touching as they moved, holding each other. He'd been awkward at first, but he had managed, hadn't he? Most of it was a good partner. And she seemed to enjoy herself.

"Well. Shall we do it again?"

"Why not?"

He took her hand and led her back onto the floor, marveling at how simple it really was, and vaguely aware, it was just barely perceptible, that she was dancing closer, discreetly leading him.

The secret was the partner, all right. With Marion, the few times he'd tried, it had been a complete botch. But then who could dance with his secretary? It was doomed from the start.

"Who are those people you're with?"

"Friends. The Strykers."

"Do you think they'd mind if I took you home?"

"We could ask."

Bollinger laughed, stepping on her, but Suzy didn't mind, not with every woman in the club watching.

Dex swirled her Coke, wondering why Milo was so quiet, he hadn't spoken ten words without being prompted.

"You don't smoke dope, do you?" she asked finally. The question wasn't serious. If he did, he'd have told her long ago, she thought. He tried to get her to do everything else.

"No," Milo said. He was on the other side of the pool, lying in the direct sun. His skin was much darker than hers, he could stay all day and not burn. "But I can get you some if you want. Hobe has a connection."

"Does Fred?"

"Does Fred what?"

"Smoke."

"Dope?"

"Yes."

"Sometimes."

"I hope he's not smoking it now," Dex said, glancing toward the house. Fred frightened her, he was already a man, and Maureen, the girl he'd brought, looked fast.

Milo lifted the washcloth he had covering his eyes. He looked at her disdainfully. "No, he's not smoking now. That, I assure you."

"All right, you don't have to get mad about it."

"I'm not mad," Milo said. He replaced the washcloth.

Dex wondered how he could be so positive. There were a lot of stories about Fred. In Grade Eleven, he'd grown a full mustache, and once at a house party, because the girl hosting it wouldn't "co-operate," he'd spit in a condom and stuck it down between the sheets in her parents' bed.

"I think I'll see. I don't want the house smelling."

Dex put her glass under the lounge chair and hitched up her bra. "Can I get you something?"

Milo didn't answer.

Had he heard her? He must have, Dex decided. She got up and went into the house, again wondering what was wrong with him. He didn't usually sulk, except when he couldn't get his way, and they hadn't had that argument today, or at least not yet.

The house was very still. No one was in the kitchen and the living room was also empty. God, if they were in a bedroom, she'd kill them, Dex thought. She started down the hall.

"Fred!" Maureen said urgently.

Dex stopped. They were in the den, the door partially open.

"*Fred*," Maureen moaned. "Oh, Fred, fuck me! Fuck me, fuck me, *fuck me*."

Dex backed off, her hand over her mouth, afraid that she was going to say something. She was shaking by the time she got outside.

Her voice was barely a whisper. "Milo, do you know what they're doing?"

He didn't answer.

"Milo! They're making love!"

"So?" Milo said. "Doesn't everybody?"

He didn't move, the washcloth still covering his eyes, and Dex thought, oh, that's what was wrong. They were arguing again. She just hadn't known it.

Joe Patino spent the day in his rented room, getting drunk on cheap wine, becoming ever more bitter. Though most Agua Calientes shunned him, he was a disgrace to their people, a drunk who had wasted his heritage, he had tenuous contacts with a few and he'd heard the talk.

Bluestone, it was said, had optioned Sun Devil Canyon to Mallory, and the boy was soon to be a millionaire.

Patino tried to imagine a million dollars and how he might get some small share of it. It only seemed fair that he should. They were related by blood. Was he not Angel's brother?

Was there some legal recourse? Some initiative...?

Words, Patino thought. The white man's words. Unlike the other Agua Calientes, he had very little education, he had trouble with words. He mouthed them, only dimly knowing their meaning, and without the will or way to test them.

He drank from the bottle and the wine spilled down the front of his shirt. He ought to do something, he thought. But what?

He was nobody and he had nothing.

... five, six, seven. Eight.

Chip hung up, sprawling back on his bed. He lay very still for a while, imagining Jody with other men, making love to them, doing dirty, perverted things. Cut open her head, and there would be nothing but pricks inside, he thought. Instead of cells, there'd be hundred of thousands of little pricks. Millions of them.

He reached for the phone again, trying to remember where he had tried last, the office or her apartment. The office, wasn't it? That was her latest excuse for not being able to see him, she had some typing to catch up on, but if it was true, why wasn't she working? He had been calling since midmorning, every half hour, the office and her apartment both, over and over, dialing a number that rang and rang, that was never answered, that mocked him.

It mocked him like her mocking words, the last time they'd been together. "You," she had said, "fuck like the Roadrunner, beep, beep."

Fuck her, Chip decided. He put the phone back and sat up, vowing that he wouldn't try again, she wasn't worth it, why chase a whacko? If he was such a lousy lay, how come he satisfied *normal* women? Lots of them.

Remembering the list, he went into the wardrobe, pulling open the top drawer. The list was in a large manila envelope marked "Research Material, Keep." He took it out, tearing off the covering pages, clippings from *The Christian Science Monitor*. One fell to the floor. "How to Make a Nuclear Reactor."

Leaving it there, Chip returned to the bedroom, reading the list as he went, skimming over it. Charlotte. Remember her? The first time, she said, trying to sit up, to see what it looked like, his penis stuck in her, and she had a cunt as big as her shoe. Diane, who didn't have any tits, and Leslie, who had only one. She didn't tell him until she was undressed. A one-night stand, it lasted six weeks, he felt so guilty. Older women, Jesus. Doreen. One tit was bigger than the other. A lot bigger.

He got back on the bed and put the list aside and found the telephone and started dialing. His finger slipped and he had to start over. He wasn't satisfied he had it right until the third run-through. He let that ring. Once, twice.

"Hullo?"

"Jerry?"

"Yuh."

"It's Chip."

A pause. "Where are you?"

"The Springs."

"Oh."

"Listen," Chip said. "You remember Maxine, the all-time dirty fuck?" He found her on the list. "She sucked balls, that was her specialty."

"No, but you'd think I would."

"Well, that's nothing. Wait till you hear … what I got now."

"I'm with a lady."

"Oh," Chip said. "Listen, I won't keep you, what I called to say, keeping a list is kind of stupid, isn't it? I mean, it's childish."

"That's what you called me to say?"

"Yeah."

A pause. "Okay."

"So I'm burning mine," Chip said, deciding at that moment. It just came into his head. "What about you?"

"I'll burn mine, too."

"You promise?"

"Sure."

"Okay," Chip said. "I'm hanging up now, and I'm going to burn my list, and then I'm going to call you back, okay?"

"I said I'd do it."

"Okay," Chip said. He hung up, looking at his hands, the palms wet with sweat.

Rona. Remember her? Back and forth, mouth, cunt, mouth, cunt.

He held the sheet at an angle and set fire to it with his lighter.

Remember the Snake? She fucked in the ocean.

Bollinger had to park his Rolls on the street. Milo's new car, a souped-up Lancia, the rear end two feet off the pavement, was in the driveway with a Corvette.

Suzy felt oddly apprehensive. Dex had said that Milo was coming over, they were going to study together, but she hadn't mentioned—what was his name?—the rough-looking character?—Fred?

The cars seemed very male. They were like an advertisement: Your daughter is entertaining men.

"You know Milo Chermak, don't you?" Suzy asked. She hadn't intended to mention him. It would be nice if Bollinger simply found Milo at the house, but now she wasn't too sure. "Dex, that's my daughter, they're sort of going together."

Bollinger tried to look interested. "Are they?"

It was too late now, but she should have telephoned Dex, to warn her she was coming home early, Suzy thought. The house might be a mess. Any more than two and they weren't studying. That was a party.

There hadn't been any real chance to call, though. Vivian had made a fuss. What about the Hampton party, which they were supposed to go on to together, and why couldn't Bollinger join them? Good God, she'd been going to make an *issue* of it, and then Bollinger, suddenly decisive, had simply whisked her away.

Very decisive, Suzy thought, remembering with a rush of pleasure. Bollinger liked her, was really interested—and now this. She should have called.

"Well, shall we have that drink...?"

Bollinger also was hesitant. The Corvette threatened. It somehow seemed rowdy. "I don't see why not."

Suzy got her keys and led the way up the walk. The house was quiet, no stereo blaring, anyway. They probably were at the pool. She unlocked the door and pushed it open for Bollinger.

"You sticking with scotch?"

"Please."

Inside, she closed the door, looking around apprehensively, relieved to see that everything was in its place. "Dex? I'm home!"

At the same instant, Fred burst out of the kitchen, carrying Maureen with her legs wrapped around his hips. They were naked, coupling on the run.

Suzy screamed.

"Oh, shit," Fred said. He released Maureen's buttocks, letting her slide off, causing her to scream, too. She hit the floor with a thud.

Fred put his hands over an enormous erection.

"You ... you pigs!" Suzy shouted, unable to control her anger. "What are you doing in my house?" She ran at Fred, trying to strike him. "Get out! *Get out!*"

Fred dodged out of the way, bumping into Maureen, and they both sprawled on the floor.

Bollinger was still frozen.

"It's okay," Fred told him, trying to explain. "We just ... didn't know you were coming."

Suzy turned her face into the wall. "Get out."

Fred scrambled to his feet, dragging Maureen with him. They ran into the den.

"Well," Bollinger said, finally finding his voice. "This is, uh, quite a surprise."

Suzy blundered down the hall, keeping her face to the wall, not having the nerve to look at him. This was impossible, it couldn't have happened, it was like a nightmare. Everything ruined. My God, what did he think?

Fred emerged from the den, pulling on his trousers. "Excuse me."

Bollinger stood aside.

His shoes still in his hand, Fred went out the door, followed a moment later by Maureen, dressed only in her panties, the rest of her clothes clutched to her breast.

She gave Bollinger a quick look. "'Bye."

Suzy stopped. Dex? Where was she? Madly, she turned back, flinging open Dex's bedroom door. Half dressed, Milo and Dex were trying to make up the bed. They looked at her, caught.

"Tramp!" Suzy shrilled. "I turn my back, and this is what happens? You turn our home into a whorehouse?"

Bollinger came down the hall, thinking that he shouldn't interfere, but she was handling this very badly.

"Whore," Suzy said, the rage knowing no bounds, Dex had ruined everything. "Whore, but it's the only way you can keep him, isn't it? You're not satisfied with what I've provided, you've got to have Chermak money!"

Bollinger reached for Suzy, inadvertently looking into the bedroom, seeing a shocked, shattered child who, he thought, would be scarred forever.

He pulled his hand back. How could she have handled it so badly...?

He turned away, going back down the hall and out of the house.

From the Racquet Club, which they left early, despite Em's protestations that it was going to get better, Sargent and Angie went on to the annual block party at Sunshine Estates. It was billed as a get-acquainted party for newcomers but was actually just a good excuse to get potted.

By the time they arrived—after stopping at the house to look in on the children—Chaney was already well on his way, disdaining the customary lampshade for a toilet seat, which he was wearing around his neck.

"It's a costume party," Chaney explained, giving Sargent a beer, "and I've come as a shit." He winked at Angie. "A good shit, though."

Angie rolled her eyes and kept on going, taking a belated offering, potato salad, to the patio. Sargent's friendship with Chaney bothered her almost as much as his deep involvement in the High Desert project. As far as she was concerned, that was something else Sargent couldn't afford, to play the fool. When he got better—if he ever did—she hoped he would be more serious-minded.

Chaney took Sargent to meet Groper, the tract's developer, who was presently building ten additional houses.

"Sargent is also in real estate," Chaney announced. "He's got a great idea, which I'm sure he'd like to share with you."

Groper, a small, intense man with the face of a badger, regarded Sargent with obvious distrust. In his world, nobody did anything for nothing.

A group gathered. Chaney's fans.

"It's to help locate open houses," Chaney said, much to Sargent's relief. For an awful moment, he thought Chaney, despite his promise, was going to mention Cathedral City. "Instead of signs and arrows, how about colored balloons, filled with helium? You tie them on a string and fly them directly over the house. Then people can see them for miles."

Groper seemed interested. "What kind of balloons?"

"With your houses, Mickey Mouse," Chaney said. He moved away, the fan club following, hooting with laughter.

"Well, fuck you very much," Groper told Sargent.

Sargent smiled and walked away. To plead innocent seemed unfair, it would spoil the joke, and he actually ought to feel flattered, he thought. Chaney normally didn't share credit for his bon mots. He must be trying to get him in good with the neighbors.

The sonofabitch.

He looked for Angie, thinking he ought to stick with her awhile, but she was already engrossed with new friends, relaxed and smiling, talking a mile a minute. It struck him that they both had more fun with tract-housing types. The Racquet Club was impressive in its way, but they belonged here, not in high society. Hadn't they learned that in Washington?

He kept circulating, making small talk, trying to keep names straight, listening to Chaney's outrages with one ear.

Someone had come in his old uniform, a bell-bottomed sailor suit with the flap in front, very proud that he could still fit in the thing. "Oh, you were out of shape then, too, huh?"

The fan club roared.

A complicated person, Sargent thought. In a group, Chaney was always "on," the life of the party, the self-appointed entertainment. Alone, just the two of them, he was often quiet and deep, almost philosophic. He was strongly committed to his convictions.

They were close friends—they talked almost every night—but this was typical now. The big hello and then he probably wouldn't seek him out again. Too busy performing.

Sargent tried once, but Chaney was putting on a private show for George Wagman's wife, Eve, and awhile later, after it was dark, he saw them sneaking off together.

Yes, complicated, and too daring for his own good, it seemed. Wagman was a brawny truck driver who could snap Chaney's spine. Why take the chance?

"Does it really matter that much?" Lois asked.

Mallory looked at her. "What?"

Lois came to sit beside him. She had changed, as promised, into something more comfortable, silk lounging pajamas that clung to the soft hills of her body.

"Why don't you admit it?" she teased. "It wasn't as good as you expected, was it? The party, I mean."

Mallory wasn't about to admit anything. He took a sip of his brandy, which she had served in a huge snifter. He couldn't seem to get the level down.

"You didn't knock 'em on their ear, but the thing is, what you've got to remember—nothing would."

"Oh?"

"Seriously," she said. "If you walked across the pool—on the water?—and one of them missed it, you know what they'd say?" She tried to mimic Vickers. "What's this I hear?"

"Yeah."

"It's true," Lois said, mimicking herself now, and Mallory had to laugh. He'd also been afraid of the press making a big thing about him being back in town, but his return had been mentioned only in passing, a few paragraphs when he wouldn't comment. Only that scandal sheet, *The Sandbox,* had given any trouble, hinting at a romance.

Lois put a hand on his arm. "What else is true—it's a good project, and it's going to go."

The sincerity with which she said it made him stop.

"And, what the hell," she added, coloring slightly at what for her was a profanity. "We've got each other."

Her hand remained on his arm.

Each other? To release himself, Mallory returned the brandy snifter to the coffee table, wondering if he might have somehow missed something.

Was the scene indeed set for romance when they returned from the Racquet Club? Low lights, soft music, a cozy gas fire, the nightcap out and waiting. Tina discreetly withdrawn for the rest of the evening.

"You look nice in that jacket," Lois said, as if she had only been touching the material. "I like to see you dressed up."

Mallory looked at her. "I like to see you in something more comfortable."

She blushed.

Mallory retrieved his drink.

"That wasn't supposed to mean," he began, and then thought, shit. He put the glass down again and took her hand, enfolding it with his fingers. "What are we doing?"

She didn't answer, afraid to speak now, waiting for him to tell her.

It could happen, Mallory thought. With his other hand, he touched her hair, lifting a strand and letting it fall.

The kitchen door banged.

Lois pulled away.

"Where are the Band-Aids?" Theo hollered. He came into the living room, grimacing with pain, shaking a bony finger. "Oh? You two back already?"

"What's wrong?" Lois asked. She got up, going to him.

"Shock." Theo told her. He made a noise, imitating, apparently, an electrical discharge.

Lois examined the finger. "It's just a bit red."

"When were you a nurse?" Theo demanded. "I want Tina to look at it."

"Then go ahead. But remember her rule. 'No blood, no Band-Aid.'"

Lois returned to the sofa, sitting a bit farther away from Mallory this time. "How's the movie?"

"Jiminy!" Theo said, remembering. "I'm missing it!" He got the remote control, turning the television on, flipping through the channels until he found himself. The resemblance was barely there. A dashing, heroic figure.

Lois had to raise her voice to be heard. "What's wrong with your set?"

"On the blink," Theo told her. He showed his damaged finger as proof. Then, to Mallory: "This was me, before they took away my manhood."

Mallory put his glasses on. "Which one's that?"

"*The Buccaneer.* With Faye Manusov and Harvey Orst. That's her now."

"We've seen this," Lois complained.

Theo got a hassock, pulling it closer to the television set. He sat down, giving no indication that he'd heard. "Now there was an actress for you. According to the gossip columns, she was sleeping with the studio chief, he was Norman Lerner at the time, they all but came out and said so, but she got there all on her own."

Lois gave up. "We could go somewhere else," she suggested.

Where? Mallory wondered. To bed? He took his glasses off, putting them away. He'd finish his brandy, and then he'd go home.

Lois didn't persist. The spell had been broken.

As St. Pierre would have said, it was written in the sand, Kismet. None of them had an alibi.

After the beating from Bluestone, he had gone back into the office, tending his cuts and bruises himself and bravely resuming work on the Old Hartford Place. He accomplished little, though, his jaw becoming increasingly more painful, and after a while he got the idea that it might be broken.

Not having a doctor—he was still too new in town—he decided to go to Desert Hospital Emergency. Unfortunately, there'd been a serious accident on the interstate, a truck driver falling asleep at the wheel and crossing the divider. He'd hit two cars and a camper before overturning and there were four dead and seven injured, two critically.

Emergency looked like a battlefield aid station.

St. Pierre sat ignored for an hour. Finally he left, without anyone taking his name or giving him a second look.

Bollinger literally fled. In a kind of panic—God, what an appalling, grubby scene!—he got in his Rolls and headed for Los

Angeles. Marion didn't expect him until the morning, when the Lear, back from Dallas, was to fly him in, but now he didn't want to wait.

If he hurried, they could have a late dinner, then spend the night together on the yacht at Marina del Rey. Marion liked the yacht—that would make it up to her.

To get her out of the way, to give him a clear run at Suzy, he had invented problems in Los Angeles, she deserved better treatment than that. If he was going to cheat, he should cheat properly, for God's sake. It wasn't as if he didn't have the money. Or the sense to choose more discreetly.

Ruth, she was a disaster, to ever think it could be serious, and now Suzy ... ?

Bollinger cringed. Whatever had possessed him? In his quest for variety, he had sacrificed good breeding, but it wouldn't happen again.

It was after eight when he got to the house in Beverly Hills. Marion wasn't there. Hours later, close to midnight, she came breezing in, surprised to see him and explaining that she'd been to a movie. Her alibi, which left him with none.

Mallory drove around aimlessly, thinking that had been a close call, hadn't it? Lois obviously had set her cap for him and he didn't know how to handle such a situation.

Cissy's best friend? That was wrong. Or was it? Face reality.

He cruised side streets, anything to keep moving, reminding himself that Cissy had been dead for several years, and wondering if it wasn't time to admit he'd always felt a certain attraction for Lois. Given the opportunity—could that attraction grow into love?

The question plagued him. Like a dead body refusing to be buried, it surfaced at every turn, demanding an answer.

Mallory finally decided that the answer was no. If the question had to be asked, the answer was no.

He continued driving aimlessly. His trouble, he thought, was his stupid pride, it always had been. If he could only put it aside just once.

In the end, he found himself in a strange neighborhood, so dark and quiet it was unreal. For a moment, he thought something was wrong, and then he realized, laughing at himself, that they were all new houses, not yet occupied.

At least he could still laugh when there was no one to see or hear him.

Joe Patino never got out of his room. At one point, he wasn't sure when, he awoke in a drunken stupor, groping for his wine bottle and finding it empty. Desperately, he searched everywhere, trying to find enough money for another, but all he could collect was eighty-three cents.

What would that buy? Nothing, and he had no credit, and there was no one from whom he could borrow. Disgusted with himself, he fell down on his bed, sobbing. He wasn't sure when blessed sleep took him again.

Mary Alice was exhausted when she got home from the Racquet Club. Billy tucked her into bed and waited for her to fall asleep and then he sneaked out of the house and headed for Cathedral City. The crash project Mary Alice had ordered was rapidly transforming the old shed and greenhouse that was to be the Casa Verde. He wanted to check the day's progress, how many more beams had been restored, how many new tiles laid and, yes, to imagine it in operation, a long line of important people clamoring to get in, all trying to catch the eye of the gracious owner and host, Billy Segundo.

Alone, he walked the place, building it in his mind, and by the time he left it was after midnight. Nobody had seen him come. And nobody saw him leave.

❧ ❧ ❧

For a change, Cleo stayed sober that evening, the memory of St. Pierre's humbling sufficient intoxication, every detail fondled, keepsakes to be treasured.

He deserved it. Oh, God, how he deserved it, and it wasn't just chance that she should be called upon as witness.

No.

The Lord worked His will in mysterious ways, Cleo decided. She remembered hearing that as a child. And that He picked people to be His instruments.

Cleo wondered. Had Bluestone been chosen to be His instrument?

Chip spent most of the evening parked outside of Jody's apartment building. Periodically, he went to the front door, buzzing to no avail, and twice he drove to a nearby pay telephone to make calls that were not answered.

Yet he knew she was home. Her bathroom window didn't have a blackout blind and the light there kept turning on and off. So often, she had to be with a man, he thought. They kept washing themselves. For such a dirty girl, she was clean.

When the man left, he'd go up, he decided. It was easy enough to get into the building. Time it right, follow another tenant in, act like he belonged, that's all.

But when the man did leave—it *had* to be him, he was very handsome, and he had that look of pleased disbelief—when he did leave, Chip drove away, too.

He didn't want to see her now.

Sargent got lost. When the block party broke up, Kaestner, another newcomer, professed to be too drunk to drive and his wife didn't have a license. Angie volunteered Sargent to take their babysitter home.

The girl lived in Desert Hot Springs. Sargent didn't pay attention to the way, content simply to follow her directions, and coming back he got hopelessly turned around, heading for Beaumont instead of Palm Springs. He got to Cabazon before realizing his mistake.

On the way back, hurrying to get home, he tried a shortcut and got turned around again. When he finally made it, the children were asleep, and Angie also had gone to bed, pretending to be?

Sargent wondered if that was why she had volunteered his services. It would take a long time before things were good between them again. If ever.

He took a beer out to the pool. Why him?

Soon Chaney came over the fence.

"How did you make out?" Sargent asked.

"Fabulous," Chaney lied.

They laughed, careful not to disturb Angie, whether or not she was asleep.

CHAPTER TEN

Thacker spotted the truck just after first light. It was parked on a side street, a block off the highway, and he wouldn't have paid any attention, there was nothing wrong with its being there, except the door on the passenger side was hanging open.

He slowed, wondering if he ought to check. It had been an easy shift, not one report to write up, and it would be a shame to spoil that. He thought of his wife, warm and wet. If she had to wake up, that was the best way, she always said. But she would be awake already if he had to write a report. As a police officer, he had two main faults. He couldn't type and he couldn't shoot straight. Not being able to type was going to get him fired someday.

Goddamn, he decided. Duty called. He stopped the cruiser and snapped on his microphone. "Bo-deen, this is Thacker. I'm checking a pickup on Third Street off Highway One-eleven in Cathedral City."

There was no answer on the radio.

"Bo-deen, this is Thacker. Do you read me?"

There was still no reply.

Jesus, Thacker thought. He'd just left Resondo, who'd been sleeping behind U B Pipe & Supply in Midway. Backing up, he turned onto Third Street, pulling in behind the truck. He wondered if he was the only one awake on the whole fucking shift. There hadn't been a squeak out of Juarez for an hour. And where the piss was Meyers?

He got out gingerly. Outside the cruiser, he always felt vulnerable, a target. He held his hand near his revolver as he approached the driver's side.

The cab was empty.

Wooosh, Thacker thought. The last moment, he had imagined someone crouched there, a sawed-off shotgun ready to blow his head off. He pulled the door open to check the registration and noticed a folded red handkerchief on the seat. He picked it up and found the ends knotted to form a loop. A sweat band?

Making a face, he was about to put it back, but then he saw the seared hole, matted with what looked like dried blood, and the strands of long black hair clinging to it.

Jesus. Jesus Christ.

Thacker went back to his cruiser to make a report.

"Bowden," he said, thumbing on the mike. "This is Thacker. I could have a possible homicide."

The radio crackled. "Say again ...?"

An hour later, several blocks back up the cove, Resondo found Bluestone sprawled face down in a ditch, shot three times at close range with a small caliber gun. He had two wounds in the chest, and a third, seemingly a *coup de grâce*, in the right temple.

Jacobi made the identification.

"Shit," he said softly, looking away.

"What's the matter?" Resondo asked. "You know him?"

Jacobi nodded. Upon Thacker's initial report, Bowden had telephoned him, saying he might have a case at last, and Jacobi had joined in the search for a body. He'd been in the next block— across an empty field—when Resondo let out a whoop.

"What's his name?"

"Miguel Patino, or at least he used to be. Lately, he took to calling himself Bluestone."

"He looks Indian."

"Half."

"Caliente?"

"Yeah."

It was what distressed Jacobi. There weren't that many, he'd have preferred to see a beaner go, but then the Patinos were star-crossed, weren't they? He'd known Angel almost intimately, having arrested him numerous times for being drunk and disorderly, and he'd watched Angel's brother, Joe, piss away a fortune. For a while, he thought Bluestone had a chance, Mallory as his guardian, but then they'd had a falling out and Mallory had gone off somewhere.

"What do you make of it?"

"Robbery, probably," Jacobi said, feeling for a wallet and not finding one. "Some hitchhiker ..." He stood up. "He shoots him and dumps the body here. He takes the truck—he's going to steal it, too—but that's dumb. He bails out at the highway and hitches another ride and now he's in Arizona."

Resondo didn't see how that figured. The body was on the east side of the road, which suggested it was dumped en route to the highway, which suggested that the hitchhiker was picked up in the cove, which suggested in turn that he was a local, not a transient. A local wouldn't take off. He'd stay here.

"You got an argument?" Jacobi wanted to know.

"Just with the Arizona part."

"Okay, then he was headed west. He's in Los Angeles by now. Does that make you any happier?"

No, Resondo thought, but he wasn't going to argue, there were all kinds of explanations. Such as the killer drove up from the highway looking for a place to dump the body and saw this and made a U-turn. What was wrong with that idea—except that a ditch was a ditch and there was one on both sides of the road?

"After a while, you get a gut feeling for these things," Jacobi said. "You want to sit on the truck? I don't want anybody touching it until Science has a look."

Resondo nodded and left, thinking he had a gut feeling, too. It was a local, not a transient. But he wasn't going to argue.

By eight-thirty, Jacobi had Mallory at the morgue, making official what both already knew to be fact. Mallory had heard the news on the radio while shaving in the bathroom of his newly rented apartment. He'd cut his lip, his first thought for himself, that it wasn't fair to learn that way, they were supposed to tell the next of kin first. The explanation—volunteered later, when he didn't care anymore, did it change anything?—was that Joe Patino had been notified first and Joe failed to mention that Mallory was back in Palm Springs.

Quigley, the medical examiner, lifted the sheet. "Is that him?"

"Yes," Mallory answered.

"That's all, then," Quigley said. He dropped the sheet and shoved the body back into the keeper.

That's all? For Christ's sake, give me a minute, Mallory thought, but the door had banged shut, and perhaps it was better that way. Freeze-frame image, the last duty society demanded he perform, and in all the other memories he carried, the little bastard always would be very much alive.

Jacobi was waiting on the steps. Mallory didn't say anything, just getting into Jacobi's car for the run back, and Jacobi didn't say anything either until they reached Cathedral City. That reminded him of the project—and the one question he had to ask.

"You, uh, don't think it had anything to do with this, do you?"

Mallory looked at him. "What do you mean?"

Jacobi wasn't sure. On the way to the morgue, Mallory had sought refuge in conversation, telling him of the option taken on Sun Devil Canyon and the plans for High Desert, all hinging on whether enough options could be bought up in Cathedral City. Obviously, a lot of money was involved.

"What I'm asking, I guess—had Bluestone gotten paid?"

Mallory shook his head. "No. We don't exercise till December."

"So he was broke?"

"Virtually."

Jacobi considered.

"What are you getting at?"

"Nothing," Jacobi decided. "Like I told you, his wallet's missing, which suggests a robbery. If he'd been paid—had a lot of money and was flashing it around—then it would be more likely to be someone local. They'd have seen it, or maybe heard about it, you know?"

"Christ," Mallory said. "The town's full of people with more money than he ever hoped to have. The reason they don't get shot, they're not so stupid as to pick up transients." Quickly, he looked away. "Or so lacking in humility. He thought he could handle anything. And he always was getting proven wrong."

I guess, Jacobi thought, not needing much to get talked into it. The transient theory made the most sense—what he'd figured himself, first off—and Mallory being back in town and Stu Bollinger in the background didn't change anything. A million dollars didn't change it, either. The kid hadn't been paid.

So what was bugging him?

That it was so routine, Jacobi decided. His first homicide in months, and it had to be straightforward, the hitchhiker did it. Routine and straightforward—and virtually beyond solution.

Mallory got the first call. Back at his apartment, getting undressed for the shower he still hadn't taken, wondering if Lois had called in his absence and if he should call her, never mind the fucking condolences, he ought to reassure her that he was okay—the phone rang and he thought it was Lois. He picked it up and he was going to tell her that he was okay and a man's muffled voice caught him totally unawares.

"Mr. Mallory? Fair warning. You could be next."

"What?"

"You could be next. So take my advice. If you want to stay alive, stop your project, get out of the canyon."

"Who is this?"

Click.

Gawd, Mallory thought, listening to the dial tone. The world was full of ghouls. Bluestone's body was still warm and the crank calls had already started.

He hung up and continued to undress. You could be next? Somebody had a bag of garbage for a head.

The phone rang again.

The same goddamn idiot? Probably, he thought. Letting it ring, he went into the bathroom, pulling the door shut and turning on the shower, the drum of the water blocking it out.

There! Let the idiot have his fun. He got the rest of his clothes off, standing naked in front of the mirror on the door, a big and powerful man despite the years, and if so—was that him there or not?—then why was he afraid to answer?

"Because," he said aloud, arguing with his reflection, "I don't want or need this kind of shit." It wasn't enough, Bluestone dead, there had to be some crank, telling him to abandon the dream? Bluestone dead, and now a shadow to fight, the Mystery Asshole? "Fuck."

Abruptly, he opened the door. The phone was still ringing.

All right. He strode back and snatched it up.

"Oh, God," Lois sobbed. "I've been calling and calling. Where were you…?"

He sat on the bed, the relief so momentary it was barely there, and then afraid and angry again, and tired, too. He knew before he asked. "Away. What's wrong?"

"A man telephoned…and he said he was warning me, that I was next."

"What man?"

"He wouldn't say. Just that I had to sell my shares."

"Your shares? Did he say to whom?"

"King," Lois cried, breaking down. "He threatened to kill me! He said I was next—and he meant Bluestone!"

"Hey," Mallory told her. "You're okay. Tina is there isn't she? And Theo?" He waited for her to stop crying. "There's nothing to worry about. It's just some stupid crank."

"How do you know?"

"I do, that's all. Now hang up and let me get dressed. I'll be over just as soon as I can."

"All right."

"Good-bye."

Frowning, Mallory put the phone down, worried that she should be so panicked, and feeling a kind of vague disappointment. He had thought she would be stronger than that. She hadn't even said she was sorry about Bluestone.

Later, in the shower, the water icy cold because he'd left it running, trying to make excuses for her—and for himself—he finally accepted the fact that it might not be a crank.

Lois could see it in Mallory's expression. "He was called, too—wasn't he?"

Mallory nodded, coming out of the den, lowering his voice so he wouldn't be heard by Theo. "Yes. Marion took it, she wouldn't put him through to Bollinger, but it was the same spiel, almost word for word."

Lois shivered. "That's everyone."

"Just about ..." Mallory consulted his list, his own name at the top, and then Lois, Suzy, Mary Alice, St. Pierre. And now Bollinger. "Except Sargent."

Lois looked at him.

"No," Mallory said, certain of that, and ashamed he'd shared the same thought. The history of mental illness ... well, he'd done crazy things once, that's all. "It's not Sargent. I'd have recognized the voice. You can't disguise a nasal twang."

"You can't?"

"No." He put an arm around her shoulder, taking her back to the sofa, where her coffee was still on the table, barely touched. "I read that somewhere. *The Hardy Boys at the Seashore?*"

"This isn't funny."

"No," Mallory said again, and it wasn't. They could be dealing with more than a crank, with someone who was trying to scuttle High Desert, with someone who was going about it in a very deliberate, effective fashion. Lois' hysterical reaction was a measure of the shock value of death threats coming immediately after Bluestone's murder. It made them realistic, she could see it happening, *you could be next,* and for her that was terrifying.

"What are we going to do?"

"Nothing, for the moment."

"Nothing…?"

Mallory nodded. He'd gotten the others to agree, for the moment, nothing. If the calls persisted, if there was anything to indicate it was more than a crank, that any of them might actually be endangered, then they would quietly bring in the authorities.

Lois was staring at him. "We've got to call the police."

"Why? Because of a crank?"

"You don't know that," she said accusingly. "If it isn't, if it's the man who…" Again, she shuddered, her coffee spilling. "Ohhh."

Mallory took the cup from her and returned it to the table.

"King," she said, "I'm frightened, and if you don't call them, I will."

He stopped, bent over. "Let's give it a chance, huh? If it gets into the newspapers…investors get death threat? That's not going to make it any easier for me to raise capital."

"Oh. And that's your main concern?"

He stood up. "It's one of them," he said carefully.

She considered for a moment. "What do the others say?"

"They agree."

"With you?"

"Yes."

She looked at him. "But you didn't consult me?"

"Well," Mallory said, just catching himself, almost saying that he didn't have to, he was the man. Half an hour ago she was crying in his arms—dear God, what were they going to do?—and now she was telling him? "You were kind of upset, weren't you?"

"That doesn't excuse it. It's my company, and I have a right to be consulted, and I don't want to be treated like some silly woman."

You're not, he was going to say, but then he realized the accusation was true, or part of it, anyway. She was a woman. Unfortunately, most of his troops were women, and they were in disarray. Suzy, before he calmed her down, had been on the verge of panic, and Mary Alice, although she professed otherwise, had sounded as if she'd peed her pants. Even Marion, the high-priced business professional, used to killings if only financial, even Marion had betrayed a certain dismay. Was that why the caller had been content to voice his threat to her rather than directly to Bollinger?

"I think." Lois said, getting up, "that we ought to have a meeting—a full and proper discussion—and then we'll decide what to do."

Mallory stared at her, not quite comprehending, not trusting himself to speak. Surely she wasn't going to fight him on this?

In the canyon, Hoover, the grader operator, shifted the lift lever again, thinking that he was imagining things, but the blade stayed dead on the ground.

He hesitated, the diesel engine throbbing, telling himself that the blade *had* to lift. It was working perfectly when he knocked off yesterday. And it couldn't get broken standing still.

What the hell...?

Frowning, he cut the engine, clambering down and going around front, staring at the shiny steel plungers which had always done his bidding without question, pushing the massive blade, lifting and turning it. Steel muscles and they always responded before and they weren't broken. So what was wrong?

Rodriguez, the foreman, watching from the shack, he'd seen the whole business, got his hard hat and came out and stood on the porch. Hoover was still staring at the blade dead on the ground.

"What's the matter?" Rodriguez yelled. "She won't go?"

Hoover shook his head.

"Why not?"

Hoover shrugged.

Oh, fuck, Rodriguez thought. There was always something. He started down the stairs, favoring his bad leg.

Aware of him coming, Hoover swung aboard again, thinking he should act like he was trying, and as he did so he saw the hacksaw, half buried in the sand on the other side. He held frozen for a moment. Was that it?

"Let me try," Rodriguez grumbled behind him.

Without replying, Hoover got down on the other side, retrieving the hacksaw from the sand. He ran his callused fingers along the worn blade. They came away with black specks. Rubber.

"It's the hose," Hoover told Rodriguez, who was up on the grader now. He showed him the hacksaw. "Somebody's cut the hose."

Rodriguez stared at him. "You're sure …?"

Hoover nodded, looking at the other equipment, Crandall's dozer, also dependent on hydraulic hose, and the scoop and the dump trunk, which they had planned to start using today, except that they weren't going to work, either. Hoover knew it in his bones. Nothing was going to work today.

When the meeting started, the battle lines already had been drawn, Mallory, St. Pierre and Sargent on one side, Lois, Suzy and Mary Alice on the other. With machinery sabotaged—several thousand dollars in damage—they obviously were dealing with more than a harmless crank. Hoses cut, instruments smashed, sugar in fuel tanks. Those weren't threats. They were violent acts.

As soon as she heard, Mary Alice changed her mind, as anxious as Lois to have the police informed, and Suzy reluctantly had to agree, not so much out of fear for herself as for Dex.

Lois took that as support enough. If it came to a vote—which she wasn't quite certain how to call—they'd have a tie and she as president of the firm ought to prevail in that case, she decided. They couldn't drift without direction just because there was a stalemate.

She looked at Mallory sitting at the other end of the long table in the board room. She tried to be as reasonable and diplomatic as she knew how. "It's no longer a question of whether we should take this person seriously. It's *how* seriously."

"Yes, but nothing has changed," Mallory contended, resisting the impulse to pound the table. "It's the same thing, scare tactics. It's what the sonofabitch wants, publicity."

"You don't know that."

"No, but logic dictates it. Whoever this is, he's making an impossible demand, isn't he? Sell our shares or else—and who are we supposed to sell to? There's no buyer, and if one came forward, it would be tantamount to admitting he initiated the calls. Isn't that so?"

"Not necessarily."

"Jesus …"

St. Pierre intervened. "Lois, please, what Mallory is trying to say, we're probably not dealing …"

She cut him off. "I *know* what he's trying to say."

"Please," St. Pierre said. "Hear me out. In all likelihood, we're not dealing with the murderer at all, but rather someone taking advantage of Bluestone's death. For whatever reason—and it could be anything, he wants the canyon left unspoiled, all right?—for whatever reason he's seized upon this opportunity to badger us. A few telephone calls, a bit of vandalism, and if we take him seriously, go running to the police, it will be in the headlines tomorrow."

"As if I didn't have enough trouble already." This from Mallory.

"It's not something we can trust to be kept quiet," St. Pierre continued, frowning at the interruption. "And, as King has said, he's at the nitty-gritty with potential investors, any or all of whom might take flight. Is hollering police any way to raise capital?"

"No," Lois told him. "But the money isn't my concern at the moment. Our lives are. Mine, if I have to be so selfish." She stopped, thinking that it was useless to argue, and that she had enough support, it wasn't just her being silly about something. And she also felt that it was a personal, not a business, matter. "If you can't understand that, let me say that I have every intention of informing the police of a threat made upon me personally, quite apart from whatever decision happens to be made at this meeting."

"Thank you."

"You're welcome."

"Damn, you're being stupid," Mallory said angrily. He shoved away. "All right, we'll concede you that. File a complaint if you're so anxious for your name in the paper." The rest was for St. Pierre. "Let's get the hell out of here."

Mary Alice patted Lois' hand. "Make your call, honey."

Lois glared at Mallory. "I fully intend to."

Mallory started for the door.

"I also think," Lois said very loudly, waiting for him to stop, "that we should consider halting the project."

Slowly, Mallory turned back.

"Until this matter is settled," she added, looking at the others. "If the police can assure us it's safe to proceed, we'll go ahead. But until we know for certain …?" Her eyes met Mallory's. "This is for your safety, too."

Mallory stood staring in disbelief. What in the name of God was she trying to do? If threats, threats alone, could stop High Desert, then they were dead for sure, lost and beyond resurrection. If that's all it took then the threats would just keep coming. They might as well abandon, forget it.

"I think it's something we should discuss," Lois said, addressing the others, "consider very carefully, and then put to a vote."

Mallory still couldn't believe his ears. *A vote?* What did she think? That her company and the project were somehow one and the same?

St. Pierre looked at him, as if to say she's your "dear friend," monsieur.

Lois blundered on. "After all, the majority rules."

"Goddamn!" Mallory thundered. "High Desert is not your company. You don't preside and you're a very modest shareholder and you're behaving like a twit. The shares decide, and I've got Bollinger and St. Pierre here, which is more than enough, there's no need for any stupid vote, we're going ahead." His fist hit the table. "And if you don't like that, too bad!"

There was a long silence. Lois sat stunned, her face drained white.

"Well," Suzy said at last. "I guess that settles that."

"Yes," Mallory told her. "We're going ahead." He took a moment to get himself under control. "Needless to say, your part in it is essential, and I would hope, despite any differences, that you'd continue with the options."

Suzy managed a brittle laugh. "Don't worry. Some of it's my money, too. Remember?"

"Yes."

Mary Alice pushed to her feet. She stood looking at Mallory. "I hope you know what you're doing."

He nodded for answer, not wishing to discuss it any further. The project was going ahead.

"You'll keep me posted?"

He nodded again.

Satisfied, she got her bag, leaving without saying good-bye, careful not to give any sign to Lois.

"Meeting adjourned?" Suzy asked.

"I think so," St. Pierre said.

They left together, quickly followed by Sargent, hurrying to catch up, bumping chairs in his haste.

Lois looked at Mallory. "How could you?" she asked.

He didn't answer, his mind elsewhere, wishing he'd been able to convince, not bully. He didn't have Bollinger, had no idea what he might do in a pinch, whether he'd come along or not, and if he did how long he'd stay.

Later, in his office, taking the first of the really frightening calls, from a suddenly wary prospective investor, Mallory decided that he'd better find out and soon about Bollinger. Mission Guaranty & Trust, a "very definite" before, was now only a maybe, Michael Spencer's excuse being that he needed a legal opinion on the option signed by Bluestone. Was the thing still binding?

"I'll check my lawyer," Mallory offered, wondering how Spencer had learned of Bluestone's death so quickly. It wasn't something that would make the newswires. The famous Palm Springs grapevine must be at work already, reaching out, via gossiping brokers, to the financial houses.

"No, I'll check with ours."

"All right," Mallory said. "Let me know." He waited for Spencer to promise he'd do that much, but the line remained oddly silent. "Hello...?"

Spencer came back on, his voice muffled, talking to someone else. "...six-thirty, my wife's picking me up." There was a pause. "King? I'm sorry, where were we?"

"That's what you were going to tell me."

"Huh? Oh, that's right. I want to check with our legal department. Listen, how's the weather there, anyway?"

"Hot."

"Lucky you. We're in a fog. Well ... keep in touch?"

Sure, Mallory thought. They said their polite good-byes and he hung up, thinking Spencer wasn't even a "maybe" anymore, he was a "faintly possible," depending not on the canyon's option so much as Bluestone's murder being solved and being shown to have no connection with High Desert. With the Mafia scare in Palm Springs, the banks, like everybody else, got very, very cautious when there was even the slightest suggestion that things might not be kosher. Mission Guaranty & Trust had lots of places to put its money. And a crock of shit wasn't one of them.

Mallory sighed, fingering a note from Jody. While he'd been talking to Spencer, Wells Fargo had called.

Marion took the phone back and offered another. "This is Tatum. He says it can't wait. And Genovese is on another line. Should I have him call back?"

Bollinger looked at his watch. "No, it's getting late there. He'll want to be off to his club." Belatedly, he turned to Mallory, asking his permission. "You don't mind, do you?"

"No, of course not," Mallory said, which was a lie. In half an hour there'd been at least a dozen calls, the result being that they had hardly talked at all. It was as if the switchboard had been given instructions to drum up interruptions.

The only thing Mallory had established thus far was that Bollinger wasn't particularly concerned about the threats and sabotage. He wanted Suzy to continue optioning property on his behalf in Cathedral City. It was, he said, juggling his phone calls, a sound and viable proposition on its own.

That seemed to be the message: While High Desert might be dependent on Cathedral City's renewal, it wouldn't be a fatal blow if High Desert, for whatever reason, failed to materialize. His own new city would still prosper.

Mallory had come to Bollinger for help and found him strangely aloof and unco-operative.

Bollinger took the phone and walked across the patio with it. "Hello, Tatum? Now, what can't wait … ?"

"It's an insurance problem," Marion explained.

Mallory stared after him, frowning. "Oh? What kind?"

"A big one."

Naturally, Mallory thought. Was there any other kind?

"Louise?" Marion said into a third phone. "He's going to talk to Genovese. Will you have him hold, please?" The rest was for Mallory. "You've got the patience of a saint."

Bollinger came walking back. "… four million, which is as high as I'm going. Tell them to take it or leave it."

Marion caught his signal. "Louise? Put him through."

She hung up and the other phone rang and she answered it. "Hello? Genovese? He's going to talk to you."

"Yes, I am prepared to go to court," Bollinger said, falling back into his chair, "and you can tell them that, too. Call me back." He hung up, putting the phone aside, looking at Mallory with a faintly quizzical expression, as if surprised to find him still there. "Really, the tempest will pass."

"It's not a tempest. I barely held the thing together this afternoon, half our shareholders wanting to bail out, and you so uninterested you weren't at the meeting."

Marion came between them with the other telephone. "Genovese."

Bollinger took it, holding it in his lap. "You managed, didn't you?"

"This time? What about next? And where do you stand exactly?"

"Where do you think? With you, of course."

Mallory wanted more than words. "You weren't this after-noon. I can see a fight coming and I need to be sure." He hesi-tated, he didn't like asking within earshot of some Genovese, however distant. "Can I have your proxy?"

Bollinger smiled. "Is that what this has been leading to?"

"Yes."

"All right, you've got it, then." Bollinger picked up the phone. "Genovese? Did you hear that? How trusting I am … and how easily taken?" He adjusted the phone, making himself more comfortable. "How is Margaret, my friend?"

The quick decision bothered Mallory, thinking that it was another indication of Bollinger's uninterest, the man didn't care. And while the proxy had been readily given, it might, in rougher days ahead, be as readily withdrawn. He sat waiting, trying to close his mind to the continuing telephone conversation, which seemed to be of a purely social nature.

"Tuesday?" Bollinger was saying. "No, that's too short notice. Don't you know anything about women? They have to shop first." The easy laughter came again. "All right. You check with yours and I'll check with mine. We'll confirm tomorrow."

Mallory looked at Marion. "Have you got something I could drink?"

"Certainly. What would you like?"

"Whiskey. A jarful."

Marion smiled and moved away. "Just relax. It's coming right up."

Mallory watched her go. A nice woman, he thought. What kept her working for the bastard? Finally, he had to smile him-self, thinking that it was the same thing that kept him waiting, temper in precarious check.

The money.

Bollinger frowned, excusing himself to Genovese, looking at Mallory. "Is there something else …?"

Mallory nodded. "Yes. How long do I have the proxy?"

"Till I take it back."

Sure, Mallory thought. So what was it worth, really? What did it *guarantee?*

"I've told you," Bollinger said impatiently. "It's a tempest."

Mallory shook his head. "It's a crock of shit."

"Well, characterize it any way you wish, it will pass. The thing you've got to do—press forward."

"Where? To the point of no return?"

"What's that supposed to mean?"

"What I've told you. Two bankers, definitely in, now they're having second thoughts, and other prospects suddenly aren't available. I could get overextended awfully easily—and then what?"

Bollinger made a snorting sound. "You're in trouble, maybe. But that's down the line, where it might be all roses, too. So why don't you get off your ass and get down there and find out which?"

"You mean gamble?"

"All business is a gamble," Bollinger said, as if lecturing some unschooled investor. "How much have you got committed? Personally, I mean?" He waited, the telephone seemingly forgotten. "A hundred thousand, isn't it?"

"Yes."

"Yes. And what have you got to gain?"

Mallory hesitated, aware of the distant eavesdropper, why should he know?

"A lot of money," Bollinger said, answering for him. "With luck, you could clear a million. Personally, I mean. The risk— if there is one—seems rather small in comparison." Smiling, he finally raised the receiver, cradling it with his shoulder. "Genovese? What do you think of all this?"

"There are other investors," Mallory said hoarsely.

Bollinger laughed. "Genovese? Did you hear that? I'm one of them, and instead of bold, decisive action—a problem's come up, you understand?—I'm offered this prattle?"

Prattle? Mallory saw red. It was an effort not to rip the phone away. He rose up, choking back his anger, thinking that he had to get the hell out.

Bollinger waved him down, a hand quickly cupping the mouthpiece. "Hold on!"

Mallory stopped.

"Before you run off. Are you going ahead with High Desert or not?"

Was he? Mallory took a breath. "I don't see how I can without firm money."

"You've as much today as you had yesterday," Bollinger reminded him. "What's changed, except you might have to find other sources for the long haul?"

"I might not be able to get it. There's no guarantee."

"There never was. Had you one, would you be sweating now?"

Mallory had to admit that was true. To begin with, he simply crashed ahead, knowing the money would be there, it had to be for a sound proposition. Having it suddenly uncertain was what gave a man the willies, though.

"Just because a couple bankers get cold feet, don't you; too," Bollinger complained. "Quite apart from what's happened, you still believe in the project, don't you? And I'm keeping my end of the bargain." He lifted the phone back to his shoulder. "You started something, finish it."

Sure, Mallory thought. That was easy for him to say, one of the richest men in the country. "Would you guarantee High Desert's completion?"

Bollinger stared at him.

"We just need your name."

"On a blank check?" Bollinger shook his head. "No, I'm not carrying the whole damn thing. That wasn't the arrangement."

Mallory was going to argue.

"I said *no!*" Bollinger told him. "There'll be no free rides. Whatever you've been led to believe, my resources do have a limit, and they'll be strained in any wholesale buying up of Cathedral City. High Desert is your responsibility and whether or not it goes ahead is entirely dependent upon your efforts. It's your project—not mine."

"Yes, but ..."

"*No!*"

Mallory looked at him, choking back the anger once more. If he argued, Bollinger might renege on his commitment in Cathedral City. The bastard had all the power. He didn't have to exercise his options there. He could pass.

Bollinger was talking to Genovese again, laughing. "Gisele? She said that?"

Mallory left to get his whiskey elsewhere.

It had been a big news day. The Middle East in turmoil, the President arguing with Congress, and the Supreme Court issuing a rash of far-reaching decisions—that, with the weather, took up the front page of *The Desert Sun.*

Bluestone's murder was dismissed with a few paragraphs inside. Jacobi was quoted as saying the killing probably was committed by a hitchhiker. He also asked for assistance. If anyone saw anything, they were urged to contact their nearest police department.

Chaney had the clipping when he came over the fence that night. He showed it to Sargent, oddly triumphant.

"Yes, I saw it," Sargent said. He hadn't known Bluestone very well. The boy had only two interests: girls, and those goddamn rocks. Still, he felt a loss. A man overboard. One of the crew gone.

"Disgusting, isn't it?" Chaney persisted.

Sargent stared at him blankly.

"Five paragraphs!" Chaney said. "If it was anyone else—any other member of your syndicate—they'd give it half the front page, right? And I don't mean Bollinger, or Mallory, either. They're 'names' in their own right. But Lois Sills? Suzy Braverman? Yourself?"

Oh, that again, Sargent thought. Chaney would stoop to any level to discredit *The Desert Sun.*

"Admit it. He was just a fucking Indian. So he's not news."

"Frankly, I doubt that's the reason."

"Then what is?"

Sargent shrugged. Deadline problems, whatever. What he did know, he'd been glad to see such a small story, no mention of High Desert. "Have you considered that they simply weren't aware?"

"Exactly. Because they didn't bother checking."

Now he scoffed. "Who with? Joe Patino?"

"Mallory. Surely to God they keep files? One phone call, and they'd know he had optioned the canyon. What I'm saying, if one of his business associates had been murdered ... ?"

Sargent gave up. He wasn't in the mood to argue the size of obituaries and he hardly qualified as a fan of *The Desert Sun,* which on previous occasions had offended his sensibilities, too. The last straw—and he still didn't know why it made him angry—was when they listed what was on the menu before identifying the guests at an important dinner for Ford. Maybe the food editor had been assigned?

"I'm right," Chaney said, taking the silence for agreement. "Wait till tomorrow. I'm going to blast them."

"You're going to what?"

"Give them hell!"

"Hold on," Sargent complained. "I thought we had an agreement? Whatever was said in this yard ... confidential?"

Chaney looked at him. "Yes, but that was before someone got murdered. You don't expect me to ignore a murder story?"

"No. But…"

"But what?" Chaney demanded. "Most of it's out, anyway. You've put two press releases in that rag, and they'll never report that Bluestone was in your syndicate unless you give them another release."

"And that's important?"

"Jesus Christ! What have I been talking about?"

Bluestone being kissed off, hardly worthy of mention, Sargent thought, and he had to admit Chaney's point. Bluestone was a major shareholder in a major project. Had any of the others been killed, himself included, there would have been more questions, and the fact would have come out and been published. Chaney shouldn't be asked to ignore something of legitimate interest in *The Sandbox*'s story on Bluestone.

"Don't worry," Chaney said. "Anything I print, it will come from other sources, not you. What I want you to understand— with somebody murdered—I'd be asking questions in any event."

"All right."

"You understand?"

"Yes."

"Good. Then there's no argument."

Sure, Sargent thought, but their nightly talks had provided Chaney with the right questions to ask. Had he not confided, Chaney, like *The Desert Sun,* might also be uninterested. The profession of outrage stemmed more from a desire to clobber the opposition than correct an injustice. Bluestone, after all, wouldn't be reading any papers.

"It's not going to hurt you, is it?" Chaney asked.

Sargent looked at him, thinking there was a pal, asking that kind of question, and he wondered if he ought to test their friendship, say yes and see what happened.

"No," Sargent said. He used to have a lot of pals but now he just had the one and he didn't want to lose him.

CHAPTER ELEVEN

Bluestone's murder was spread all over the front page of *The Sandbox*. Chaney had gone into as much grisly detail as possible, calculated to inflame, and had revealed that Bluestone—at Mallory's "strong urgings," he reported—had recently optioned Sun Devil Canyon to Mallory and Bollinger. Names of the other syndicate members weren't mentioned until far down in the story.

Out of deference to him? Sargent wondered, reading it. Or was it simply that Chaney had chosen those two for his whipping boys? If he was suggesting there was more than met the eye in the High Desert project—and that certainly seemed to be his intent—then it made sense to restrict the number of supposed villains. Lois, Suzy, St. Pierre, Mary Alice, plus himself. The list got too long. It didn't sound feasible.

But two scoundrels?

Yes, his readers might swallow that, all right. Especially when one was a politician with a not altogether clean slate and the other a billionaire who refused to admit he'd amassed enough.

Actually, it was quite good, as clever a piece of character assassination as he'd seen done, purely by innuendo, in a long, long time, Sargent had to admit. He was just as happy to be mentioned in passing. And without reference to his m-m-mental illness.

"What's he trying to do?" Angie asked anguishedly.

"Sell papers," Sargent told her. "Any cause, however doubtful..." He smiled to mask his concern—this could cause trouble for the project—glancing at the editorial headlined "Two Systems?" "What's for dinner?"

"We're going to Em's."

"Again? The kids get on her nerves."

"She insisted."

"Well, you can say no, can't you?"

"Yes, but it was you who accepted."

"Oh." Sargent said, looking at her. "This is pretty strong stuff. Did you read the editorial?"

She shook her head.

"Quote—'Bluestone was a man of means and attainment. After all, half a university education isn't half bad for an Indian.' That last part is in brackets. Then:

"'If one of his wealthy business associates had been murdered, there'd be a big fuss, the power structure would be up in arms, the police would be doing something.'

"'Yet the establishment press barely sees fit to make mention of the case. There is no indication of community concern. The police act bored.'

"'Is it simply discrimination? Or is there perhaps some other explanation? Is it possible that certain persons of power and influence are being protected?'"

Angie made a face. "What persons?"

"If anyone else had written it, I'd say there weren't any," Sargent told her. "That's an old editorial writer's trick. You offer your readers two evils, hoping they'll take the lesser." Abruptly, he took her hand, pulling her down into his lap. "But with the diatribe accompanying it? He means Bollinger, obviously. And Mallory, too. Although I don't know what power and influence the poor bugger is supposed to wield."

"Why do you say that?"

"Say what?"

"Poor bugger."

Why indeed? Sargent wondered. Because, after this broadside, the project could be in more trouble, and Mallory had everything riding on it? "I don't know. I just feel sorry for him, I guess."

Angie snuggled closer. "I think he's a fink. Chaney, I mean."

"You do?"

"Yes, he's hurting us, we're in High Desert, and I don't think you should see him tonight."

Sargent didn't answer.

"You could come to bed early for once," Angie told him.

"Certain persons of power and influence ...?"

Clements threw the newspaper on Jacobi's desk, the editorial circled by an angry black swath, the pen pressed so hard that its felt tip had broken.

"Who in the hell is this sonofabitch talking about?"

Jacobi read Chaney's diatribe while Clements, nominally his superior, a captain in overall charge of the Indio substation, made a mental list of all the items that didn't belong on Jacobi's desk. The piggy bank, for instance. And the stuffed frog.

"Goddamn," Jacobi said, unhappy with the reference to bored police, "he kicks everybody in the ass but the Indians. Remember when they were the bad guys?"

Clements pointed to the circled editorial. "Forget that. Who are we supposed to be protecting?"

"Bollinger, I suppose," Jacobi said at last.

"Yeah, Bollinger," Clements complained, "and do you want to tell me why the first time I hear he's involved, it's in a telephone call from Riverside?"

Jacobi shrugged. Homicides were his department. He felt no obligation to keep Clements posted, and Bollinger wasn't involved anyway, or at least only in the most peripheral way.

"That's not much of an answer."

No, it wasn't, Jacobi thought. He offered to return the newspaper, and then, when it was refused, decided on the wastepaper basket. "Who called? Yemana?"

"Yeah."

"What did you tell him?"

"I said I'd talk to you."

"Why didn't you tell him to talk to me?"

"Because he doesn't talk to you, remember?"

Jacobi sighed. Yemana, the sheriff, threw a fit at any hint of "The Fix," even at the traffic ticket level. Like Tom Kendra, the new police chief in Palm Springs, he was strictly by the book, refusing to interfere in any way with the normal operation of the judicial system. People still remembered the fuss over the $30,000 check presented by friends and admirers to departing Police Chief Bob White.

The money was raised at a star-studded testimonial dinner which several city council members had tried to stop. They felt the police chief had been well paid and the gift would be seen as a payoff. Was the $30,000 for "thirty years of fantastic service," as White's admirers claimed, or, as the Los Angeles *Times* asked, was it for special favors granted over the years to the rich and the famous and to personal friends?

Yemana's other bugaboo was the Mafia. There were a large number of people living in the Palm Springs area who had past or present connections with organized crime.

The sheriff's office, working with a federal grant, had identified about fifty persons associated in some way, shape or form with publicly identified organized crime figures. But mobsters couldn't be stopped from moving in—they had a right to buy property, didn't they?—and, thus far, there was no indication they were engaging in illegal activities in the county.

Yemana lived in mortal fear that they might start. A hoodlum under every bed.

"Did the Master have any suggestions?"

"For one thing, he thought you might solve the case," Clements said, smiling for the first time. "That would clear Bollinger, and it wouldn't hurt our reputation, either. You still think it was a hitchhiker, do you?"

"Yes."

"What have you done?"

"The usual. There's a routine …"

"Sure," Clements said. "It's a routine case, so you handle it in a routine way."

Jacobi didn't argue. He was guilty as charged, going in with a preconceived notion, concentrating on the one theory and not exploring other avenues. Only once, driving Mallory through Cathedral City, had he been tempted to ask that fateful question—"Where were you last night?"—and he had decided not to for the wrong reason. Fuck, he was a cop, and tender sensibilities, they didn't enter into it, and neither did how rich and powerful a man might be, even one as rich and powerful as Stu Bollinger.

"Listen," Clements said. "I don't care. What Yemana wants— and what I want too—is an arrest and conviction." He motioned to the wastepaper basket. "That kind of shit? It makes big waves, you know? It's like they say, 'The bigger the lie …' and the only way to deal with it is to prove he's wrong."

Jacobi almost laughed. An arrest and conviction? Jesus Christ, it was a hitchhiker, a thousand to one, and the sonofabitch was in Arizona by now, or—as Resondo preferred—Los Angeles.

"Okay. The power of the press. Some silly scribbler starts making vague accusations in a throwaway newspaper and we start chasing our tails. There's just one thing, though. What if…?"

Clements frowned.

Yeah, the unspeakable, Jacobi thought. What if, in their unseemly rush, they discovered this vicious, premeditated murder was the work of a leading member of Palm Springs' high society?

"Don't complicate it," Clements told him. "Just get us the killer, okay?" He started for the door. "And while you're at it, get rid of that fucking frog."

Spisak went through the whole routine, locking his office door, taking the phone off the hook. The only difference, this time, was that Ivy was in the outer office, wondering what the hell he was doing.

Mallory wondered, too. "If this is to say I told you so, I'll kill you."

"No," Spisak assured him, wishing it was only that. He pulled open his middle drawer, removing what Mallory could see, across the desk, was a Last Will & Testament. "I've got good news and bad news."

Mallory waited.

"First the good news. Bluestone left a will, which I had advised him, on several occasions, as being a wise thing to do. The bad news is that you are the sole heir."

"May I?" Mallory said after a while. He took the will and read it. There were just the two pages of a standard dime-store form. He, Mallory, was being left all of Miguel Patino's land and chattels. Sun Devil Canyon, identified only by its legal description, headed the brief list, which also included the cabin and the pickup truck. "Is this legal?"

"I'm afraid so."

Mallory read it through again, noting that it had been made out the previous June, and that the witness was Millie, the girl he had interrupted in coitus. Well, he had done the lady wrong, he thought. She wasn't only interested in the money.

"I can appreciate that you are hardly jubilant," Spisak was saying. "We, uh, both know what the reaction is going to be." He leaned back, gesturing helplessly. "I just wish there was something I could do."

Mallory looked at him, passing the document back. He hadn't asked, and already he was being turned down. Was that what friends were for?

"I can't," Spisak said.

"Why not?" Mallory demanded, suddenly angry. "You've thirty days to file for probate, haven't you?"

"Legally, yes ..."

"Then sit on it that long."

"I can't."

"Damn you! Why not?"

Spisak made the same helpless gesture. "That's pretty plain, isn't it? In view of the nature of the death ...?"

Yes, it was plain enough, Mallory thought. Spisak was covering his ass. If it ever came to it—and how well do you really know your friends?—he didn't want to be considered an accessory.

"You think I haven't agonized? Two days, I've been sitting on the fucking thing."

And twenty-eight more, that would kill you, would it? Mallory wondered. He still didn't think he was asking so much. Just time, that's all. Give the police a chance to solve the murder, let the dust settle. "Does Ivy know?"

Spisak nodded. "About the will, yes."

"But not what it says?"

"No."

Then the bastard, he ought to sit on it, Mallory thought again. Hadn't he admitted what the reaction would be when the will was made public? Immediately, he, Mallory, would be a suspect in the murder, in the public mind anyway. He, Mallory, would be the storm center of a far worse scandal than before, and that's all it would take for his fellow investors to run for the hills, led by Lois.

"For Christ's sake, understand," Spisak complained. "I've got a reputation too, you know. I've always done what's right, followed my conscience, and this late … ?" His eyes finally met Mallory's. "It's hard to stop now."

Mallory looked at him for a long moment. This late? Spisak seemed to be aging as he watched. Of all the things they'd done together, nothing had been what you could call dishonorable, he thought. Except when it came to ladies.

"Okay," Mallory said. "Let your conscience be your guide." He got up, waiting for the door to be unlocked.

After Mallory left, Spisak called in Ivy, giving her the will.

"Lock this up somewhere, will you?" he asked.

Ivy nodded, returning to the outer office, where she put on her glasses and began reading, still angry that Mallory had seen the will before she had. She was a confidential secretary. There'd never been any secrets.

Spisak came and stood in the doorway. "What do you think?" he asked when she had finished.

"I don't blame you, I guess," she said. Not looking at him, she crossed to the wall safe, working the combination. "Do you want to make up some story?—that we didn't know we had it?"

There was no reply.

"I can say it was my fault," she said. "I misfiled it, not realizing it was a will, it came with a bunch of other papers, and they'll just have to accept…" She turned, his silence like a scream that wouldn't end. "Then what is it you want?"

A little understanding, Spisak thought. "On the way in this morning, I stopped off at the court house. It's already filed for probate."

Her face softened.

"I didn't want him changing my mind. And I also called Jacobi, so he's been duly informed."

"I see."

"Yes, and I also told Williams, *The Desert Sun*'s court reporter, to make sure it comes out in *The Sun* first, not *The Sandbox*. I hate that sonofabitch Chaney—and anyway, there's nothing to hide."

"No..."

"No," Spisak repeated. "You try to hide things, sooner or later, you get found out, and then that only makes it worse. Mallory, he ought to understand that. A grown man. I'm doing him a favor."

Ivy put the will in the safe.

"What are friends for?" Spisak demanded. He went back into his office, closing the door. If he was going to cry, that was his business.

Jacobi stopped his car. There was a lone figure on the canyon floor, working with a small concrete mixer and a pile of stones, building what appeared to be some sort of cairn. Mallory?

It must be, there was no one else around, but it was odd to find him with his shirt off, Jacobi thought. Unskilled labor came at four dollars an hour. Things couldn't be that tough. Yet.

He shrugged—the first of many questions, all to be answered—and eased off the brake. The car started to roll again. The engine wouldn't be needed the rest of the way.

Mallory was leaning on his shovel when Jacobi got to the bottom. The pile of stones had become bricks and the supposed cairn was the beginning of some sort of column.

They had to start somewhere. The post for the first "No Trespassing" sign?

"Hullo," Jacobi called, piling out. "I thought work couldn't get going again until at least tomorrow?"

"It doesn't," Mallory said. He let the shovel fall, picking up his shirt, using it to mop the sweat. "This is the ground-breaking ceremony. I thought..." He smiled, coming forward to shake hands. "I thought it might do me some good. Stuck in an office, a man can rot, you know? What's happened?"

"Nothing."

"Oh? You coming all this way, I was expecting some sort of news."

Jacobi shook his head, looking around the canyon, trying to visualize what Mallory had in mind. Most new desert communities were built and sold in the same way, and he doubted if this one would be any exception.

Phase One. The entrance is the first thing. A wide, ornate, imposing gateway with a boulevard down the middle and palms planted on either side. Then they build the clubhouse and it serves as the sales office where would-be buyers may examine a large model of the development. The model shows everything in infinite detail—all the streets and houses and swimming pools; the golf course, the tennis courts, the "lake," the park, the green zones. Next, they build half a dozen model homes around a cul de sac, varying in appearance, size and cost but somehow having a reassuring sameness about them. These half-dozen homes— along with the scale model and a little imagination—present a pretty fair picture of what is being offered. Finally, flags are put up. brochures are printed, advertisements are placed in the paper and there's a grand opening—a first offering—and if all goes well over the next month or so enough buyers will sign on the dotted line to enable a start on Phase Two.

"Where are you putting the entrance?"

"You're standing in it."

Jacobi couldn't help laughing. The bricks were used and Mallory's workmanship uneven. It reminded him of the old gate at the Mesa.

"Expecting something a bit more grand, were you?"

"Yes."

"Sorry," Mallory said, "but we're keeping it simple, just a country lane. It winds down and comes through here and past an old bell tower that's going to be over there somewhere and that's all. Nothing fancy, except the houses themselves, of course. We'll be setting the standard with the first one." He put his shirt aside, pointing. "Over there—beyond those rock outcroppings?—that's where we're putting the Old Hartford Place."

Jacobi was confused. Was everything going to be old? It sounded as if they were creating instant history.

"You didn't know this was a former estate?"

"No."

"Yes," Mallory said, laughing. "Once a date plantation. St. Pierre's idea, he thinks it will give us tone, but I say he's asking for trouble. They'll be wanting to know why we didn't leave some trees. Then what do we tell them?"

"A date plantation?"

"It sounded better than an orange grove."

"Yes, but this is a little high for dates, isn't it?"

"Maybe that's why Hartford went broke."

Jesus, Jacobi thought. Entrepreneurs. He looked at the rock outcroppings, where Angel's crazy drawings, beautiful in their wild way, didn't square with the newly created history of the place. They couldn't have it both ways.

"What's the fairy-tale behind them?"

"There isn't one. They've got to go."

"Oh?" Jacobi said. "What does ..." He stopped, realizing that was the wrong tense. "Bluestone. I guess he wasn't too happy with that?"

"No. There were some discussions."

Jacobi turned back. "What kind of discussions?"

"Heated ones," Mallory told him, frowning. The conversation had suddenly veered. "What are you doing up here, anyway?"

"Visiting. Is there somewhere we can get out of the sun?"

"There's the shack."

"All right."

Mallory retrieved his shirt, leading the way. He wondered why he felt annoyed, he knew this was coming; it had to, after the will.

"Am I being questioned?"

"Yes."

Inside the shack, Mallory put a pot of water on the stove, getting out the coffee he'd brought with him. There also was milk and bread and meat in the fridge. He'd planned to spend the day.

"You going to read me my rights?"

"You've the right to remain silent," Jacobi told him. He sat backward in a kitchen chair, hooking his cowboy boots in the rungs, knees raised like a grasshopper. Thick fingers removed a notebook and cigar from his jacket's breast pocket. The pages flipped. "The last Friday in October, between ten and midnight ... where were you?"

"Is that when Bluestone was killed?"

"Approximately."

Mallory tried to remember. The Racquet Club party, then back to Lois' place, the lights low and music playing softly, a couple more drinks and they'd have been in each other's arms—except for Theo.

"I was driving around aimlessly because a television set broke down and a seduction went phffft."

"I beg your pardon?"

"I can't account."

Jacobi looked at him, the cigar half unwrapped, the task interrupted. After the hitchhiker, who was in either Arizona or Los Angeles, and who wasn't going to be caught in any event, Mallory was his prime suspect. When Bluestone died, Mallory became a millionaire, and while he might deny it, how could he prove he didn't know the terms of Bluestone's will?

More damning, though, was the fact that until Mallory put the High Desert syndicate together, Bluestone was rich on paper only. It had taken Mallory to turn the paper into cash. Was it merely fate which dictated the cash flow to him so swiftly? Or did he perhaps give fate a push?

"I said I can't account," Mallory told him, too loudly.

Jacobi nodded. He exchanged the cigar for a pen and wrote that in his notebook. And, finally, he thought, there was Mallory's celebrated temper, the violence lurking just below the surface, ready to burst forth at the most modest provocation.

Marion put down the phone. "He's a policeman."

"In cowboy boots?" Bollinger demanded.

Marion joined him at the one-way window, in time to see Jacobi settle into a lounge chair at the swimming pool, the scrollwork boots highly visible and incongruous.

"Apparently," she said.

Bollinger studied Jacobi for a moment, as puzzled by the western garb as the decal on the car, which had been left blocking the driveway.

"What's he want with Chip?"

"I don't know. Harry says Chip left word to let him in, that's all."

"He made an appointment?"

"Apparently."

Bollinger frowned, switching on the patio channel, and the room filled with Jacobi's gravelly voice, sounding oddly apologetic.

"... to talk about girls, if you don't mind."

Marion turned, intending to leave, but Bollinger took hold of her arm, a silent but firm order that she remain.

Chip's voice: "Whatever. I've nothing to hide."

Jacobi (suddenly very official): "All right. This Jody Walsh. I understand you had a relationship with her?"

Chip: "We dated."

Jacobi: "Seriously?"

Chip (after a pause): "That depends on what you mean."

Jacobi: "No, it depends on what you mean."

Chip: "Then I'd say yes, it was serious. Or on my part, anyway."

Jacobi: "But she wasn't ... ?"

Chip: "Apparently not."

Jacobi: "Why do you say that?"

Chip: "Well, as you obviously know, the relationship ... broke up."

Jacobi: "Her idea?"

Chip: "It wasn't mine."

Jacobi: "What about Bluestone?"

Chip (carefully): "What about him?"

Bollinger stiffened. Marion sensed it, embarrassed for him, and for herself, too. Why was she listening?

Jacobi: "I thought it might have been Bluestone's idea."

Chip: "Oh ...?"

Jacobi: "Yes. I'm still not too clear on where your romance ended and his started."

Chip (angrily): "He didn't break us up, if that's what you're suggesting."

Jacobi: "Then what did?"

Chip: "Nothing."

Jacobi: "I see."

Chip (defiantly): "I didn't satisfy her, all right? I didn't satisfy her ... sexually."

Marion reached to turn it off but Bollinger restrained her.

Jacobi: "If it makes you feel any better, Bluestone apparently didn't, either. They dated what—just the two or three times?"

Chip: "Does it matter?"

Jacobi: "That's what I was going to ask you."

Chip: "If I was jealous?" (A long pause) "Shit! What is this? Are you accusing me ...?"

Jacobi: "No, I'm just trying to eliminate you, that's all. Where were you Friday night—between say ten and twelve?"

Chip: "Is that when he was murdered?"

Jacobi: "I asked where you were."

Chip (hesitantly): "Outside her apartment."

Jacobi: "The whole two hours?"

Chip: "Yes."

Jacobi (after a pause): "You were waiting for her, were you?"

Chip: "She was with someone, and I was waiting for him to leave."

Jacobi: "A man?"

Chip: "Yes. He was with her several hours. And I didn't kill him."

Jacobi (thoughtfully): "A girl like that—you can't kill 'em all."

Bollinger turned it off.

In Chip's apartment, waiting for Jacobi to finish his questioning, whereupon he'd have some questions of his own, Bollinger noticed a piece of charred paper in the fireplace. He stooped to retrieve it, angry that the maid wasn't being thorough, and thinking that it was strange to be there at all, it was still far too warm for Chip to be having fires.

Upon closer examination he saw that it was, or had been, a list of names, all of them girls, it seemed. Some were still legible. Franell. Charlotte. Betty Boop (a nickname, apparently?). Norma Flagst ... it ended there.

Bollinger frowned. Flagstaff? Chip had dated a Norma Flagstaff. A nice girl, from a good family, and then there'd been that unfortunate ...

The frown deepening, Bollinger returned the charred paper to the fireplace, in the same position it had been before. Instead of waiting for Chip, he left the apartment immediately, already knowing what he might have to do, but not quite certain as to how he should go about it.

Jacobi found St. Pierre bent over his drawing board in his kitchen workshop at The King Mallory Company. He stood silently watching, feeling as he had upon seeing Mallory at work on the canyon floor, that here was a man building and his job was to tear down.

"Who is it?" St. Pierre asked. He didn't turn around.

"The police."

"The ... police?"

"Homicide," Jacobi said, opening his wallet. He held it up with the badge displayed. "The Riverside County Sheriff's Department."

"Uhhh," St. Pierre breathed, a small moan. "I'm sorry. I thought it was..." Slowly, he twirled on his stool, trying not to laugh, this probably was about Bluestone. "I thought it was in connection with my wife."

Jacobi shook his head, disappointed by the pushed-in face. He had wanted him more handsome. Anybody could fuck some ugly bastard's castaway.

"Good," St. Pierre said. He changed hands with his pencil. "I'm sorry. I didn't get your name."

"Jacobi," Jacobi told him. He pretended not to notice the proffered hand and moved around to examine St. Pierre's work. It was a half-completed drawing of a Spanish mansion. "What have we got here? The Old Hartford Place?"

"Yes. How did you know?"

"I've been talking to Mallory."

"Right. About Bluestone's murder, I suppose. You did say Homicide ... ?"

You fucking know I did, Jacobi thought. He disliked people who asked questions for which they already had answers. There was so much that wasn't known in the constant quest for knowledge. Why would anyone waste questions?

"A nasty thing."

"What?"

"The murder."

"Was it?"

St. Pierre looked at him, wondering what the hell, it was an odd way to start an inquiry, but then he was used to the Mounties, more formal.

"What happened to your eye?"

"My eye ...?"

"Your face, then. It's all cut and bruised. You look like someone's been knocking on you."

Involuntarily, St. Pierre felt his blackened right eye, the only mark he still carried from the one-sided brawl with Bluestone. The other bruises and small cuts had healed. He was fast that way.

"In a fight, were you?"

St. Pierre wondered how he knew. Cleo had been the only witness, and it wasn't something she was liable to report. He'd lost, hadn't he? It was only if he'd won—if an assault and battery charge was possible—that she might go running to the police.

"Well ...?"

St. Pierre hesitated. The next morning, embarrassed—no, mortified—he'd made the usual excuse, it was from a doorknob, and no one had been so impolite as to press him on it. Then, when the news came. Bluestone found shot to death, his battered puss had been completely forgotten and he'd been just as glad and he'd left it that way. Cleo was the only one who knew and she'd never connect the fight and the murder in a million years. She didn't read the papers. She wouldn't even know Bluestone was dead.

He'd forgotten about it—the fight hadn't occurred—and the sleight of mind had been so successful, what better demonstration than this now: when he'd heard the word "police," he'd felt for his wallet. He was guilty of withholding separation payments, yes. But he hadn't shot anyone.

"Something Mallory mentioned," Jacobi said, trying another tack, "was that Bluestone wasn't happy about Angel's rock drawings having to go. He said there were several heated arguments."

He knew, St. Pierre thought. He could see bruises that had gone, cuts that had healed, *and he knew.*

"Were there arguments?"

"Yes."

"Would you characterize them as heated?"

"Yes."

"Did it come to the point where he popped you in the eye?"

"*Yes.*"

"Well." Jacobi said, getting out his notebook, "that wasn't so hard, was it?" The pen came next. "When was this little tiff?"

"Friday afternoon."

Jacobi paused, surprised by that admission. "The day of the murder?"

"Yes, but ..."

"What time?"

Christ, St. Pierre thought. What was this, a confession? "I'm not certain. Four, five o'clock ..."

"Where?"

"Here. Outside. I was working and he came in and I didn't want to argue anymore so I tried to leave and he ... grabbed hold of me."

"Any witnesses?"

"No," St. Pierre said, determined to hold back that much. Bring Cleo into this and he really was in trouble. In her version, he'd be a sore loser, threatening to get even.

"Is that why you didn't report it?"

"Would you?" St. Pierre demanded. Had he been challenged, he'd have admitted she was there, but now the worst was over. "I didn't because it had no bearing and because I don't look for trouble and because I wasn't asked."

Jacobi considered. That seemed reasonable enough. In the same position, he'd be inclined to keep quiet himself. "All right. But how about later? Anyone who can vouch for you then?"

St. Pierre didn't realize he had let go of his pencil until it clattered on the floor. "... when Bluestone was killed?"

Jacobi nodded, bending to get it.

"I'm sorry," St. Pierre said. He took the pencil back, dismayed to see that his hand was shaking. "I don't like being a murder suspect, that's all."

"Nobody does," Jacobi assured him. "Especially when they're guilty." He paused briefly, smiling. "Consider yourself lucky. Can you imagine how the killer feels?"

"No."

"Guilty, probably. This would be between ten and twelve. Where were you then?"

"Desert Hospital. I thought my jaw might be broken and I went to Emergency."

"Why so late? I thought the fight was at four?"

"The pain was becoming worse."

"All right. And who treated you?"

"No one. They were too busy. There'd been an accident."

Jacobi looked up from his notebook. "So you just sat around for two hours?"

"That's right," St. Pierre told him, feeling foolish. Why had he waited so long? "I thought they'd get through."

Jacobi thought for a moment. "There's somebody who saw you, though? Someone who'll say you were there?"

St. Pierre shook his head. No, there wasn't. Not in that carnage.

Jacobi put him down as another prime suspect. He wasn't exactly sure why, except that a man who'd lie about a date plantation, he'd lie about anything.

Carson, the jailer, a fat white turnip who never saw the sun, spent a long time examining the release order and its attached bail receipt.

"Peyser!" he yelled finally.

Peyser looked up from his comic book.

"You want to get Patino? It seems he's going bye-bye."

Peyser nodded and got the keys.

"What's the use of us locking him up?" Carson asked, turning back to Jacobi, "if you're going to bail him out?"

"I want to talk to him," Jacobi explained, polite for the moment. There was some information he wanted. "If that's all right with you ... ?"

Carson jerked and jabbed a fat thumb toward the heavy steel door that Peyser was opening. "You could have talked to him in there."

"Naw," Jacobi said, smiling. "You might not let me out."

Carson stared at him, not denying it.

"I haven't seen the arrest report," Jacobi said. "Do you know what it's all about?"

"The usual. Drunk."

"Yeah, I know the charge. But I was wondering ... were you here when he was booked?"

"No. I was at the President's Prayer Breakfast."

"Did he say anything?" Jacobi asked, keeping his temper with difficulty. "What I'm getting at—some expression of grief—or maybe remorse?—for a relative's untimely death?"

"Oh, you think he might have done that?" Carson said, a question of his own. He brightened perceptibly. "It figures, doesn't it?"

"Did he say anything?" Jacobi repeated.

Carson thought a moment, then shook his head. "Naw. Nothing about Bluestone. But that don't mean he ain't just the type."

Jacobi sighed, thinking Carson was wasted as a jailer, he'd make a good all-round law enforcement officer. And judge and jury, and executioner, too.

"It would be good riddance." Carson said. "There's never any other Calientes in here. It's always the Patinos, they give the band a bad name."

That reminded Jacobi of what else he wanted to ask. "Was he in here Friday night?"

"The night of the murder? No, he wasn't, come to think of it." The pig eyes lit up. "Hey, hey, hey."

Jesus. Jacobi thought. Where did they find them? Or was it the other way around?

The lockup door opened and Peyser pushed Joe Patino out. He looked around unsurely, rubbing his eyes with one hand, holding his pants up with the other.

Carson pulled open a drawer.

"I'll sign," Jacobi offered.

Carson passed him a manila envelope. "He just makes an X."

"Oh, then you can," Jacobi said, smiling. He tore open the envelope and tossed Patino his belt. "Catch … !"

Patino caught it, surprisingly agile, it seemed, but actually it was just practice.

"You remember me?" Jacobi wanted to know.

"Uhhh," Patino grunted, squinting at him. He fumbled the belt through its first slot. "Am I supposed to?"

Jacobi took a pair of doubtful glasses from the envelope and fitted them over Patino's flat nose.

"Oh." There was a smile of recognition. "Yeah, I remember, all right. You kick Angel's ass a lot."

The same, Jacobi thought. He folded the envelope and stuffed it in a jacket pocket.

"You're the one who bailed me out?"

"Yeah."

"How did you know I was here?"

"It's your second home, isn't it? Come on, let's go."

Patino was suddenly suspicious. "Where?"

"Just the fuck out of here," Jacobi told him, aware of Carson and Peyser watching and listening. "Come on."

Patino hung back, fearful now. Impatiently, Jacobi took hold of an arm, dragging him out of the booking room.

"No!" Patino shouted, trying to struggle free. "You got the wrong guy! I didn't do it!"

Jacobi got a better grip, twisting his arm behind his back, steering him by the scruff of the neck, speechless with pain. He marched him out of the station that way, going out the back door.

"Now." Jacobi said. He let go of Patino's arm, swinging him around, grabbing hold of his shirt front instead. "Why are you the wrong guy? You've got proof of that?"

Patino closed his eyes. "I want a lawyer."

Jacobi looked around. There was a big cactus growing against the wall, a bundle of long, sharp knives.

"One last time. Where's your proof?"

"I want a lawyer."

Jacobi grunted, backing Patino toward the wall, pushing him into the cactus as hard as he could. Patino screamed.

"You killed him, didn't you?" Jacobi demanded. "He wouldn't give you any more money, so you argued, shot him?"

"No…"

"You found out about the will? Mallory got everything and you got nothing? That's why?"

"No."

"Then prove it, goddamn you. The night he was killed. Where were you?"

"Me?" Patino sobbed. "When I'm drunk?" He clawed ineffectively at Jacobi's twisting fist. "When I'm drunk…I can't remember."

Jacobi released him. Fuck, he thought, it went on and on, all of them with some cause, however unjust. Where did it end?

Sargent took Jacobi into the back yard, giving him Chaney's normally reserved chair, except that Chaney wasn't coming tonight, Angie didn't want him around anymore.

"Do you want a beer or something...?"

Jacobi shook his head. "No. I'm on duty."

Sargent wondered why that should sound ominous. Though he had missed the name, he'd caught the part about "Detective Sergeant, Homicide," and he knew this visit must have something to do with Bluestone. He just hadn't imagined until this moment that it might have anything to do with him. There could be questions about Bluestone's dealings with Mallory, perhaps, or about his relationships with others in the office, such as Jody and Chip. But nothing—as "on duty" threatened—to do with him.

"This is ... about Bluestone, I take it?"

"Yes," Jacobi said. He fitted himself in the chair, stretching and crossing his legs. "First off, I thought he'd been done in by a hitchhiker, you know? But now I'm not so sure. I've been talking to his friends and associates and asking them all the same question—do you know who'd benefit from having him dead?"

Sargent hesitated. There was Mallory, of course. But if a homicide detective didn't know that by now, there was no helping him.

"Apart from Mallory," Jacobi added, as if reading his mind. "And not necessarily on that scale, either. In my business, there ought to be a saying the opposite to the one about the forest for the trees."

"The obvious gets in the way, does it?"

"Not normally. But when it does, it does. If you know what I mean."

Yes and no, Sargent thought, feeling even more endangered, the question had been too easily dodged. So what had the man really come to ask?

Surely not ...?

Jacobi got out his cigar, which he had been playing with all day, yet to commit to his mouth.

Sargent was suddenly hot and uncomfortable. He took off his new sports jacket, a loud green disaster which Em had presented to him after dinner, saying that if he refused to buy new clothes she'd do it for him, and they'd all look like this, too.

"What brought me to the desert," Sargent said, getting it over with, "was a nervous breakdown, and I probably can't account for my whereabouts at the time of the murder, and to answer your other question—no, I don't know who else would benefit."

Jacobi sighed. To be so inept, he must be tired, he thought. He ought to have called it a day with Patino. "You won't be falsely lulled? Well, you're right. I didn't come to share confidences."

Immediately, he put away the cigar, exchanging it for the telex from Washington. "Cards on the table. St. Pierre, Miss Walsh and yourself, you're all new arrivals, so to speak. So I took the liberty of checking with—what's a good euphemism?—the hometown authorities."

Sargent waited. He wasn't going to admit anything.

"It says here," Jacobi said, getting it unfolded, "that you were a political humorist. You wrote a column for the Washington *Star,* something called 'Play-Doh's Republic.'" He looked up, as if expecting it to be denied, it was that bad. "Which made me suspicious immediately. Anyone who can find humor in politics ... ?"

Sargent still didn't answer.

"Okay," Jacobi told him. "But just correct me when I'm wrong, will you? You had a mental breakdown, and you committed yourself to an institution ..."

"That's wrong."

Jacobi looked up again. "Is it?"

"Yes," Sargent said, wondering how his resolve could have vanished so quickly, but that had always been a sore point. "I was tricked."

"Tricked ...?"

"That's right. You see, I thought my wife was crazy, that it was she who needed treatment, and so when I signed in it was just to demonstrate how easy it would be for her to do so. But then—the bastards—they held me to it."

Jacobi thought for a moment. "That doesn't sound like much of a trick."

"No," Sargent admitted, managing to smile, "and they wouldn't have gotten away with it, either. Except for my condition."

"I see. Then you admit that you were ... well, crackers?"

"I'm afraid I must. It was an open institution, no locks or other restraints, and I spent several days trying to break out, and goddamn if I could."

Jacobi consulted the telex again. "You were only in a week."

"Yes, but I had calmed down by then, and I didn't wish further treatment—or not there, anyway—and so they more or less had to let me go. As I said, it was an open institution."

"They'd have preferred that you stay?"

"Yes. for a while."

"How long?"

"I don't really know. That would depend on my progress, I suppose."

"Or lack of it?" Jacobi demanded. "What I can never understand—how do you people get back on the street before you're well? All right, it was an open institution, but they could transfer you, couldn't they?—to some place that did have locks?"

Oh, God. The typical keeper, Sargent thought. He was too familiar with the attitude to be more than annoyed. "It's an inexact science, but the gamble was warranted, be assured. The crisis had passed. I left reasonably subdued—there'd been a week of heavy sedation, of sleep—and no threat to anyone but myself. When I say I needed further treatment, it was for the impending aftereffect, which is a long, deep depression."

Jacobi snorted. "I still think they had proper cause to detain you."

"I don't know what you've got there," Sargent said, meaning the telex, "but the hospital's records should simply show that I signed out AMA—against medical advice. Is that what it says?"

"No. It says you voluntarily underwent treatment and were released."

"May I see it?"

"No."

"Fuck. And you want my co-operation … ?"

"It might be to your benefit," Jacobi counseled. "With me especially, it's true what they say, 'A little information can be a dangerous thing.' And all I seem to know so far—you were released from the funny farm not fully recovered."

"Which worries you, does it?"

"Frankly, yes. Seeing why you went in."

Jesus, Sargent thought. "Let's hear it."

Jacobi consulted the telex once more. "You were becoming violent, which is not normally your nature."

"Really? Does it give specifics?"

"Yes," Jacobi said, looking around and lowering his voice. "You pushed your wife, knocking her to the floor."

"Does it say she was trying to force her way into my hotel suite?"

"No. It says you had kidnaped your children."

"Does it say it was for their own protection and that I released them immediately?"

"Yes, but it also says you smashed a lot of liquor bottles, and that you tore a telephone out by the roots, and that you threatened to kill the Pope, if, and I quote, 'His Holiness doesn't stop the war in Ireland.'"

"Where did you get that shit?"

"Are you denying it?"

"No, I'm saying it's shit."

"It's your mother-in-law, if you must know," Jacobi said, deciding that it was time to lose his temper. He handed over the telex. "Do you see what she also claims? That you blew twenty-five thousand of somebody else's money buying the life story of Klaus Altmann Barbie, a Nazi fugitive hiding out in Bolivia, intending—through trick wording in the contract—to get exclusive world rights to the *real* Barbie Dolls—Naked Nazi and his Jewish girl friend Naked Nancy?"

Sargent read beyond that to the end. At least there wasn't any mention of his planning to sell the tattoos one number at a time. "So ...?"

"You tell me."

Right, fair enough, Sargent decided. However briefly, he had been Looney Tunes, demonstrating a degree of violence, and—under the present circumstances—the gentleman's question was valid: Did he still get these fits?

"This was a manic high," Sargent explained, handing the telex back. "For whatever reason, I was affected with an excessive enthusiasm. I wanted to do ... well, in the end, *everything*, I suppose. It's hard to explain. I was like a snowball rolling downhill, faster and faster, gathering force and momentum, larger and larger, out of control—except that *I* was going uphill." He paused, remembering. "To the top of the world. Or so I thought, anyway. And it was a marvelous feeling. I was ... gleeful."

Jacobi nodded carefully, wishing again that he had waited till another day. He hadn't come prepared for a lengthy confession. Just a simple yes or no—that's all he wanted.

"You asked," Sargent reminded him, seeing the expression. "I was neglecting my work, directing all my energies, and not a small amount of money, to various grandiose schemes. People became concerned, especially my wife, her mother. They tried to oppose and frustrate me and I got annoyed. So there were scenes—loud, but nothing really desperate, you read that shit—and then a lawyer got involved, and then a doctor, and then, finally, I signed in, okay?"

Jacobi nodded.

"What triggered the mania? I'm not sure, but frustration, I suspect. I've an aunt here—Em, my psychiatrist—and she perhaps has put it best, that all my life I'd been a watcher, not a *do*-er.

So maybe I saved up and exploded? That's one theory, anyway, and another is a chemical imbalance, brought on by what they're not exactly sure, and still another—my own—is that it's a virus. But what you want to know is, has it happened again and have I been quietly rampaging? The answer is no—there are no quiet rampages."

"You're through?" Jacobi asked hopefully.

"Yes."

Thank God, Jacobi thought. He folded the telex, returning it to his pocket, and he got his cigar, biting off the end. "Then I'll be going."

Sargent got up with him, relieved but surprised. "That's all?"

"Yeah. You've already said you couldn't account for the time of the murder, didn't you?"

"I said I *probably* couldn't."

"Oh," Jacobi said, pausing. He took the cigar out of his mouth. "This would be between ten and midnight. Can you account for that period?"

"No."

Jacobi considered briefly. That's what he had wanted, a simple yes or no, but it didn't make the answer any more palatable, another ideal murder suspect, once a nut always a nut, no matter how they pretended otherwise. "Well, I guess you were right, huh?"

Sargent hesitated. "There's an explanation."

Jacobi was waiting. "All right. Let's hear it."

"I was lost."

Aren't we all? Jacobi thought, tipping his Stetson good-bye.

Bollinger took the call on his private line, which only he, not even Marion, answered. He'd been waiting.

"I got it," Lombardi said. "Norma Flagstaff, found murdered in the Paramount Hotel, Culver City, 8 June 1975. And still unsolved."

"Yes. that was the one," Bollinger said. "They've, uh, no idea who did it. I suppose?"

"Naw. Whoever, he got clean away. Too bad, too. I took a look at some of the pictures."

"What do they think was the motive?"

"Jealousy. She was a very pretty girl, and it seems she slept around a lot. so what they figure, somebody got mad."

Bollinger didn't answer.

"Is there anything else I can do for you?" Lombardi asked, mindful of his handsome retainer.

"No," Bollinger decided. "I was just ... inquiring for a friend."

He was staring again.

Like Em before her, Angie watched from a window, wondering if he'd ever really get better. She made sure the children were asleep and then went out into the yard.

"I'm okay," Sargent said, hearing her.

That made it worse. If he was, he wouldn't feel it necessary to reassure her. would he? Even before the question was asked?

Angie took a chair beside him.

"Really, I am," Sargent insisted. "I'd tell you if I wasn't." He got his glass, surprised to find it almost full, the beer tasting warm and flat. How long had it been sitting there? Or, more to the point, how long had he left it there, forgotten?

"Okay," Angie said. "Just as long as we can talk about it. Last time ... we didn't talk."

No. Sargent thought. Just screamed a lot. He put the glass down. The last time? That was a coincidence. When he heard her come out, he'd been thinking of the same thing.

The last time.

Question: Was he drifting into another manic state?

The last time, it had caught him so incredibly off guard. Though others saw the warning signs, he was in it before he knew what was happening, and then it was too late for him to stop. He was gone—and he had to run until he fell.

"What do you want to talk about?"

"How you feel, I guess," Angie said. She took his hand, an unusual initiative.

"I feel fine."

"You're sure?"

"Yes."

"Then why were you staring?"

"I wasn't. I was thinking."

Oh, Angie thought, afraid to ask what about, he got such strange ideas. It was best to talk just in general terms.

"You're not depressed?"

"No."

That's what made him afraid. He ought to be depressed, so much going wrong, but it hadn't gotten him down. He was still up, hanging in there, and the way he felt, whatever came along he could handle it.

A changed man. The Cathedral City caper had been like a tonic for him. He was deeply involved and he was getting rusty tools working again. At long last, his mind was focusing outward, concentrating on new and impersonal challenges, not forever reviewing his own unfathomable past.

Angie let go of his hand. "Okay ..."

"If you're worried," Sargent said, trying to sound casual, "why don't I give you a proxy to vote my shares?"

She looked at him unsurely. "In the High Desert project?"

He nodded, smiling. "What other shares do I have?"

She still didn't understand. "Why?"

"Like I said, if you're worried," he told her. "It's a lot of money, and if you'd feel more secure, making the decisions ...?"

Angie took a moment. "You don't?"

"I feel secure enough to let you," Sargent said.

She was going to protest—part of the therapy, he had to take on obligations—but then she remembered what had brought her outside. He'd been staring again.

"All right. Let's do that, then." She tried to think of some excuse to leave. "Can I get you anything?"

He shook his head. "No. I still have a beer going."

She smiled, the relief showing, which he misunderstood, thinking it was about getting the proxy. He decided it was a good idea. When he was—what did the cop say, crackers?—the main thing that worried her, it became an obsession, was her future security.

The question persisted. If he felt so up, as if he could handle anything they threw at him, Bluestone's murder and the threatening phone calls, and Lois and Suzy and Mary Alice wanting to bail out and now sabotage and a bully-boy cop digging up old garbage ... was he drifting?

Sargent wordered if he ought to phone a doctor and make an appointment. If he had to be put away again, he should go before the harm was done, not afterward.

Jacobi found himself on Dillon Road, which wasn't the way home. How had he strayed? he wondered. It had been a long, hard day. All he wanted to do was fall into bed and die.

Up ahead, a flickering neon sign beckoned, half of the letters missing: *The St r Br t Mot l*

Well, the inner man, perhaps he knew better. Correction: All he wanted to do was fall into bed and get laid and die.

Jacobi smiled and turned into the StarBrite. As always, a light was on in Cleo's unit, showing through the cracks in the drawn blind.

He parked in the last stall where his car wouldn't be visible from the street and walked back and knocked softly.

"Jacobi?" Cleo asked after a moment. There was sleep in her voice, and some gin, too.

"Yeah."

She unlocked the door and let him in, keeping her face averted. "What time is it?"

The first question, always, Jacobi thought. Not how are you, or glad to see you. But she was, though. He was sure of that. "Late."

Her face still averted, she went into the bathroom.

Jacobi sat down, pulling off his boots, looking around. The small, dismal room was also predictable. It never changed.

You'd think she would put a picture up. Something.

"I met your husband today."

The splashing stopped. "Elliott ... ?"

"You remember his name?" Jacobi said. He stood his boots beside the door.

Cleo came out of the bathroom, drying her face. "I thought you said you couldn't help."

"This wasn't on your behalf," Jacobi told her. "It was about a small matter of murder. Tell me truthfully now—do you think he's the killer type?"

Cleo looked at him.

"I'm asking out of personal interest. Nothing to do with the investigation. If he found out about us ... would he be liable to make a fuss?"

Cleo laughed. "Elliott? God, no!"

Jacobi felt himself relax. So, he hadn't come to get laid, either? It was to have that assurance?—a woman who had lived with him, driven him beyond the point of endurance, she would know.

"What brought all this on?"

"I told you—the murder."

"What murder?"

"Bluestone's. Don't you read the paper?"

Cleo put her towel aside. "What are you saying? That Elliott is mixed up in ..." She stopped, unable to go on. A murder?

Christ, she didn't, Jacobi thought. She didn't even read. "No. Or at least I don't think so. If you'd pick up a paper once in a while, you'd know why I haven't been around, I've finally got a case. Come here."

Cleo held back, tightening her housecoat. "Tell me the truth. I want to know. Is he?"

The truth? Jacobi shook his head. Sure, if he had the faintest glimmering. "Listen, all I know, I've got a dead Indian and I'm questioning his business associates and Elliott is one of several, that's all. There's nothing more than that. Okay?"

"An Indian ... ?"

"Yes." Impatiently, he went to her, one huge hand cupping the back of her head, the other untying the housecoat. "Relax, will you? I honestly didn't come to talk."

Cleo surrendered only her body. Her mind was still focused on the word "Indian," which was now taking the form of Bluestone, the name supplied by Jacobi, and now there was Elliott, too: Bluestone's swift fist hammering at him, and finally he was on his hands and knees, dripping blood.

Jacobi moved inside the housecoat, taking a nipple between his fingers, feeling it harden. He could smell the mouthwash on the gin. At first, that had offended him, she always had a buzz on, but now he thought it was to his advantage, it left her without any inhibitions at all. She let him do as he pleased and she did what he asked. And sometimes she took the initiative.

"I saw them fighting."

"Who?"

"Elliott ... and the Indian."

Jacobi released her. How could she have? St. Pierre claimed there were no witnesses.

"Friday afternoon," Cleo said. "In front of the office. I was parked across the street—I wanted to talk to him, you know?— and the Indian boy went in and then they came out together and they were arguing. I ran over—'I've got you now,' I said—and

Elliott tried to go back inside but the boy wouldn't let him. And Elliott slapped me."

"Slapped you?"

"Yes. He knocked me down. That's when the boy grabbed him, and they started fighting, punching each other."

"And...?"

"The boy won. He kept hitting Elliott in the chest, knocking the breath out of him. And Elliott couldn't fight anymore. He just... went down, and he quit."

"What time was this?"

"I don't know. The afternoon."

"Four o'clock?"

"I'm not sure. About then."

Well, she had to be telling the truth, Jacobi decided. St. Pierre told the same story, he just left her out, that's all. He said there were no witnesses. But why?

"After the fight... what happened?"

Nothing, Cleo thought, feeling empty. That was the trouble. The sight of him humbled—down on his knees, bleeding—she had thought that would sustain her, but instead it whetted her hate, it made her want to see him suffer more.

"Was anything said?"

"Yes. Elliott said he'd kill him."

Jacobi wondered. Was that the truth of it? The reason St. Pierre didn't want him to know that Cleo had been present?

"What were his exact words?"

"He said, 'I'll kill you.' He called him a bastard, and then said, 'I'll kill you.'"

Jacobi sat down on the sofa bed. Maybe, he thought. Knocked about, a man might say that, all right. But he didn't trust Cleo in any testimony she might give against St. Pierre. The sole purpose of her life was to drag him down.

"But he didn't do it, though," Cleo said, changing her mind. It didn't make sense to put Elliott in jail. How could she torment him then?—and she would never get her money.

Before Jacobi could move, she clapped her housecoat about his head, captured against her crotch. She heaved, finding his mouth.

"It's me you want," Cleo said, laughing. "The fight gave me the idea. If Bluestone was killed, Elliott would be blamed..."

They fell back on the sofa, entangled. "I shot him—how many times?—and later I went to Elliott, trying to blackmail him, but he's such a bastard, he said ... Ohhhhh!"

Afterward, falling asleep, Jacobi thought maybe she really did it, that would be a clever red herring, a patently false confession, but what would be her motive, the timeless one of revenge?

Another suspect.

CHAPTER TWELVE

Vickers, the Conduit, the man through whom the rich made their wishes known, asked the question very, very seriously. "Are you out of your fucking mind?"

Jacobi just stared at him, thinking that he looked like the stuffed frog he kept on his office desk, except that Vickers was eating a strawberry shortcake ice-cream cone, not playing the mandolin.

"Let me answer for you," Vickers said, deciding to be blunt. "Either you are, which makes it easy, we'll simply have you committed, or else you are stupid, which makes it difficult." Briefly, the washed-out eyes appeared, slits in the folds of flesh. "But not impossible."

Jacobi continued to stare, thinking it was a strange place to be what was it, bribed or threatened? They were at a table in Baskin-Robbins around the corner from the Spa Hotel, where Vickers, to stay alive, lived.

"Are you threatening me?"

"Not I," Vickers said, his frog tongue flicking, "not I."

"Then who is?"

"Who do you think?"

There was only one other choice. The magic name Vickers had mentioned in suggesting it might be helpful if they had a little chat. "Bollinger ... ?"

"You went to his home," Vickers said. "You questioned his son without observing due process. You practically accused him of murder."

Jacobi was going to protest.

"The exact words," Vickers said quickly, cutting him off, "were and I quote, 'A girl like that—you can't kill them all.'"

Had he said that? Something like it, Jacobi thought, very close anyway, but he couldn't swear to it and he wondered how Vickers could. *The exact words.* As remembered by Chip, who had been angry, defiant and—at the end of the questioning— shaken and afraid?

Vickers was waiting. "You deny it?"

"No, I don't deny it," Jacobi said after a while, "and if that's all it takes to make Stu Bollinger crap his pants, he's going to be swimming in a sea of shit before this is over. That spoiled kid of his is a suspect in a murder case and he isn't going to receive any special favors from me. He gets leaned on like all the rest."

"No."

Jacobi frowned. "What do you mean, *no?*"

"No," Vickers repeated. "No, he's not a suspect, and no he's not going to get leaned on."

What the fuck? Jacobi thought, almost laughing. "Listen, Vickers, I appreciate who you are, a big man in the scheme of things, but you aren't telling me how to handle a murder investigation and ..."

"Not I," Vickers said, tongue flicking, "not I."

"Nor Bollinger," Jacobi told him, laughing now, "and as for threatening me, that's a fucking joke. I don't threaten." He stopped, thinking he ought to be angry, but it was too ridiculous for that. "It really doesn't bother me if Stu Bollinger stomps his buckled shoe."

Vickers paused with his ice-cream cone. "He's not threatening you. That was a poor choice of word on my part. Or was it you who used it ... ?" He twisted the cone, not wanting it to drip, trying to think of a better word, more precise, exact. "He's telling you."

Jacobi laughed again. "Is he? Well, like I said, either way, it doesn't bother me, Vickers. You tell him to keep stomping that buckled shoe—and maybe, like Rumplestiltskin, he'll disappear."

There was just a flicker of disappointment in the washed-out eyes. "All right, I'll tell him you said that," Vickers said, popping the last of the cone into his mouth. He sucked it down and found a dollar and left it for a tip. His voice was a whisper. "Have a nice funeral."

Jacobi remained at the table, watching Vickers squeeze past the line at the crowded counter, a fat man who looked like the stuffed frog on his desk, the one people didn't believe was real until you showed them the asshole. Jacobi sat watching and wondering. Was Vickers real?

Vickers went outside and headed back toward the Spa Hotel.

Jacobi sat thinking. After a moment, he got up, following him out. He caught up at the corner.

"Listen," Jacobi said, grabbing Vickers' arm.

"If you have any apologies," Vickers said, pushing the button for the pedestrian crossing, "I'd make them to Mr. Bollinger personally, and instead of driving over, I'd crawl."

"You think you're ... ?"

"Pregnant," Dex said again, louder this time.

Suzy sat down, feeling as if she'd been punched in the stomach. For a long moment, she couldn't speak. She just sat there, blaming herself.

"How long has it been?" she asked then.

"Two weeks."

Suzy tried to think. Dex's periods were very regular. A day or so off. That's all.

"Almost three," Dex said, not permitting any escape.

"Well," Suzy breathed, "you ought to see a doctor then, shouldn't you? There's a simple urine test. He'll have the results in a few hours." Finally, she looked up, the question barely audible, because she was accusing herself. "It ... *is* Milo?"

"Yes, of course," Dex told her. "It's who you wanted, isn't it?"

Suzy shook her head. "No."

"It's what you said, that you'd rather have me sleeping with him than going out with a nobody."

"No!"

"That's funny," Dex said, staring her down. "I could have sworn ..." Abruptly, she turned away, leaving the living room.

Suzy called after her. "Dex! It was said in anger. You know I didn't ..."

The bathroom door slammed on her words.

"... mean it," Suzy finished, knowing she was lying. She had meant it. Dex was her Golden Girl. When she took a man, he'd have to be someone special, from a good family, well off and social, and ... *damn!*

"Dex," Suzy said outside the bathroom door, "you're trying to punish me, and that's not fair. I've only wanted what is best for you. And if you're going to sleep with a boy, if you think you're old enough and that's what you want to do, there are precautions you can take."

There was no answer.

"Dex! You're trying to punish me. *There are precautions!*"

Finally, the door opened, and Dex handed Suzy a glass, half full of yellow liquid.

"It's piss, Mother," Dex told her, "and you can have it analyzed, because I'm late for school."

Joe Patino went to The King Mallory Company with a copy of *The Desert Sun* stuffed under his shirt, hiding it like a secret, as if no one else read. He was inside before Sargent could lock the door.

"I want to see Mallory." he announced, weaving drunkenly. "Tell him…" He staggered, almost falling, grabbing a desk for support. "Tell him his partner is here."

Sargent tried to turn him around. "Come on, out you go, you're drunk."

"Sure," Patino said, twisting away. "I'm always drunk. Why not?" He made it to a swivel chair, collapsing. "You tell him to come here. We've got some talking to do."

"He's not seeing you in that condition."

Patino laughed, throwing back his head. "Mallory!" he shouted. "You fucking sonofabitch, you're not screwing Joe Patino, you hear me, *Mallory!*"

Lois came out of Mallory's office, her face gray. "What in the world is going on here?" she demanded.

Sargent shrugged helplessly. "All I know is he wants to see Mallory."

"Yes," Lois said stiffly. "I heard." She looked at Patino, shaking her head in disgust. "King? Do you want to take care of this… creature?"

Mallory appeared behind her. "Who is it? Joe?"

"You're fucking right it's Joe," Patino told him. "Now we're partners, we're on a first-name basis, hunh? I can call you King?"

Lois shuddered. "Get rid of him."

"Hey, a softer fuck, please," Mallory said. He moved around Lois. "Jesus. It's barely noon. How can you be blind this early?"

Patino pulled the newspaper from under his shirt, opening it up, showing the headline. "I'm not blind."

No, Mallory thought, stopping abruptly. Nobody was, unfortunately. Neither bankers nor friends, neither angels nor drunks. He'd just had it out with Lois, one more time, and now Joe Patino?

"What's the matter?" Mallory asked tiredly. "Are you embarrassed, too?"

"I want a piece," Patino told him.

"What?"

"A piece," Patino repeated. "What it says here, Bluestone left you all his money, and I don't get anything?"

Mallory didn't answer. Too busy with his own problems, he hadn't even thought of Patino, had forgotten he existed. And yet he was related, wasn't he? He had a claim.

"I'm blood!" Patino shouted. "You fucking bastard, you better give me some, Mallory. You give me some ... or else!"

Maybe, Mallory thought. Later, when it was settled, if it ever was settled, maybe he would give the poor drunken bastard something.

"King, *please*," Lois said shrilly. "Get him out of here."

"No," Patino told her. "Old Joe, he's not going anywhere." He looked at Mallory, rocking in the chair, suddenly sly. "How much is it worth, I don't cause you trouble, partner? What I was thinking, if I went to court, filed a suit, challenged the will ... ?"

Mallory almost laughed. "I was thinking of doing that myself."

Patino missed the joke. "Naw. You don't want to do that. Lawyers? Fighting ...? Listen, I'm drunk, you can take advantage of me, let's just figure it out and shake hands here. We'll do it right now—an out-of-court settlement."

"No thanks," Mallory said, changing his mind, wondering why there'd been that moment of charity, he wasn't getting any himself these days. "You'd only piss it away, and besides, when I start getting charitable, I'll pick my own causes." He made a motion. "Move it."

"No. I'm staying. We make a settlement now."

Mallory opened the office door, wedging it, and then went back to Patino, swinging him around in the swivel chair.

Patino clutched the arms. "No! I'm staying!"

Mallory ran with him, rushing the chair across the floor, bumping it over the threshold. Screaming, Patino pitched out, sprawling headlong down the stairs.

Sargent stood watching, unable to react, frozen. This was the one thing he still couldn't handle. Scenes.

After a moment, Mallory went out, ostensibly to see if Patino was still alive, but actually to retrieve the chair.

Patino moaned. "You bastard. You fucking ... *bastard!*"

Mallory decided he was all right. He brought the chair back inside and locked the door.

Sargent finally found his voice. "He's not hurt ...?"

Mallory ignored him, looking at Lois, wondering if she was satisfied.

Lois looked away. "It doesn't solve anything, does it?"

No, Mallory decided. It didn't. He went back to his office, locking that door, too.

Outside, Joe Patino struggled to his feet. He wanted to fight, but he couldn't, he was too drunk. He raised a fist, shaking it at the faces behind the glass, a last act of defiance, letting Mallory know that he wasn't beaten, that Sun Devil Canyon rightfully belonged to him and that he was going to prove his claim. He was blood.

Jacobi drove up onto the top of the dump, passing a shack patched together out of discards, following the red arrows pointing to the disposal area. There was a bulldozer working there and a couple of old trucks backed into the mess with Chicanos unloading them. And farther down the line, as promised, Bollinger's new Chevy Blazer.

Should I start crawling now? Jacobi wondered.

As if in answer, Bollinger rose up from behind the cab, looking strangely out of place despite the overalls and the armful of trash, instantly recognizable as a board chairman slumming. He paused, nodding slightly, then dumped his burden over the side, sending up a puff of dust.

Jacobi parked his car farther down the line and got out and walked back.

The stench of garbage was thick in his nostrils. An unlikely place for a billionaire to suggest for a meeting, which was exactly why Bollinger had proposed it. Jacobi thought. If he ever had to testify to it, who would believe him?

Briefly, he regretted not having a witness at a discreet distance, but this was a personal, not a police, problem. He knew his fellow officers too well to trust them with the care and protection of his precious hide. He'd do a better job of it. And he always worked best alone.

The whole idea was ridiculous, absurd, but if it ever did come to the point where he thought Bollinger seriously intended to have him killed, he'd waste the sonofabitch first. So he was like his adversary in that respect. He preferred to keep this just between the two of them.

"Well," Bollinger said, staring down at him from the Blazer's bed. "it's not Lord Fletcher's, but at least we can talk privately." He bent for another armful of trash. "Want to lend a hand?"

Jacobi, who had never met him before, he didn't keep that kind of company, shook his head no, annoyed that Bollinger should be so perfectly cast, representing exactly what he was.

"Suit yourself."

Rich. Jacobi thought, watching the trash spill at his feet, and cultured and distinguished, and powerful...which made him dangerous.

"Now, what's this about a misunderstanding?" Bollinger asked, the question coming out of the puff of dust.

"First, let's make sure we have one," Jacobi suggested, the answer he'd rehearsed. "Sometimes, working through intermediaries, things can be misinterpreted. So that's why I wanted to talk to you personally. I thought if I explained exactly what I'm doing, and if I answered any questions you might have, then your concern might be alleviated, in which case there wouldn't be any misunderstanding."

Bollinger got another armful of trash. He stood holding it. "I'll make it easy for you. Is Chip a suspect in Bluestone's murder or not?"

"Yes and no," Jacobi said, which had also been rehearsed.

"What's that supposed to mean?"

"Maybe, maybe not. What I know so far—Bluestone took his girl, and the night of the murder, he can't account for himself."

Bollinger frowned. "Took his girl? You mean Jody?"

"Yes. Chip denies it, he says they broke up first, that Bluestone just got her on the rebound, but I've got too many people who tell it otherwise, including Jody."

Bollinger's expression hadn't changed. He was still frowning. "I'd be inclined to believe Chip. He had a lot to offer the girl. And what was she going to get from some Indian?"

Jacobi took the precaution of backing off a bit further. "A proper fuck, apparently."

There was no show of anger, but the frown remained, deepening. "You're suggesting Chip couldn't give her one?"

"That's what she says."

"Oh? And what does Chip say?"

"He admits it. The one thing they agree on. He couldn't satisfy her sexually."

Bollinger considered. "It sounds like they're having a good fight."

Jacobi shrugged. He wasn't going to argue, just state his case, that's all.

"He never had any trouble before," Bollinger said, making it sound like a complaint.

"Maybe this one's different."

"Why should she be?" Still frowning, Bollinger opened his arms where he stood, half the load falling back into the truck. "What the hell does she want?"

"I've told you."

"Yes," Bollinger said, as if finally accepting it. He clambered out of the Blazer. The frown persisted, and the edge of complaint in his voice, too. "This is the first I'd heard…"

"I'm sorry."

"No, don't be," he said quickly. "I expect you to be frank. That's why you're here." He pulled the zipper on the overalls, revealing a golf shirt beneath it, his initials embroidered on the pocket, SB. "If I don't know, I can't help, can I?"

"I guess not."

"I can't," Bollinger said, preferring that answer. He pulled the Blazer's door open and eased up onto the seat, sitting sideways against the wheel, facing out at Jacobi, left standing in the sun.

Jacobi waited, disturbed that Bollinger's sole concern, thus far, was the slur against Chip's sexual prowess. How about the boy's lack of an alibi? Maybe, Jacobi thought, Bollinger didn't see that as a problem, or at least not one that couldn't be solved.

Bollinger caught his breath, not used to the physical exertion. His only exercise was golf and an occasional game of tennis in which the ball by unstated agreement was hit to him.

"The odd thing," he mused, "I got those two together. Introduced them at a party. I thought…" He shrugged, almost smiling. "She seemed like a nice enough girl."

"She is," Jacobi assured him.

"Oh? You made her sound … well, like a tramp."

"Not by today's standards. She may sleep around, but she's kept her amateur standing."

"Still, if there were other men …?"

"Not at the time," Jacobi said. "At the time, there was just Bluestone and Jody was using him both ways, to get off and to maybe build a fire under Chip. It seems she still had hopes."

Bollinger's frown was back. He started to say something and then changed his mind.

"The thing is," Jacobi said, "whatever the truth of the matter, it looks bad. All right, maybe Bluestone didn't break up the romance, but it looked that way to the others in the office. Bluestone, he'd been sniffing around Jody for quite awhile—and so what are people supposed to think? They see Jody on Chip's arm one day and the next day she's on Bluestone's? Hell, what would you think?"

Bollinger waved that off. He wanted it over with.

"And the other thing," Jacobi said, obliging, "no matter how Chip rationalizes his actions now, he was jealous and he showed it. Everybody in the office tells the same story. He was jealous—and he was hurt and angry."

"Did they fight?"

"No, nothing like that. It was the situation more than any one incident. Two roosters with one hen, and Bluestone, unfortunately, doing all the crowing."

"Chip didn't threaten him?"

"No, he didn't."

"Well," Bollinger decided, looking relieved. "It doesn't sound like you've got much of a case."

"I'm not building a case," Jacobi told him. "Yet ..." Purposely, he let the suggestion hang, dangling like bait.

The frown was suddenly back. "You're suggesting you might?"

"Yes and no," Jacobi said, the answer he'd rehearsed. "If further information comes to light, I could be obliged to, down the line." He paused, letting that dangle, too. "You see, as much as I'd like to reassure you, I've nothing yet that says Chip didn't do it, or what would be just as good, proof that somebody else did. It's an open case, subject to further investigation, and any of the principals who can't account for their whereabouts ... well, they remain vulnerable, that's all."

"Vulnerable?"

"Subject to further questioning," Jacobi corrected, thinking Bollinger had seized upon the word. He didn't like the way things were going. "Chip says he spent the night of the murder sitting in his car outside Jody's apartment. I'd prefer he was whacking off behind the barn, just as long as someone saw him."

Bollinger snorted. "That part doesn't bother me. Friday night? If called upon, I couldn't account for my whereabouts either, but that doesn't make me vulnerable."

All right, Jacobi thought, he'd used the wrong word, and he was sorry and if necessary he'd apologize. He had the distinct impression that he was, suddenly, the fuckee.

"But Chip is?" Bollinger persisted. "He had a motive, jealousy, and if further information comes to light ...?"

Jacobi turned and walked away. The sonofabitch, he was the one who was so goddamn stupid.

Bollinger got the Blazer started, swinging around and driving after him, shouting as he came up alongside. "How much do you want?"

Jacobi didn't answer. He kept walking toward his car.

"How much?"

Jacobi climbed up into the mountain of garbage where Bollinger couldn't follow in the Blazer. The recorder had to be in the cab, he decided, and Bollinger had got a bit on him, but not enough. There had been just a suggestion: "*I'm not building a case. Yet ...*"

Bollinger got out of the Blazer, starting up after Jacobi, who by now was almost at the top. Down the line, the dozer operator was waving them off, thinking they were scavengers.

Bollinger finally made it to the top. stopping to get his breath. "All right. We'll talk private."

Jacobi merely nodded. He wasn't taking any chances.

"What I think," Bollinger said, looking at the dozer operator, "is that you've got a good thing going, Deputy. A murder you can't solve and a rich kid you can pin it on. What do you think?"

Again, Jacobi didn't reply, shrugging instead.

"At least admit it's tempting," Bollinger told him, "and that it might be fairly easy, too. Say you found the murder weapon, and then you arranged to find it again, only this time among Chip's possessions? That's all it would take to put him away. There'd just be one question. How much would Daddy be willing to pay?"

Bollinger glanced at the dozer operator, who had stopped his machine now, getting off and coming over. "The answer, if that's what you came up here to find out, the answer is *anything*. Deputy. He's my son, my only son, and I'll pay any price to protect him. so just tell me how much, that's all. Tell me your price—and I'll willingly pay it."

Jacobi shrugged once more, smiling faintly now, aware of Bollinger's growing desperation.

"All right," Bollinger said, the smile deciding him, "I said any price, and I meant it. I'd prefer to buy you, but if you'd rather be killed, that's your choice."

"Kill me?" Jacobi said, the words out before he could stop them. Was the man mad? "You're threatening to kill me … unless I stop investigating your son?"

"You heard me," Bollinger told him. "I don't care if Chip's guilty, find someone else to pin it on, frame them and make it stick. You've ample candidates. Cleo, for instance, a worthless drunk, who'd miss her. or that nut case, Sargent? Pick any of the several and do it and do it right." He paused for just a moment, his voice flat, emotionless. "If you do, you're rich, and if you don't, you're dead."

"You're serious …?"

"Yes."

Jacobi almost laughed despite himself. The man had to be mad. "Mr. Bollinger, I'm sorry, but if the evidence supports a charge against Chip, he'll be arrested and arraigned, and neither you nor all your money will be able to slow or stop the process."

"You're wrong," Bollinger said softly. "I've millions, hundreds of millions, and it's the kind of money that can buy anybody. Sheriffs, district attorneys, judges …" He glanced at the approaching dozer operator and then turned back. "Hell, given the right circumstances, it can buy a governor, a President. And you're saying it can't buy you?"

Jacobi still wanted to laugh. "Mr. Bollinger, I'm sorry, but that's exactly what I'm saying."

"Then you're dead, Deputy," Bollinger told him. He turned and started back down.

The dozer operator, flushed with anger, was waiting at the bottom, prepared to ream him out, but he changed his mind when he got a closer look. Bollinger was somebody special even slopping through grabage. He moved aside and let him pass.

Bollinger swung aboard the Blazer, starting it up, spinning away. The dust climbed in his wake.

Jacobi stood watching, unable to believe what he had heard, he could put the crazy sonofabitch away. He let him clear the disposal area and then started down himself.

The dozer operator thought he ought to say something. They weren't supposed to be up there, scavenging or not. "You lose something?" he asked.

Jacobi didn't answer. He got in his car, sliding behind the wheel, stripping the tape recorder from beneath his shirt. He ran the tape back and turned up the volume and punched the play button.

There was nothing on it. Not even static.

Yeah, Jacobi thought, turning around slowly, looking at the climbing dust. He'd lost something, all right. His virginity.

Lois took the corner too fast, the Rolls rocking perilously, tires squealing. For an awful instant, she thought it was going to overturn, but the car righted itself and somehow remained in the proper lane. She slowed immediately.

What was she trying to do, kill herself? For another awful instant, that loomed as an alternative to breaking with Mallory, which was going to happen if he didn't abandon High Desert.

Murder and business didn't mix, not in Palm Springs. *The Desert Sun* had played it down, but the story was still the talk of the town, a different version under every hair dryer, and across every cocktail glass, too. That was the trouble with people who didn't have enough to keep them occupied. They talked.

Mavis, for instance, saying she knew there was going to be trouble the day Mary Alice came home married to a Mexican, and how could she, Lois, lower herself to be associated, but then business was business, wasn't it? And the shark's smile as she walked away. Mavis had never walked away before. She wouldn't dare.

Business was business. What was that supposed to mean? That she'd do anything for a buck? And what was anything?

Lois shuddered. Pinny Donaldson, one of her best friends, had seriously asked if she needed the money, wouldn't it be better not to be involved, and Marie Farris, who used to be a friend, had suggested she might not want to come to her party, there was so much gossip she didn't want her, Lois, embarrassed. She'd tried to make it sound as if the concern was only for her, but that wasn't it, of course. Marie's first concern was for herself and she was very selective in whom she invited to her parties and no matter how she tried to make it sound the invitation had been withdrawn.

Unbelievably, it had been withdrawn. Wagging tongues were creating a scandal and destroying her socially. Mallory had to choose. High Desert or her.

He had to *understand.*

He would, she decided, composing herself, and she put all thought of self-destruction out of her mind. She wasn't that kind of a woman. She was strong and she knew what she wanted and she was also intelligent enough to know that if she didn't get it, it wasn't the end of the world.

Later, knocking on Mallory's door, the fingers of the ever-present white gloves flapping in her fist, she was still trying to imbed that idea in a deep dark recess where it couldn't be pried out. It wasn't the end of the world.

Mallory answered wearing a scruffy bathrobe and that's all. He wasn't expecting company. Especially not her.

"Oh," he said, wishing he'd used the peekhole. The door was wide open and it was too late to dematerialize. "It's you."

"Yes." She waited to be invited in.

Mallory stood looking at her. A nice, solid, well-preserved woman, faultlessly dressed and groomed, pleasant if not beautiful, intelligent if not wise. And all he saw was trouble.

"May I...?"

"Of course," Mallory said, getting out of the way.

She smiled and entered, looking around apprehensively. It was her first time in the apartment, which he had moved into without consulting her, another sore point.

"So...this is it?"

Mallory merely nodded, thinking that wasn't something he could argue, and he wasn't going to apologize, either. He closed the door, first tightening his robe, glancing both ways down the hall. When he turned back, she was examining the picture over the fireplace.

Everybody did. It was massive, too large to ignore, a line drawing in a thin black frame, a naked lady in repose. She was on her back, legs crossed at the knee, a martini in one hand, cigarette hanging from her mouth, and her vagina was a motel door with a picturesque canopy. A miniature taxi was parked out front. A miniature gentleman was walking away from it, headed for the motel door, a raincoat over his arm, carrying a suitcase, giving the impression that he'd be staying awhile.

"Mmmmm," Lois said, moving on to a smaller picture.

Two hands clasped, the fingers entangled, or rather that was the impression from a distance. Upon closer inspection, the hands became bodies, the fingers limbs. A deformed couple. Copulating.

"They came with the place," Mallory explained.

"I hope so," Lois told him, afraid to look further. She found a chair and perched on it and got out her cigarettes. "You don't mind me dropping by? I thought..." Belatedly, he took the proffered lighter. "I thought, since you wouldn't come to me, that I had better come to you."

Mallory lit her cigarette.

"And ask you, what's wrong?" Lois finished, exhaling.

"I don't summons," Mallory said. He felt the weight of the lighter, then dropped it into her open bag.

She looked at him. "It was hardly a summons."

"It sounded like it."

"Well, I'm sorry..."

"And it was," Mallory complained, deciding not to let her off. He could remember the exact words: "I think we'd better have a talk. When can you get here?"

"All right, then. But I didn't mean it that way."

He still wasn't satisfied. "You seem to have gotten the idea that I work for you, and I don't. We've a partnership."

"I understand."

"I hope so. I don't mind working with people, but not for them."

"All right."

Yes, that's what you keep saying, Mallory thought, but it wasn't all right. He sat down, wanting to tell her to leave. "Anyway, you're here."

Lois smoked her cigarette. Her face was flushed, partly from the drinks, she'd had two before leaving home, but mostly because he was being impossible. Her whole world was at stake—and he was worried about business decorum?

"I don't want to be involved," she said finally.

"In what?"

"A scandal."

Mallory suppressed a sigh. That again? Of course she didn't. No one did. But how *not* to be involved, damn it?

"And I'm not going to be, either," she said. "It's what I came to tell you. I want the High Desert project stopped. Completely ... or else."

Mallory closed his eyes, squeezing the bridge of his nose between thumb and middle finger, trying to blot out one annoyance with another, a practice derived from the vet who came to the ranch when he was a boy. Old Mac had a twitch—a loop of chain on a stick—and he would put a horse's ear in it and twist a couple of times.

Referred pain. "The horse's ear, it hurt so much," Mac had advised, grinning through yellow teeth, "he don't care if you stick a thumb in his eye."

"Did you hear me?" Lois demanded. "I want High Desert stopped, shut down completely, and I don't want any further involvement with Cathedral City, either. If Stu Bollinger wants the stupid place, let him buy it himself. I'm not doing his dirty work for him."

"We've discussed this before," Mallory said, trying to be patient. "High Desert is going ahead, it's not your decision. And as to Cathedral City, we've got an agreement with him, that we're to act as his agents, and there is quite a sum of money involved ..."

She screamed at him. "I said ... *or else!*"

Reluctantly, he opened his eyes, taking his hand away from his face. He looked at her for a long moment, feeling more disappointed than angry. "Or else what?"

"You'll have to resign."

He took another moment. "From the company, you mean?"

"Yes. I own it, don't I? Or is that also a syndicate decision?"

"No, it's your company." he said, laughing briefly and stupidly. "You can do what you want there." He stood up with an effort, still looking at her. but seeing a stranger. "Very well. You have my resignation. But that doesn't stop High Desert."

"No." she admitted. "I'm sure you'll persist, somehow." She got her purse, stubbing out her cigarette, making it look like an execution. "But not with my money."

The vehemence disturbed him. "It might not be that easy to divest," he warned.

"Oh? You're going to fight me on that, too?"

"Well, your shares aren't bonds, you can't just turn them in, and I don't know that you're going to find a ready buyer."

Lois hesitated, thinking it was criminal how little she knew. Jock did all the business, everything, and when he died, the men he had appointed took over, accountants, brokers and lawyers, and they did everything. She didn't even know how to clip a coupon.

"Then I'll talk to my lawyers." she decided, getting her purse and gloves. "And this time I'll listen to them." She got up, finally meeting his eyes, seeing how he liked that. Pelican, the young man assigned to her at Gregory and Brace, had strongly advised against the real estate firm, and she hadn't even consulted him on buying the High Desert shares. She'd used her mad money. "You'll be getting a call."

Mallory didn't answer. This was silly. Lawyers … ?

"And." Lois reminded him, sensing victory, "you owe me some money, which I want paid back."

He still didn't answer.

"Now, if you don't mind."

"You'll get it," Mallory promised, finally finding his voice, "but it will take a few days. I'll have to arrange a loan. I … I'm sorry."

Lois looked at him, the pained, bewildered expression. Was he? "Damn you." she said, the tears starting.

Mallory turned away. Jesus, he thought. So that was it, after all? And here it comes.

"I love you."

"Sure."

"I do," Lois said, sobbing. "I always have. From the first day." The rest was an accusation. "Before Cissy."

Mallory stood rooted. Don't be ridiculous, that's what he had intended to say. the answer he had formulated weeks before, which he had practiced, but now the words wouldn't form. No one wanted to be ridiculous. He didn't, and she wasn't.

"I don't know," he began. "I've tried to be honest. Lately. I've felt the same stirrings, I guess, but I wanted to be sure." He slowly turned to face her. "And I didn't want to be bought, damn it. I'm not a car or some chest of drawers, Mrs. Sills. I'm a man—and I'm not for sale."

The last was all that registered.

"All right," she told him, putting her handkerchief away. "Offer withdrawn." And she meant it. She didn't want him, couldn't accept him. if he came tainted by another scandal, if it meant destroying the whole way of life she had established for herself.

Face wet with tears, she turned and ran, struggling with the door but getting it open, plunging down the hall and into the night and out of his life.

Mallory went to close the door. One of her gloves was on the threshold. He stooped, picking it up, putting it in his bathrobe pocket. He held it there, suddenly very lonely.

Jacobi got his phone, dialing direct to Los Angeles, the LAPD's Public Information Division.

"Chaplin," somebody said.

"Listen," Jacobi told him, "I'm a member of the Writers Guild, I'm doing a TV script, a cop's got a tape recorder stuck under his shirt, so he can secretly record a suspect's conversation."

"Yeah...?"

"Okay, so what I want to know, is there any way the suspect can prevent that tape from recording, say electronically, or with a dose of radiation?"

"No."

"You're sure? I want to be authentic, you know?"

"Positive."

"Okay, then could he erase it afterward?"

"Well, it's done by a magnet."

"Yeah, I know how it's usually done, but can the suspect do it, from a distance, not physically touching the machine?"

"No."

"You're sure?"

"Just a minute. I'll talk to my boss."

Jacobi waited, listening to a muffled conversation.

"No way," he told him. "It can't be done."

"I was thinking," Jacobi said, "you hear about those X-ray inspections at airport terminals, film getting exposed—do you think it could be something like that?"

"No. Not with tape. There's no way we know of how it could be done."

Jacobi hung up, looking at his tape recorder, thinking there *was* a way, goddamn it. Bollinger had done it to him. He stared at the ceiling for a while, uncomfortably aware of all the corpses in the desert up at Yucca, the rotted corpses of all the smart guys, big and small, who didn't believe it when a man with a lot of money said all he had to do was pick up a telephone.

Frowning, he placed another call, this time to Phil Grady, a district attorney with the Organized Crime Unit in Orange County, figuring he could take the chance. Grady owed him a couple of favors. And he wasn't the kind who talked.

"Grady," Grady said.

"Phil, it's me," Jacobi told him. "Question: I'm secretly taping a suspect, from maybe two, three feet. Is there any way he can fuck my tape so I can't record him?"

"No."

"Is there any way he can erase after I record?"

"From the same distance? No."

"You're sure? No equipment you're aware of that will do it?"

"None whatsoever that I know of at all. You got a problem?"

"Two of them."

"Want to tell me about them?"

"No, but thanks anyway," Jacobi said, not inclined to take it any further, or to check with higher echelons. It was the boys on the street who used the stuff. "I'll see you around."

Worried now, he hung up, thinking that he wasn't ever going to solve the mystery, and it wasn't what was really bothering him anyway.

There were other matters more pressing. Such as what Bollinger had on his tape. How to erase *that*? If it was anyone else, Jacobi mused, he'd just drop around, kick his ass real good, take his tape recorder away from him and, like Richard Nixon was alleged to have done, push the erase button.

But Bollinger wasn't just anyone, and he was coming on very, very strong. He'd taken the trouble to find out about Cleo, a likely candidate for a frame-up, as was Sargent. And he hadn't minced any words when he said he wanted it done: Lay off Chip, find another killer, or else. Frame someone, and if he didn't, he, Jacobi, was dead.

Idle threat?

Maybe, maybe not. The man had power—he could buy a President, he said. And he had some sophisticated stuff—one of the ways he made his fortune?—that even Grady didn't know about. But the main thing, what made him worrisome, was all that money.

Jacobi stared at the ceiling, thinking of the corpses up at Yucca, smart guys, big and small, cops among them, who didn't believe it when a man with a lot of money said all he had to do was pick up the telephone.

There was a knock on the motel door.

Cleo stirred, sleepy drunk, she'd been waiting for him, all her inhibitions gone.

"Jacobi … ?"

The door rattled.

Sighing, Cleo slipped out of bed, switching off the light and feeling her way in the dark, taking the chain off and turning the knob until the latch released. She kept her face averted.

"You're late," she whispered, not complaining, she was happy to have him whenever he wanted her. She touched his arm, a promise, and went into the bathroom, still feeling her way, she didn't want him seeing her mussed up.

In the bathroom, she kept the light off, not wanting to see herself, either. She brushed her teeth and swirled with mouthwash. He didn't mind her drinking, he liked her with a buzz on, he said, but he'd also remarked about her smelling like a gin mill, so she always was very careful about not offending him with her breath.

They loved by touch, seeing only shadows, the smells not their own. By touch … and sounds.

She came out of the bathroom, opening her housecoat and letting it fall, dropping back onto the bed with her legs open and waiting.

She raised a hand. "Where are you …?"

Like a gift, something was pressed into her open palm, small, round and hard. She closed her fingers around it, wondering what it could be, and then, too late, she felt other fingers at her throat.

"Ja …!" she screamed, a death gurgle.

CHAPTER THIRTEEN

Trabish, the owner of the StarBrite, thought something was suspicious when he went out to clean the swimming pool. Cleo's door was partly open, which was unusual, she normally slept until noon at least, unless Jacobi came around to saw off a piece.

He'd better check, Trabish decided. Jacobi's car wasn't about and he hadn't heard it come in the night. A light sleeper, he knew the regulars. Flying Phil, who came to see Jason, every Tuesday and Friday, and Pender Cabs, which came all the time, taking Doreen on her appointed rounds.

Trabish put his skimmer down and went around the pool and called softly at the open door. "Mrs. St. Pierre...?"

There was no answer. He looked inside, knowing immediately that she was dead, a broken doll on the rumpled sofa bed, staring blindly and her neck askew.

"Awww," Trabish said, backing off. He waited a moment, making sure he was all right, he had a heart condition, and then he ran for the office. He couldn't figure how it had happened. He was a light sleeper—and he hadn't heard a thing.

Jacobi parked in the street. There was an ambulance in the StarBrite's lot, backed in at an awkward angle, blocking the entrance.

Trabish met him on the sidewalk. "I tried to get hold of you first."

"That's okay," Jacobi told him, not stopping. He went around to the rear of the ambulance, where the attendants were lifting Cleo inside, a lump under a gray blanket.

They paused, recognizing him.

Lieutenant Jerry Sung, Jacobi's equivalent on the Palm Springs Police Department, came over and stood in the way, shaking his head no.

"Okay," Jacobi said again.

The attendants gave the stretcher a final shove and closed the doors on it. They looked at Jacobi, uncertain as to what was appropriate and deciding it would be best to say nothing. They separated, heading up front on opposite sides, disappearing into the cab.

Sung made a coughing sound. "I'm, uh, sorry."

"It's okay," Jacobi said, the last time. He stood watching the ambulance leave, lights flashing incongruously.

"You feel like talking?"

"Sure."

Kessler, a homicide detective, came out of Cleo's unit, followed by Quigley, the medical examiner.

"You guys can go now," Sung told them.

Kessler frowned.

"I said fuck off," Sung said.

Kessler hesitated, ready to argue, but Quigley nudged him with his black bag.

"I'll drop you," Quigley offered.

After a moment, Kessler followed him to his car.

Sung walked over to the swimming pool, sitting at a rusted table. He felt his nose, as if to see if it was still there.

Quigley's Plymouth bumped out of the StarBrite's parking lot.

Trabish, who had been watching it all, went back into his office, the screen door banging shut.

"I understand," Sung said, feeling his nose, "that the lady was one of your punchboards. True or false?"

Jacobi came back from wherever he'd been. "True."

"I beg your pardon?"

"Yeah, I was whacking her," Jacobi said. He got a chair, pulling up to the table, so he wouldn't have to shout. "A couple three times a week. Pretty regular."

Sung looked toward the office. "That's what he said. Friend of yours?"

"I know him."

"Mmmmm," Sung mused. He took a button from his pocket, feeling it like he'd felt his nose. "She was strangled sometime during the night. After one-thirty. Doreen, the popsie in number four, she heard her singing to herself then." He rolled the button in his fingers, showing it. "No sign of forced entry. Did she keep the chain on?"

Jacobi nodded.

"It was off. so maybe she knew him, I was thinking her husband, your friend mentioned she was unhappily married, or maybe she just thought it was you. Do you think that's possible?"

"It's possible."

"I was thinking her husband," Sung said again, "but Quigley thinks we're looking for a professional, clean and quick. Like someone who'd done it plenty of times." He put the button on the table. "Ever see that before?"

Jacobi picked it up, a dappled green, about the size of a nickel. It looked like it might have come off a sports jacket. It wasn't his. "No."

"It was in her hand," Sung said, taking it back. He thought for a moment. "What else? She was naked, but not sexually assaulted, and there were no signs of a struggle, which is another indication that she may have known him, and that's about all so far, I guess. Unless you've got any ideas?"

Jacobi shook his head.

"Well, think on it," Sung suggested. He returned the button to his pocket, waiting. They still had lots to talk about.

Jacobi looked past him, to Cleo's open door. He was going to miss her. For a not too pretty lady with a drinking problem, she sure knew how to please a guy. "Incidentally, what was she singing?"

"You mean when Doreen heard her last night?"

"Yeah."

"I dunno," Sung said, feeling his nose. "Is it important?"

No, Jacobi decided. He was just wondering, that's all.

Tina knocked on Lois' bedroom door, slowly counting to five before she entered, a precaution that wasn't necessary.

"Ma'am...?"

Lois stirred, clutching a pillow, the only thing Tina had ever found her holding.

"I wouldn't bother you," Tina said, taking a business card from her apron pocket, "except that he said it was extremely important." She looked at the card, unable to read it, the room was too dark. "He's a lawyer."

The question was barely audible. "A who?"

"A lawyer," Tina repeated. "Something Ferguson, and he said to tell you, it's about High Desert."

Lois was suddenly wide awake. She sat up, pushing pillows aside, looking past Tina to her bedroom door, which had been left open.

"He's downstairs," Tina assured her, moving over to the window, "and I wouldn't worry about him, a good wind and he'd blow away." Behind the drapes, she lifted the blackout blind a crack, reading. "Donald Ferguson, Hestor and Maylor, a Professional Corporation..."

"Give it to me."

Tina surrendered the card.

"And turn on the light."

Tina turned on the bedside lamp.

"Ohhhh," Lois said, forgetting she didn't have her glasses. They could be anywhere. She'd come home crying and throwing things. "What else does it say?"

"There's just a phone number, and the office is on Palm Canyon."

Lois frowned, her head aching, it always did when she tried to sleep late. The firm's name wasn't familiar, but that didn't mean anything, she thought. She was just barely aware of Melvin Belli.

"What will I tell him?"

"To wait," Lois decided, curiosity overcoming her fear. She found her robe, getting out of bed. "But I want you there when I talk to him, and Theo, too."

Tina nodded. She waited until Lois went into the bathroom and then raised the blind and pulled the drapes, letting the sun flood in, changing night to day. The room was littered with clothes dropped in flight.

"Do you want me to put out something for you?"

There was no answer.

Tina picked up a shoe, then let it drop. Picking up wasn't her job.

In the bathroom, Lois patted her face dry, examining her puffy eyes, swollen from crying herself to sleep. She thought of Mallory. Was it really over?

Yes. It was. *It had to be.*

Lois put the face towel aside, picking up a brush, pulling it through her hair.

Downstairs, Ferguson paced the foyer, a thin, pale young man who had parted company with Hestor and Maylor a full three months before. He was on his own now.

Theo watched him with one eye. Before going up, Tina had consulted with him. Ever since the first anonymous telephone call, Lois had been afraid of her own shadow, and after last night ... ?

Fetch her down, Theo had ordered. He had a premonition. "You don't remember me, do you?"

Ferguson shook his head.

"I used to be a star," Theo told him.

Ferguson smiled, pacing. He hoped Lois wasn't checking on him.

Tina appeared on the landing. "She'll just be awhile."

"Thank you," Ferguson said.

"You're supposed to wait."

He nodded. "Thank you."

Theo watched him with one eye.

To cover his nervousness, Ferguson put his attaché case on a side table, popping the latches open, making sure, which was ridiculous, that they still worked. There was no reason for them not to work. They'd never stuck or anything.

"You're supposed to wait, too," Tina told Theo.

In the bathroom, Lois finished brushing her hair, deciding that she'd just go down in her robe. For a brief instant, she thought of getting Jock's gun, a small automatic, which she kept in a cookie tin in her jewelry drawer.

But that would be silly. She'd fired it only a couple of times, eyes closed on a target range, and the young man downstairs, whatever he had to say about High Desert, surely couldn't mean her any harm. Did criminals come with calling cards?

Sighing, she turned away from the mirror, thinking about Mallory again, reliving their confrontation. She went downstairs wondering how she was supposed to fight him. She couldn't let him drag her into the muck.

Ferguson was waiting. "Mrs. Sills...?"

Lois nodded.

"My name's Ferguson. I'm an attorney."

"Yes, my housekeeper told me," Lois said, wondering why he was so nervous. "Now, what's this all about?"

"Well," Ferguson began, aware of all of them watching. "I'm acting on behalf of certain persons who wish to remain anonymous."

"Anonymous … ?"

"With what's been happening, I know how that sounds," Ferguson said quickly, "but I want to assure you, these are law-abiding citizens and this is a legitimate offer." He laughed, a kind of titter. "I suppose you want to know what offer?"

"It would help," Theo grumbled.

"Well," Ferguson said. He got his attaché case. "My group, or rather the persons I'm representing. I'm simply their attorney, wish to purchase a controlling interest in the High Desert project. If you'd like to sell, they'll buy your shares at par value."

Theo shook his head. "She's not dealing with people who won't show their faces. And if you're the guy who …"

"Please," Ferguson said. He opened the case, removing a sheet of paper, which he offered to anyone who would take it. "It's all explained here."

Lois suddenly felt relieved and good. The way out, she thought, and she didn't care who the people were, or what their motive was or anything else, just as long as it was a legitimate offer.

"Tina, get my glasses," she said, and she took the piece of paper from young Ferguson's trembling hand.

"Murdered …?"

St. Pierre sat down heavily, the breath taken from him, as if struck by a physical blow.

"Yes, last night sometime," Jerry Sung said, carefully taking note of St. Pierre's reaction. Normally, he'd have had a friend or relative break the news, that would have made it easier, but he wanted to see the reaction. Shocked, like St. Pierre couldn't possibly have known, unless he was a very accomplished actor, and there weren't that many around. "I'm … well, I'm sorry."

St. Pierre finally got his breath. "How … ?"

"Strangled," Sung said, deciding to get it over with.

"Where … ?"

"The StarBrite."

"Who …?"

"We don't know yet," Sung said, looking around. The condo was luxurious, expensively furnished, in sharp contrast to Cleo's mean motel room. "Can I get you something? A drink of water?"

St. Pierre shook his head. "No. I'll be … all right."

Sung sat down, looking around, struck by the contrast. He felt his nose. "You've a nice place here."

"Yes. a friend's," St. Pierre said. "The StarBrite? That's what … a motel?"

Sung looked at him. "Yes. she was staying there." He hesitated, frowning. "You didn't know?"

St. Pierre shook his head. "No. We were separated."

Sung nodded, looking around again, thinking that St. Pierre, even if this was a friend's place, had managed to get the better of the deal.

"She wasn't supposed to be down here," St. Pierre said, feeling obliged to explain. "She had a perfectly good town house in Toronto, and a small farm in the country, and …" He stopped abruptly, realizing that he wasn't explaining, but rather defending. "Nobody asked her to stay at … some motel."

Again, Sung nodded, still looking around, thinking that if she'd been so well fixed in Canada, she ought to have had a better place than the StarBrite.

"Maybe it was all she could afford?"

St. Pierre didn't answer. He didn't have to defend, he decided.

"Trabish," Sung said, substituting him for Jacobi, a professional courtesy, "the StarBrite's manager, he says you were withholding separation payments, and that's why she was down here, trying to collect." He paused, turning back. "Is that right?"

St. Pierre still didn't answer.

"Is it?" Sung demanded, feeling his nose.

"Yes," St. Pierre said finally.

"Yes," Sung repeated. "A town house, a farm ... they can be expensive. To keep up, I mean. Repairs, taxes." He got up. restless. "You can lose them if you don't pay your taxes. And how do you pay your taxes if you don't have any money?"

St. Pierre was ready for him now. "You work."

"You work," Sung repeated. He stood looking at St. Pierre for a long moment, the expensive clothes that went with the luxurious condo, a friend's borrowed place or not, he'd managed the better of the deal. "What kind of work does your wife ... excuse me, what kind of work did your wife do?"

"None. She didn't work. She thought it was beneath her."

Sung considered. "Some women, they get to her age, no training or experience, sometimes it's difficult for them to get work."

"She could get training," St. Pierre said, suddenly angry, what the hell did this Chinaman know, he hadn't lived with the bitch all those years, watching her spending it and asking for more, never satisfied.

"Yes, I suppose you're right," Sung admitted. "She could have, and it's too bad she didn't, isn't it?" He started for the hall closet, feeling the button in his pocket, the same way he had been feeling his nose. "If she had, she'd still be with us, wouldn't she?"

St. Pierre put his head in his hands. For a long time he had wished Cleo dead, and now he was supposed to feel guilty?

Negative? Suzy put the phone down, feeling oddly disappointed. She'd had time to think, calmly and rationally, and she had decided, had the test been positive, Dex pregnant by Milo, that it wouldn't be the end of the world exactly.

The Chermaks were staunch Catholics, pillars of the Church. Abortion was absolutely out. Dex would have to have the baby. If not the Chermaks, she, Suzy, would insist on it, and the child wouldn't be given up to strangers, either. Dex would keep the child—and they'd have to get married.

Dex was too young, of course, and her education would be interrupted, probably never resumed, yet teen-age marriages work, lots of them, and who needed to go to college if she was marrying the heir to millions, and besides, think of the baby's welfare, its birthright...

Suzy frowned, wondering what was wrong with her, the test was negative, there wasn't going to be a baby.

The Lear landed hard, which was Potter's trademark, although otherwise he was a good pilot. Bollinger waited for the engines to reverse before he opened his eyes. He'd survived another, he thought.

Marion smiled at him. "Have you decided what to do about Lois?"

For answer, Bollinger fingered the message which Grady had handed back after they departed Dallas.

URGENT SEE YOU UPON ARRIVAL

"You think she's waiting out there?"

"It sounds like it."

"Well, if she sees us, there's no avoiding it, I suppose. But let's not go looking for her."

"All right."

Marion unfastened her seat belt, wondering what was going on. surely he wasn't at it again, so soon after Suzy Braverman? The idea came, and went. Lois had her sights on Mallory, and Bollinger was being very, very good to her. Marion, these days.

This trip, for example. He hadn't done anything he couldn't have accomplished on the telephone and there was no need for her to have gone along except for the fun, of which there had been quite a lot.

Marion wondered. Was he being *too good?* The idea came, and went.

Bollinger was looking out his window. "She's there, all right."

Marion got up, leaning across him. As the Lear turned, she caught a glimpse of a woman in a camel-colored coat standing in front of the Combs Gates executive terminal.

"We could go out the back way."

"No. That would be too obvious. Let's just get it over with."

"All right," Marion said, thinking that he didn't want to avoid her very badly, and also wondering how he knew it was her. From this distance, it could be any woman. Unless he knew she owned a camel-colored coat?

"Better still, have Harry bring her over. I'd rather talk here than in the limousine, and we won't be obliged to drop her off, just in case she didn't bring her car."

"All right," Marion said again. Twice denied, her suspicions were aroused once more, the idea that this was planned, or at least expected.

In front of Combs Gates, Lois watched the Lear taxi to the north apron. She didn't know if it was Bollinger's or not. The Palm Springs airport had dozens of them coming in every day.

But he was due, Lois thought, looking at her watch. Blodgett had given her the estimated arrival time and had promised to get through a message that she'd be waiting. Now, if he'd only listen to reason.

Mary Alice had. And Suzy. With Bollinger, she'd almost have the majority control that Ferguson's group wanted, just Angie left to convince.

Make him listen, Lois prayed, thinking that God helped those who helped themselves, and it had been a surprise—no, a shock, actually—to discover how much inner strength she possessed.

She wasn't a fighter. Things came too easy, they always had. And she didn't have a business head. Jock took care of everything, even in death.

But she was measuring up, Lois thought. On the north apron, a limousine started, backing out from between parked aircraft, coming toward her, and she headed for it confidently.

In the Lear, Bollinger lost sight of her again, just as Harry was stopping. He motioned to Marion, indicating that she should turn up the volume.

There was the sound of a power window being lowered.

Harry's voice: "Mrs. Sills ... ?"

No answer, so she'd be nodding.

Harry: "If you'd like, Mr. Bollinger will talk to you in the plane."

Lois: "Anywhere is fine."

"Okay, turn it off," Bollinger said. He'd heard enough to know that she was determined.

Rather than turn around, Harry backed up down the line, getting into position as the Lear pulled in.

Bollinger moved to another window, watching as Harry got out, opening the limousine's left rear door, then the trunk.

"Is there something I should know?" Marion asked.

Bollinger thought for a moment. "Yes. She drinks tea."

Damn him, Marion thought. She waited for the jet's whine to stop, then opened the door, the steps folding out with it.

Bollinger smiled, moving from the window, greeting Lois as she finally emerged from the limousine, where she'd been hiding from the noise. "Hullo! What's this all about? We don't usually rate a welcoming party."

"You don't mind, though?"

"No, of course not." He extended a hand. "Come on ..."

She went to him, taking it, and he pulled her aboard, as easily as he would a child.

"Thank you," Lois said, catching her breath. She looked around the plane's luxurious interior, finding Marion. "Hello."

"Mrs. Sills," Marion said formally. She busied herself in the galley.

Bollinger directed Lois to the sofa. "Would you like something? Marion was going to make a cup of tea."

"Well, if it's being made," Lois told him. She sat up straighter, the sofa tending to pull her into its depths. "I'm sorry to bother you this way, but it is important."

"Urgent," Bollinger reminded her.

"Yes," Lois said quickly. "So much has happened in the brief time you've been away. Cleo, that's Elliott St. Pierre's wife, was found murdered this morning, strangled in some awful motel ..."

Bollinger nodded sympathetically. "Yes. We saw it on the wire."

"And King inherited all of Bluestone's estate," Lois continued, rushing along, "everything including the canyon, and the newspapers are making a big thing about it, as if to suggest ..." Her voice trailed off. "Well, you know what newspapers can be like."

Bollinger nodded again. "Yes, we know. It was on the wire." He looked at her, as if to ask, Is that all?

Lois tried to get herself organized. "What's happened ... an anonymous group, they won't reveal their identities, but they're quite legitimate, I'm assured, wants to buy a controlling interest in the High Desert project. They're offering to buy any and all shares at par value—the only proviso being that they obtain control."

Potter came out of the cockpit, head bent low. He squeezed past Marion, acknowledging Lois with a look. "Grady will finish up. okay?" he told Bollinger. "I've got a lady waiting."

"Sure." Grady grumbled, stuffing a bulging briefcase with more papers.

Bollinger ignored them. "And I take it you'd like to sell?"

"Yes, very much." Lois said. "I've discussed the offer with Mary Alice and Suzy, and they're agreeable, too. And I think I may be able to convince Angie."

"Angie ... ?"

"Sargent's wife. He gave her his proxy."

"I see." Bollinger said. He got up and closed the cockpit door. "Despite what's happened. Mallory and St. Pierre, they're as firmly opposed to selling as ever, I imagine?"

"Yes," Lois admitted. "But if you came with us…" She stopped, thinking that she didn't have to explain.

Bollinger moved back to his chair, looking out the window, checking on Harry. Oblivious, he was standing beside the limousine, hands clasped behind his back, waiting. Potter was off at a gallop.

"If I came over, what it sounds like, we'd have a tie."

"Yes," Lois admitted again, "but it wouldn't be just us women then, we'd have one of the men, too. And someone of your stature…?" She did her best to smile naturally. "I think that would impress Angie."

"Mmmmm," Bollinger said. "Cleo's murder. Do the police think there's a connection?"

"With High Desert?" Lois shrugged helplessly. "I don't know, but with the threats being made, the sabotage at the site…" She looked at him, trying to compose herself, thinking that she had to argue the plain, stark, emotionless facts. "I'm not panicking, but I do have a reputation to protect, just as you yourself have, and what I'm saying is, neither of us should be involved. It's untenable."

"Mmmmm," Bollinger said. "I suppose." He considered for a moment. "What is it you want exactly? My agreement to accept this anonymous group's offer?"

"Yes."

"But I've given Mallory my proxy."

"Then take it back. Give it to me."

"You'll go against him?"

"I already have."

"Yes. but now you're going to break him? And you know how strongly he believes in the thing?"

"Blindly. He's being stupid. What is it? Just another subdivision, that's all, and he's trying to make it more than that, something that it isn't, and he's going to drag us all down."

"Well," Bollinger said, still looking at Harry, "we can't have that, can we?" He took another moment to make up his mind. "All right. You can have the proxy. Marion will see to the details tomorrow. You do what you think is right, and just keep me out of it, I prefer to stay in the background."

"Thank you," Lois murmured. She stood up unsteadily, turning to Marion, hoping to find—what?—forgiveness? *Break him,* Bollinger had said, and it wasn't until now, hearing him say it that way, that she fully comprehended what she wanted. Would another woman understand?

"You're not staying?"

"No."

Marion had the tea ready, about to ask that she reconsider, but Bollinger made a motion, meaning let her go.

"Thank you," Lois repeated. Still unsteady, she crossed to the door, taking the steps very carefully, then heading for the terminal with as much haste as her precious dignity would allow.

The cabin was silent for a long moment.

"You're never satisfied," Marion said finally. "You're going for it all, aren't you? Cathedral City, and High Desert, too?"

Bollinger smiled, "Why would you say that?"

"Because you manipulate people," Marion told him, an accusation.

Bollinger glanced back out the window. Lois was almost running, Harry stock-still beside the limousine, oblivious. That wasn't always true, but he tried, Bollinger thought. He sure tried.

"Yes," Suzy told Lois, taking the phone into the bathroom, "of course I'm still on your side, and I do agree, we've got to sell High Desert. It's just…"

"What?"

"Well," Suzy said, sitting on the throne, "I didn't realize you were going to close the real estate office, too. I thought you'd keep that going."

"No," Lois said firmly. "It's no business for me, I don't know the first thing."

"I could be broker." Suzy suggested. "Remember when we first talked? You weren't sure about King. And you said then..."

"No," Lois repeated. "It was a very stupid idea, all of it, and I'm sorry, but that's final." She paused, her voice softening. "There are lots of other firms. You won't have any trouble getting on someplace else."

No, Suzy thought, not much, except that Bollinger wasn't interested in her anymore, and if George Spector still wanted to cause trouble...

"Would you?"

"No, of course not," Suzy said. There was no sense arguing. The only reason Lois had started the firm was to get Mallory. "And don't worry, I haven't changed my mind, I'll vote to sell."

She hung up. thinking that she *had* to sell, take her money and run, because she was going to need it now. It was all she had and she was going to need it. Everything had gone wrong.

The front door slammed, Dex home from school. Suzy put the phone aside and went out to meet her.

"Well?" Dex demanded.

"It was positive," Suzy told her. "Congratulations, you're going to have a baby."

"Oh," Dex said softly. She looked down at her stomach, imagining the child starting there, the tiniest child imaginable.

Suzy went back into the bathroom and locked the door. Dex wouldn't check with the doctor, and the Chermaks wouldn't check either, she thought. It wasn't something anyone would lie about, and Milo would admit sleeping with Dex, not taking precautions, and so they'd simply accept it as fact. It wasn't something anyone would lie about.

The Chermaks, pillars of the Church, they couldn't conceive of such a lie, and they would want an immediate marriage, Milo at Harvard, Dex with him, before the baby "showed."

And they would want a marriage. Otherwise, Suzy thought, another lie to tell them, Dex would have the baby out of wedlock, give it the Chermak name, sue for Chermak support.

Lies, all lies, but if she could manage it before Dex got her period, there was going to be a wedding, goddamn it. Her Golden Girl—and Milo Chermak.

Angie went into the back yard, where Sargent was sprawled in his hammock, staring into the night sky.

"Do you want to hear the latest?"

Sargent pretended not to have heard the question.

"That was Lois on the phone," Angie said. "She got to Bollinger, and he's given her his proxy, so now she can vote his shares, too. Do you know what that means?"

Sargent still didn't respond.

"Thanks a lot," Angie said. "I'm in the middle."

Sargent finally looked at her. "What ...?"

"It's how it works out. Lois, Suzy, Mary Alice and Bollinger—that's twelve thousand shares. Mallory, who has Bluestone's, along with St. Pierre and me—that's also twelve thousand."

"Oh. It sounds like a tie."

"Not really," Angie complained. She opened up a director's chair, wondering if she should sit down, another decision. "I still haven't really decided. I think Mallory is right, we shouldn't give in to blackmail, but Lois has a point, too, we could lose everything if we don't sell. She says too much has gone wrong and people won't build in the canyon now and that there's never going to be a High Desert."

"And what do you think?"

"I don't know. The only thing I'm sure of ... I don't like being in the middle."

Angrily, she closed the director's chair, putting it back under cover.

"Well," Sargent told her, turning away, "you wanted my vote."

"I didn't want it. You gave it to me."

"All right," Sargent conceded. "I gave it to you." He thought for a moment, trying to figure out what she did want. Was it just to complain or did she want help? "Do you want to give it back?"

"No."

"Then how about the benefit of my brilliant advice?"

Angie hesitated. "Have you got any?"

Sure, Sargent thought. If you're worried about losing your investment, sell. If you still believe in the project, don't. Anything else was crap. And either way it didn't matter.

"There's a meeting tomorrow," Angie said after a while. "We're all supposed to be there. Ferguson, that's the lawyer, he's going to formally present the offer, and then we're going to vote whether or not to accept it." She looked at him, wondering how he could just lie there. "Everyone else has made up their mind. So it's up to me."

She was back in the house, the door slammed shut, before what she was telling him finally registered, that she alone—holding the swing vote—was going to decide what happened.

And that wasn't fair, Sargent thought, not moving. Angie had come after the fact. She had nothing to do with starting High Desert. Why should she hold the power to stop it?

Fuck. How had that happened?

Bollinger. He switched. He changed his mind. He must want to sell, he wouldn't have switched otherwise, but it meant an awkward situation, the project split down the middle, and it didn't give Lois her way. it just created a stalemate.

Mallory won in a stalemate. Ferguson's group wanted majority control or nothing. This was one situation where a tie wasn't a tie. All Bollinger accomplished by switching was to ... what?

Sargent sat up, thinking that Mallory won, and unfortunately he lost. too. They all did. "Angie?"

He remembered that she had gone inside. He swung off the hammock, following her into the house, finding the children glued to the television, as always.

"Why aren't you guys in bed?" he wanted to know.

"We're watching 'Love, American Style,'" the Squish explained.

He shook his head—how old was she, eight?—and went down the hall to what was called, euphemistically, the master bedroom. Angie was in the bathroom, already undressed, the tub water running. He pushed the door open wider. She looked at him, not saying anything.

"I think you should vote to sell," he told her.

She just looked at him, getting into the tub, testing the water, making it warmer.

"I was thinking," he said, "if you don't sell, how's the project going to go ahead, split down the middle. Lois and Mallory with equal votes and fighting every inch of the way? Nothing is going to get done then, nobody able to make a decision, and the whole thing could just grind to a halt."

She slid down into the tub. "Why didn't you think of that earlier?"

"I don't know. Because I just thought of it now?"

She slid deeper, flat on her back, only her face out of the water.

"There may not be another chance," he said. "If the project gets into serious trouble, Ferguson's group might come back with another offer, but it probably would be a lot lower, and what I'm saying is, it might not come back. So where the fuck are we then?" He waited, and then told her when she didn't answer. "Dead, and Bollinger picks up the pieces, taking it all for himself. He gets Cathedral City, and High Desert, too."

Angie sank deeper. "I'm going to the meeting tomorrow, and I'm going to listen to what everybody has to say, and then I'm going to make up my mind."

Okay, Sargent thought. He was too late. Five minutes ago, when she asked, he could have told her anything, she would have agreed and done it. But he hadn't come through—he wasn't there when she needed him—and so he was just too late.

"How come the kids are still watching television?"

She shrugged, barely moving, but it was enough to make a wave, the water washing over her face, and she sank deeper, staying under.

He went back into the living room. "Your mother says you're supposed to turn that off."

"Okay," the Squish said. "Just as soon as this is over."

He went outside, thinking again that he was too late, and wondering if he would ever get well, accept his r-r-responsibilities. When would anything ever matter again?

The Squish was watching "Love, American Style," High Desert was headed down the drain, and he really didn't care. As a matter of fact, he felt pretty damn good. Strangely buoyant, positive, confident.

Too confident ...?"

Sargent sprawled in his hammock and toyed with the idea of somehow triggering another manic high. If he drove himself again, working ever harder, faster and longer, run amuck to the brink of exhaustion, could he flaw his body chemistry and produce some variant peptide in his brain hormones? Might he once more achieve that glorious state where nothing is impossible?—no challenge too great, no odds too long, no problem beyond solution?

Sherlock Holmes.

The last time, Sargent remembered, thinking he ought to blush, he had imagined himself to be Jesus (a common mania, apparently, beating out Napoleon, someone said, ten to one).

He'd come back to save the world through manipulation of the communications industry. This time he'd merely be Sherlock Holmes.

Yes. Holmes. That would be enough. Plus a hat with two peaks. Or perhaps two peaked caps, worn at the same time, one on top of the other, one of them backward. Anyway, thus equipped, he'd soon solve the mystery of Sun Devil Canyon.

The thing to figure out was what Ferguson's (or was it actually Bollinger's?) anonymous group really wanted. Majority control of the syndicate bought them nothing tangible. The murders, sabotage and continuing threats of violence already had High Desert at a standstill. With Mallory and St. Pierre ousted, the project would collapse for sure, leaving everything back at square one. an empty canyon.

Ferguson's people (or were they Bollinger's?) could start over, of course. But why pay good money for all that trouble and scandal? There were other canyons, and lots of empty desert, too. Didn't it make more sense to start with a clean slate and build elsewhere?

Sargent tried to think. Perhaps, as Chaney suggested, they wanted to keep the canyon in its natural state, but that didn't make sense, either. There were other canyons, equally beautiful, even more accessible. Palm Canyon, for instance.

No. There had to be another explanation. Question: What did anybody want with an empty canyon?

Answer: It wasn't empty.

Hey, say that again, Sargent told himself, imagining that he was drifting into another manic high, far beyond the realm of ordinary mortals, higher and higher and higher.

The canyon isn't empty.

Jacobi drifted into sleep. A ditty from a childhood game kept running through his mind.

Button/Button/Who's got the button?

That's easy: Lieutenant Jerry Sung has the button. He's holding it. Evidence.

Button/Button/Who *had* the button?

That's hard.

Jacobi drifted into sleep, gone now. away. But his cop's mind was still working, sorting through thousands of images, sorting and sifting, holding, rejecting. His cop's mind was still at work and at last it came upon the image of an awful green sports jacket being removed because the wearer was suddenly uncomfortable.

CHAPTER FOURTEEN

First light, and Joe Patino was in Sun Devil Canyon, starting down the newly widened road, spurred by a last explosion of energy. He ran, laughing crazily, throwing himself down the road, heart pounding and lungs burning.

At the bottom, he fell gasping. His legs cramped and he writhed in pain. He screamed, clawing at the knotted muscles, struggling to his feet again, hobbling around in a tortured circle.

The rifle fell from his shoulder, plunging into the sand, buried as he thrashed about. The bullets for it spilled from his jacket and were lost.

He stayed at the spot, circling in a mad dance, screaming.

Gradually, the cramps eased, and he slowly wound down, lowering himself to the ground, sprawling on his back, exhausted.

Fuck, what an entrance, he thought, laughing at himself. He sure as hell was an Indian. Hadn't that been a war dance...?

Aiyee! Old Joe Patino on the warpath, stomping and screaming, in a frenzy. Better watch out, white man. You betchum. You die.

Sure.

Laughing, he waited for a while, making sure the cramps had passed, and then he carefully turned onto his stomach, searching out the rifle. He found it and seized the stock and raised it in victory.

Sure...

He put the rifle down, thinking that was the trouble with being sober, reality intruded. He had started out drunk—had to be, or he wouldn't have taken that first crooked, fatal step—and he had walked all night and somehow he had made it and now he was sober.

Suddenly frightened, he sat up, pulling off the knapsack. He tore it open and dumped out the contents, sighing with relief when he saw the bottle. Without that, he'd never make it back home.

Reluctantly now, hands trembling, he put the bottle back, at the bottom, covering it with his other provisions. He'd brought only what was in the cupboard. Sardines, beans, cling peaches, spaghetti and wax paper. Oh, and a fork, but no can opener?—and what was the wax paper for?

With a sigh, he put the knapsack aside. What was anything for? Except the bottle. Drunk, it had seemed like a pretty good idea. He'd been to two lawyers and both had advised against challenging Bluestone's will, so the only solution, if he was man enough to try, was to seize the canyon. And here he was.

You're seized, he thought, looking around. The property of Joseph Patino, to whom you rightfully belong. The first trespasser, bang!

Sure.

He shook his head, standing up with an effort, suddenly aware that his feet were very sore, probably blistered and bleeding. How far had he walked? Ten miles anyway. He'd been at it all night. Skulking across the desert. Hiding in the wash. Drunk.

What a goddamn stupid fool!

He retrieved the knapsack, picking up the rifle at the same time, and one of the bullets that had spilled from his jacket. He looked around for more but couldn't immediately see any. He considered searching, they'd be somewhere here, in the circle, but then he thought hell, he didn't need them. He never hunted anymore. His hand was too unsteady.

Painfully, he hadn't realized it, he hurt all over, Patino started across the canyon floor, headed for the shelter of the rock outcroppings and Angel's drawings. He'd sleep there, he decided. He didn't want to be caught around the shack or the machinery.

The drawings took the first rays of the rising sun.

You betchum, Patino thought bitterly. Bluestone may have failed in his battle to save those historic Indian masterpieces. But not good old Joe.

Sure.

Too late, Jacobi pulled into Sargent's driveway, the Morris Minor convertible gone, and Sargent with it. Jacobi sensed that. The thrill of anticipation, what fed him, was lacking.

Brodie came around the house on screeching Hotwheels. The boy braked scant inches away, staring at him.

"Your father home?" Jacobi asked.

Brodie shook his head. "No, he went away."

See? Jacobi thought. He got out of the car. "Do you know where he went?"

"Naw," Brodie said. Backing up, he was gone.

Jacobi headed for the house, knocking on the front door, which was partially open. There was no answer. He tried again, louder this time, but there was still no response.

He pushed the door open. "Hello … ?"

Nothing.

He hesitated, he didn't have a warrant, there hadn't been time, and then he thought, shit, when did he ever go by the rules? He went inside and down the hall, poking his head in doorways, finding the master bedroom at the end. He opened the wardrobe sliding door and found the awful green sports jacket. He pulled it off its hanger and turned around and held it up to the light. There were two buttons in front, about the size of a nickel, dapple green. There should have been three. One was missing.

Button/Button/Who's got the button?

Jacobi folded the jacket over his arm and went back outside to his car. He got in and turned up the transmitter.

"Hello, Bowden?" he said, thumbing the mike. "This is Jacobi. Do you read me?"

The radio sputtered. "…bi. Go ahead."

"Bowden," Jacobi said, aware of Angie approaching, coming around the corner of the neighboring house. "I'll be getting a suspicion of murder warrant on a Sargent, James G., and I want an APB."

There was more static. "…spell it, please. Sergeant James Gee?"

"Bowden. I'll telephone you." Jacobi said, putting the mike back. He looked at Angie, who had stopped, stricken. His window was open and she must have heard. "Yeah, it's me again."

"What did you say?" she demanded. Behind her, a school bus made the turn, explaining where she had been, seeing her girls off.

"I'm sorry," Jacobi said, meaning it, "but I've got to take him in. where is he?"

She shook her head. *"No!"*

"Yes," he insisted, getting out, "and it's going to look better if he comes willingly." He stopped, concerned that she was suddenly pale. "Do you know where he went?"

Angie felt her knees start to buckle. "Jim…?"

Jacobi caught her, grabbing her arms, and she sagged against him, a dead weight. For a moment, he thought she had fainted, but then her fingers dug into his jacket, holding tightly.

"You okay?"

"Yes," Angie whispered, her head swimming. "Just…give me a minute."

Jacobi stood holding her. Brodie came back on his Hotwheels, circling noisily, watching.

"Do you want to lie down?"

"No. I'm all right."

Brodie stopped, staring at them.

"Mommy's okay," Angie said inanely, letting go of Jacobi. "She just tripped."

Jacobi kept hold of an arm. "We'd better go in the house."

Angie nodded, letting him lead her, and Brodie took off again, roaring down the sidewalk.

"Do you know where he went?" Jacobi asked again.

"No," Angie said. "He was gone when I got up."

"When was that?"

"About seven, to get the girls ready for school."

"Had they seen him?"

"No."

"And was there a note or anything?"

"No, nothing."

Nothing, her mind screamed, and Sargent was gone without explanation, a warrant being issued for his arrest, murder, and it was like the last time, she had no security, and what about the children?

Inside the house, Jacobi got her into a chair, then went to the telephone, calling Bowden.

She watched dully. "What are you doing?"

"Putting out an all points bulletin."

"Oh."

"If he shows up, I want you to call me," Jacobi told her, waiting for Bowden to answer. "I'm going to give you a number."

Angie shook her head. "I'm not going to be here."

"Why not?"

"There's a meeting. We're voting on whether or not to sell out."

"The High Desert syndicate?"

"Yes. We've had an offer."

Bowden answered. "Radio room."

"Hold on," Jacobi said, cupping a hand over the phone. If, finally, a purchaser had come into the open, it was a meeting he didn't want to miss. "Would you mind if I came along?"

Angie shrugged. "If you want."

Sargent glanced at Chaney, thinking he was strangely quiet, he hadn't said a word since they'd left Builder's Supply, and this was *supposed* to be an adventure.

They were going prospecting.

Sargent's idea, he'd awakened Chaney with it, sneaking over the back fence while it was still dark, unable to sleep himself, he hadn't slept at all. Once the wild theory struck, *the canyon isn't empty*, that had been impossible, he'd tossed and turned for hours, convinced there was some rich mineral deposit, that would explain everything, riches beyond the dreams of avarice, as Ross used to say.

Maybe that was it, Chaney was mad at getting up too early, Sargent thought. His idea had been to go then, to sneak away before dawn, but as it turned out they didn't have a shovel between them, so they'd had to sit out in front of Builder's Supply till seven-thirty, waiting for it to open.

Or maybe, Sargent thought, wanting an explanation, it was because he'd been arguing his case forever, long after he'd obviously convinced Chaney it was worth checking out, they were going, weren't they? They had a pick and shovels banging around in the back of the Morris. And they were going.

"Did I tell you Dex Braverman is getting married?" he asked, changing the subject. He waited for a moment. "To Milo Chermak, so it's worth a mention in your column."

Chaney grunted. "She's kind of young, isn't she?"

"Uh, huh. But I think she got knocked up."

"And that's the item?"

"No," Sargent said, "the item is it's a mixed marriage, a Catholic and a Jew, and they're going to a priest for counseling, so they can get married in the Church. Mallory had been through the same shit—he had to switch, to marry his wife, you know?—and so he bumps into Milo, this is after he'd heard, and he starts giving Milo advice on how to handle Father Whoever over at Our Lady of Solitude. Mallory tells him, 'Milo, I went through that same shit, don't argue with him, just agree to anything he says, it's all fucking nonsense anyway, why let it spoil your happiness?' And Milo says, "Thanks, but I'm the Catholic.'"

"That's the item?"

"I'm the Catholic," Sargent repeated, laughing. "I'm the Catholic." He had to slow down, fearful of driving off the road. "I wish I had a picture of Mallory's face at that moment."

"He must be an asshole. Doesn't he know Braverman is a Jewish name?"

"Sure. But Braverman was Suzy's last husband. Hell, she's had four, and Dex's father was the second, I think."

"Suzy isn't Jewish?"

"No, and Mallory thought Dex wasn't, either, but it turns out that Suzy's second husband, or Dex's father, at any rate, he was Jewish."

"Maybe that's the item?"

Forget it, Sargent thought. He concentrated on driving, the road a mess because of the heavy equipment that had gone in and was now sitting idle, and which was more support, if he needed it, for his theory. Once that equipment started tearing up the canyon floor...?

He looked at his watch. It was eight o'clock, and the meeting started at nine and probably would take only an hour or so before Ferguson's offer got put to a vote. Not much time to do anything, it would be hopeless if he didn't know where to start, but he did, of course. Angel's rocks.

If there was anything to find, he was pretty sure that's where it would be. That, Holmes, would explain why Bluestone fought so hard to save Angel's drawings, and it also would explain why he was murdered. He knew too much.

Was that why Chaney was so quiet? Yes, probably, Sargent decided. The knowledge that they also might know too much. It had sounded like a great adventure back in the safety of Sunshine Estates. But now, almost at the canyon, with the possibility that the killer or killers might be waiting...?

Well, in and out, he reminded himself, which was all that Chaney had agreed to do. They'd stay long enough to collect some ore samples from the rock outcroppings and then get the hell out.

It was worth the chance. If he found something interesting, even a hint of it, he'd turn the meeting around, stop the sale until they knew what they were doing. Otherwise, he'd just have to go there empty-handed, hoping he could argue persuasively enough that they ought to have a geologist check the canyon before selling. It was going to be difficult without something to show. He already could hear Angie, "Why didn't you think of that earlier?" And so it was worth the chance. In and out. Quick.

Alone, he wouldn't do it, he wasn't that brave, he wasn't brave at all, but he had Chaney with him, and Chaney, despite his silence, had a gun.

The meeting started early. Ferguson, looking younger than his years, faced the two groups he had to contend with, all of them older and all, he sensed, more determined. What he would take from this, if successful, was a modest fee, and Lois Sills had her reputation to salvage, and Jack "King" Mallory a dream he wanted to save. And the others?

All something, Ferguson thought, more than his modest fee—if he was successful.

"Well. Since we're all here ... shall we get started?"

No one replied, but there was no objection, either. Ferguson snapped open his attaché case and removed six copies of his client's conditional offer to buy Sun Devil Canyon. He moved among the two groups, passing one to each, Lois, Suzy and Mary Alice on one side of the office, and Mallory, St. Pierre and Angie on the other, divided as their votes were divided, for the moment at a stalemate.

With Bollinger's proxy in hand, Lois held six thousand shares, Mary Alice had five thousand, Suzy one thousand. Twelve thousand shares ready to sell. Mallory also had six thousand shares, Bluestone's and his own, and St. Pierre had five thousand and Angie had Sargent's proxy, representing another thousand. Twelve thousand shares not prepared to sell. Not all of them, anyway. Not yet.

"If you'll read this," Ferguson said, speaking to Angie, "I think you'll find it self-explanatory, my client is offering to buy any and all shares at par value, provided he obtains majority control in the transaction." He paused, looking at her, knowing that she was the key, the only one he had any real chance of switching. Mallory and St. Pierre were dead set against him. "And if you have any questions, I'll be only too happy to answer them, of course."

Mallory spoke up. "Answer this one. Who's your client?"

"As I said," Ferguson told him, so often now he had it memorized, "I'm not at liberty to identify my clients, nor disclose their intentions insofar as the High Desert project or Sun Devil Canyon itself."

"No," Mallory said angrily. "Because they're goddamn blackmailers, that's why." He looked at Lois, daring her to challenge that. "Goddamn blackmailers, picking easy prey, women without any backbone."

Lois kept her eyes averted.

"Shut up, King," Mary Alice told him. "We're here to listen to this young man's offer, and then we are going to discuss it, reasonably and intelligently—if that's possible with you present—and then we are going to vote." She looked at Ferguson. "Get on with it."

Ferguson nodded, wondering where to start, he hadn't gotten any courtroom experience at Hestor and Maylor, they'd kept him in a tiny office without windows, doing research for the firm's partners, and he had never once faced a jury of any kind, never had to single out one juror, addressing her and her alone, as he was about to do now with Angie, because she was the key.

Angie sat waiting. She was going to listen, she thought. She was going to listen to what everybody had to say—and then she was going to make up her mind.

Behind her, Jacobi moved, getting into a better position, so that he wouldn't be visible from the street.

She was going to listen. Angie thought, aware of Jacobi's purpose, and then she was going to make up her mind, and she also remembered Sargent's warning, that a continuing stalemate would leave the project split down the middle, nothing getting done and the thing slowly dying, the shares decreasing in value, and she remembered, too, the last time Sargent was put away, she had no security, and what about the children?

"If you'll read this," Ferguson said, starting again, speaking to Angie.

Sargent drove into the canyon cautiously, watching for some sign of movement, any suggestion of something that didn't belong. The stillness was eerie, it looked like a painting. Nothing moved.

"What do you think?"

Chaney shrugged, fingering his gun, a French-made pistol which, in defense of his country, he had removed from a dead Cong.

"It looks okay to me," Sargent said, more to convince himself. "If there's a killer anywhere, he's probably at the meeting, trying to buy this place, right?"

Chaney still didn't answer.

Crapping himself, like me, Sargent thought. He turned off the rutted road, driving into the shelter of the sabotaged grader, switching off the motor and listening to the silence. There was nothing.

"Well. Shall we get at it?"

Chaney nodded, getting out on his side, taking a shovel from the back. After a moment, Sargent followed, wishing Chaney would say something, the silence was beginning to get to him. He collected the pick and the other shovel.

Chaney was waiting.

"Let's try the leading edge of that second outcrop," Sargent suggested, pointing. "It looks pretty loose." He started toward it, glancing back after a few steps. "You coming?"

Chaney shook his head.

Sargent stopped, puzzled. "What's the matter? You want to try someplace else?"

Again, Chaney shook his head, letting go of his shovel, taking the safety off the pistol, which he had loaded with dumdums.

Aw. shit, Sargent thought. How could he be so stupid? No wonder he hadn't gotten any threatening call, he'd have recognized Chaney's voice, right off. And if he did any digging this bright and sunny day, it would be his own grave, wouldn't it?

"Yeah," Chaney said finally, getting himself ready. "I'm afraid I'm the guy."

Sargent looked at him. He managed only the one word.

"*Why?*"

"I don't know," Chaney admitted. "It just...happened." Briefly, he considered firing, getting it over with, but then he decided he should explain. He owed a pal that much. "You were right. There is ore. Pitchblende."

"And that's worth killing for?" Sargent demanded, suddenly outraged. "There's no way you're going to get it."

"I don't want it," Chaney said. "Bluestone did. When he found it—he was using one of the dozers, trying to dig out the rocks, save Angel's drawings—when he found it, he came to me, the crusading newspaper editor, the protector of the little man. He figured Mallory was fucking him. And that I'd help him."

Sargent could feel the anger boiling up inside. He'd gone for help. too. He'd trusted him.

"I tried to, at first," Chaney said, making it sound like an apology. "I didn't know what he had—he's the one who thought it might be pitchblende—but I've got a Marine buddy who did know, he used to work with Edison and now he's with the Anti-Nuclear Movement, and Chester shit when he saw the sample. It was rich."

Sargent started toward him.

Frowning, Chaney raised the pistol, ready to blow Sargent's head off. "You want to hear this or not? You're standing on what is probably one of the richest finds in North America. When Chester asked for more samples, I came out here with Bluestone, digging around some more with the dozer, and the goddamn stuff was everywhere. *Stay!*"

Sargent stopped, frozen.

"I'm trying to explain, all right? When Chester did his tests, it was all high-grade ore, about as pure as it gets, and that's when he asked me, what I thought about sitting on it. When he left Edison, *why* he left Edison, it was to oppose nuclear proliferation and he knew I felt the same way and this was a chance to do something about it, we just wouldn't tell anyone. So he asked me. And I asked Bluestone."

Chaney raised his left hand, cupping the pistol, steadying it. "I tried to reason with the sonofabitch. It was *his* uranium and he could leave it here where it wasn't going to hurt anybody or he could make a lot of money selling it for nuclear bombs and power plants, and what did he think was right, you know? I mean we've already got enough bombs to blow the world apart a couple times and sooner or later one of those power plants is going to go blooie and who the fuck needs that? I tried to reason, but he got stubborn, all he could see were the dollar signs, all the money he was going to make, and I don't know, I just got mad, I guess. We started arguing and I saw it wasn't any use and I had the gun and I used it."

Sargent remained frozen, thinking the same thing, that it was useless.

"After that," Chaney said, his shoulders hunching, "I was committed, you know? I had to stop High Desert—otherwise, why did I shoot him?—so I started making those anonymous calls and fucking with the machinery and trying to figure who might take the canyon off your hands without disturbing it and finally it came to me, who the rightful owners were, the Agua Calientes." For the first time, he smiled, faintly. "That's who is buying the canyon this morning. The Agua Caliente Indian band."

The smile gave Sargent a small flicker of hope. What was he suggesting? That they knew, and made a deal? "They agree with you, do they?"

"They were open to suggestion, on account of how nice I'd been to them in *The Sandbox*, and they agreed that it ought to be kept in its natural state, preserved as a park, and if they do that, leave things alone, they'll probably never discover the ore, nobody will. The closest it comes to the surface, it's under three feet of overburden, so nobody's going to get any gamma readings, and anyway, the stuffs so pure, it's almost all alpha radiation. Instruments aren't going to pick up anything. If it's found again—it'll be by luck."

Oh, Sargent thought, the small flicker snuffed out, and he was desperate, anything now, stealing seconds. "What about Cleo?"

Chaney shook his head, steadying the pistol. Killing her, that wasn't something he wanted to explain, not to Sargent. When Bluestone had that fight with St. Pierre, vainly trying to buy more time, he, Chaney, had been crouched down in Bluestone's truck, and he thought Cleo might have spotted him. If so, she was the one person, apart from Chester, who knew they'd had any contact, and he was afraid that she might remember and mention it to Jacobi. So...

You kill once, it's not so hard the next time, Chaney thought, taking careful aim. And Bluestone wasn't first, of course. He'd done a lot of killing, too much of it, in Nam. It came easy, like stepping on a bug. But he didn't enjoy it—*there's the difference*—and he wanted to stop and the best way to do that was to stop worrying about getting caught. And the only way to do that was to put the blame on somebody else.

Why pick on a pal? Well, it was convenient, easy to steal a button from him, and he also was a suitable candidate, on account of the history of m-m-mental illness, but the main thing, what really decided it, was the fear that if you let him sit around thinking long enough he was going to figure it all out and fry you.

Joe Patino loomed up behind the rocks, his bottle in one hand, the rifle in the other. He thought he'd heard somebody talking. He shouted drunkenly. "Hey...!"

Chaney whirled. All he saw was the rifle. He squeezed off three shots in quick succession. The third hit, and Joe Patino's head exploded.

Sargent lunged with the shovel, the point digging cruelly into Chaney's ribs. He screamed in agony, dropping the pistol. Sargent scooped it up, the thought that he was saving himself only half formulated, and not thinking at all that he might kill to do so, but when Chaney rose lunging, face contorted in pain and rage, he pulled the trigger and there was another explosion and Chaney's chest opened with a spew of blood.

No, Sargent thought. *No.* He stood staring down at what he had done, some inner voice arguing that it wasn't his fault, he'd heard all those war stories, about hand-to-hand combat, and he'd never had that kind of training, he only wrestled with his kids, and he had been afraid. You couldn't blame him for that, the voice argued. At one time or another, everyone was afraid, even Chaney.

He turned and ran for the Morris.

Ferguson looked at his tally of votes to sell, which Lois had demanded and led off, after a tearful shouting match with Mallory.

Lois Sills	1,000
Stu Bollinger (by proxy)	5,000
Mary Alice Chambers	5,000
Suzy Braverman	1,000
Total	12,000

Not enough, Ferguson thought, looking at Angie, wondering if she'd ever make up her mind, and whether he should take a chance and push her. Like Jacobi, the cop who had invited himself, explaining he was providing security, Angie kept looking out into the street, as if the answer—how she should vote—was somehow out there.

Ferguson was starting to get the uneasy feeling that the answer was in the street and that it was going to come bursting in and that it was going to be no.

He waited, the wall clock ticking, the minutes passing. The office was very quiet except for the ticking clock. No one had any arguments left.

"I'm sorry," Ferguson said at last, making up his mind, he was going to take a chance and push her. "I'm not prepared to wait any longer. Two more minutes—and then the offer is withdrawn."

Lois started to protest.

"Two minutes," Ferguson repeated, cutting her off. He removed his wrist watch and placed it on the desk in front of him. He waited for the second hand to come around to twelve and started counting from there. "Two minutes...and you've passed up what under the circumstances is a surprisingly generous and, as I have warned, not-to-be-repeated offer."

Lois turned to Angie. *"Please!"*

Angie wavered. Where was Sargent, who could tell her it was all a mistake, he wasn't guilty of any murder, that was silly, so stupid, and she didn't have to worry about security, the children would be taken care of, and then she could vote with Mallory, who was strong and brave and correct, they shouldn't give in to blackmail.... Where was her husband?

"One minute." Shrugging his thin shoulders, Ferguson closed his attaché case, snapping the locks shut. He looked outside, another warning that he was leaving, and saw the Morris turn into the parking lot.

Lois was begging now. "Angie, for God's sake. *Please...*"

Angie closed her eyes. "All right."

"Which is it?" Ferguson asked, sensing victory. He looked through the window again, at Sargent running across the parking lot, starting up the steps. "Is this gentleman someone who can come back later?"

Sargent opened the door on what seemed like wax figures. They had all turned to look at him, oddly rigid in that moment, a tableau.

Frozen in time? he wondered, stilled by some higher force, made to wait for the news he brought? I've just killed a man—and we're all millionaires.

Jacobi, who didn't belong in the picture, an intruder, spoiling the arrangement, pushed off the wall with his easy cowboy grace.

"I've been waiting for you, boy," he said casually, the handcuffs coming out.

Sargent looked at him. How did he know...? Stupidly, he was going to ask, and then he decided, swept by relief, that there must have been someone besides Patino hiding in the canyon. Thank

God, a witness, who had followed him out, telephoned from Cathedral City. And the sheriff's department had radioed Jacobi.

"Wait!" Angie screamed. Her hand over her mouth, she ran to Sargent, taking hold of his arm. "It's all right. It's just some stupid mistake." Desperately, she pulled him closer, burying her head in his chest. "Jim, tell him. He's wrong!"

Ferguson looked from them to Jacobi. "Is this something we can do later?"

"I don't think so," Jacobi said. He got Sargent untangled from Angie, pulling his arms behind his back, snapping the cuffs on expertly.

"But you're interrupting a business meeting," Ferguson protested. "This young lady hasn't voted."

Sargent looked at the sea of faces. There was something wrong. They didn't know about Chaney.

Suddenly frightened, Sargent tried to pull free. "What is this?"

Jacobi thought he'd never ask. "It's for Cleo," he told him, satisfied. "I'm arresting you for her murder." He lowered his voice, whispering gruffly, a secret. "You made a mistake, wearing your new coat. She tore a button off."

St. Pierre looked up. "Cleo?"

"Please!" Ferguson said loudly. He'd lost control, everyone talking at once. "May I have your attention, *please!*"

Sargent finally understood. He hadn't left a button with Cleo, but Chaney had, on purpose, one of his, and even though Chaney had confessed the rest of it, a murder frame-up wasn't something he would want to tell a pal.

Jesus Christ. Like Angie, Sargent wanted to cry, who was going to believe him, especially after what had just happened back in the canyon?

"Come on," Jacobi said.

Sargent looked at the sea of faces. Angie, whom he couldn't help, he never could, not ever. Mallory, whose dream was ruined, there never was going to be a High Desert, the project would be forgotten as soon as the graders hit the ore. St. Pierre, who didn't have to stay and fight, he could walk away from it, his running days were over. And Lois and Suzy and Mary Alice, ladies in distress, they thought, but no matter what happened now, their reputations and purses were still intact, so he couldn't help them, either.

Every one of them had enough money and it wasn't going to help to give them more.

Despairingly, Sargent searched the sea of faces, thinking he had to help someone, he couldn't help himself, and he realized—with an almost overwhelming sense of sadness—that the only one he could help was Chaney.

"Why I interrupted," Sargent told Ferguson, "my wife here, she holds a proxy, the shares are actually in my name, and it's my intention to instruct her to sell them to you ... *if.*"

The room fell silent, Mallory looking away, betrayed.

"Two things," Sargent said. "You represent the Agua Caliente Tribal Council. If we sell them the canyon, they plan to keep it in its natural state, preserved as a park. Have I got that correct?"

Ferguson nodded. If someone else had revealed it, he was no longer bound, and it also seemed that his client's purpose, after much difficulty, was about to be accomplished.

"Yes or no?"

"Yes," Ferguson said quietly.

"Could that be a part of our agreement? That the canyon be kept as a park—in perpetuity?"

"Yes. the council has already stated to me that it wants the land placed in trust, nothing to be built there."

"A trust," Sargent said. "All right, I vote to sell." He looked at St. Pierre. "You might as well, too. You heard him. They're not going to be building anything."

St. Pierre's pushed-in face was still creased with doubt. "Did you kill her?"

Sargent almost laughed. Already he felt cleansed. "No. Of course not."

"I didn't think so," St. Pierre said. "Very well, we'll give it back to the Indians." He turned to Mallory. "I'm sorry, but I think we've lost, old boy."

Mallory was looking at Lois, his defeat tempered, however slightly, by a new respect for her. Far from "buying" him, she'd fought him, beat him. Maybe she was as much her own woman as he was his own man. Or used to be.

"Well?" Ferguson prompted.

"All right, damn you," Mallory said, looking at Lois, gutted in the public square one last time, and feeling very, very lonely.

CHAPTER FIFTEEN

The important thing, Father O'Flanagan thought, ever mindful of a diminishing flock, was that they were gaining another Christian—and from the Jews, too. He gazed fondly upon the shiny countenance of Milo Chermak, for whom he had waived *everything*, and if the bishop complained, so be it. The thought of losing the Chermak tithe made Father O'Flanagan's stomach twist. That, and his diet. He hadn't eaten anything but the Eucharist since Sunday.

"She'll be here," Father O'Flanagan said softly, looking out over a full church.

Ten blocks from there, Hank Goldfarb, who had come all the way from Spokane to give his daughter away, drove Suzy's Oldsmobile into a Kentucky Fried Chicken parking lot. "Give her a dime," he ordered.

Suzy shook her head.

"I *am* menstruating," Dex told her mother.

"You're spotting," Suzy said, unwavering. "I told you, it's all the excitement. You're simply having a little false alarm, that's all." She looked at her former husband, remembering why she hated him. "Hank, if you don't get us to that church, I'm going to kill you."

"Give her a dime."

"No!"

"Somebody will," Dex wailed. Before Suzy could react, she was out of the car, wedding gown flying.

Hank reached back, meaning to stop Suzy from following, but it wasn't necessary, Suzy wasn't going to chase her, wrestle in the restaurant. Nothing was going to stop Dex from making the call—hadn't she known that half an hour ago?—it was out of her hands, in God's, and maybe the doctor wouldn't be in his office, or his nurse wouldn't tell.

Hank turned back, not wanting to look at her. He knew now. "This is so like you."

Suzy didn't answer. She wasn't going to speak again. Never.

After an eternity, Dex returned to the car, getting in the front seat this time, looking oddly composed, almost serene.

"It was negative," she told her father.

Hank sighed. "What do you want to do, honey?"

While this drama unfolded, Trabish, the proprietor of the StarBrite Motel, was checking in a gentleman with a pushed-in face, a man who sounded, even to Trabish's tin ear, French.

Trabish read the name printed so clearly, the man must be an artist, a draftsman? *St. Pierre.*

"We, uh, had a lady die in this room," Trabish said, letting go of the card. He knew the answer before he asked the question. "The same name. Is that why you asked for it?"

St. Pierre nodded. "I was her husband."

"Oh," Trabish said. Reluctantly, he got the key. "If you, uh, just want to look around ... you don't have to pay."

"Thanks, but I might be awhile," St. Pierre told him. He took his wallet. "How much?"

"Eight dollars."

St. Pierre put them on the counter, a five and three ones.

"Plus tax," Trabish said, stalling. For a moment, he had the ridiculous idea that this might be the killer, returning to the scene of the crime, intent on destroying some vital piece of evidence overlooked by the police. But would he tell his real name?

"How much is that?"

"Forty-eight cents."

St. Pierre put another dollar on the counter.

"Were you, uh, looking for something?" Trabish asked. He made change, surrendering the key. "The cops took everything. And I cleaned the place out pretty good."

St. Pierre didn't reply. Yes, he was looking for something, but how to tell this stupid little man, how could he understand, it was punishment? He took the key and went out.

Waiting, Father O'Flanagan opened his Bible, permitting him to look furtively at his watch, which showed twelve minutes past the appointed hour. Normally, he would not be here, he thought, listening to people cough. He'd be in the sanctuary watching—he had ten bucks on it—the Raiders kick the shit out of the Rams.

A common occurrence—who hears more lies than a priest?—Father O'Flanagan had been misinformed. An altar boy had said the bride was here. So he had come forward, of course. And the boy would be altered, all right.

"She'll be here," Father O'Flanagan said softly, starting to pray.

Finally, after what seemed for absolute ever, Suzy entered the church, taking the arm of a grateful usher, letting him quickly escort her to her pew. The murmur of voices hushed as she kneeled and bowed her head.

At the rear, Hank was in the church now, whispering to another usher, asking him to point out Howard Chermak. He hurried forward—the one who looked like Howard Cosell?—and gave him the note and stood waiting for an answer.

Chermak unfolded it. *Dex isn't pregnant. Do you want to stop the marriage?*

Ruth was blind without her glasses. She kept staring ahead. "What does it say?"

Chermak folded the note, giving it back to Hank, indicating Milo. "Tell him."

Hank hesitated, his courage lost, conscious of every eye staring, the silence a roar. He crumpled the note.

Dex, watching from the door, hated them all, couldn't they even do that? She steeled herself and started down the aisle.

Abruptly, the organ began playing, the first few notes and that's all, she was running and already at the altar.

Milo waited.

"I'm not pregnant," Dex said, moving into position beside him. "I never was." She paused, getting her breath, wondering how to explain it simply. "You know what my mother's like?"

"Jesus Christ," Milo said. He closed his eyes. "Did you have to wait till now?"

"I just found out."

"Now?"

"Now," Dex repeated, afraid she was going to get the giggles. The whole thing suddenly struck her as very, very funny. Were they actually having this conversation, with everyone listening?

"Jesus Christ."

"What I think we ought to decide," Dex said, looking at Father O'Flanagan, who also struck her as very funny, "is whether we still want to get married. I've had time to think about it. and my answer is yes and no."

Milo finally turned to face her.

"Yes, I want to get married," Dex told him, "but no, not now. I don't want to rush into it, I'd prefer to wait." She paused. "The only thing, if we call off this wedding, we're never going to get married, so I guess what we should be asking is, do we love each other?"

Milo decided he was never going to find another girl like her. "I do."

Dex took his hand, serene.

"May we begin?" Father O'Flanagan asked in a choked voice.

Later, no one could say who was first, it simply began, that's all, a ripple of applause, and within moments everyone was standing, clapping joyously.

Suzy stayed on her knees, head bowed. Praying, it appeared, but she was thinking about showing a house, a very expensive one. to a rich, lecherous client, and he was making a pass and she was telling him to stick it in his ear, she didn't have to sell real estate for a living, she had a beautiful daughter who had married well.

May we begin? Father O'Flanagan demanded of God in His heaven, did He want him to miss the game?

There was, Trabish decided, his conscience getting the best of him. the Cadillac. It was still in his, Trabish's, name, Cleo had never put the transfer through, and Jacobi had told him to keep it. But still...

Trabish left his office and went to what was formerly Cleo's unit. He knocked on the door.

"Yes?" St. Pierre said.

"She had a car," Trabish said loudly, hoping Doreen would hear, evidence of his honesty. "Do you want it?"

Lying on the bed, thinking how he had made her live, in poverty, St. Pierre shook his head.

"It's a Cadillac."

That thing? No, St. Pierre thought. "You keep it."

Trabish went away, feeling righteous, but then he remembered. He went back and knocked again.

"What about the dog?" he shouted.

St. Pierre sat up. A dog? He *hated* dogs. He swung off the bed and cautiously opened the door.

"Hold on," Trabish said. He went around the side of the motel, where the Cadillac was parked, a temporary kennel. When he returned, he was carrying Mouse, at arm's length.

"She left this, too."

St. Pierre felt his hackles rise, what a ratty mongrel, eyes too close together, pinching the nose. It reminded him of Cleo.

"Is it a bitch?"

"Yes, but she's been fixed."

Just like Cleo, St. Pierre thought, reaching out apprehensively.

Trabish handed Mouse over. "Careful, she's got a habit of pissing on you."

Oh, good, St. Pierre thought, feeling better already. It was written in the sand. Kismet.

"And so then I said," Milo reported, his champagne glass trembling in his hand, "but I'm the Catholic."

The laughter rolled at him, in a wave.

"Finally," Milo added, coming to the end, "I want to thank my mother and father, for making me the kind of person who could get a girl like Dex."

More laughter, and then, when they realized he had finished, applause.

Mallory eased out of the crowd, going to the bar for a proper drink, he never did like champagne. The night he'd come back, cowering behind the *Times*, Lois had been waiting with a bucket of it, harder than usual to swallow, he was celebrating under false pretenses then, he didn't want to stay. His drink for inappropriate occasions. Funny to have it in hand again—when he didn't want to leave?

The bartenders beamed at him, Mexican boys in crisp white jackets, barely old enough to serve themselves. "Señor?"

"Teacher's. Over lots of ice. And just a splash of soda."

"Si." The brown hands flashed, producing it in moments, properly. "Will there be anything else, señor?"

Mallory shook his head, wondering what was wrong with him, he must be star-crossed. Billy had been in that limo, too, coming fearfully and with less chance of success, and taste this drink, will you? Mixed properly.

Not without jealousy, he looked around Billy's new restaurant, Casa Verde, which the wedding guests had converged on from Our Lady of Solitude. Mary Alice had suggested it for the reception ("offered," was the word she used) rather than one of the usual places, the Canyon or the Gene Autry Hotel. Suzy had thought it wise not to say no.

Everybody compromised, Mallory thought. Except him. He was going back to Oregon, to sit in the rain at Newport. There was nothing for him there, and Billy had this handsome restaurant which, unlikely as it first seemed, was going to be a success. He'd seen that in the faces of his fellow guests. They'd come to laugh, and they'd been pleasantly surprised.

Outside, the place still looked like a storage shed, there was no changing that, but the interior had been completely transformed, achieving—what was it?—a certain charming and seedy opulence. Where it never existed before, a wide balcony swept around two walls, and the huge stretch of flat emptiness in the middle had become three levels, a central dining area open to the roof, a more secluded bar and dance floor, and then all sorts of interesting nooks and crannies for private suppers.

Despite the grand scale, the massive fireplace and impossibly large wagon-wheel chandeliers, there also was an intimacy about it, with something to hold and please the eye wherever one looked, be it a wall niche for a Madonna's head or the hand-painted ceramic bowls in the washroom.

Mallory thought it irresistible, amazed, as always, at what Spanish hands could do with such basics as bricks and timbers, tiles and stucco. Some wrought iron here and a bullfight poster there and you had his idea of heaven. It would serve all seasons, cool and inviting in summer, warm and cheery on crisp winter nights.

Yes, a success, goddamn it! That these and others would be back he had no doubt. Even with a crowd this size, the service was faultless, the food excellent. Royal offerings of peasant fare.

Finally, Gwen Sommerset had invaded the kitchen, returning breathless with the news that the chef was Ramon, hired away from La Quinta. Trust Mary Alice.

Next week, when Casa Verde officially opened, there'd be a lineup.

And for him ... ?

Mallory fitted into an archway and finished his drink, wondering if he should have another, he'd be in tears if he kept this up. Milo and Dex slicing the cake, Suzy watching tearfully, she'd finally gotten rid of the little bitch, and Billy so proud he was going to bust his tuxedo, Mary Alice hovering over him like a mother, her Date Fluff on the menu. And Lois.

Across the restaurant, their eyes met briefly, and Mallory felt himself stiffen, not realizing she was present, he hadn't seen her at the wedding, hadn't spoken to her since the meeting. He turned away and went back to the bar.

Lewis examined her in the limousine's rearview mirror.

"You, uh, remember me?" he asked. "I brought you out last summer—from Los Angeles."

She flicked a look at him. "When I moved, you mean?"

"Yeah."

"I guess," she said absently, settling in her seat. "You look familiar."

She didn't remember, Lewis thought. "I remember you," he told her, thinking that she was the most beautiful woman he'd ever met, bar none, "from all the luggage."

She smiled, leaning back, closing her eyes. "Yes, there is a lot, isn't there? How long will it be?"

Lewis checked his list. Jody Walsh, to the Beverly Hills Hotel. That made her, let's figure this out, the last to be dropped off. "Oh, about three hours."

She nodded.

Lewis eased out into the traffic. "Things, uh, didn't work out for you here, hunh?"

"Not exactly," she admitted.

"So what are you going to do now?"

She shrugged, pretending not to know, but it was all planned, actually. She'd sleep late—she needed her sleep—and she'd have breakfast/lunch in the Polo Lounge, and then she'd sit around the pool for a while, showing off her body and her tan, making all the rich bitches jealous. And there'd be a man. There always was, for the Empress.

Lewis, who aspired, he was in this job for the contacts, decided there was no harm asking. You could never tell, he thought. You could never, ever, tell. "If you're not doing anything ... maybe we could get together later?"

She looked at him, or rather at the boil on his neck.

"Maybe," she lied.

One for the road, and that's all, Mallory thought. As he got his drink, Lois joined him at the bar, smiling tentatively. "I heard you were going away," she said, "and I was hoping, before you left, that I could have a small dinner party."

"Thanks, but that's really not necessary."

"So that a few favorite friends could say farewell," Lois added, as if he hadn't heard. "Our ill-fated syndicate members. Spisak, Em ..." She looked at him, the hurt showing. "Would you let me do that much?"

"Really, it's not necessary."

"Perhaps not," she admitted. "Still, I would like to."

No doubt, Mallory thought. Despite a broken heart, she would do her best, holding forth in a determinedly sprightly fashion, and he would be miserable the whole goddamn time. He drank his scotch.

"Well," Lois said finally. She started to move away, making room for others coming to the bar. "I guess it's good-bye, then." She offered her hand. "I'll say it now."

Mallory stared into his glass. "The reason I'm indefinite, Mrs. Sills," he told her, suddenly making up his mind, "is that I may not be going anywhere, I might stay."

"Oh?" She withdrew her hand, holding it with the other. He nodded. "Yes. I've decided, the years I have left, what I need now, it's fewer pretensions. My reputation, as such, is already made. Climbing mountains isn't going to help my friends see me any clearer. And as to getting rich? Oh, I might make it. I suppose— tunnel vision, total concentration, blind to life and its joys—but who is a million dollars going to impress, except me and fools and strangers? So what I think I'll do is ... I think I'll just relax and enjoy." At last he looked at her. "And there's this person I know, an old friend, we go back a way, there's a chance, depending how she feels, that we might do it together."

"Oh?"

She kept saying that, Mallory thought, wondering how he was supposed to be more explicit, people crowding them from all sides, which was his fault for choosing a bar for his little speech, but any other time and he wouldn't be making it. He seldom compromised.

"What I want from this arrangement," he told her, "is what I intend to bring, love and patience."

She flushed, barely able to speak. "Is this a proposal ... ?"

"Yes."

"Yes," Lois said joyously. "Yes, yes, *yes!*"

Not caring that she might object, he was going to be the man of the house, Mallory kissed her, right in front of everybody.

Sargent looked up, startled to see Jacobi, he'd approached as silently as, once upon a time, did Chaney.

"Oh. You again ... ?"

"Yes," Jacobi admitted. He sat down in the chair, which, in former times, was Chaney's. "How come you're not at the wedding?"

Sargent eased back in the hammock. "I don't go to weddings."

"Nor to funerals?" No, Sargent thought, not answering. Nor to funerals. He didn't go to weddings, and he didn't go to funerals, either.

"You didn't miss much," Jacobi said. "They just dig a hole in the ground and put the casket in it. The minister says something inappropriate." He paused, trying to remember. "'... returned to the land, which he loved.' And then he closes his prayer book—and that's all."

No, Sargent thought, still not answering, it didn't sound like much. He could have done a better job, he knew the man, they were pals.

"Only five or six people showed up," Jacobi said, getting out a cigar, "none of whom I knew. A thin girl with haunted eyes, that would be his wife, probably—what was her name?—Win?"

"I didn't know his wife."

"You didn't?"

"No. All I knew was, she taught school, and she was very organized, and that she operated a Booby Box."

Jacobi paused with his cigar. "You mean a booby hatch?"

"No, quite the opposite," Sargent said, "but the one could eventually lead to the other, I suppose." He thought for a moment. "Maybe that explains it?"

Uh, uh, Jacobi thought. Nothing would explain it. Sargent, once certified, now free as a bird, Yemana believed his story, and Blankenship, the district attorney, he believed it, too. They *had to,* they said, after the tribal council confirmed it was Chaney's suggestion that they buy the canyon and turn it into a park, but he, Jacobi, would never be sure about Sargent.

No, huh? Sargent mused, uncomfortable in the silence. He wondered if he could last much longer. Jacobi was that kind of cop, stubborn. He would persist, and he, Sargent, who wasn't strong, wasn't better yet, not healed completely, he, Sargent, in the face of that persistence, might reveal Chaney's secret.

The silence went on, and on.

"What I really came to tell you," Jacobi said at last, unfolding from the chair, "the case is closed." He took hold of Sargent's hand, turning it palm up, clasping it. "Case closed, and take care, huh?"

Before Sargent could think of an answer, Jacobi was out of the yard and back in his car, gone to look for another murder, one he could solve.

Bollinger was a little drunk. Normally, he was very careful about his alcoholic intake, he had an image of authority to preserve, but this was a special occasion, or rather two of them. Chip, son and heir, was safe in the fold again, completely cleared of that murder suspect nonsense, which Bollinger knew was going to happen all along, he'd been wrong to try to interfere, but he had just wanted to *make sure*, that's all, and when you were as rich as he was, you could afford to make mistakes. The other thing—let's have a party?—he owned Cathedral City.

He summoned the Boys. Chermak, Benson, Sommerset and Rex Wills. Marion couldn't find McGregor, he'd disappeared somewhere, and Goldman hadn't come to the wedding, he was in Europe.

"I want to show you something."

Obediently, they followed him outside, bringing their drinks with them, moving single file down the narrow sidewalk.

Bollinger stopped at the corner. He looked back, making certain no one else had come out of the Casa Verde. Sommerset's wife was always tracking him, afraid he might enjoy himself.

"You see this goddamn town?" Bollinger said, turning slowly, arms upheld. "I own it. The whole goddamn thing."

They stared at him, not quite comprehending. Did he mean the people or the real estate?

"Are you bragging or complaining?" Chermak asked finally. He felt a certain need for levity. He hadn't lost a son, he'd gained a legend. They'd be talking about the wedding for years.

Benson, the diplomat, quickly intervened, sensing Bollinger's impending dismay. There'd been a little flicker of surprise in the all-confident gray eyes, as if he had asked for something, and the answer—beyond comprehension—had been no. "Wait a minute. This sounds interesting. You *own* it...?"

"Practically. I've taken options, everything this side of the industrial area, or almost everything, anyway. There've been a few holdouts."

"That was you?" Sommerset said, more confused than ever. He'd heard about the optioning—Suzy Braverman, working out of The King Mallory Company—but it had sounded crazy and he'd never thought to connect it with Bollinger. "What the hell for?"

Benson looked about, thinking the same thing, although he'd never put it that way. Speculation? He was going to ask, but that didn't make sense, Cathedral City couldn't be turned around, it was too ... well, *tacky*.

"Yes, I know what you're thinking," Bollinger said, "but hear this.... It's all coming down." He waited, expecting them to grasp the idea immediately, the empty land immensely more valuable, the potential for redevelopment almost limitless. But his announcement had been met with an uneasy silence. "What's wrong?"

Sommerset tossed down the rest of his drink. He glanced back, making sure his wife hadn't followed. "You're, uh, not going to tear down Gloria's, are you?"

Bollinger didn't understand.

"The massage parlor," Sommerset said, grinning foolishly. He glanced over his shoulder again. "Just between us girls, I get it off there every Thursday. Very nicely. The best."

"A massage parlor?"

"An institution."

"Jesus Christ," Bollinger said. "I'm talking about a fifty million dollar deal..." He felt suddenly helpless. "Are you serious?"

"If you're asking me," Sommerset said, continuing to look over his shoulder, "what's more important, that's easy. It's Gloria's." When he turned back, he wasn't grinning anymore. "Okay?"

Bollinger stared at him unsurely.

"He's got a point," Chermak said. This was something he wasn't going to mention, but now that it was out, why not? "Ruth buys a lot of her stuff at Famous Fashions. It's top label, New York. Paris—but it's one third what she'd pay at Saks Fifth Avenue."

"She buys her clothes here?"

"Sometimes."

"Well," Bollinger said, completely baffled. Chermak was making even less sense than Sommerset. What did they expect him to do? If it would help, he'd give Ruth a clothing allowance, for Christ's sake. Build a whorehouse...

"Listen," Rex Wills told him. "Don't get us wrong. It's not a bad idea. It's just... well, why fool with the place, that's all?" He motioned with his glass. "This didn't just happen. It's here because people want it, and if you tear it down, they're only going to build it someplace else. So why don't you just leave it alone?"

Bollinger thought for a moment. "Every town needs a Cathedral City? Even Palm Springs?"

"*Especially* Palm Springs," Rex Wills said.

Bollinger looked to Benson, always the diplomat, about to intervene, but Bollinger decided, for the second time that day, that he was entitled to a few mistakes.

"Oh, shut up, Benson." Bollinger said. He led the way back to the Casa Verde, leaving Cathedral City looking pretty much the way it always did, the way Sargent—and Chaney, too—had left Sun Devil Canyon.

Later, when Angie and Em returned from the wedding, Sargent showed Angie the button, which Jacobi had pressed into his hand.

Angie took it matter-of-factly. "I'll sew it back on."

Looking at Sargent, hearing him actually laugh. Em felt herself vindicated, that she had been right all along, the sun could cure anything, even the blahs.

www.ingramcontent.com/pod-product-compliance
Lightning Source LLC
Chambersburg PA
CBHW022237020726
47496CB00004B/938